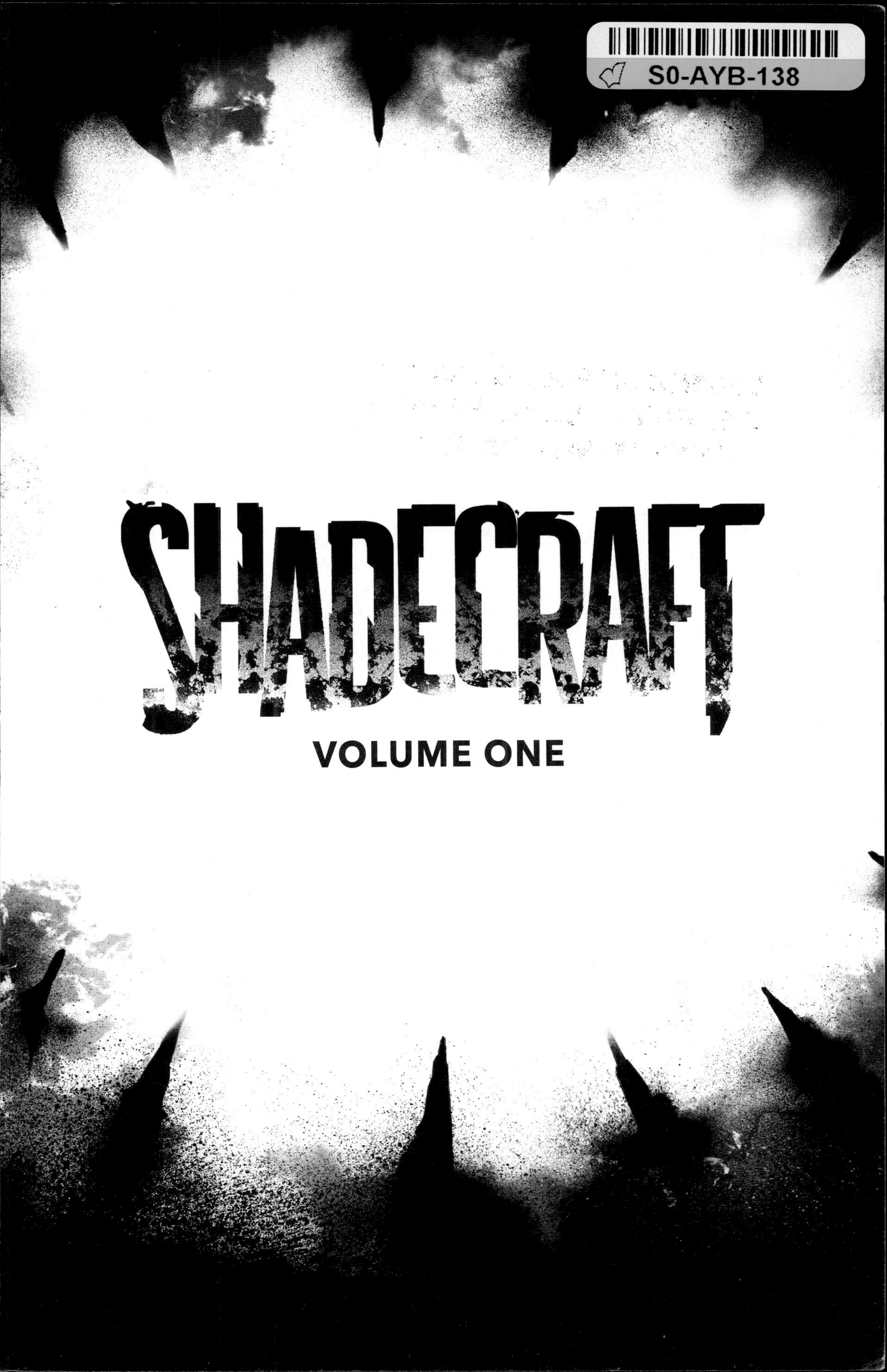

SHADECRAFT

VOLUME ONE

IMAGE COMICS, INC.
TODD McFARLANE: President
JIM VALENTINO: Vice President
MARC SILVESTRI: Chief Executive Officer
ERIK LARSEN: Chief Financial Officer
ROBERT KIRKMAN: Chief Operating Officer

ERIC STEPHENSON: Publisher / Chief Creative Officer
NICOLE LAPALME: Controller
LEANNA CAUNTER: Accounting Analyst
SUE KORPELA: Accounting & HR Manager
MARLA EIZIK: Talent Liaison
JEFF BOISON: Director of Sales & Publishing Planning
DIRK WOOD: Director of International Sales & Licensing
ALEX COX: Director of Direct Market Sales
CHLOE RAMOS: Book Market & Library Sales Manager
EMILIO BAUTISTA: Digital Sales Coordinator
JON SCHLAFFMAN: Specialty Sales Coordinator
KAT SALAZAR: Director of PR & Marketing
DREW FITZGERALD: Marketing Content Associate
HEATHER DOORNINK: Production Director
DREW GILL: Art Director
HILARY DILORETO: Print Manager
TRICIA RAMOS: Traffic Manager
MELISSA GIFFORD: Content Manager
ERIKA SCHNATZ: Senior Production Artist
RYAN BREWER: Production Artist
DEANNA PHELPS: Production Artist
IMAGECOMICS.COM

JOE HENDERSON
WRITER

LEE GARBETT
ARTIST

ANTONIO FABELA
COLOR ARTIST

SIMON BOWLAND
LETTERER

RICK LOPEZ JR
EDITOR

ERIKA SCHNATZ
PRODUCTION

COLLECTS SHADECRAFT #1-5

SHADECRAFT CREATED BY JOE HENDERSON & LEE GARBETT

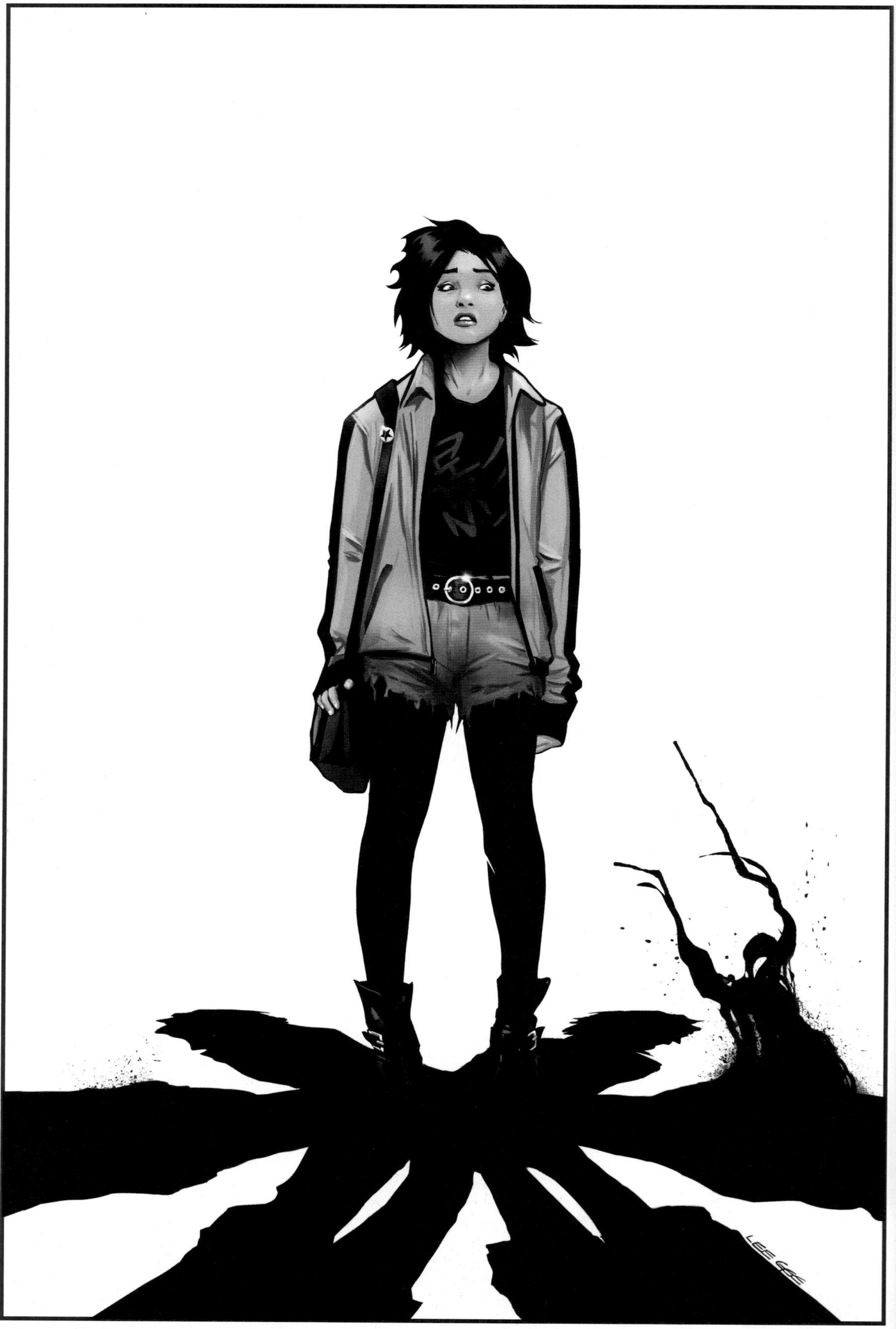

CHAPTER ONE

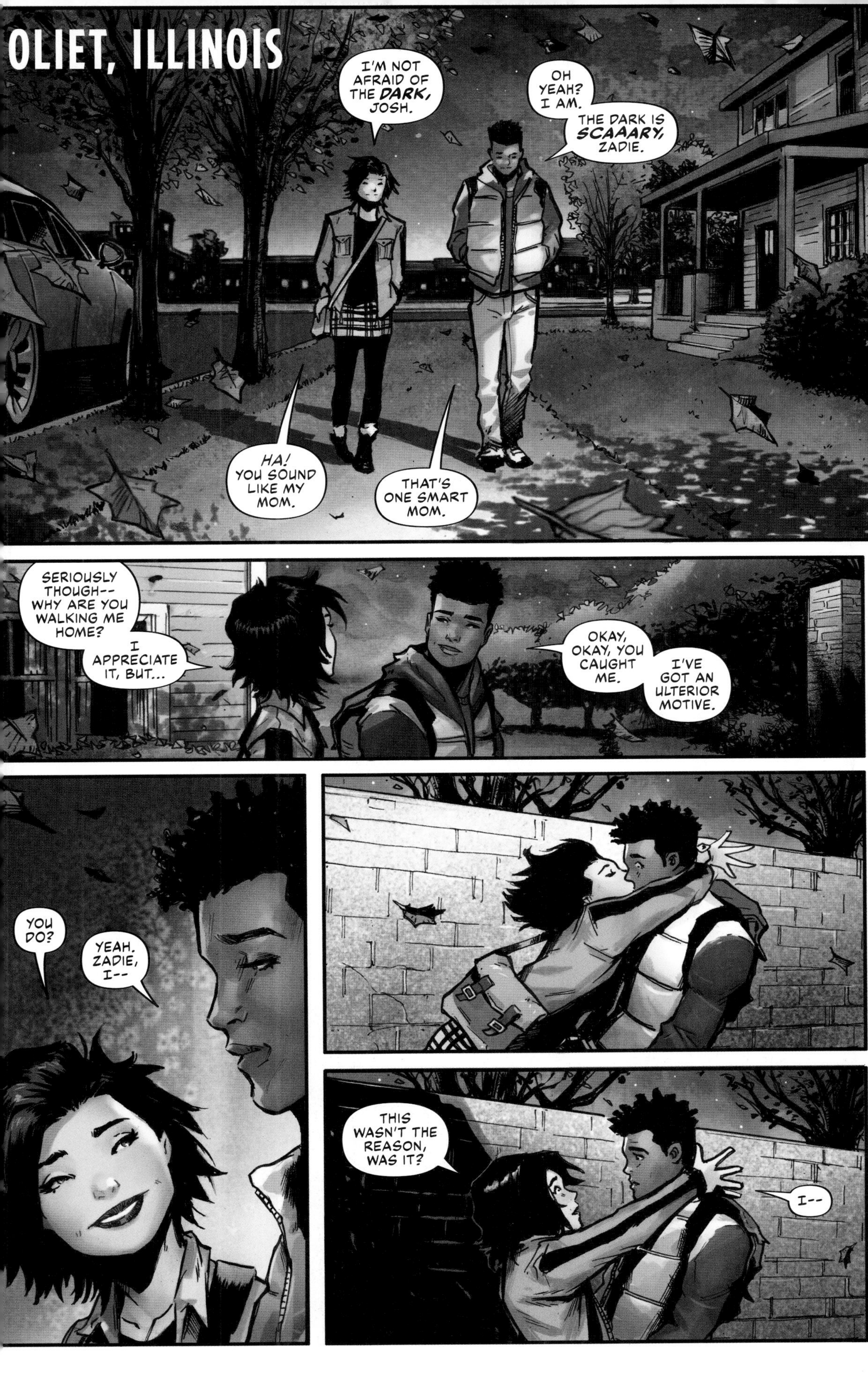

OLIET, ILLINOIS
I'M NOT AFRAID OF THE DARK, JOSH.
OH YEAH? I AM.
THE DARK IS SCAAARY, ZADIE.
HA! YOU SOUND LIKE MY MOM.
THAT'S ONE SMART MOM.
SERIOUSLY THOUGH-- WHY ARE YOU WALKING ME HOME?
I APPRECIATE IT, BUT...
OKAY, OKAY, YOU CAUGHT ME.
I'VE GOT AN ULTERIOR MOTIVE.
YOU DO?
YEAH. ZADIE, I--
THIS WASN'T THE REASON, WAS IT?
I--

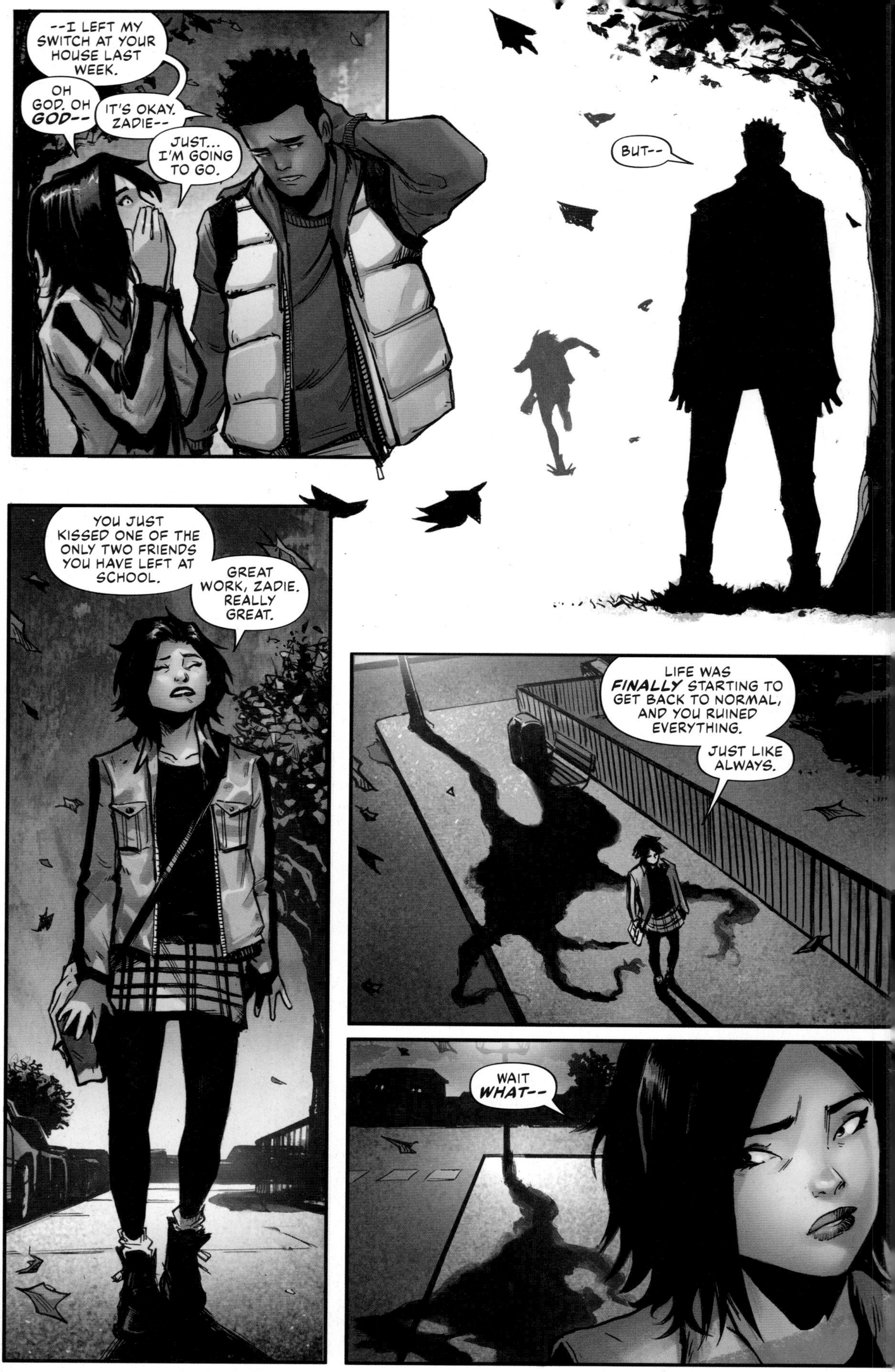
--I LEFT MY SWITCH AT YOUR HOUSE LAST WEEK.
OH GOD. OH GOD--
IT'S OKAY. ZADIE--
JUST... I'M GOING TO GO.
BUT--
YOU JUST KISSED ONE OF THE ONLY TWO FRIENDS YOU HAVE LEFT AT SCHOOL.
GREAT WORK, ZADIE. REALLY GREAT.
LIFE WAS FINALLY STARTING TO GET BACK TO NORMAL, AND YOU RUINED EVERYTHING.
JUST LIKE ALWAYS.
WAIT WHAT--

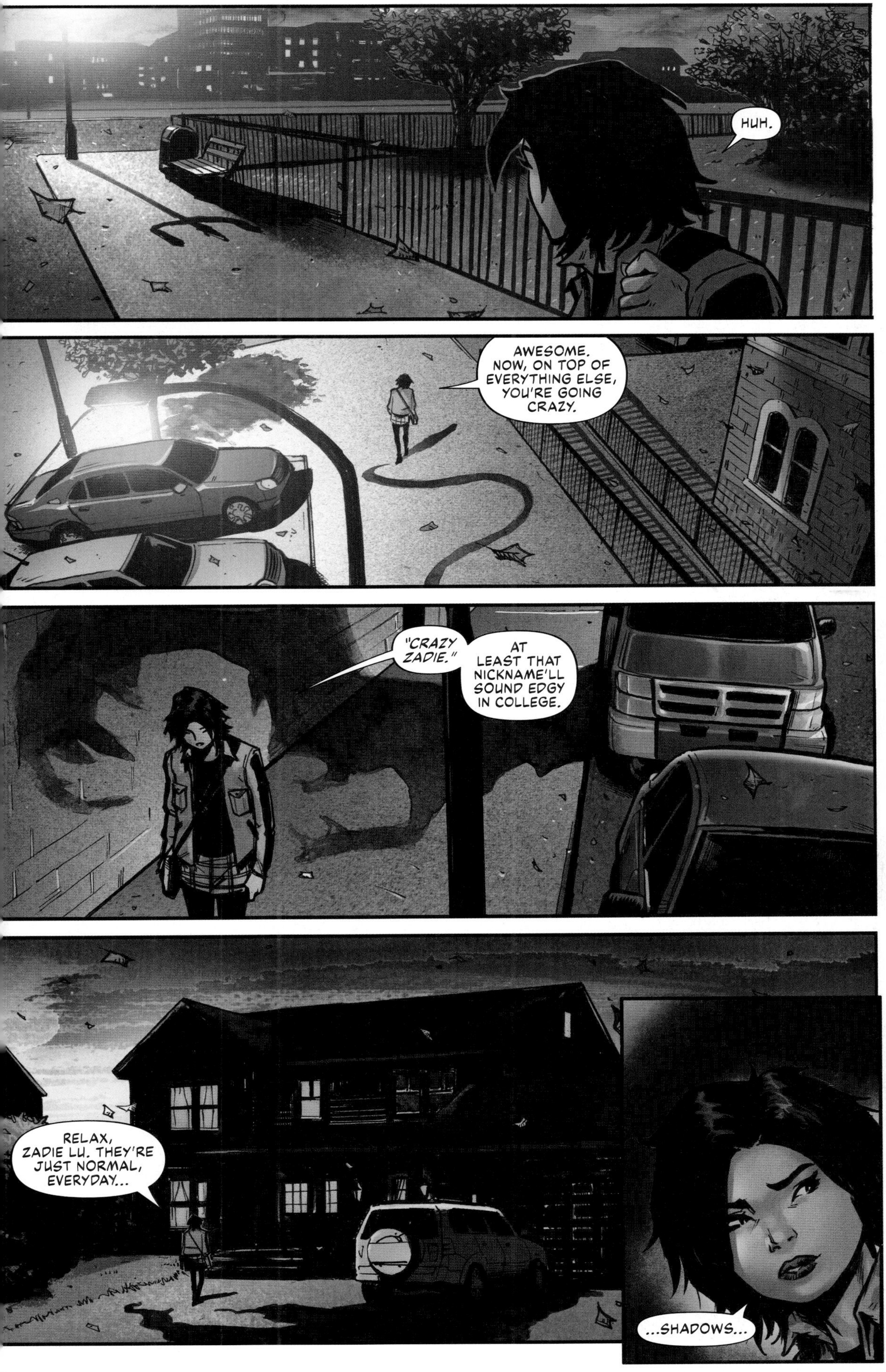
HUH.
AWESOME. NOW, ON TOP OF EVERYTHING ELSE, YOU'RE GOING CRAZY.
"CRAZY ZADIE."
AT LEAST THAT NICKNAME'LL SOUND EDGY IN COLLEGE.
RELAX, ZADIE LU. THEY'RE JUST NORMAL, EVERYDAY...
...SHADOWS...

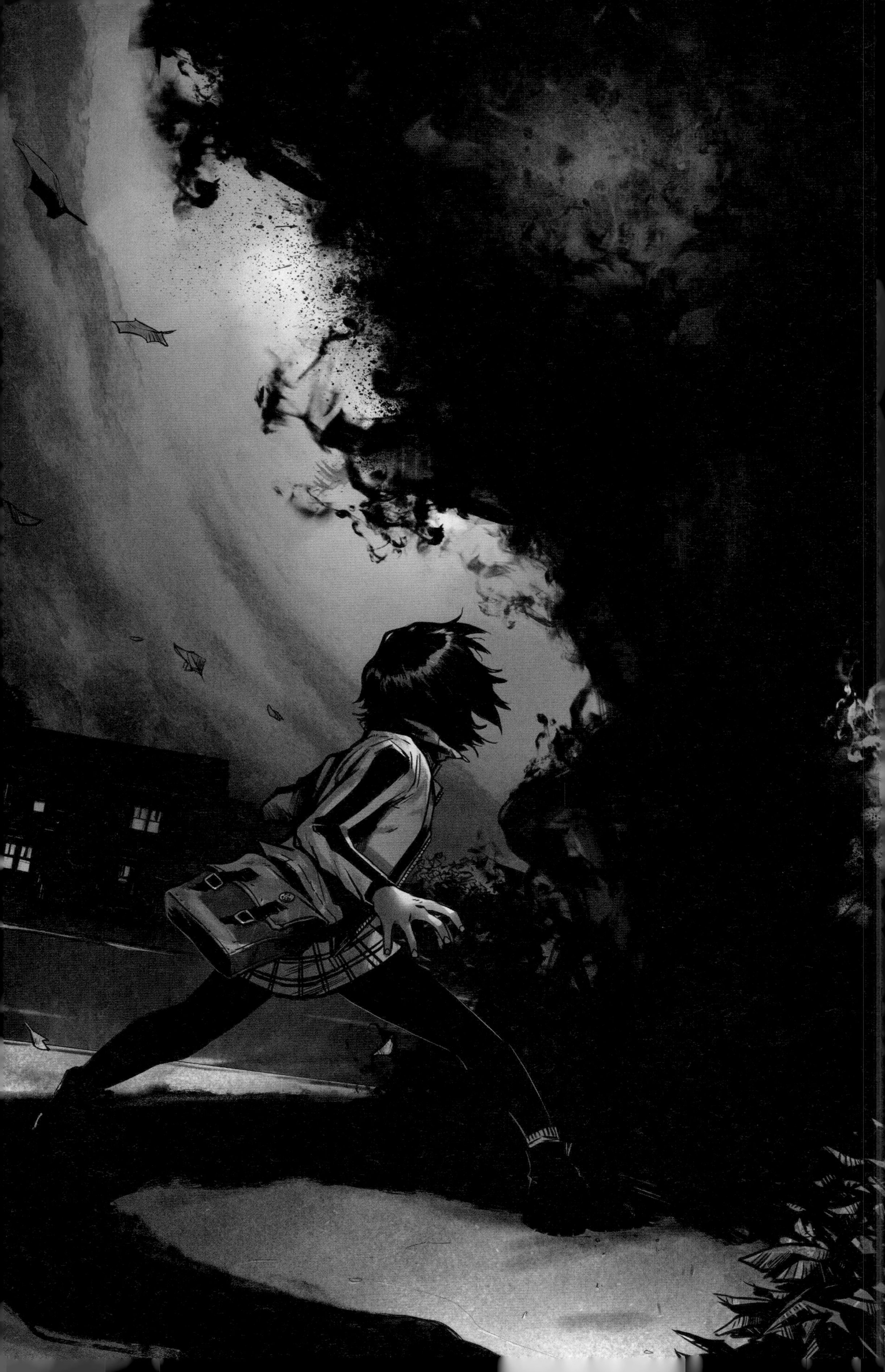

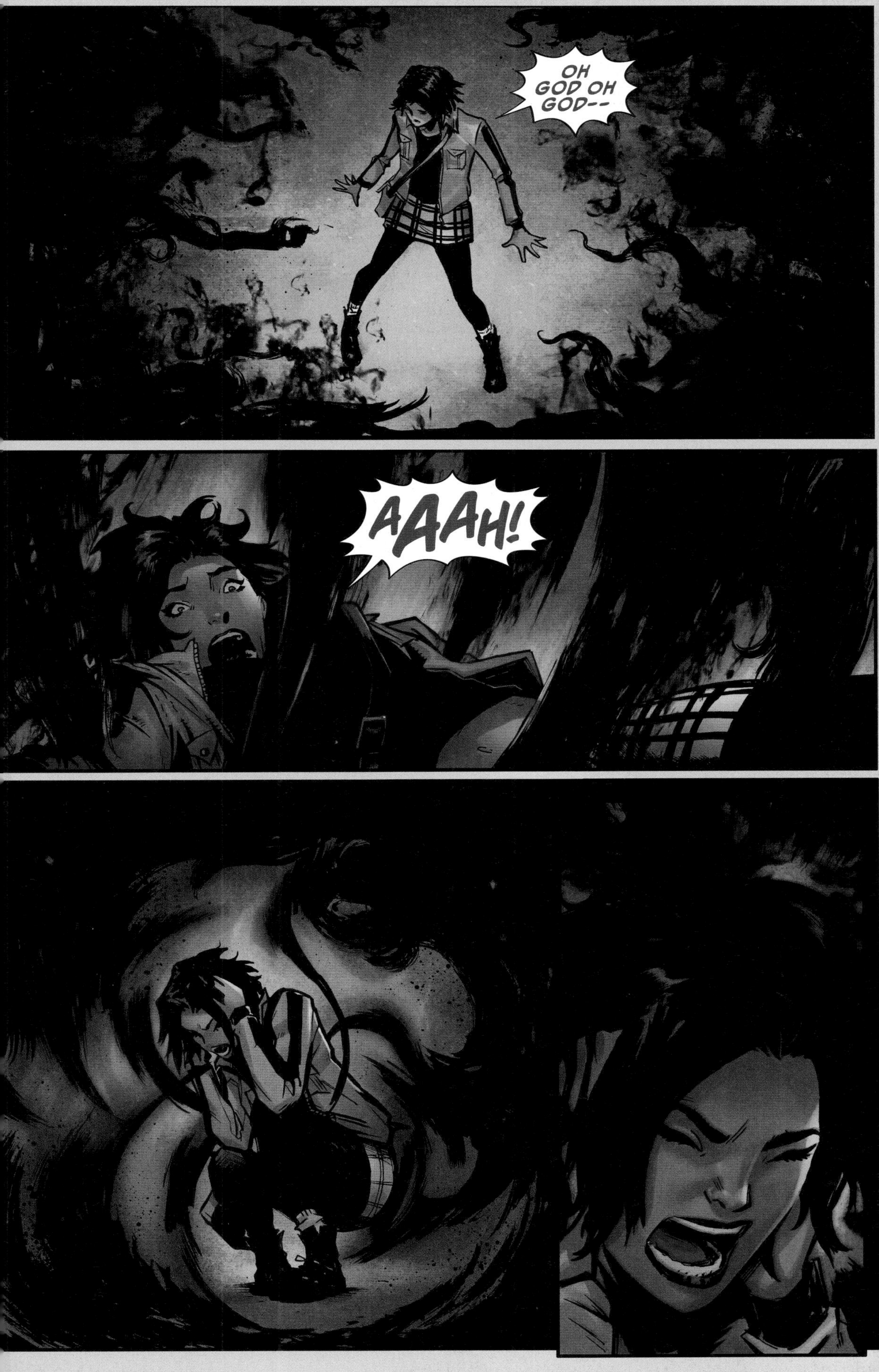
OH GOD OH GOD--
AAAH!

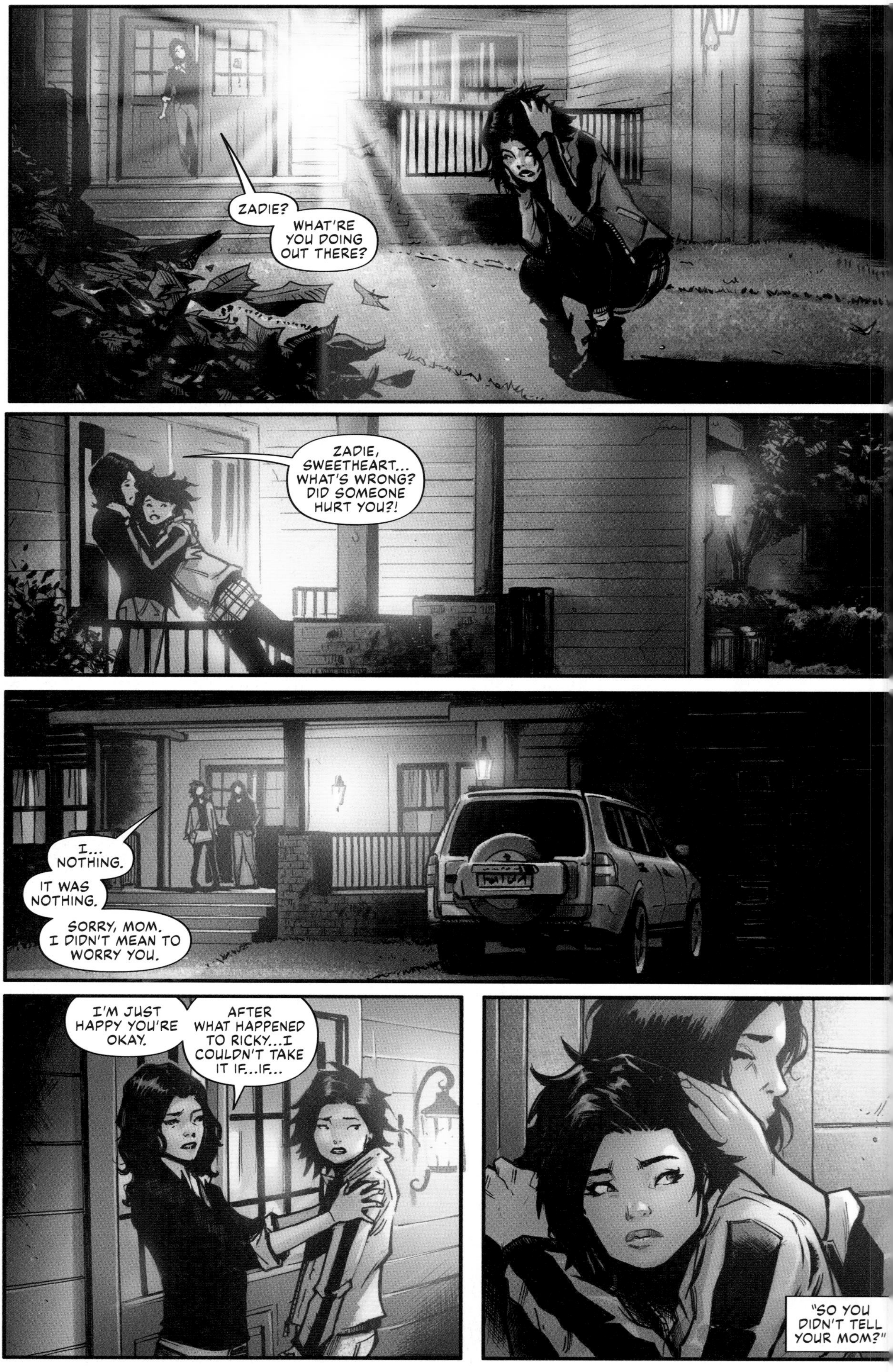
ZADIE?
WHAT'RE YOU DOING OUT THERE?
ZADIE, SWEETHEART... WHAT'S WRONG? DID SOMEONE HURT YOU?!
I... NOTHING.
IT WAS NOTHING.
SORRY, MOM. I DIDN'T MEAN TO WORRY YOU.
I'M JUST HAPPY YOU'RE OKAY.
AFTER WHAT HAPPENED TO RICKY...I COULDN'T TAKE IT IF...IF...
"SO YOU DIDN'T TELL YOUR MOM?"

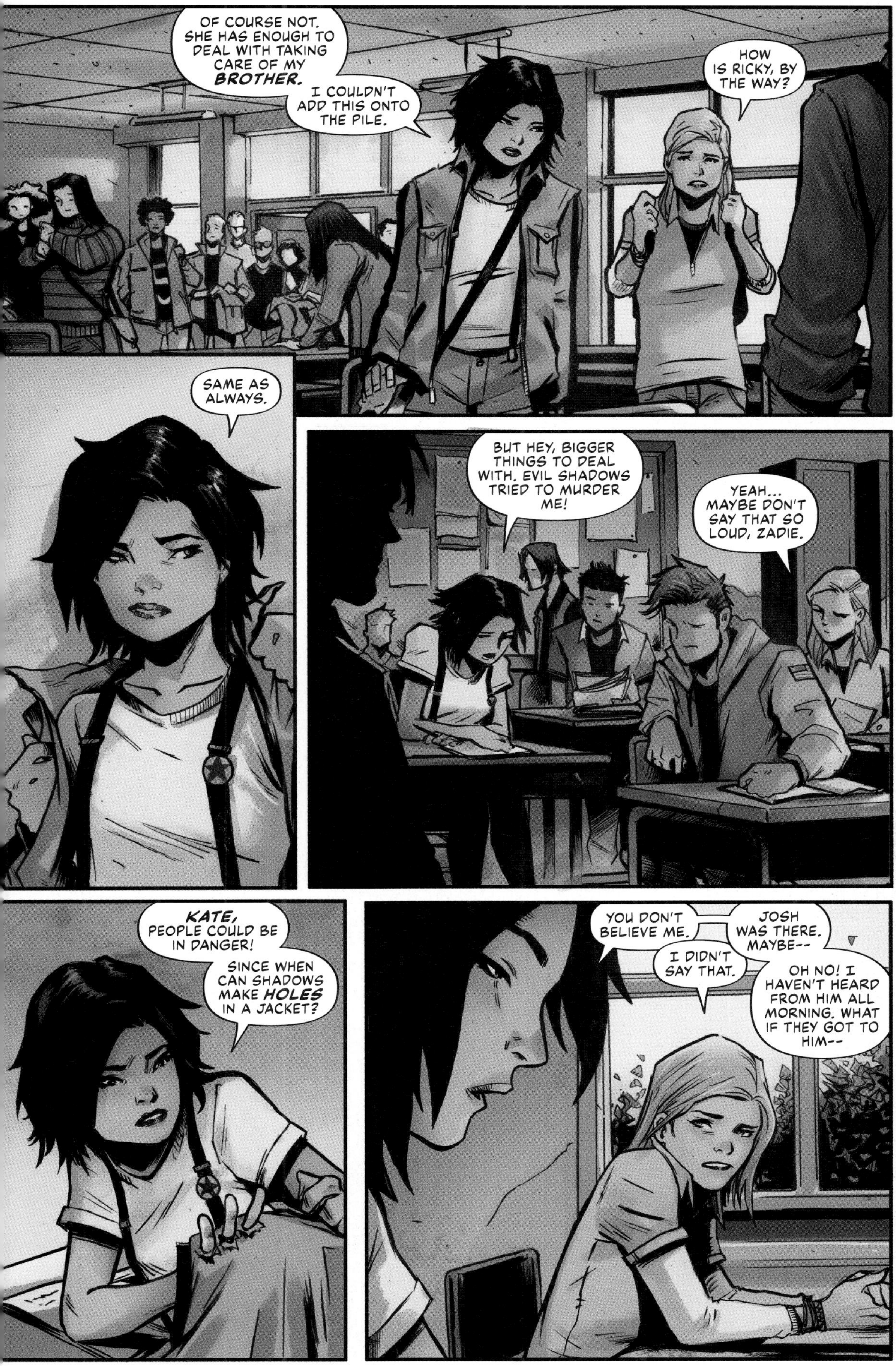

OF COURSE NOT. SHE HAS ENOUGH TO DEAL WITH TAKING CARE OF MY *BROTHER.*
I COULDN'T ADD THIS ONTO THE PILE.
HOW IS RICKY, BY THE WAY?
SAME AS ALWAYS.
BUT HEY, BIGGER THINGS TO DEAL WITH. EVIL SHADOWS TRIED TO MURDER ME!
YEAH... MAYBE DON'T SAY THAT SO LOUD, ZADIE.
KATE, PEOPLE COULD BE IN DANGER!
SINCE WHEN CAN SHADOWS MAKE *HOLES* IN A JACKET?
YOU DON'T BELIEVE ME.
I DIDN'T SAY THAT.
JOSH WAS THERE. MAYBE--
OH NO! I HAVEN'T HEARD FROM HIM ALL MORNING. WHAT IF THEY GOT TO HIM--

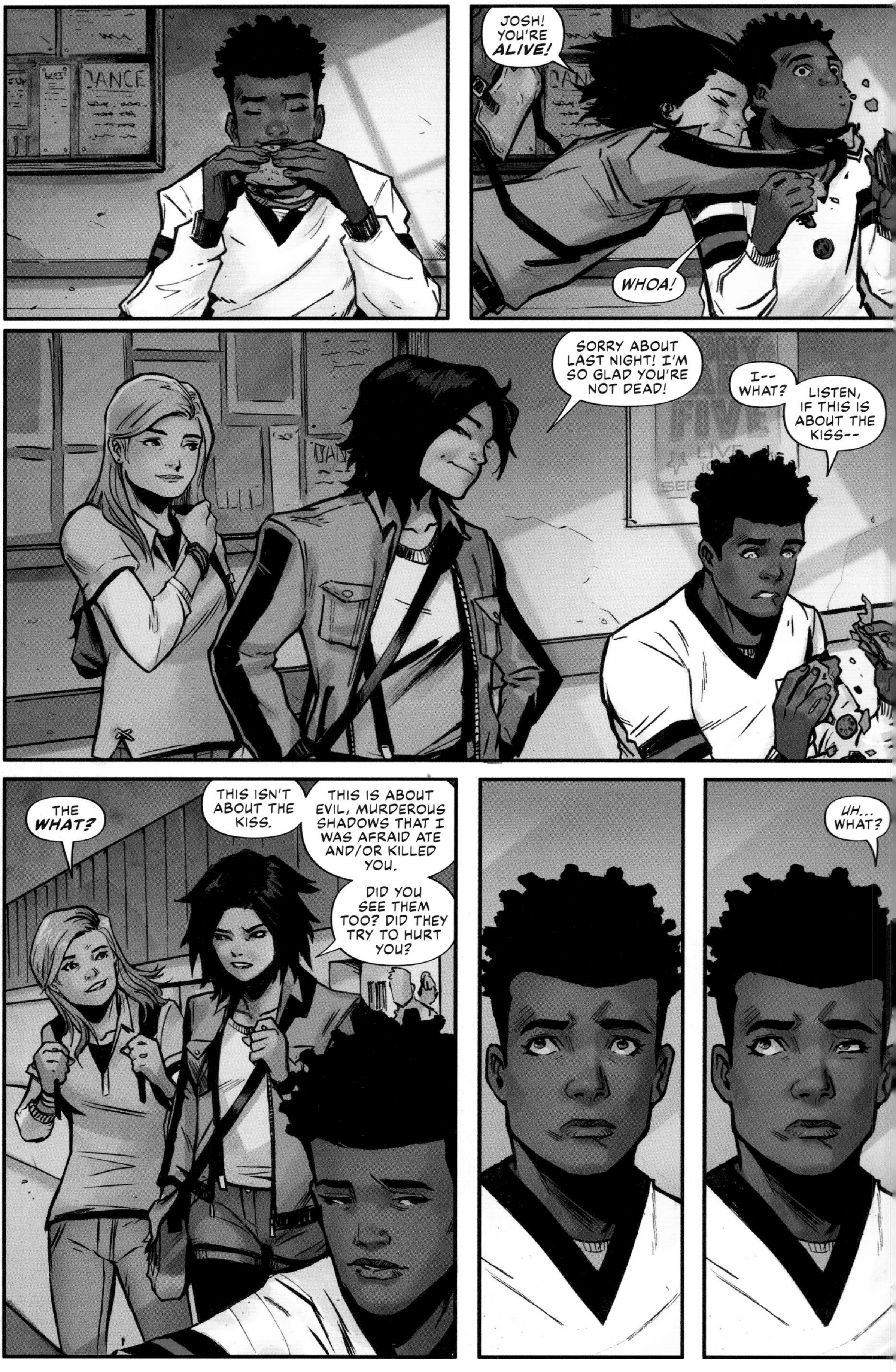

JOSH! YOU'RE ALIVE!
WHOA!
SORRY ABOUT LAST NIGHT! I'M SO GLAD YOU'RE NOT DEAD!
I-- WHAT?
LISTEN, IF THIS IS ABOUT THE KISS--
THE WHAT?
THIS ISN'T ABOUT THE KISS.
THIS IS ABOUT EVIL, MURDEROUS SHADOWS THAT I WAS AFRAID ATE AND/OR KILLED YOU.
DID YOU SEE THEM TOO? DID THEY TRY TO HURT YOU?
UH... WHAT?

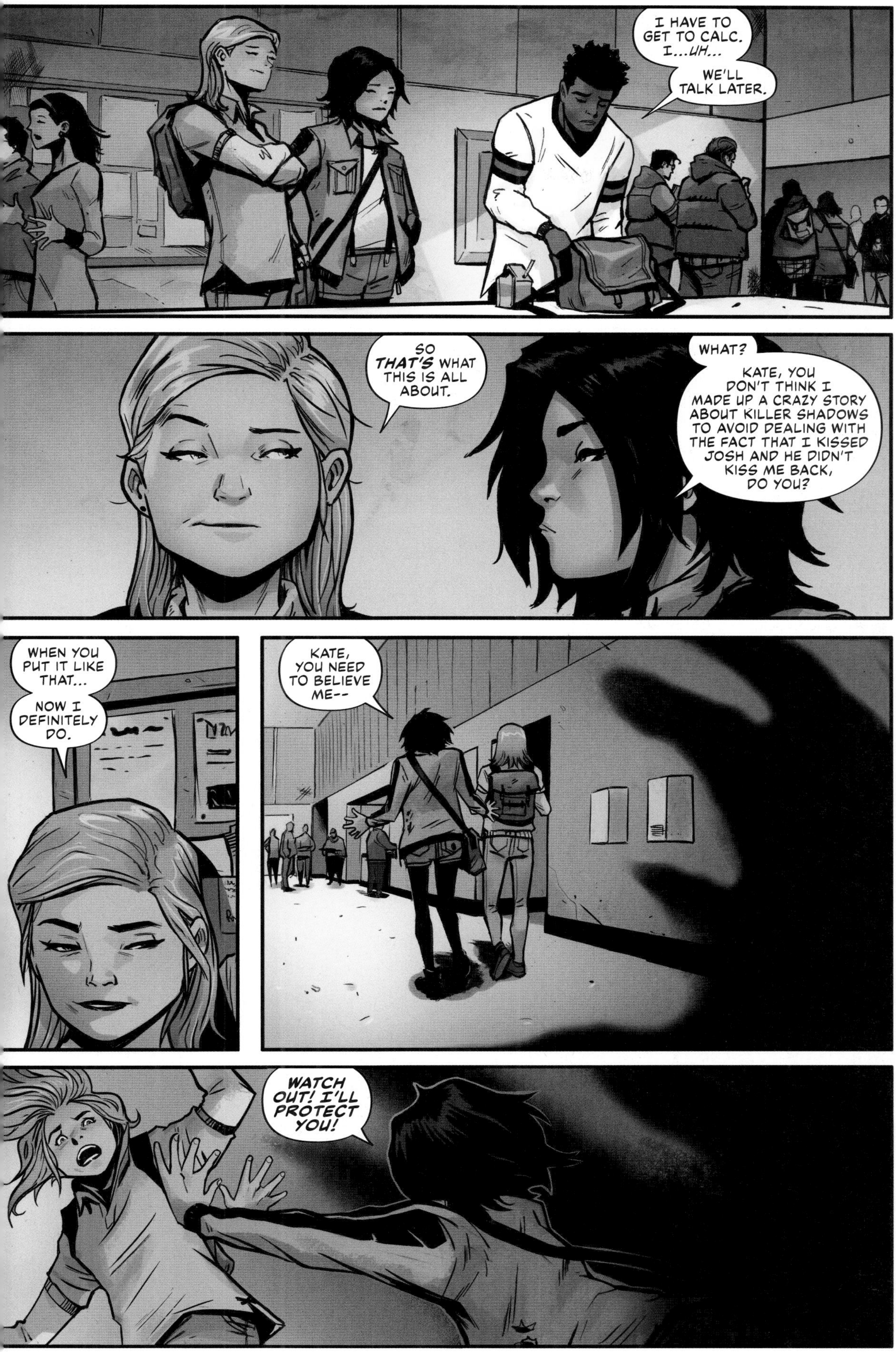
I HAVE TO GET TO CALC. I...UH...
WE'LL TALK LATER.
SO THAT'S WHAT THIS IS ALL ABOUT.
WHAT?
KATE, YOU DON'T THINK I MADE UP A CRAZY STORY ABOUT KILLER SHADOWS TO AVOID DEALING WITH THE FACT THAT I KISSED JOSH AND HE DIDN'T KISS ME BACK, DO YOU?
WHEN YOU PUT IT LIKE THAT...
NOW I DEFINITELY DO.
KATE, YOU NEED TO BELIEVE ME--
WATCH OUT! I'LL PROTECT YOU!

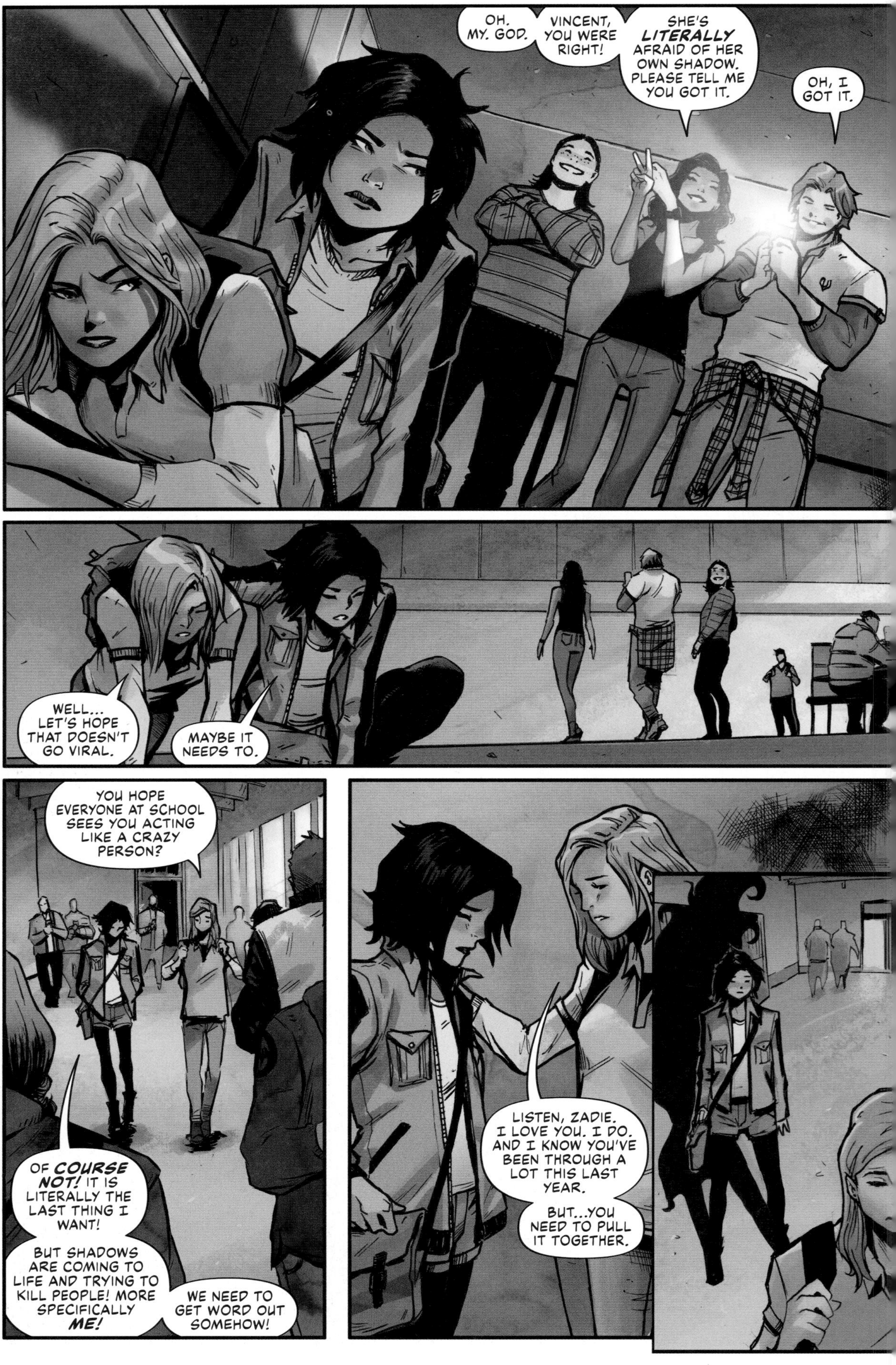

OH. MY. GOD.
VINCENT, YOU WERE RIGHT!
SHE'S *LITERALLY* AFRAID OF HER OWN SHADOW. PLEASE TELL ME YOU GOT IT.
OH, I GOT IT.
WELL... LET'S HOPE THAT DOESN'T GO VIRAL.
MAYBE IT NEEDS TO.
YOU HOPE EVERYONE AT SCHOOL SEES YOU ACTING LIKE A CRAZY PERSON?
OF *COURSE NOT!* IT IS LITERALLY THE LAST THING I WANT!
BUT SHADOWS ARE COMING TO LIFE AND TRYING TO KILL PEOPLE! MORE SPECIFICALLY *ME!*
WE NEED TO GET WORD OUT SOMEHOW!
LISTEN, ZADIE. I LOVE YOU. I DO. AND I KNOW YOU'VE BEEN THROUGH A LOT THIS LAST YEAR.
BUT...YOU NEED TO PULL IT TOGETHER.

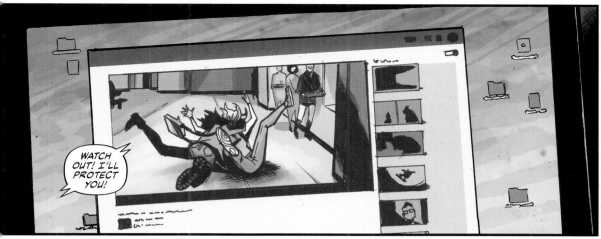

WATCH OUT! I'LL PROTECT YOU!

OOF.

AAAAND NOW I SEE THE NICKNAMES.

"CRAZY ZADIE." CALLED IT.

OH. WOW. THOSE ARE MUCH WORSE.

MAYBE I *HAVE* FINALLY LOST IT.

WHAT DO YOU THINK, RICKY?

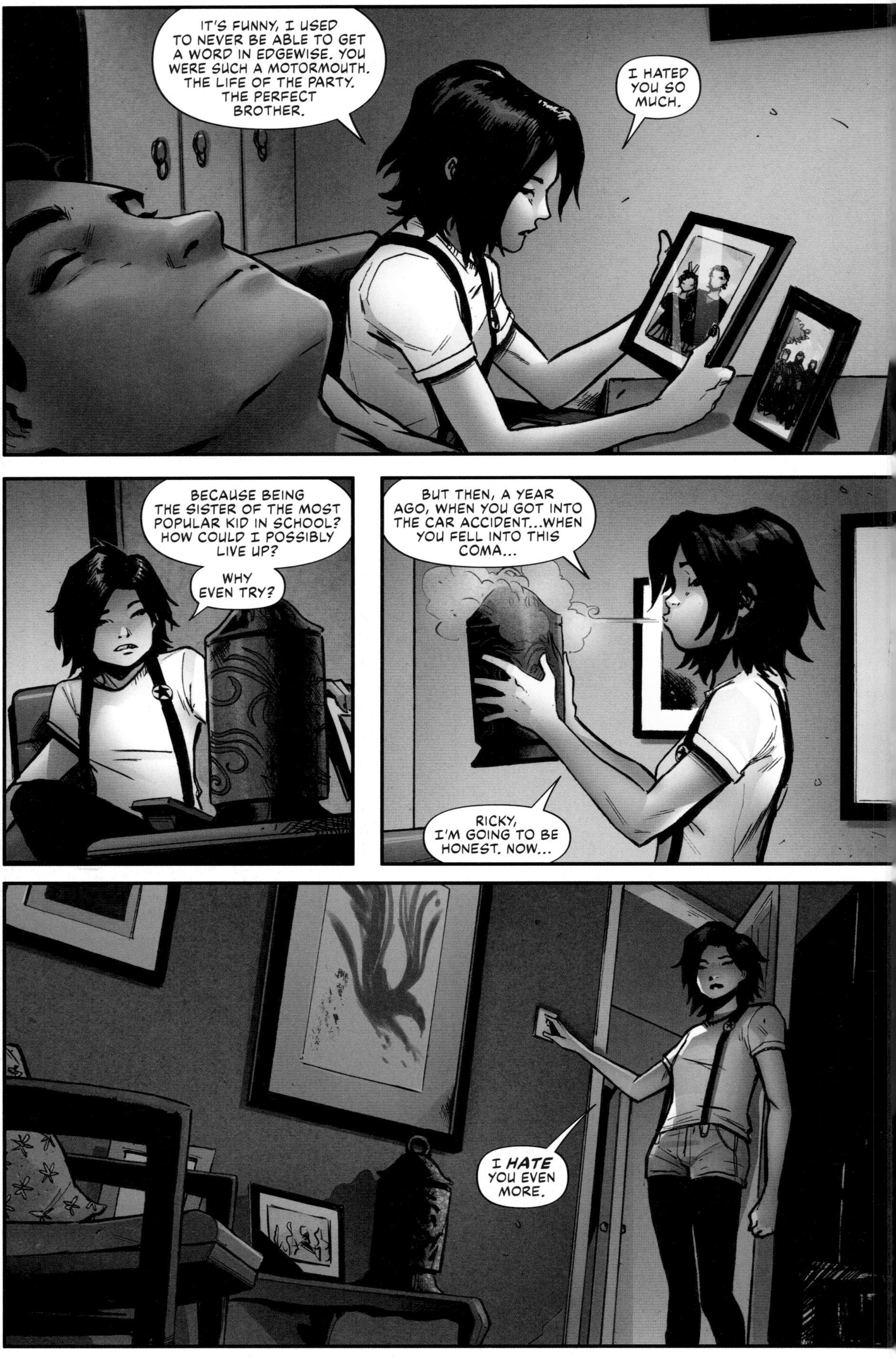
IT'S FUNNY, I USED TO NEVER BE ABLE TO GET A WORD IN EDGEWISE. YOU WERE SUCH A MOTORMOUTH. THE LIFE OF THE PARTY. THE PERFECT BROTHER.
I HATED YOU SO MUCH.
BECAUSE BEING THE SISTER OF THE MOST POPULAR KID IN SCHOOL? HOW COULD I POSSIBLY LIVE UP?
WHY EVEN TRY?
BUT THEN, A YEAR AGO, WHEN YOU GOT INTO THE CAR ACCIDENT...WHEN YOU FELL INTO THIS COMA...
RICKY, I'M GOING TO BE HONEST. NOW...
I HATE YOU EVEN MORE.

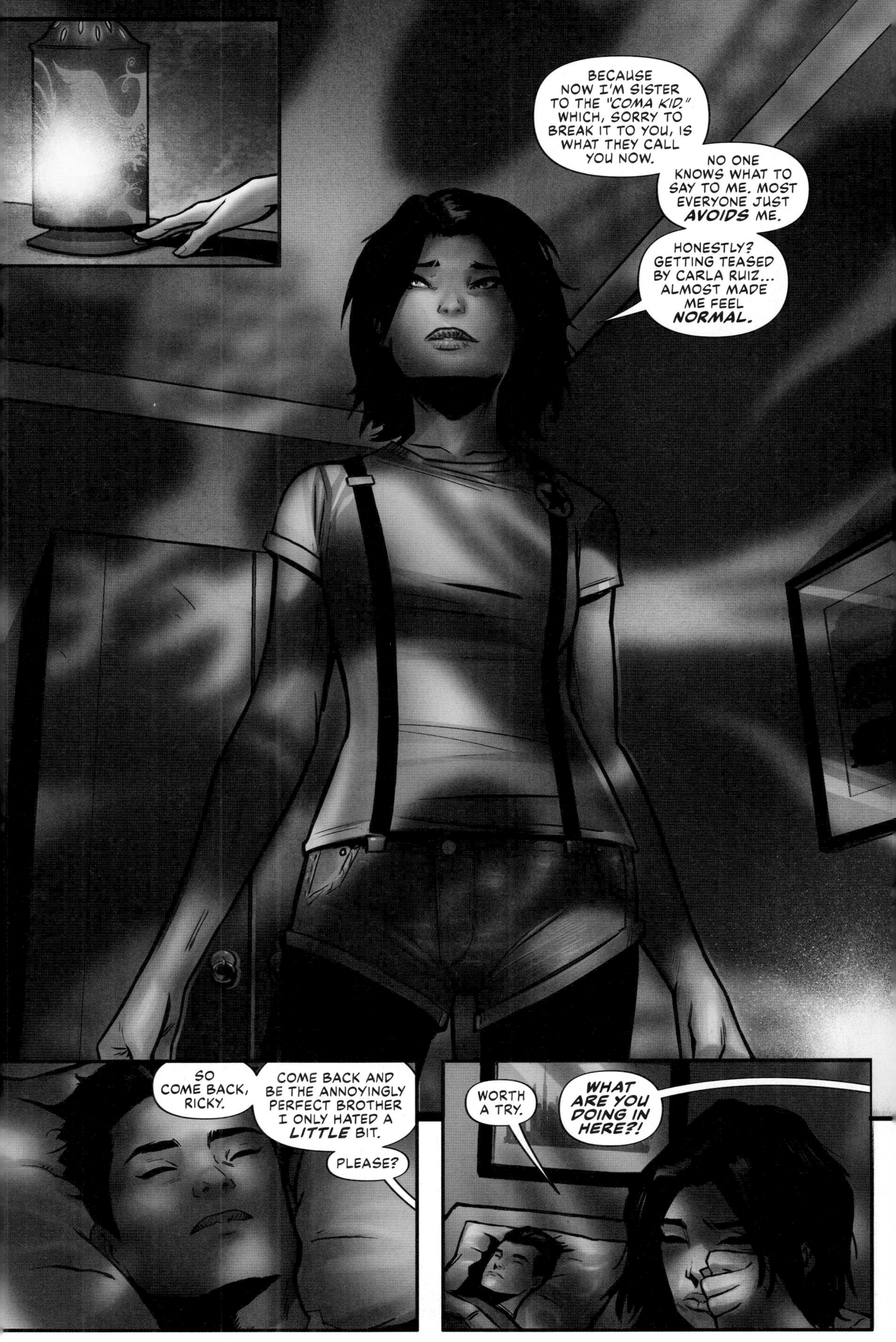
BECAUSE NOW I'M SISTER TO THE "COMA KID," WHICH, SORRY TO BREAK IT TO YOU, IS WHAT THEY CALL YOU NOW.
NO ONE KNOWS WHAT TO SAY TO ME. MOST EVERYONE JUST AVOIDS ME.
HONESTLY? GETTING TEASED BY CARLA RUIZ... ALMOST MADE ME FEEL NORMAL.
SO COME BACK, RICKY.
COME BACK AND BE THE ANNOYINGLY PERFECT BROTHER I ONLY HATED A LITTLE BIT.
PLEASE?
WORTH A TRY.
WHAT ARE YOU DOING IN HERE?!

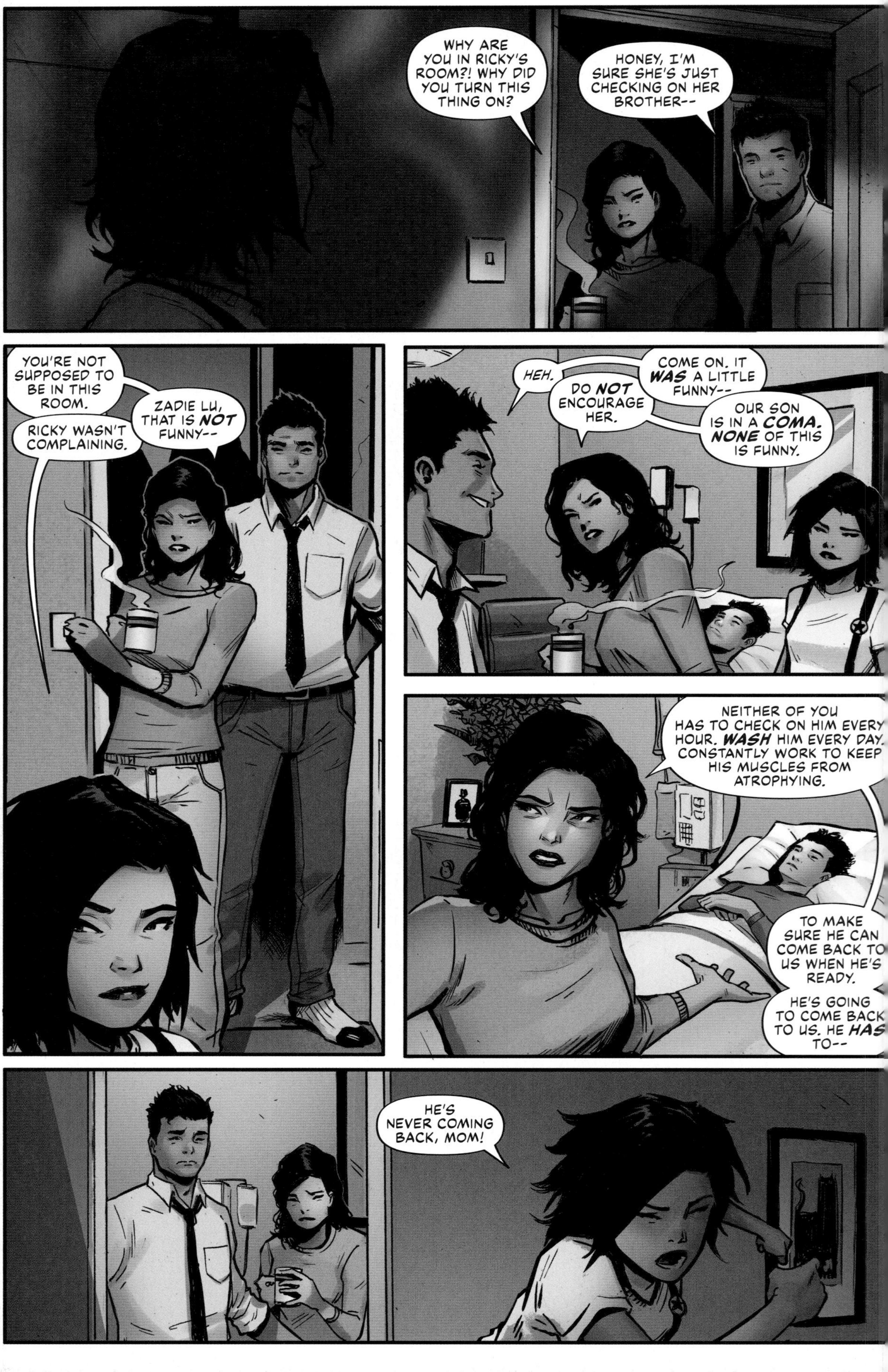
WHY ARE YOU IN RICKY'S ROOM?! WHY DID YOU TURN THIS THING ON?
HONEY, I'M SURE SHE'S JUST CHECKING ON HER BROTHER--
YOU'RE NOT SUPPOSED TO BE IN THIS ROOM.
ZADIE LU, THAT IS NOT FUNNY--
RICKY WASN'T COMPLAINING.
HEH.
COME ON. IT WAS A LITTLE FUNNY--
DO NOT ENCOURAGE HER.
OUR SON IS IN A COMA. NONE OF THIS IS FUNNY.
NEITHER OF YOU HAS TO CHECK ON HIM EVERY HOUR. WASH HIM EVERY DAY. CONSTANTLY WORK TO KEEP HIS MUSCLES FROM ATROPHYING.
TO MAKE SURE HE CAN COME BACK TO US WHEN HE'S READY.
HE'S GOING TO COME BACK TO US. HE HAS TO--
HE'S NEVER COMING BACK, MOM!

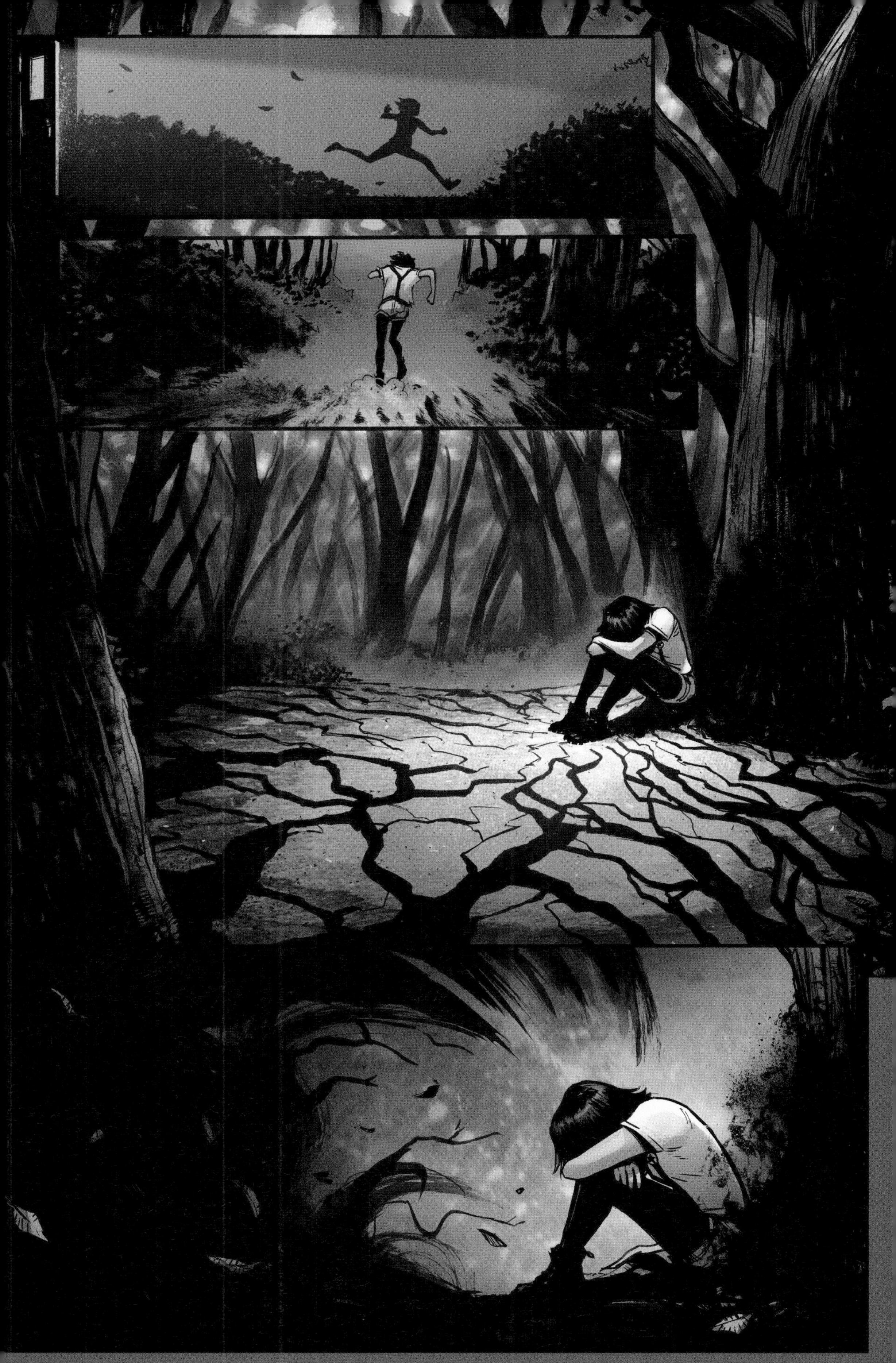

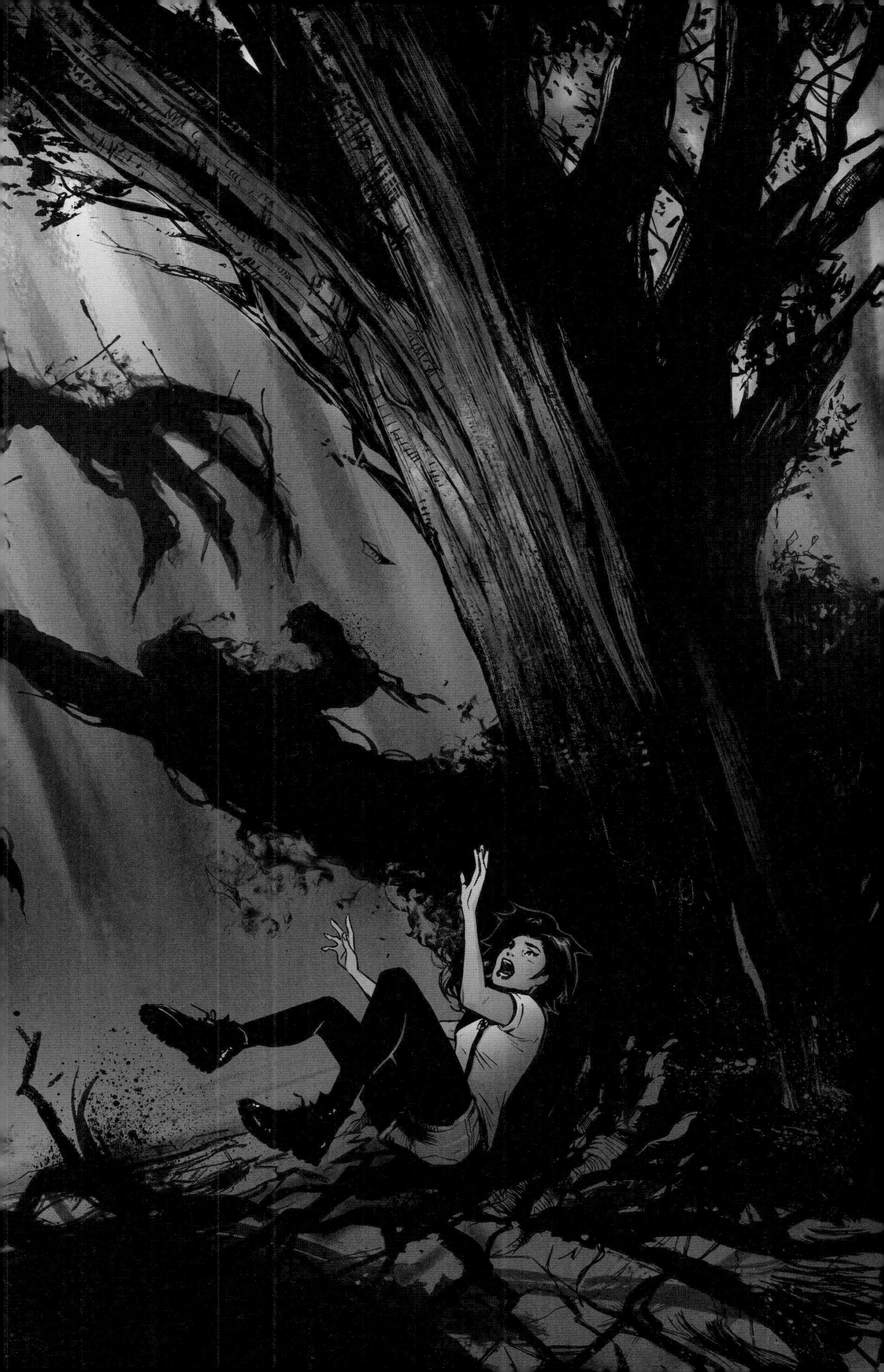

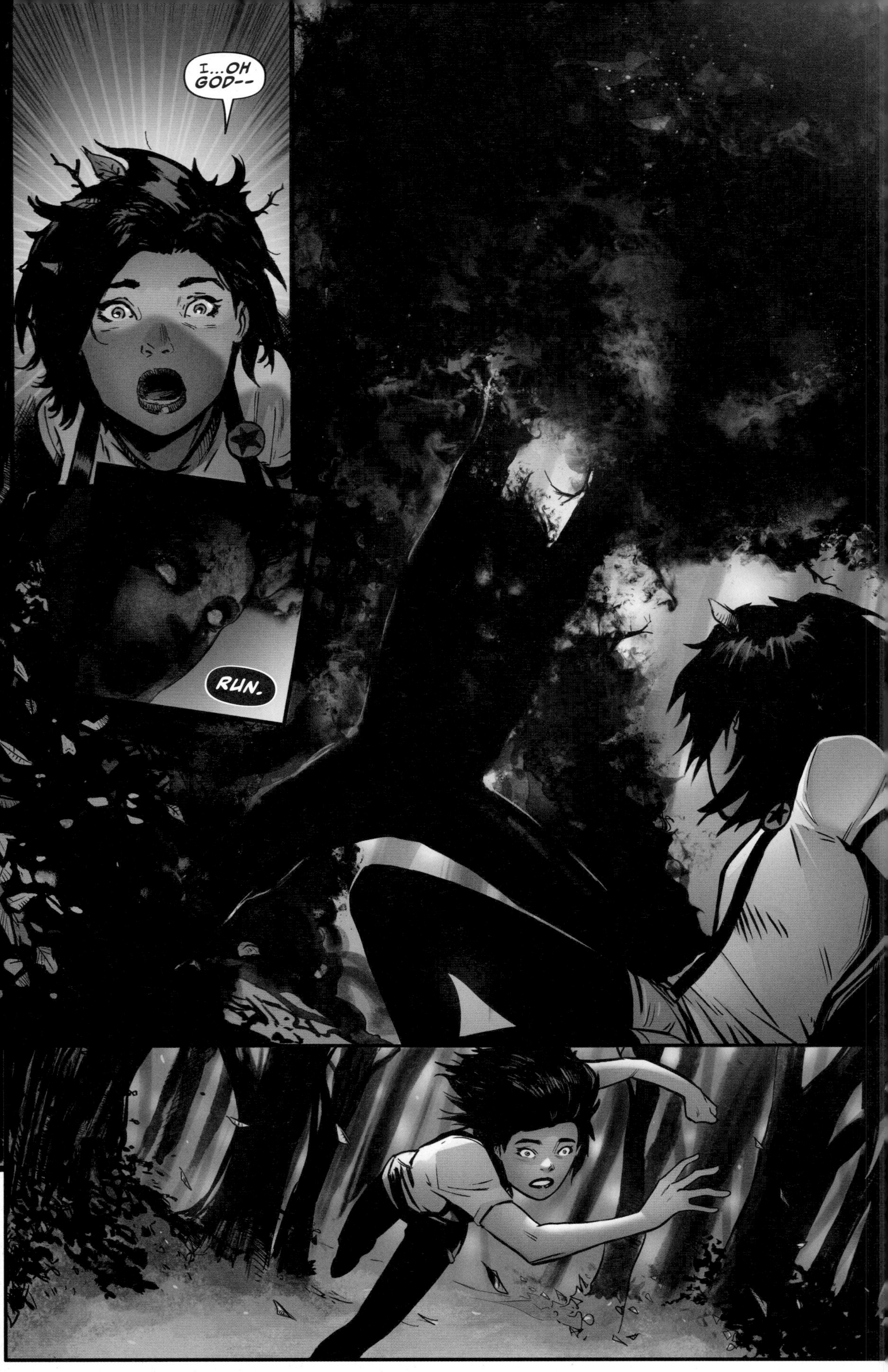
I...OH GOD--
RUN.

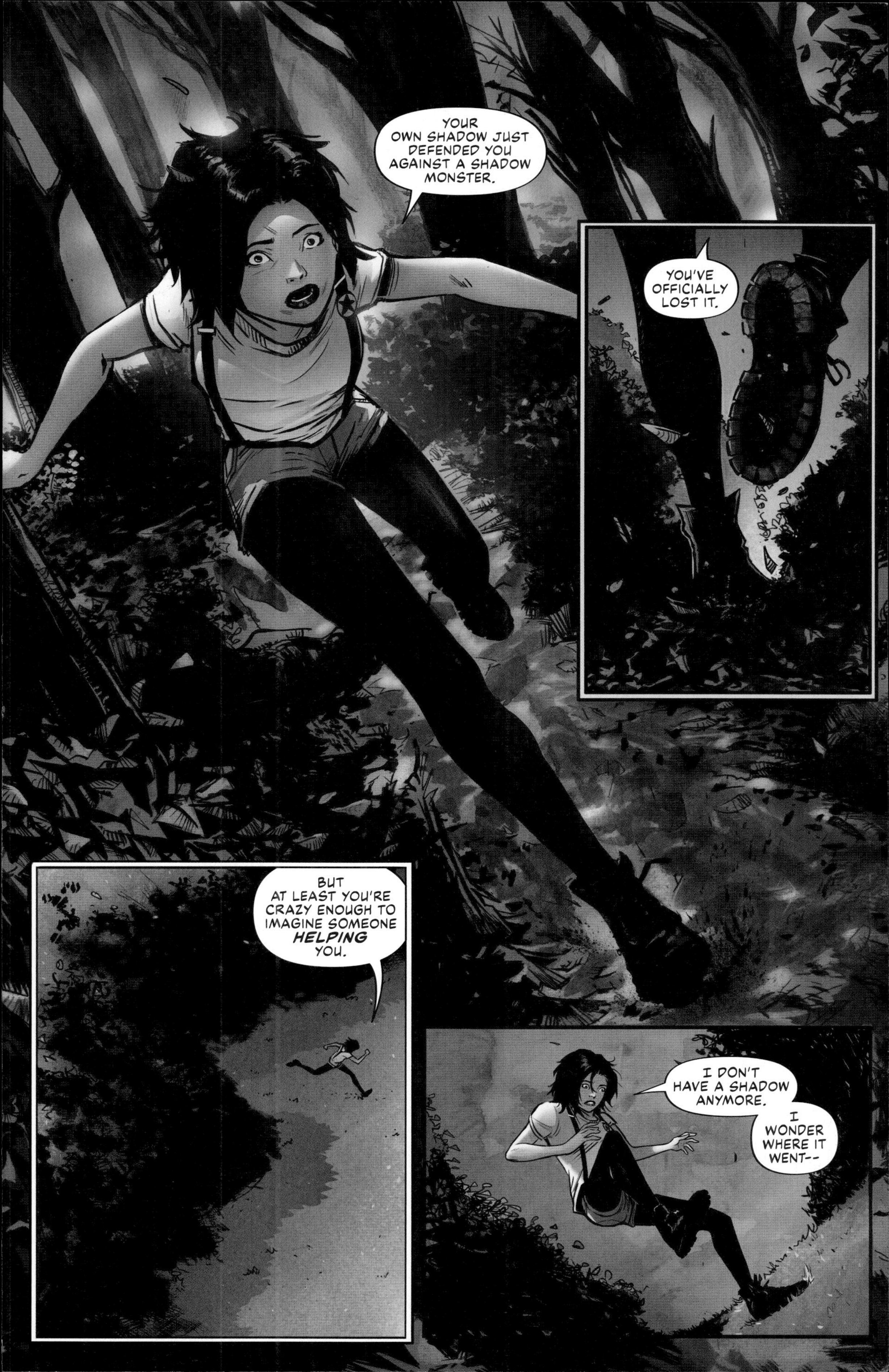
YOUR OWN SHADOW JUST DEFENDED YOU AGAINST A SHADOW MONSTER.
YOU'VE OFFICIALLY LOST IT.
BUT AT LEAST YOU'RE CRAZY ENOUGH TO IMAGINE SOMEONE *HELPING* YOU.
I DON'T HAVE A SHADOW ANYMORE.
I WONDER WHERE IT WENT--

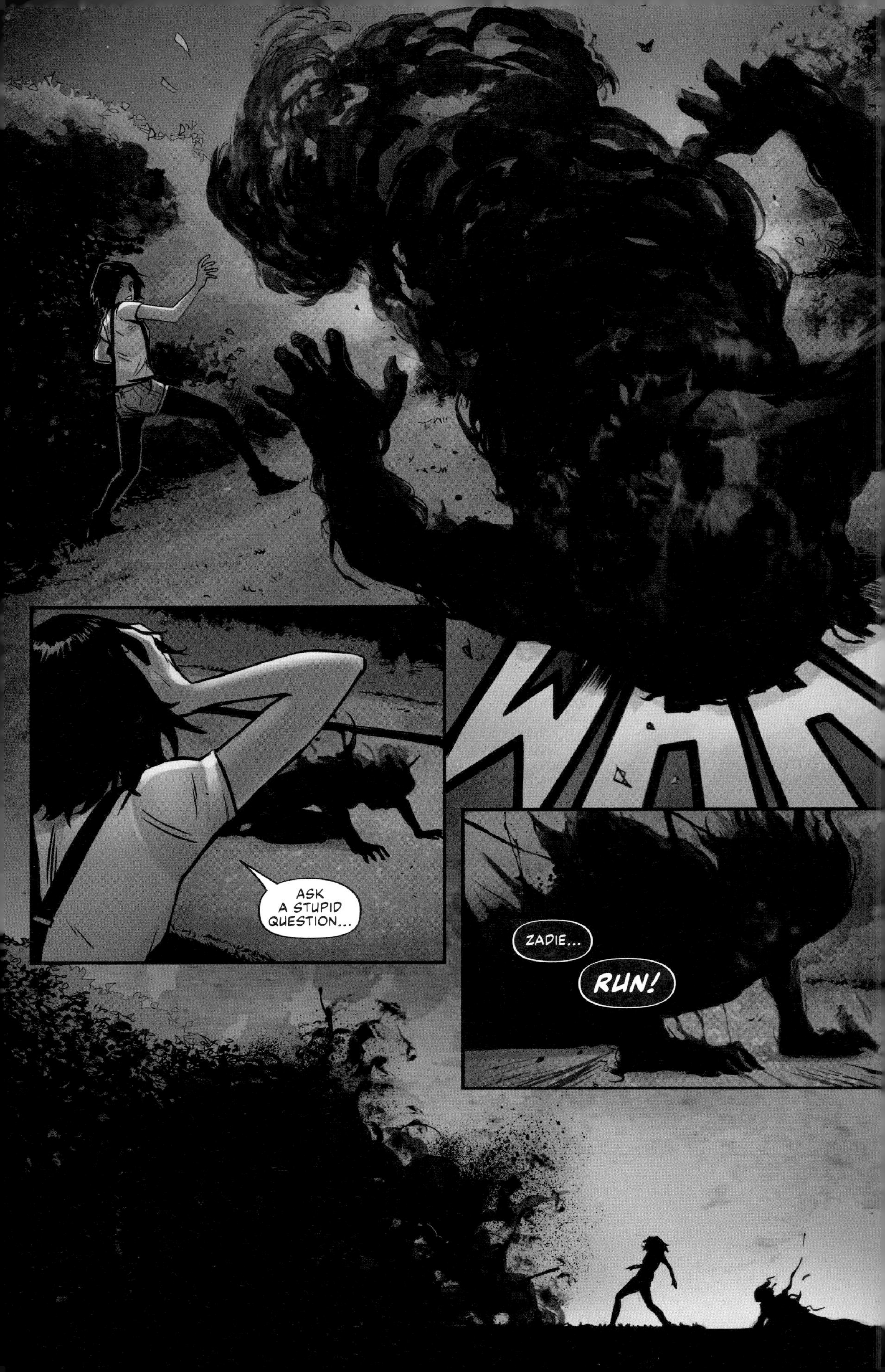
ASK A STUPID QUESTION...
ZADIE...
RUN!

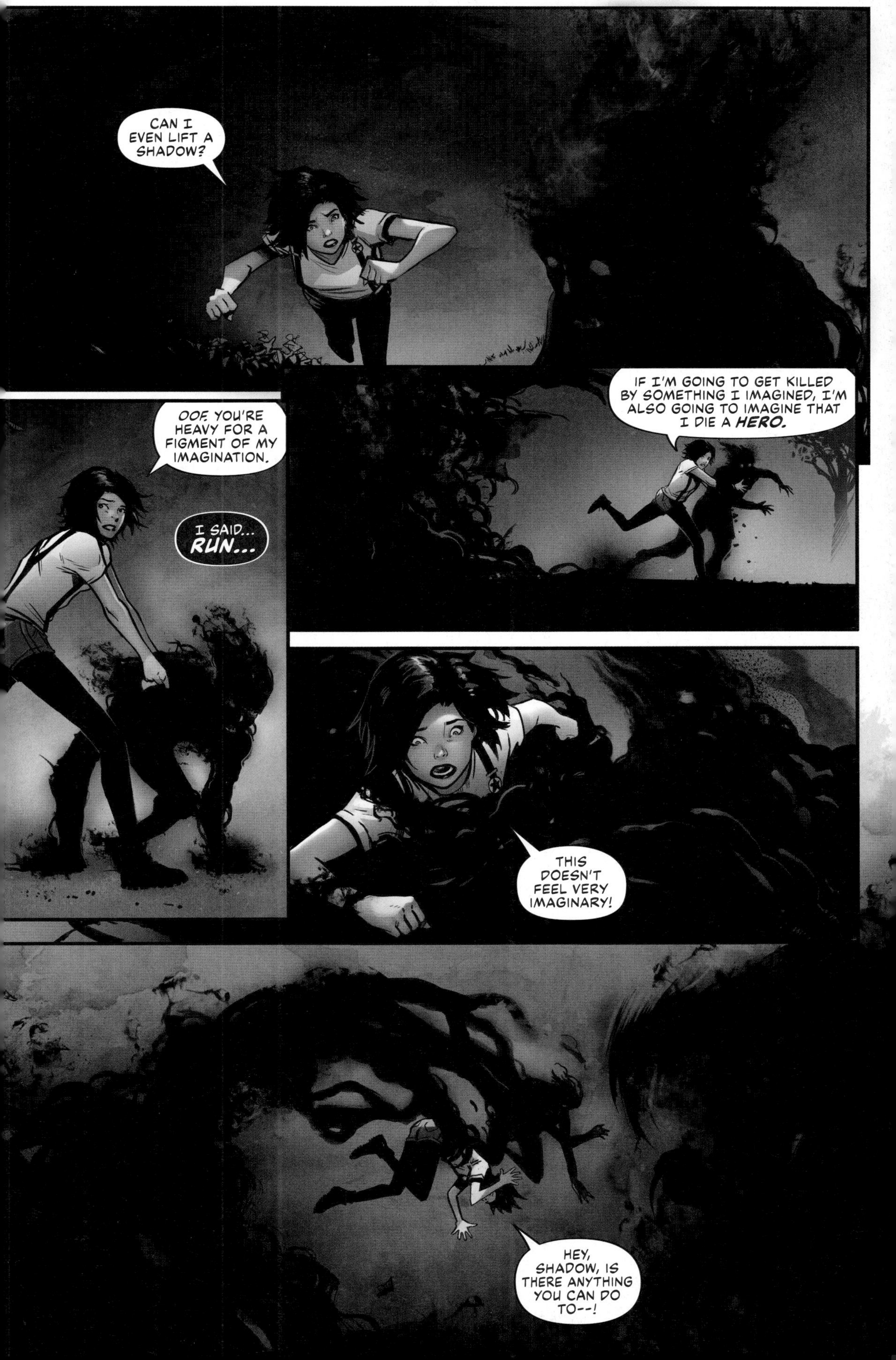
CAN I EVEN LIFT A SHADOW?
OOF. YOU'RE HEAVY FOR A FIGMENT OF MY IMAGINATION.
I SAID... RUN...
IF I'M GOING TO GET KILLED BY SOMETHING I IMAGINED, I'M ALSO GOING TO IMAGINE THAT I DIE A HERO.
THIS DOESN'T FEEL VERY IMAGINARY!
HEY, SHADOW, IS THERE ANYTHING YOU CAN DO TO--!

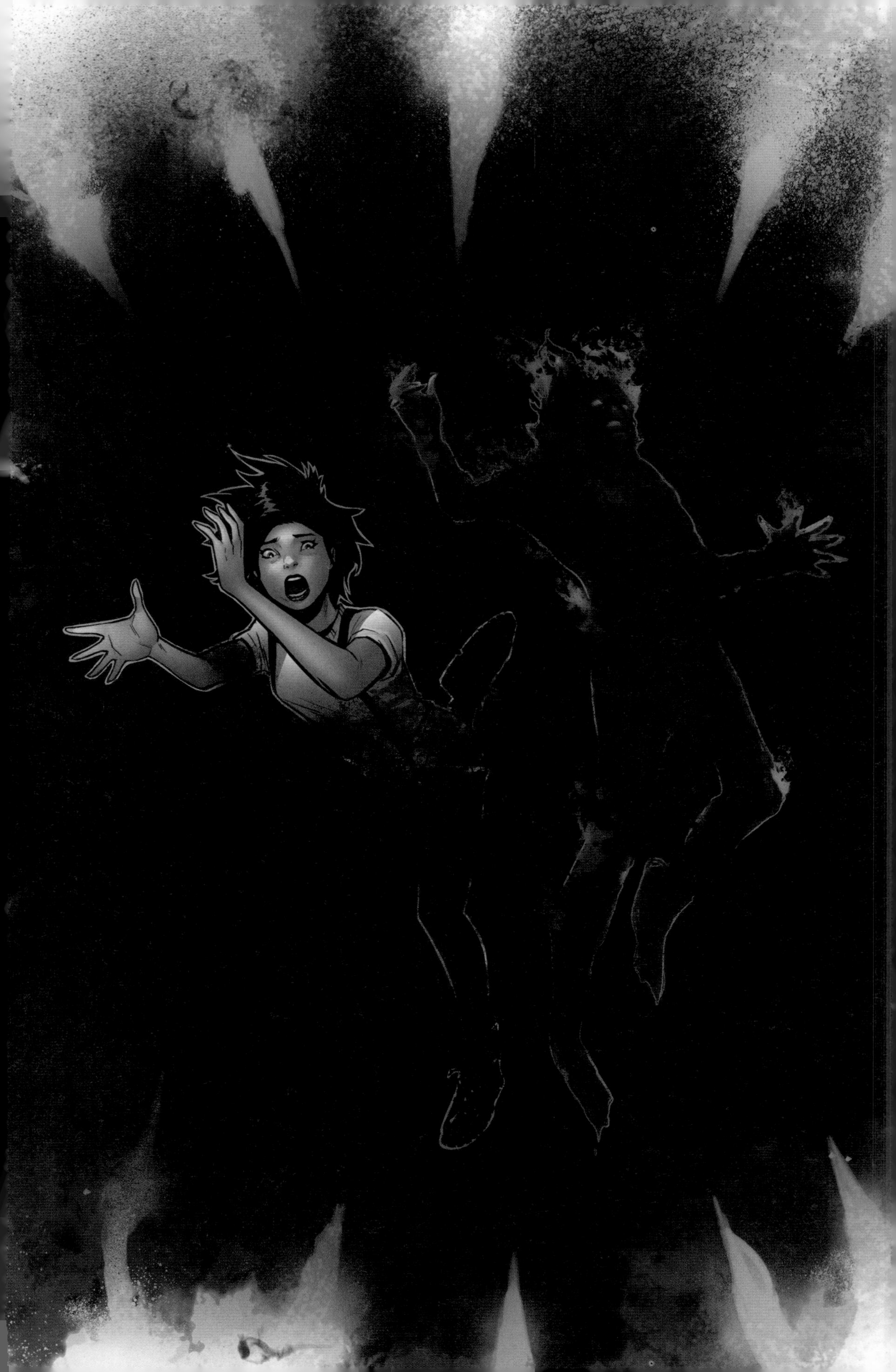

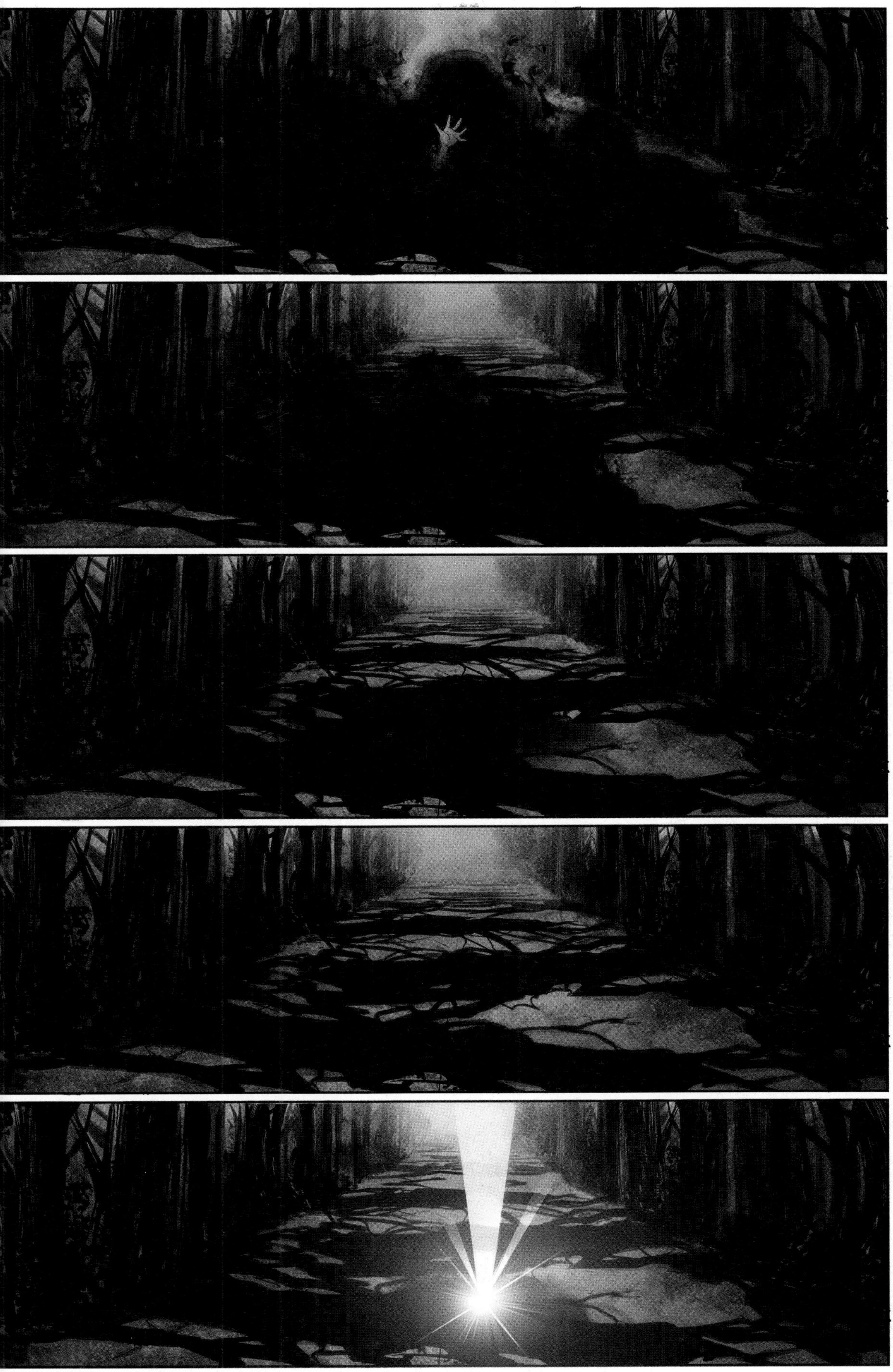

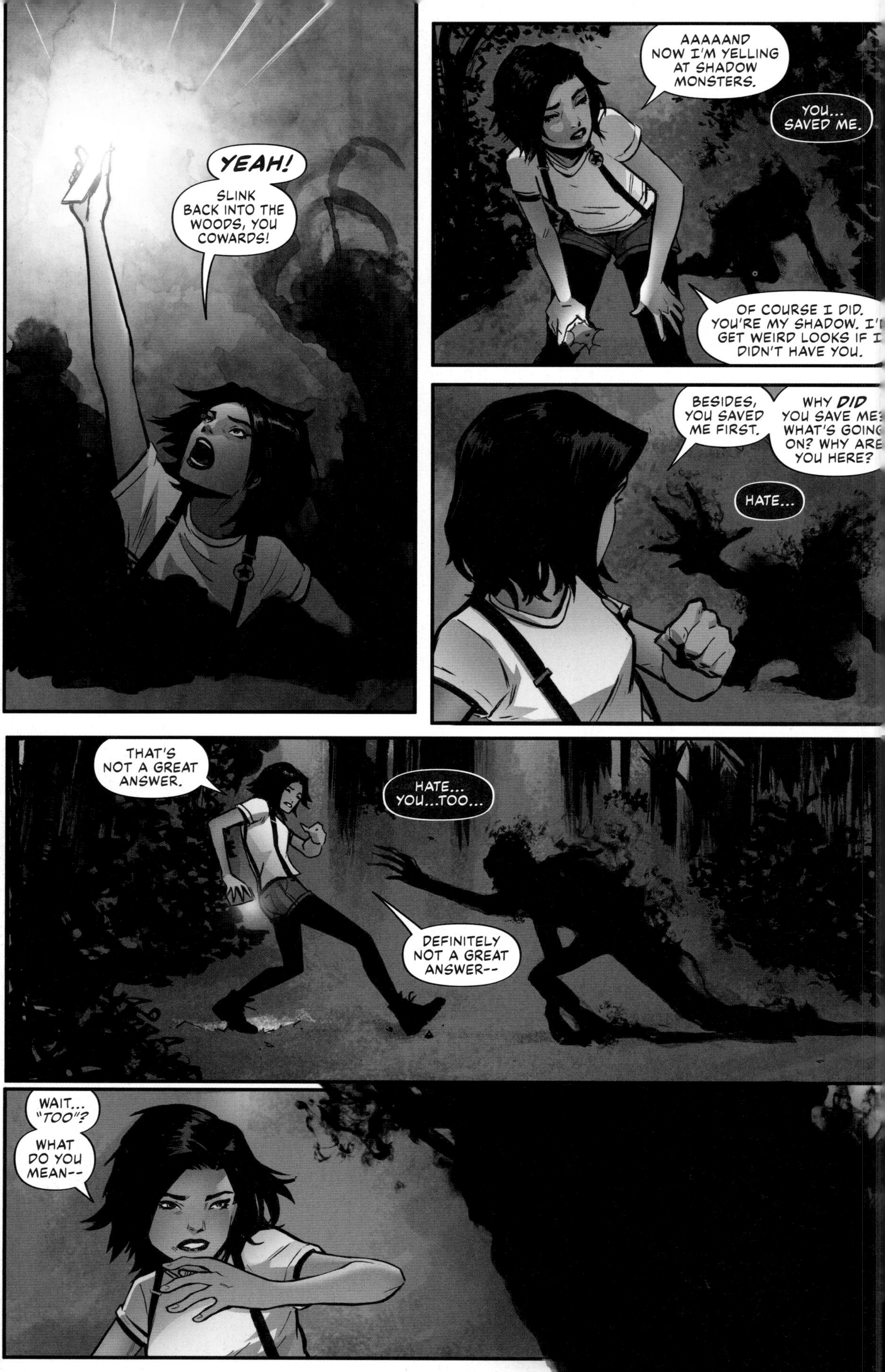

YEAH!
SLINK BACK INTO THE WOODS, YOU COWARDS!
AAAAAND NOW I'M YELLING AT SHADOW MONSTERS.
YOU... SAVED ME.
OF COURSE I DID. YOU'RE MY SHADOW. I'D GET WEIRD LOOKS IF I DIDN'T HAVE YOU.
BESIDES, YOU SAVED ME FIRST.
WHY DID YOU SAVE ME? WHAT'S GOING ON? WHY ARE YOU HERE?
HATE...
THAT'S NOT A GREAT ANSWER.
HATE... YOU...TOO...
DEFINITELY NOT A GREAT ANSWER--
WAIT... "TOO"?
WHAT DO YOU MEAN--

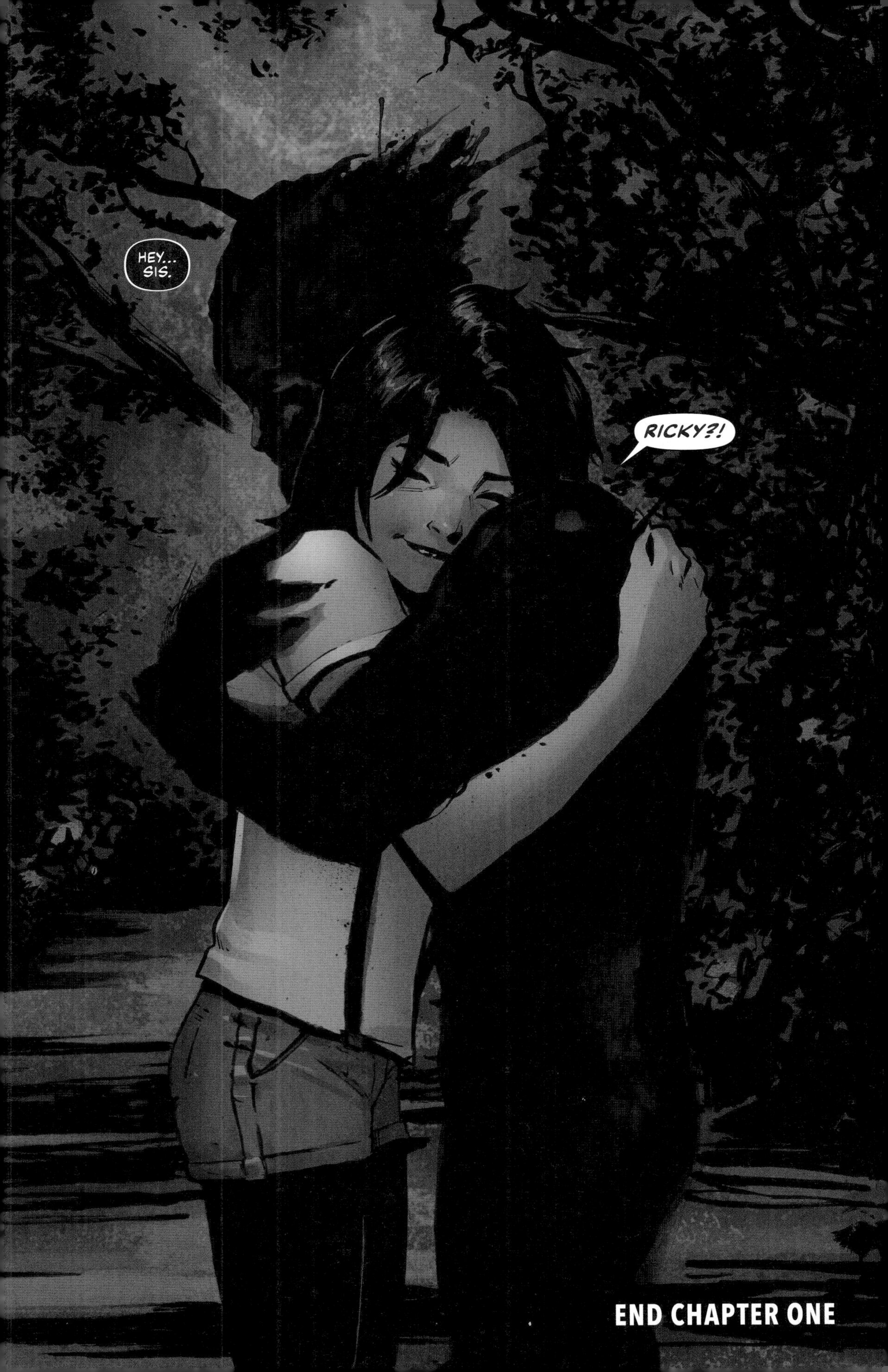
HEY... SIS.
RICKY?!
END CHAPTER ONE

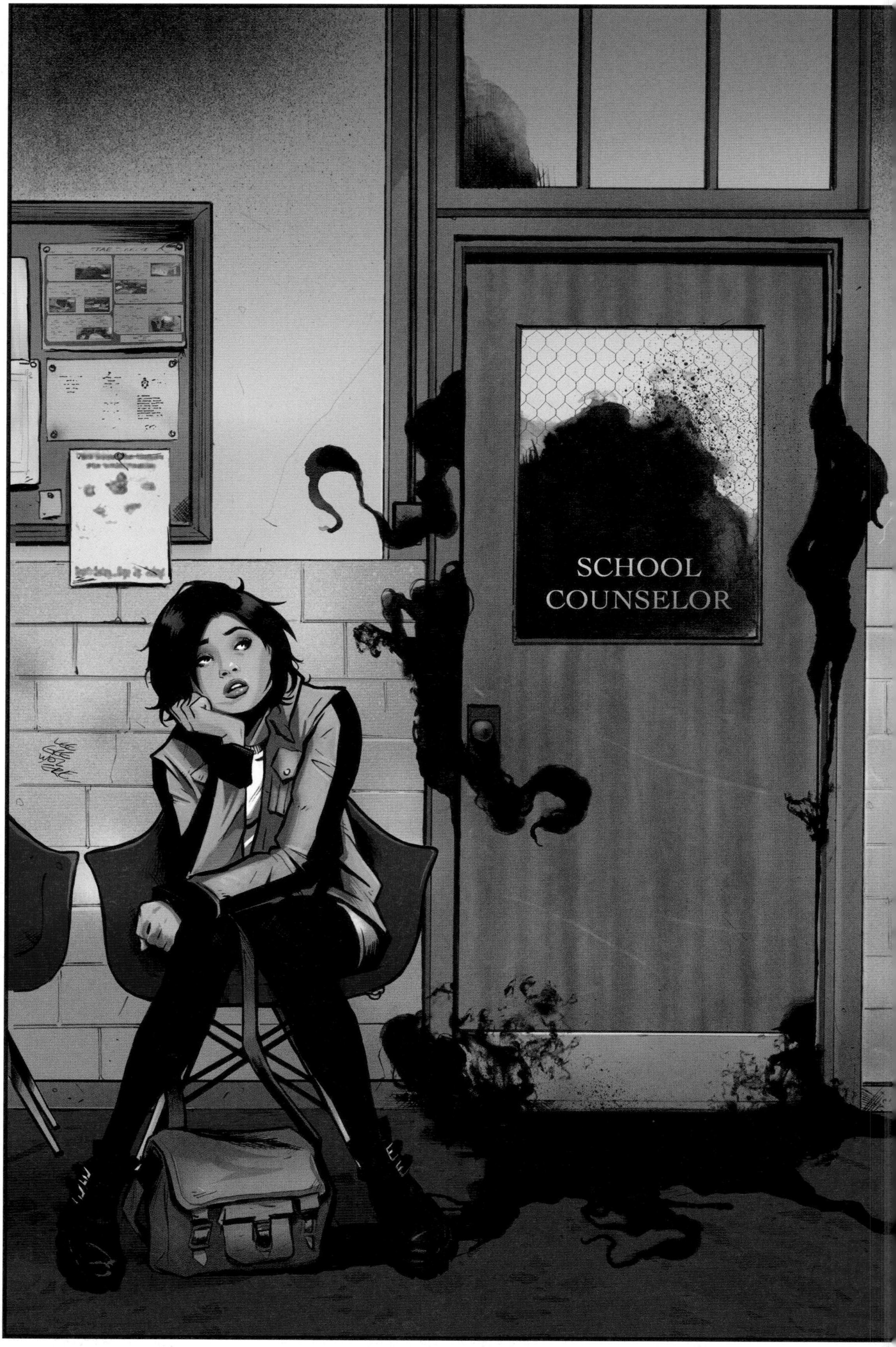
SCHOOL
COUNSELOR

CHAPTER TWO

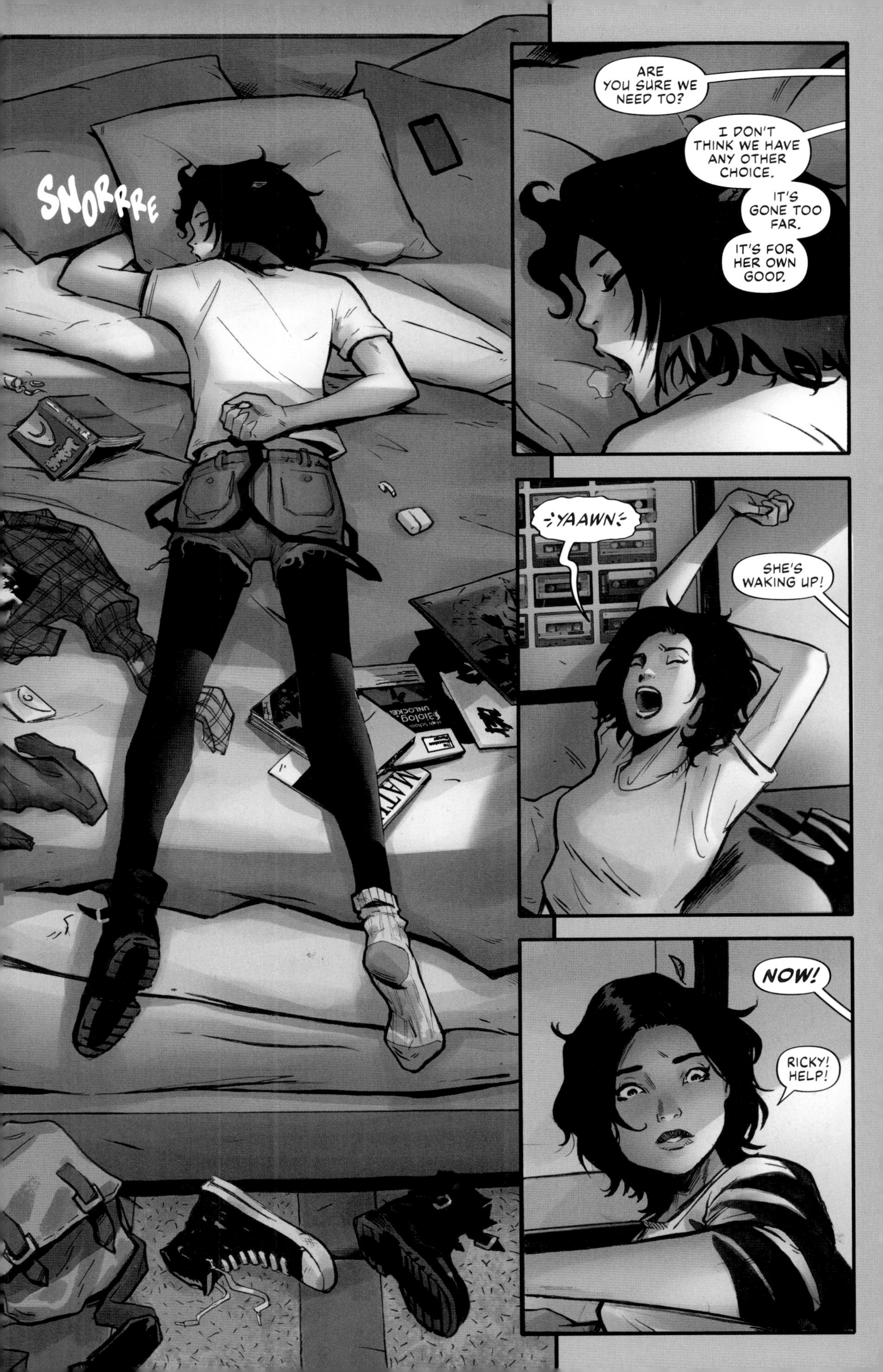
SNORRRE
ARE YOU SURE WE NEED TO?
I DON'T THINK WE HAVE ANY OTHER CHOICE.
IT'S GONE TOO FAR.
IT'S FOR HER OWN GOOD.
YAAWN
SHE'S WAKING UP!
NOW!
RICKY! HELP!

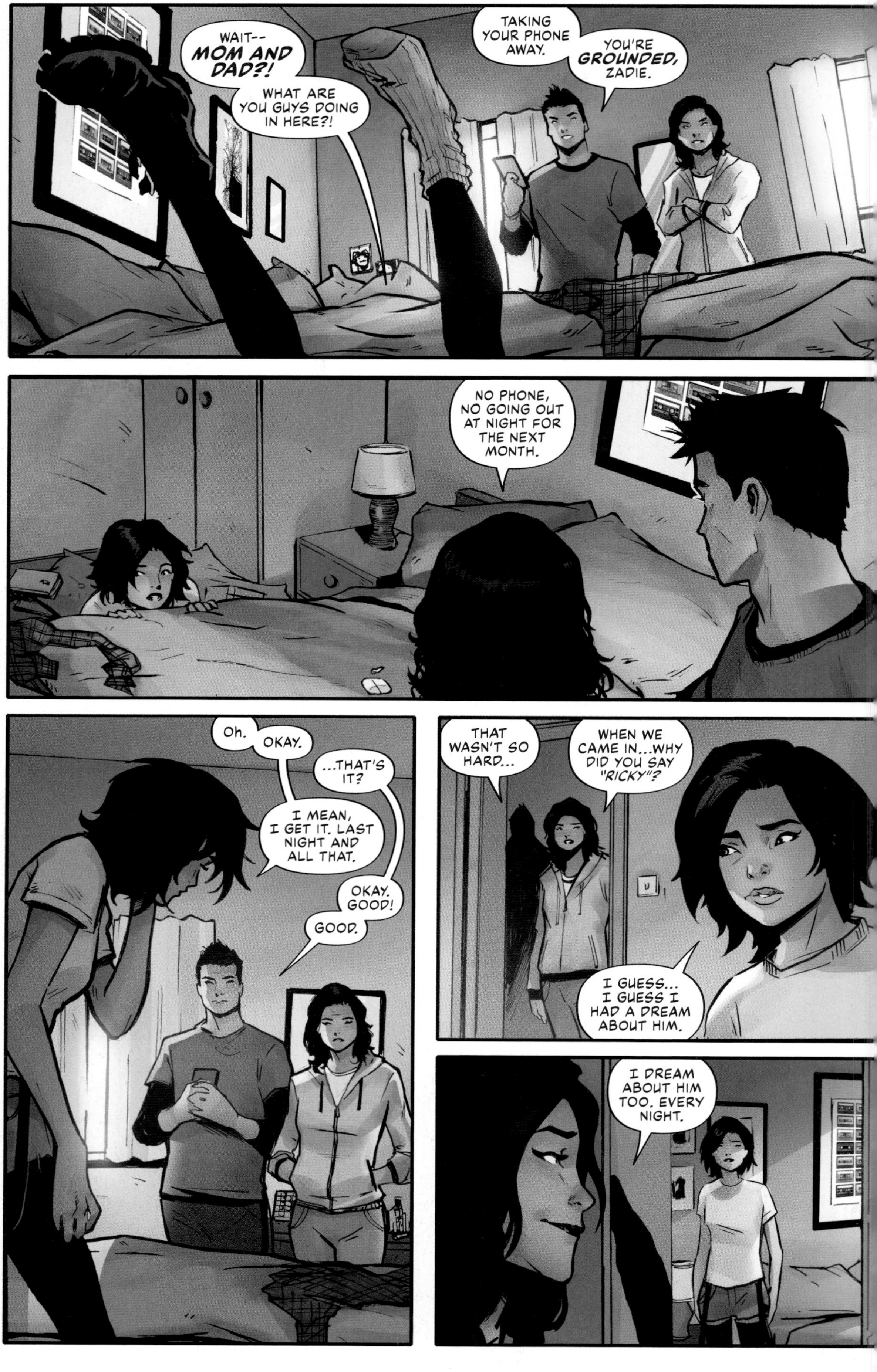
WAIT-- MOM AND DAD?!
WHAT ARE YOU GUYS DOING IN HERE?!
TAKING YOUR PHONE AWAY.
YOU'RE GROUNDED, ZADIE.
NO PHONE, NO GOING OUT AT NIGHT FOR THE NEXT MONTH.
Oh.
OKAY.
...THAT'S IT?
I MEAN, I GET IT. LAST NIGHT AND ALL THAT.
OKAY. GOOD!
GOOD.
THAT WASN'T SO HARD...
WHEN WE CAME IN...WHY DID YOU SAY "RICKY"?
I GUESS... I GUESS I HAD A DREAM ABOUT HIM.
I DREAM ABOUT HIM TOO. EVERY NIGHT.

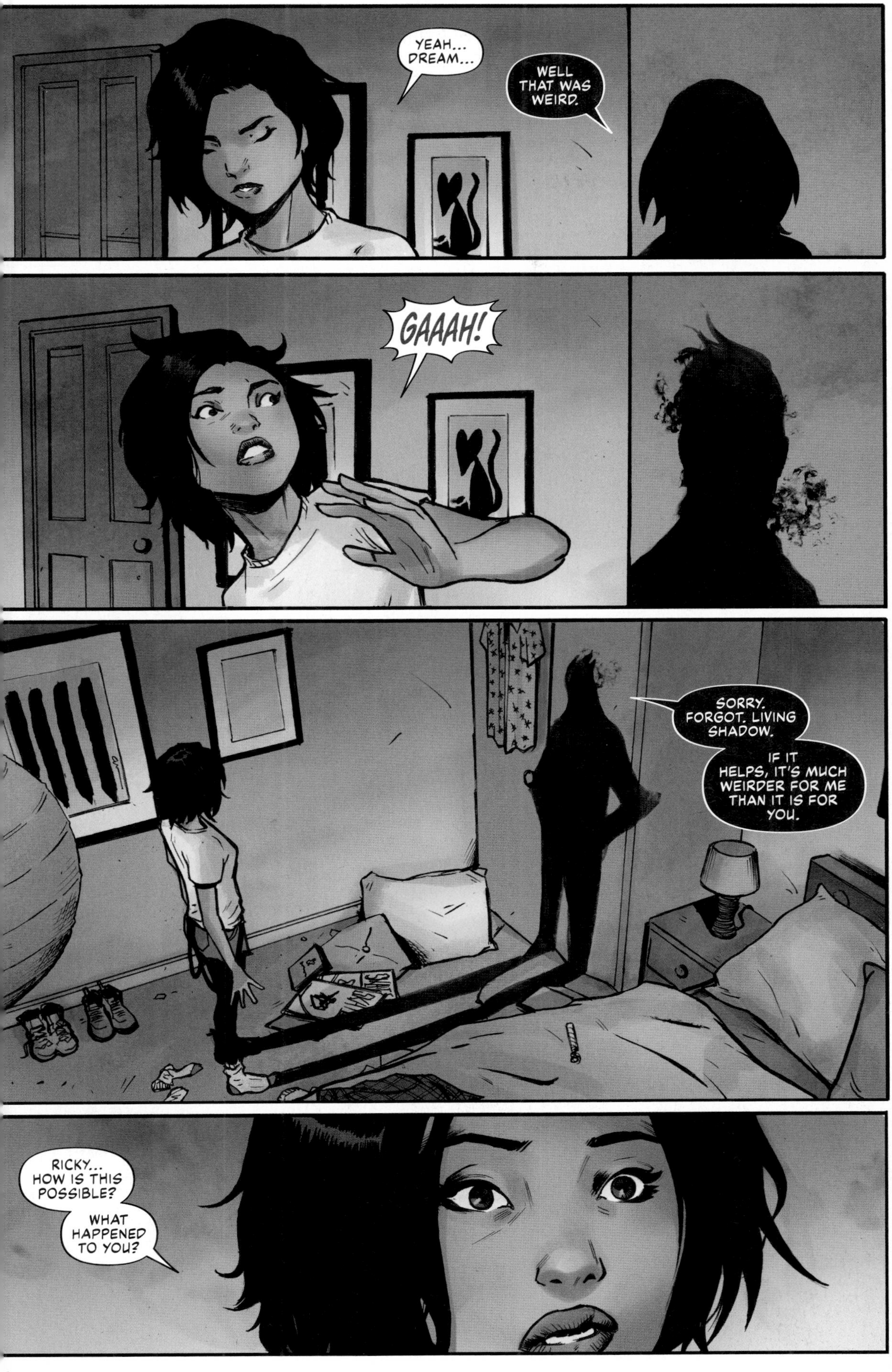
YEAH... DREAM...
WELL THAT WAS WEIRD.
GAAAH!
SORRY. FORGOT. LIVING SHADOW.
IF IT HELPS, IT'S MUCH WEIRDER FOR ME THAN IT IS FOR YOU.
RICKY... HOW IS THIS POSSIBLE?
WHAT HAPPENED TO YOU?

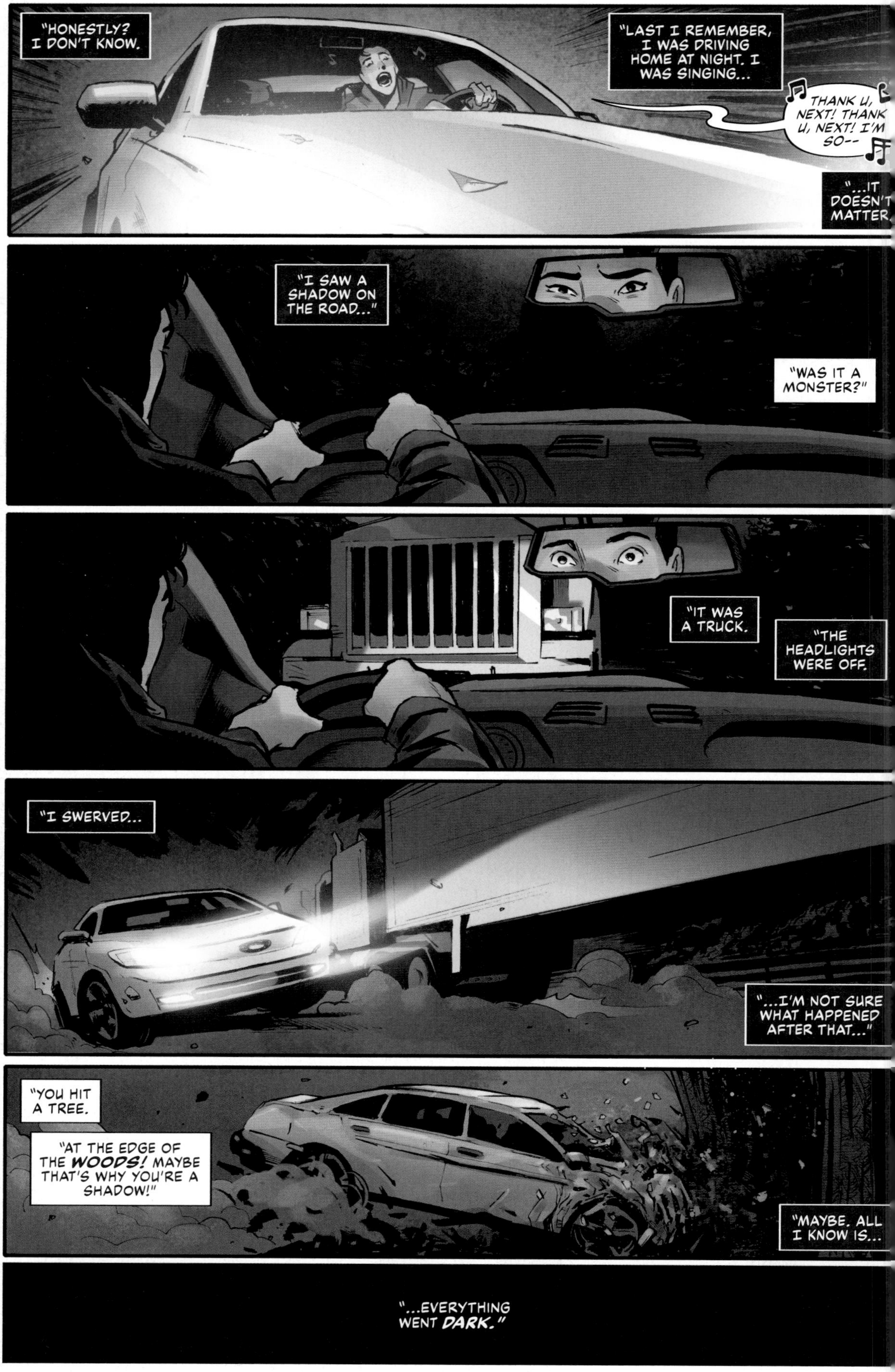
"HONESTLY? I DON'T KNOW.
"LAST I REMEMBER, I WAS DRIVING HOME AT NIGHT. I WAS SINGING...
THANK U, NEXT! THANK U, NEXT! I'M SO--
"...IT DOESN'T MATTER.
"I SAW A SHADOW ON THE ROAD..."
"WAS IT A MONSTER?"
"IT WAS A TRUCK.
"THE HEADLIGHTS WERE OFF.
"I SWERVED...
"...I'M NOT SURE WHAT HAPPENED AFTER THAT..."
"YOU HIT A TREE.
"AT THE EDGE OF THE WOODS! MAYBE THAT'S WHY YOU'RE A SHADOW!"
"MAYBE. ALL I KNOW IS...
"...EVERYTHING WENT DARK."

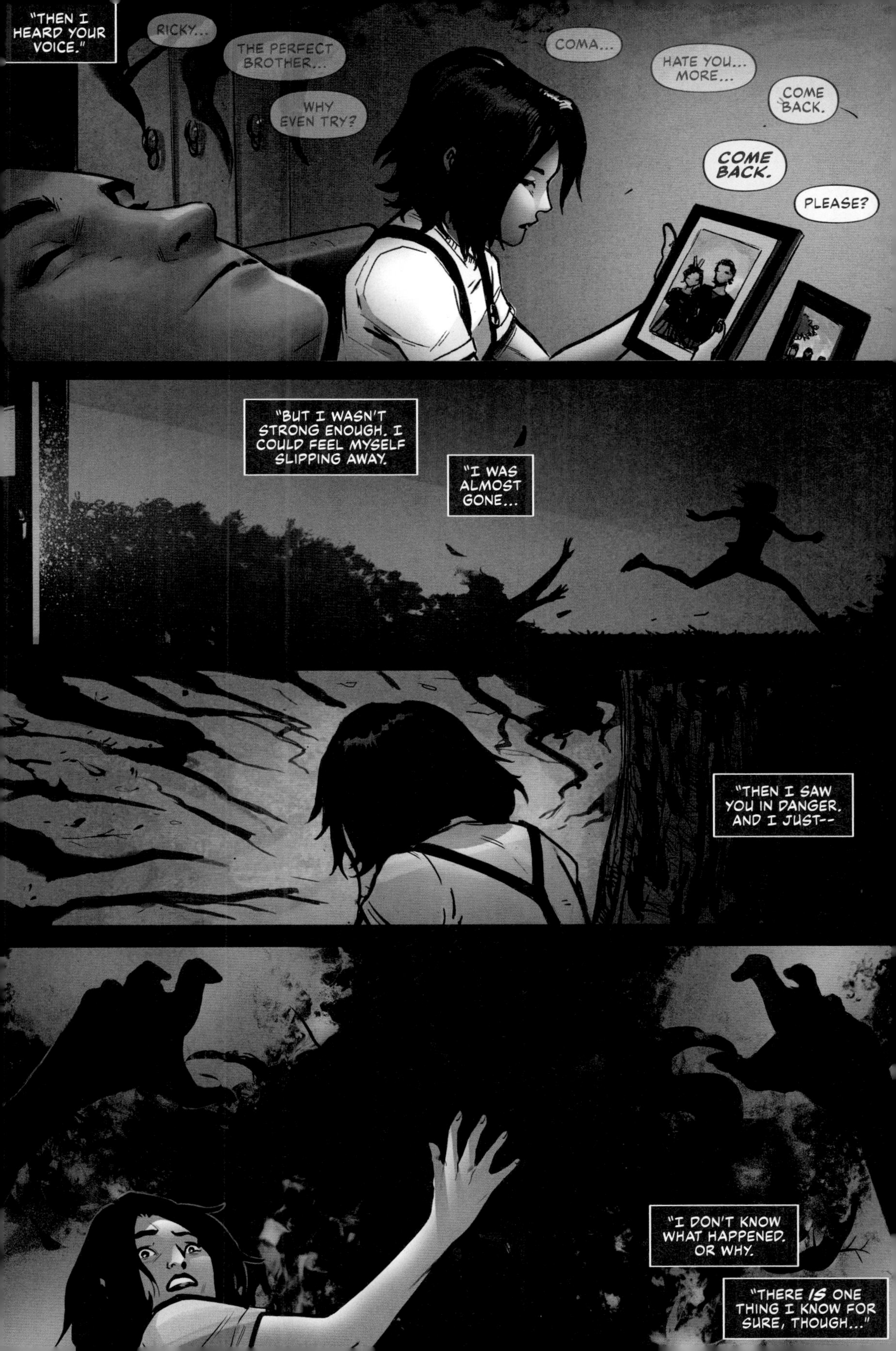
"THEN I HEARD YOUR VOICE."
RICKY...
THE PERFECT BROTHER...
WHY EVEN TRY?
COMA...
HATE YOU... MORE...
COME BACK.
COME BACK.
PLEASE?
"BUT I WASN'T STRONG ENOUGH. I COULD FEEL MYSELF SLIPPING AWAY.
"I WAS ALMOST GONE...
"THEN I SAW YOU IN DANGER. AND I JUST--
"I DON'T KNOW WHAT HAPPENED. OR WHY.
"THERE *IS* ONE THING I KNOW FOR SURE, THOUGH..."

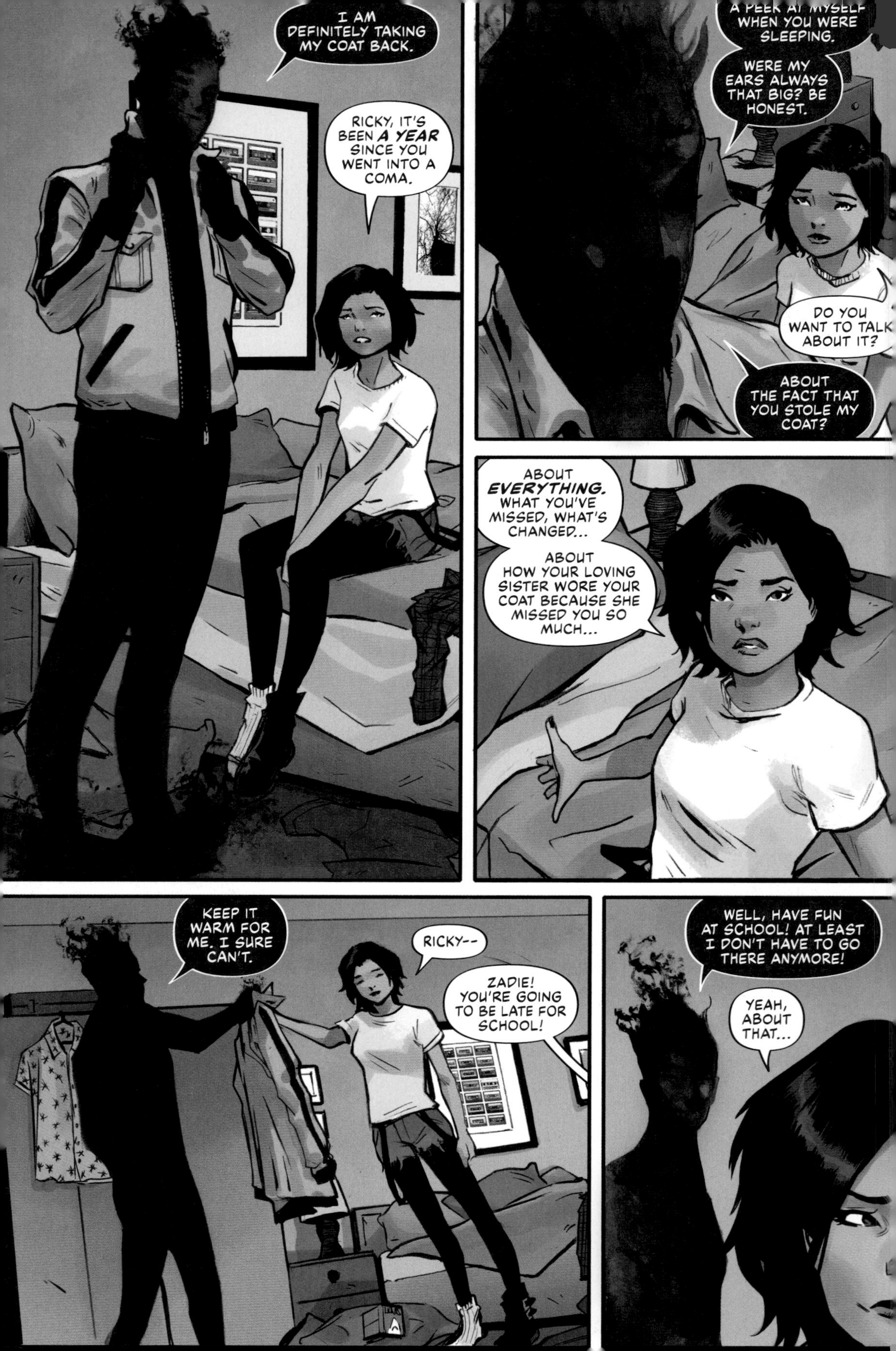
I AM DEFINITELY TAKING MY COAT BACK.
RICKY, IT'S BEEN *A YEAR* SINCE YOU WENT INTO A COMA.
A PEEK AT MYSELF WHEN YOU WERE SLEEPING.
WERE MY EARS ALWAYS THAT BIG? BE HONEST.
DO YOU WANT TO TALK ABOUT IT?
ABOUT THE FACT THAT YOU STOLE MY COAT?
ABOUT *EVERYTHING.* WHAT YOU'VE MISSED, WHAT'S CHANGED...
ABOUT HOW YOUR LOVING SISTER WORE YOUR COAT BECAUSE SHE MISSED YOU SO MUCH...
KEEP IT WARM FOR ME. I SURE CAN'T.
RICKY--
ZADIE! YOU'RE GOING TO BE LATE FOR SCHOOL!
WELL, HAVE FUN AT SCHOOL! AT LEAST I DON'T HAVE TO GO THERE ANYMORE!
YEAH, ABOUT THAT...

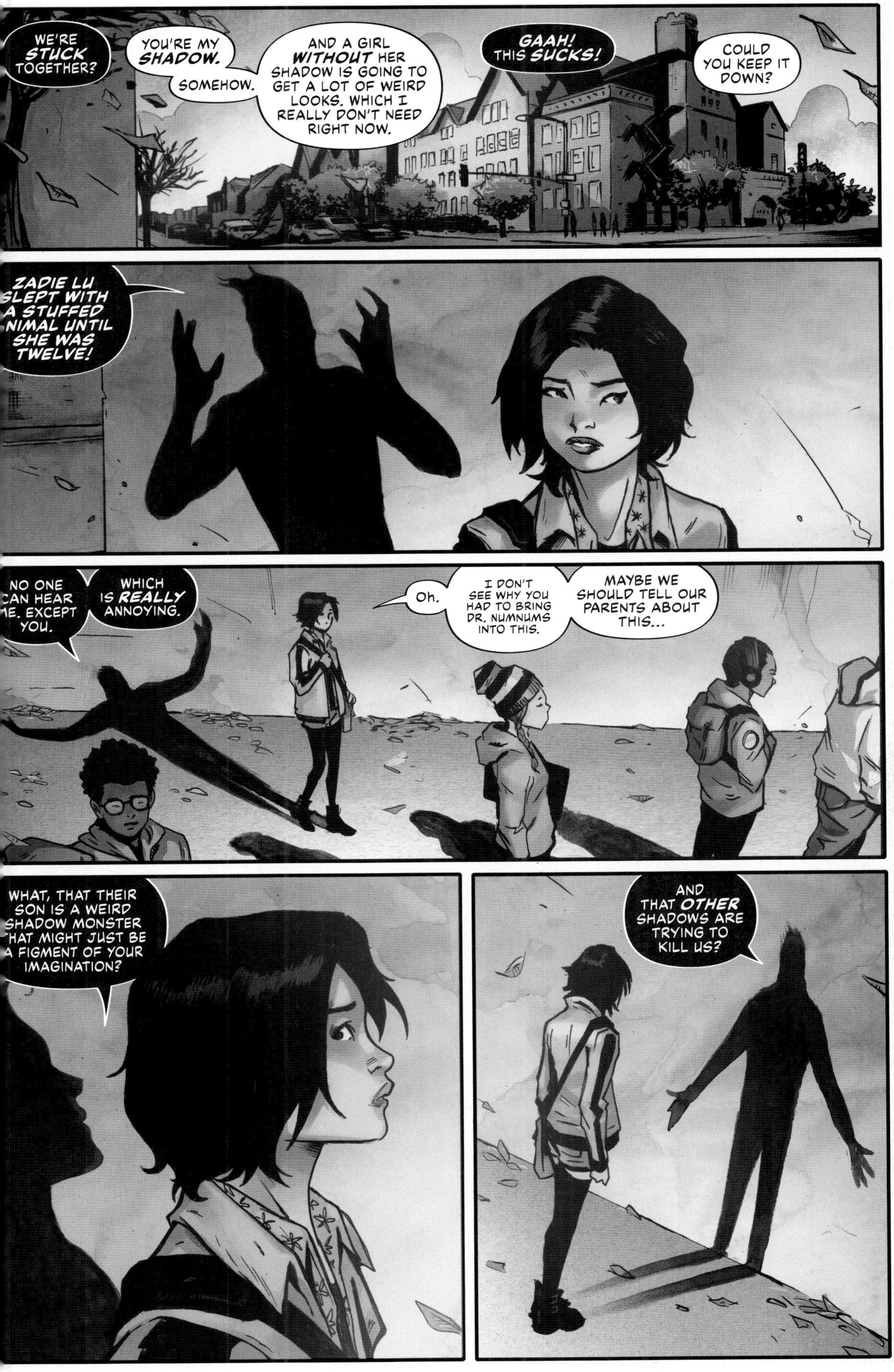
WE'RE STUCK TOGETHER?
YOU'RE MY SHADOW.
SOMEHOW.
AND A GIRL WITHOUT HER SHADOW IS GOING TO GET A LOT OF WEIRD LOOKS. WHICH I REALLY DON'T NEED RIGHT NOW.
GAAH! THIS SUCKS!
COULD YOU KEEP IT DOWN?
ZADIE LU SLEPT WITH A STUFFED NIMAL UNTIL SHE WAS TWELVE!
NO ONE CAN HEAR ME. EXCEPT YOU.
WHICH IS REALLY ANNOYING.
Oh.
I DON'T SEE WHY YOU HAD TO BRING DR. NUMNUMS INTO THIS.
MAYBE WE SHOULD TELL OUR PARENTS ABOUT THIS...
WHAT, THAT THEIR SON IS A WEIRD SHADOW MONSTER THAT MIGHT JUST BE A FIGMENT OF YOUR IMAGINATION?
AND THAT OTHER SHADOWS ARE TRYING TO KILL US?

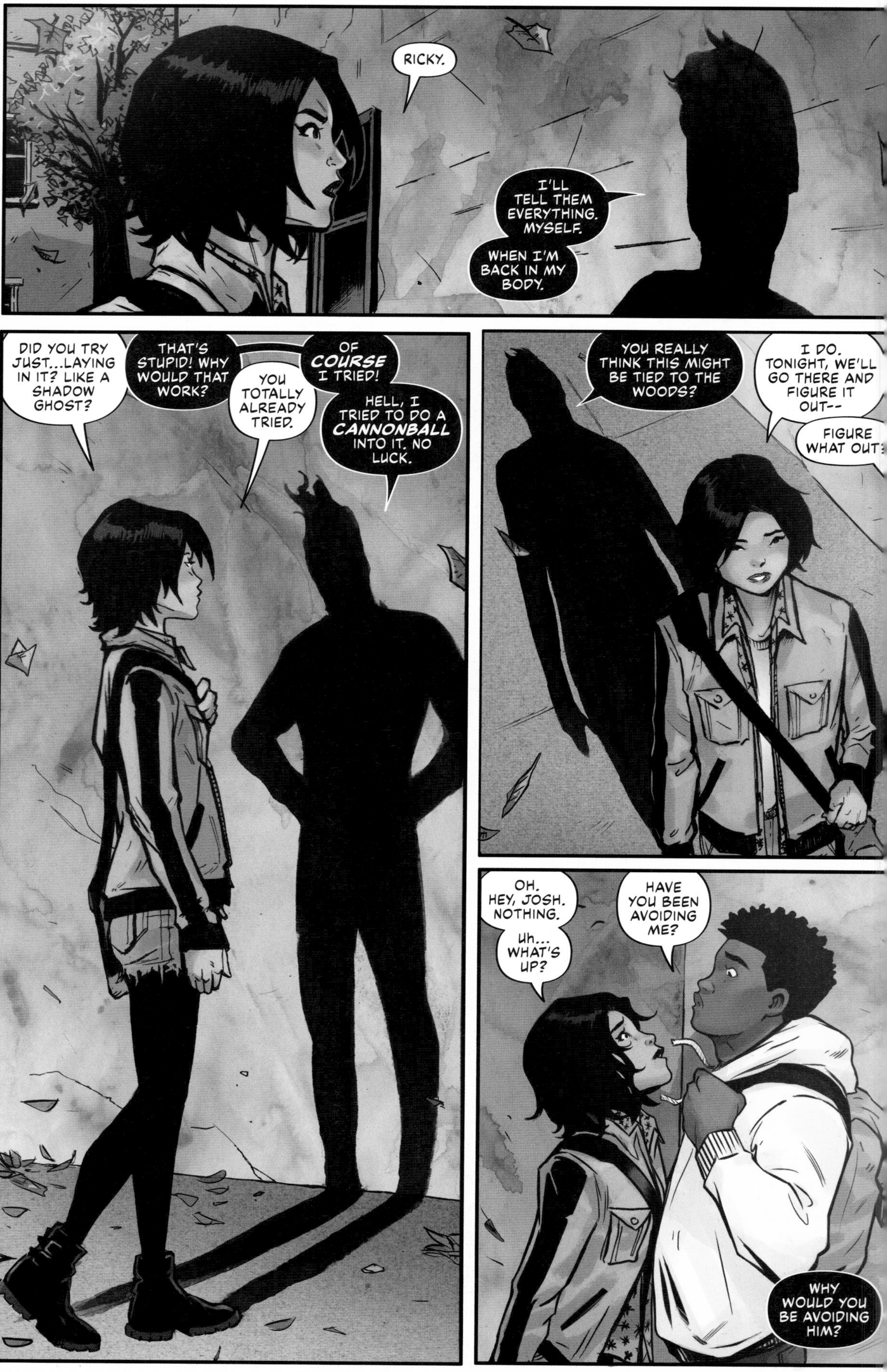
RICKY.
I'LL TELL THEM EVERYTHING. MYSELF.
WHEN I'M BACK IN MY BODY.
DID YOU TRY JUST...LAYING IN IT? LIKE A SHADOW GHOST?
THAT'S STUPID! WHY WOULD THAT WORK?
YOU TOTALLY ALREADY TRIED.
OF *COURSE* I TRIED!
HELL, I TRIED TO DO A *CANNONBALL* INTO IT. NO LUCK.
YOU REALLY THINK THIS MIGHT BE TIED TO THE WOODS?
I DO. TONIGHT, WE'LL GO THERE AND FIGURE IT OUT--
FIGURE WHAT OUT?
OH. HEY, JOSH. NOTHING.
uh... WHAT'S UP?
HAVE YOU BEEN AVOIDING ME?
WHY WOULD YOU BE AVOIDING HIM?

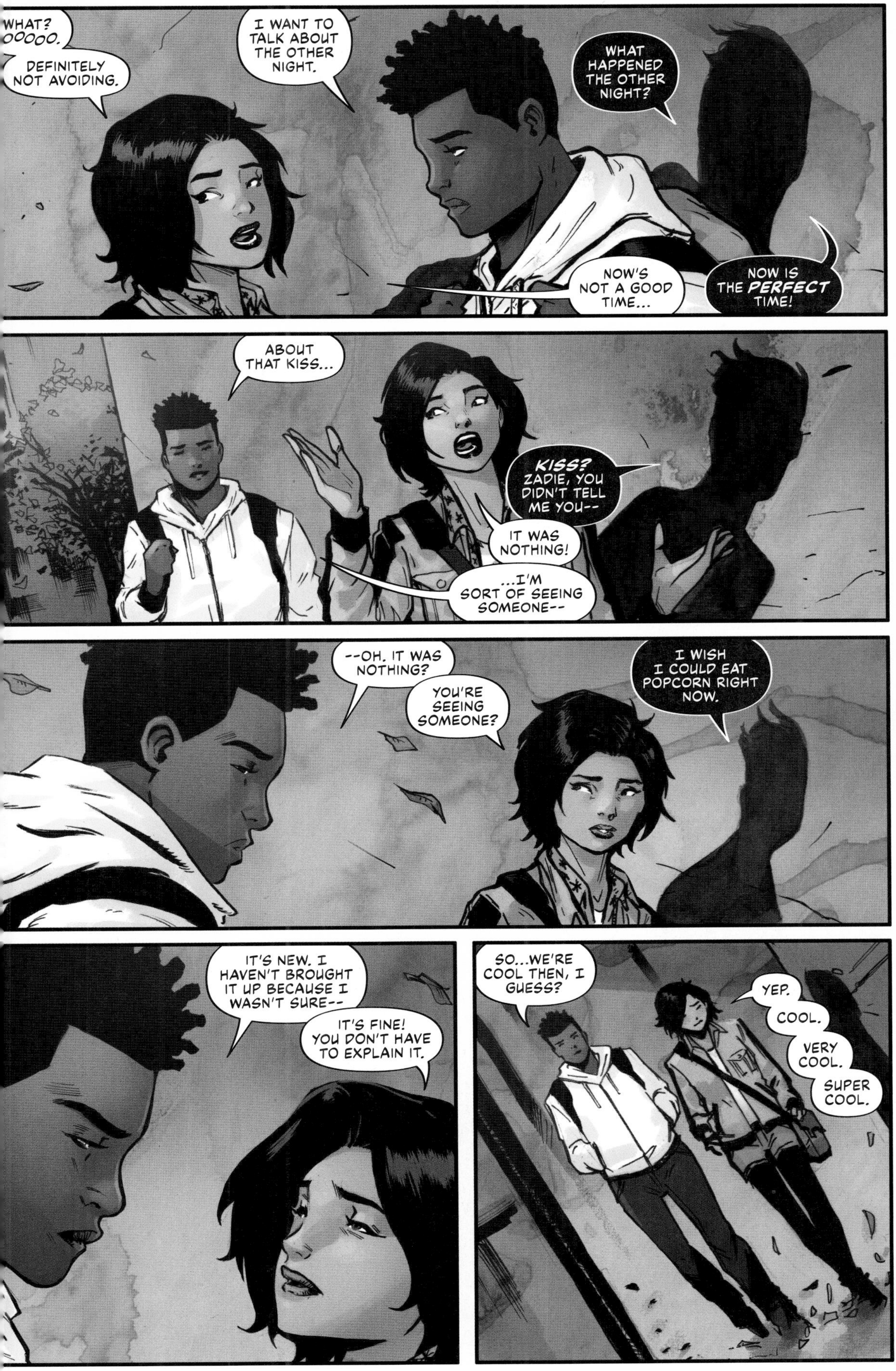
WHAT? OOOOO.
DEFINITELY NOT AVOIDING.
I WANT TO TALK ABOUT THE OTHER NIGHT.
WHAT HAPPENED THE OTHER NIGHT?
NOW'S NOT A GOOD TIME...
NOW IS THE PERFECT TIME!
ABOUT THAT KISS...
KISS? ZADIE, YOU DIDN'T TELL ME YOU--
IT WAS NOTHING!
...I'M SORT OF SEEING SOMEONE--
--OH. IT WAS NOTHING?
YOU'RE SEEING SOMEONE?
I WISH I COULD EAT POPCORN RIGHT NOW.
IT'S NEW. I HAVEN'T BROUGHT IT UP BECAUSE I WASN'T SURE--
IT'S FINE! YOU DON'T HAVE TO EXPLAIN IT.
SO...WE'RE COOL THEN, I GUESS?
YEP.
COOL.
VERY COOL.
SUPER COOL.

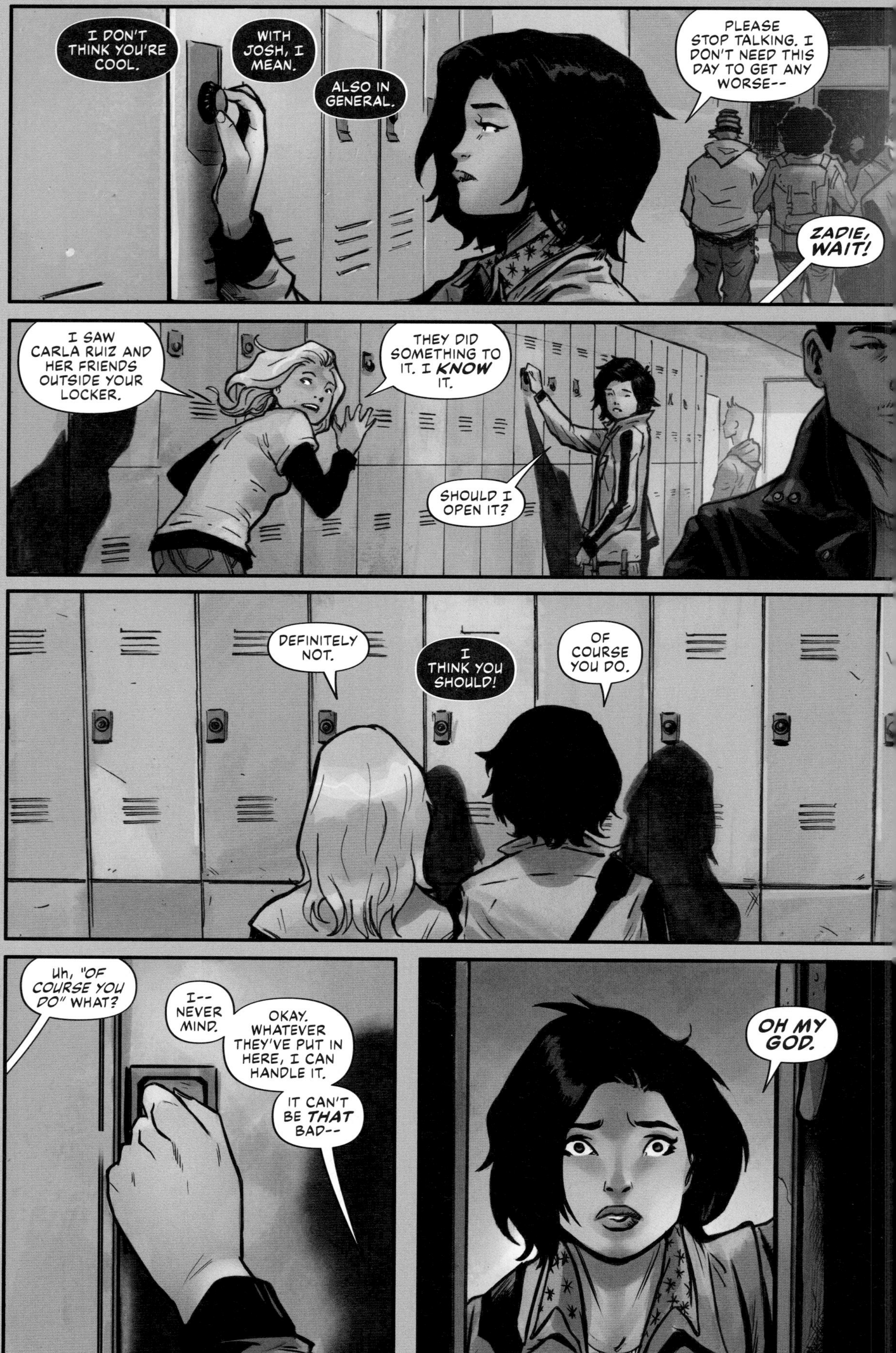
I DON'T THINK YOU'RE COOL.
WITH JOSH, I MEAN.
ALSO IN GENERAL.
PLEASE STOP TALKING. I DON'T NEED THIS DAY TO GET ANY WORSE--
ZADIE, WAIT!
I SAW CARLA RUIZ AND HER FRIENDS OUTSIDE YOUR LOCKER.
THEY DID SOMETHING TO IT. I KNOW IT.
SHOULD I OPEN IT?
DEFINITELY NOT.
I THINK YOU SHOULD!
OF COURSE YOU DO.
Uh, "OF COURSE YOU DO" WHAT?
I-- NEVER MIND.
OKAY. WHATEVER THEY'VE PUT IN HERE, I CAN HANDLE IT.
IT CAN'T BE THAT BAD--
OH MY GOD.

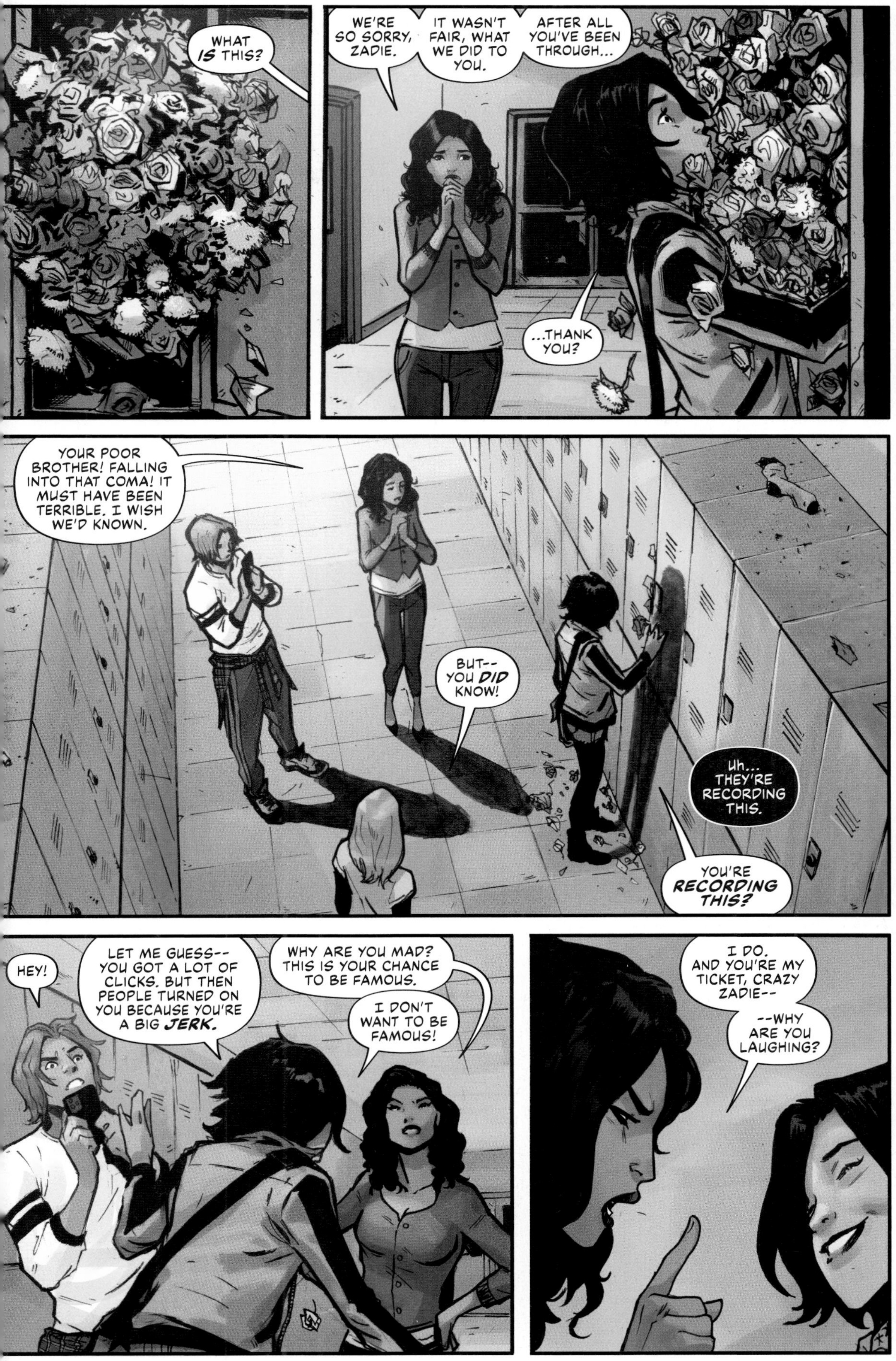

WHAT *IS* THIS?
WE'RE SO SORRY, ZADIE.
IT WASN'T FAIR, WHAT WE DID TO YOU.
AFTER ALL YOU'VE BEEN THROUGH...
...THANK YOU?
YOUR POOR BROTHER! FALLING INTO THAT COMA! IT MUST HAVE BEEN TERRIBLE. I WISH WE'D KNOWN.
BUT-- YOU *DID* KNOW!
Uh... THEY'RE RECORDING THIS.
YOU'RE ***RECORDING THIS?***
HEY!
LET ME GUESS-- YOU GOT A LOT OF CLICKS. BUT THEN PEOPLE TURNED ON YOU BECAUSE YOU'RE A BIG ***JERK.***
WHY ARE YOU MAD? THIS IS YOUR CHANCE TO BE FAMOUS.
I DON'T WANT TO BE FAMOUS!
I DO. AND YOU'RE MY TICKET, CRAZY ZADIE--
--WHY ARE YOU LAUGHING?

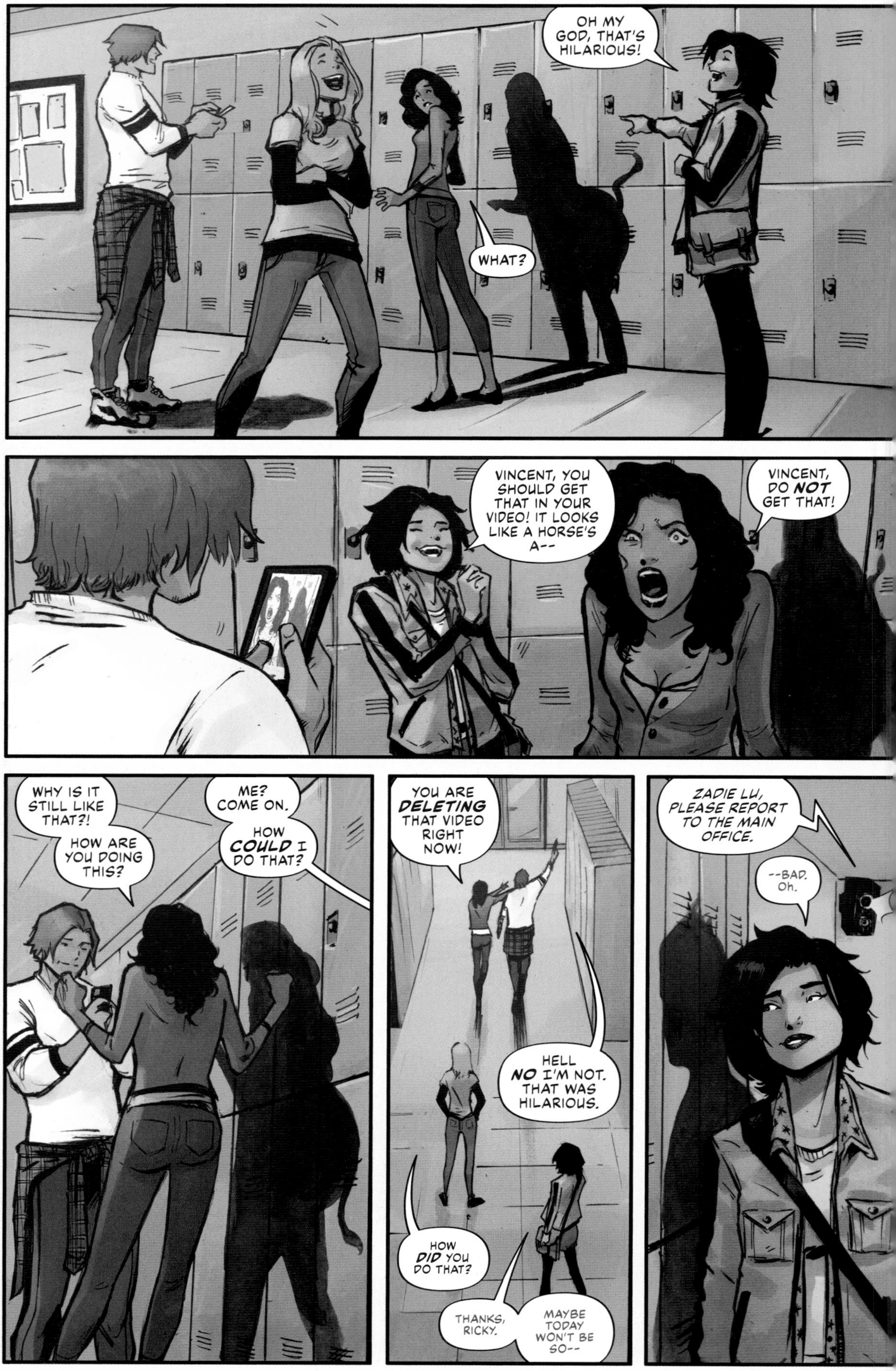
OH MY GOD, THAT'S HILARIOUS!
WHAT?
VINCENT, YOU SHOULD GET THAT IN YOUR VIDEO! IT LOOKS LIKE A HORSE'S A--
VINCENT, DO NOT GET THAT!
WHY IS IT STILL LIKE THAT?!
HOW ARE YOU DOING THIS?
ME? COME ON.
HOW COULD I DO THAT?
YOU ARE DELETING THAT VIDEO RIGHT NOW!
HELL NO I'M NOT. THAT WAS HILARIOUS.
HOW DID YOU DO THAT?
THANKS, RICKY.
MAYBE TODAY WON'T BE SO--
ZADIE LU, PLEASE REPORT TO THE MAIN OFFICE.
--BAD. Oh.

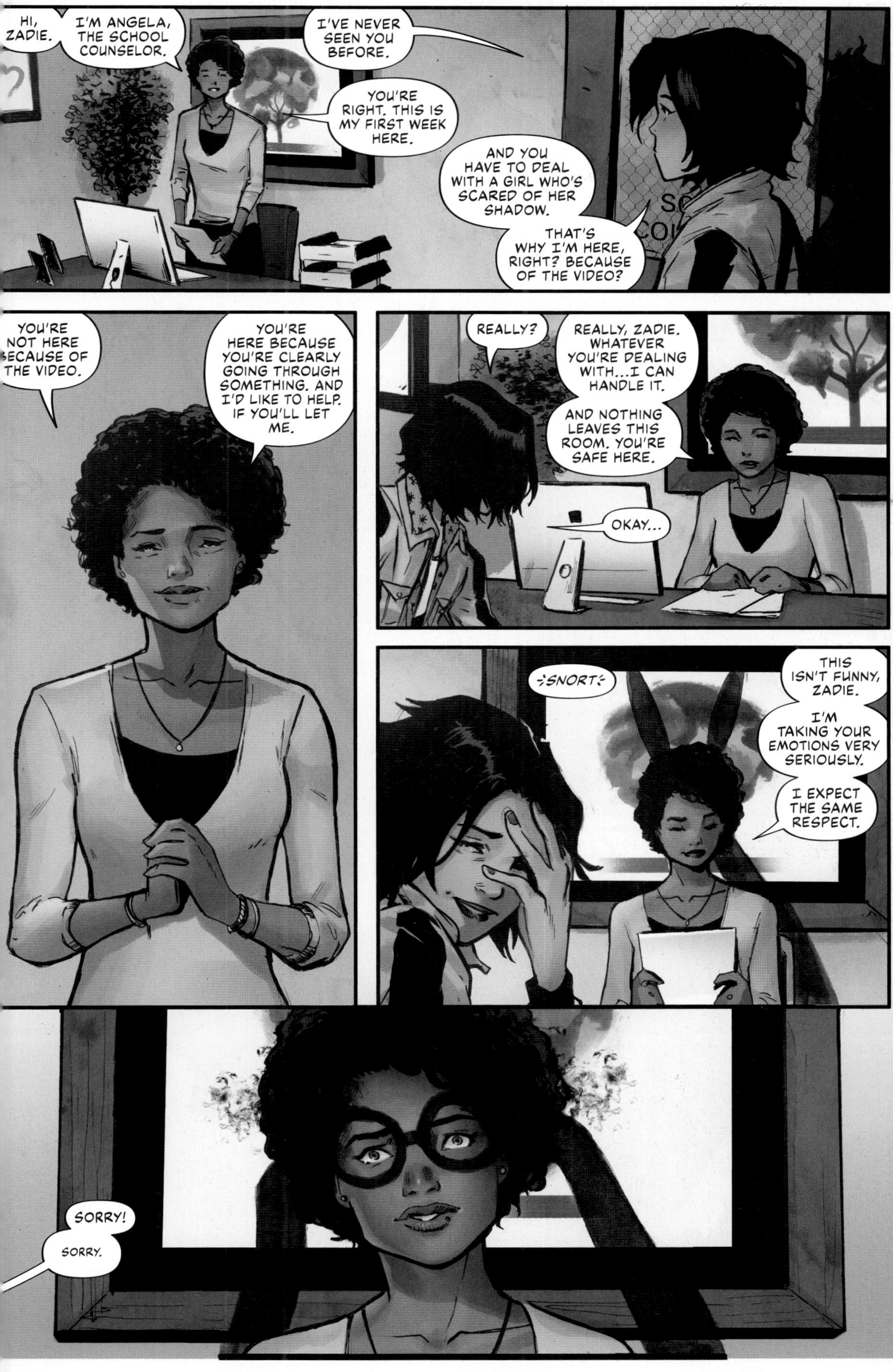
HI, ZADIE.
I'M ANGELA, THE SCHOOL COUNSELOR.
I'VE NEVER SEEN YOU BEFORE.
YOU'RE RIGHT. THIS IS MY FIRST WEEK HERE.
AND YOU HAVE TO DEAL WITH A GIRL WHO'S SCARED OF HER SHADOW.
THAT'S WHY I'M HERE, RIGHT? BECAUSE OF THE VIDEO?
YOU'RE NOT HERE BECAUSE OF THE VIDEO.
YOU'RE HERE BECAUSE YOU'RE CLEARLY GOING THROUGH SOMETHING. AND I'D LIKE TO HELP. IF YOU'LL LET ME.
REALLY?
REALLY, ZADIE. WHATEVER YOU'RE DEALING WITH...I CAN HANDLE IT.
AND NOTHING LEAVES THIS ROOM. YOU'RE SAFE HERE.
OKAY...
SNORT
THIS ISN'T FUNNY, ZADIE.
I'M TAKING YOUR EMOTIONS VERY SERIOUSLY.
I EXPECT THE SAME RESPECT.
SORRY!
SORRY.

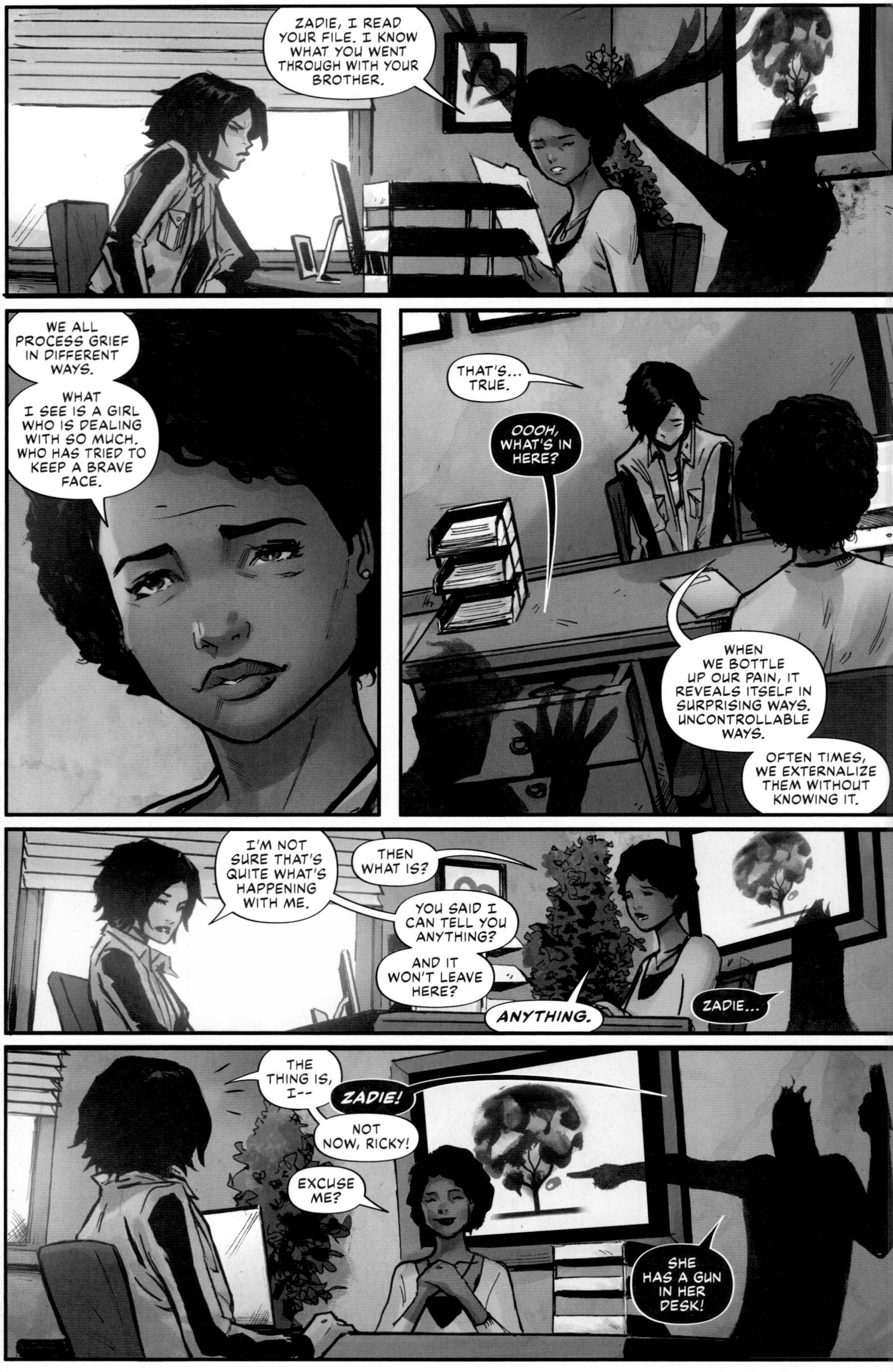
ZADIE, I READ YOUR FILE. I KNOW WHAT YOU WENT THROUGH WITH YOUR BROTHER.
WE ALL PROCESS GRIEF IN DIFFERENT WAYS.
WHAT I SEE IS A GIRL WHO IS DEALING WITH SO MUCH. WHO HAS TRIED TO KEEP A BRAVE FACE.
THAT'S... TRUE.
OOOH, WHAT'S IN HERE?
WHEN WE BOTTLE UP OUR PAIN, IT REVEALS ITSELF IN SURPRISING WAYS. UNCONTROLLABLE WAYS.
OFTEN TIMES, WE EXTERNALIZE THEM WITHOUT KNOWING IT.
I'M NOT SURE THAT'S QUITE WHAT'S HAPPENING WITH ME.
THEN WHAT IS?
YOU SAID I CAN TELL YOU ANYTHING?
AND IT WON'T LEAVE HERE?
ANYTHING.
ZADIE...
THE THING IS, I--
ZADIE!
NOT NOW, RICKY!
EXCUSE ME?
SHE HAS A GUN IN HER DESK!

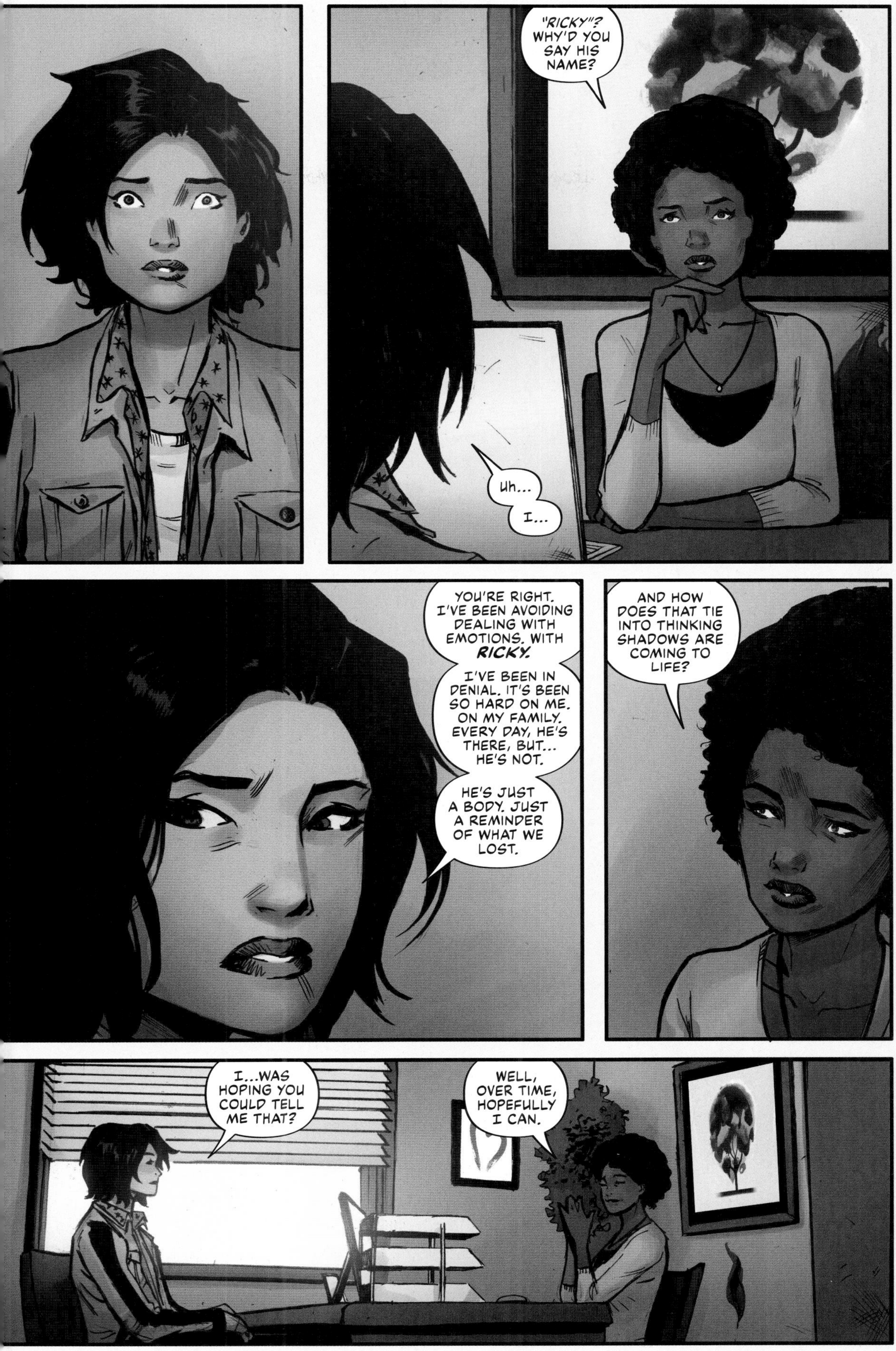
"RICKY"? WHY'D YOU SAY HIS NAME?
Uh...
I...
YOU'RE RIGHT. I'VE BEEN AVOIDING DEALING WITH EMOTIONS. WITH RICKY.
I'VE BEEN IN DENIAL. IT'S BEEN SO HARD ON ME. ON MY FAMILY. EVERY DAY, HE'S THERE, BUT... HE'S NOT.
HE'S JUST A BODY. JUST A REMINDER OF WHAT WE LOST.
AND HOW DOES THAT TIE INTO THINKING SHADOWS ARE COMING TO LIFE?
I...WAS HOPING YOU COULD TELL ME THAT?
WELL, OVER TIME, HOPEFULLY I CAN.

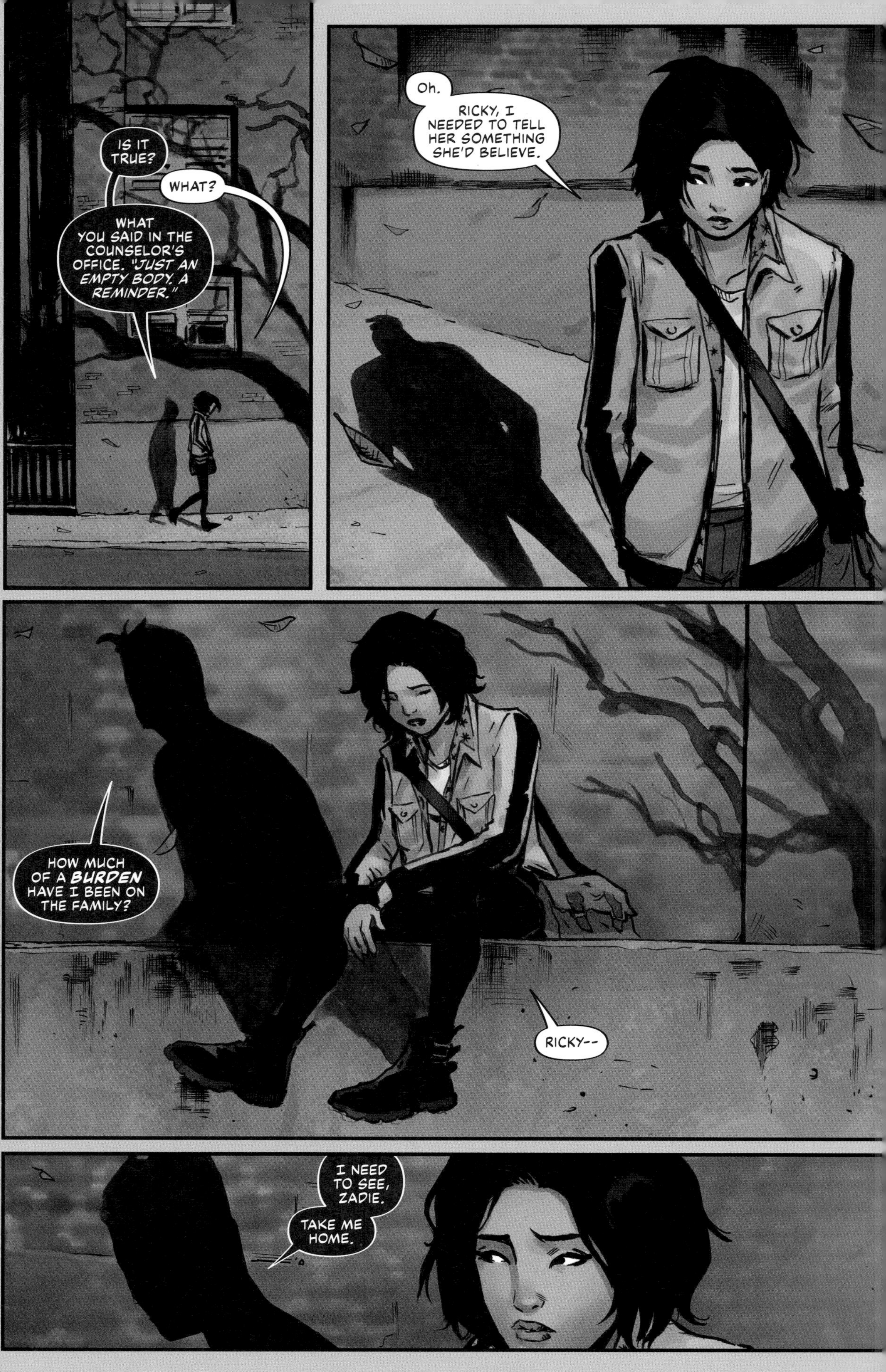
IS IT TRUE?
WHAT?
WHAT YOU SAID IN THE COUNSELOR'S OFFICE. "JUST AN EMPTY BODY. A REMINDER."
Oh.
RICKY, I NEEDED TO TELL HER SOMETHING SHE'D BELIEVE.
HOW MUCH OF A BURDEN HAVE I BEEN ON THE FAMILY?
RICKY--
I NEED TO SEE, ZADIE.
TAKE ME HOME.

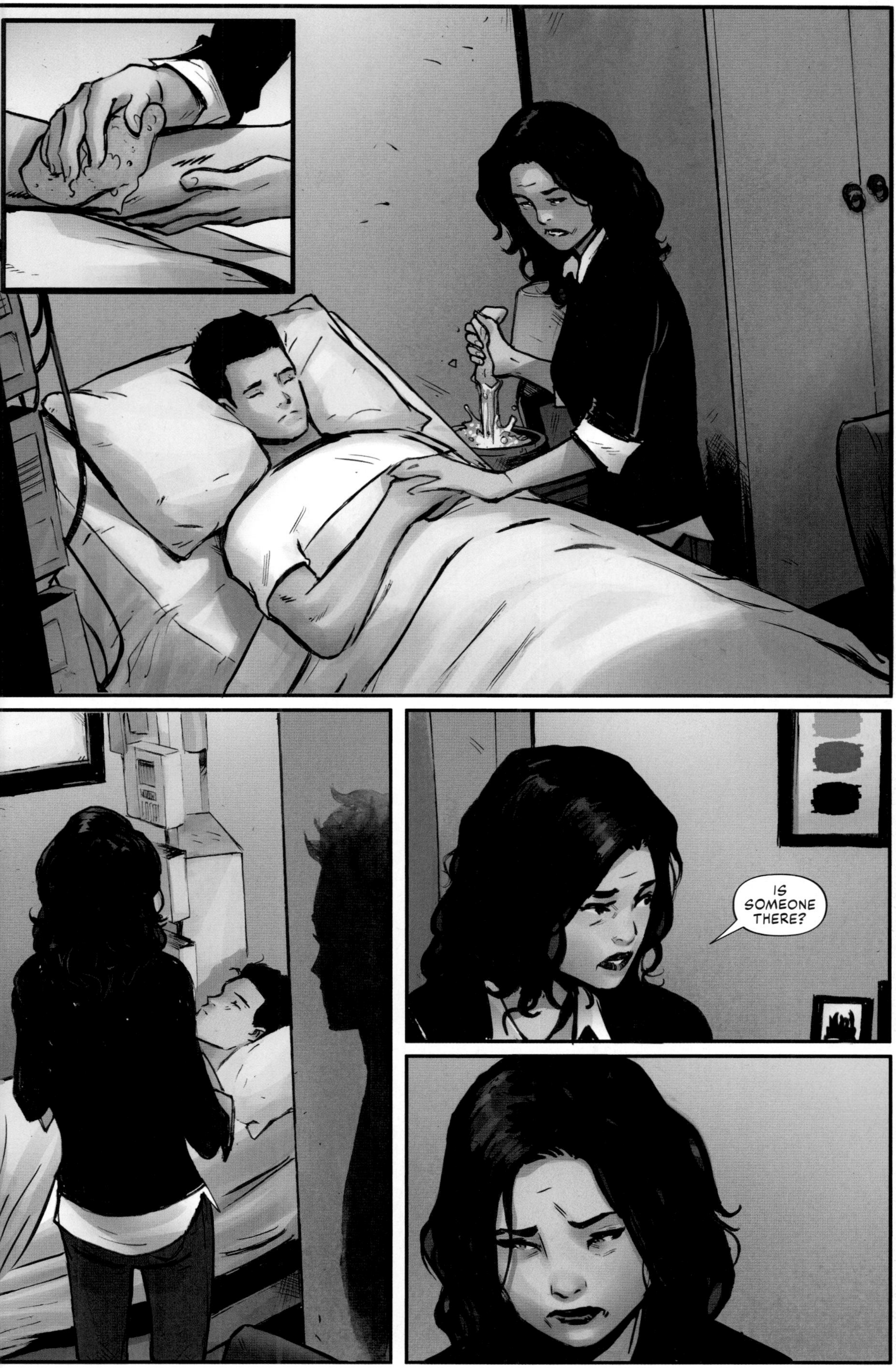
IS SOMEONE THERE?

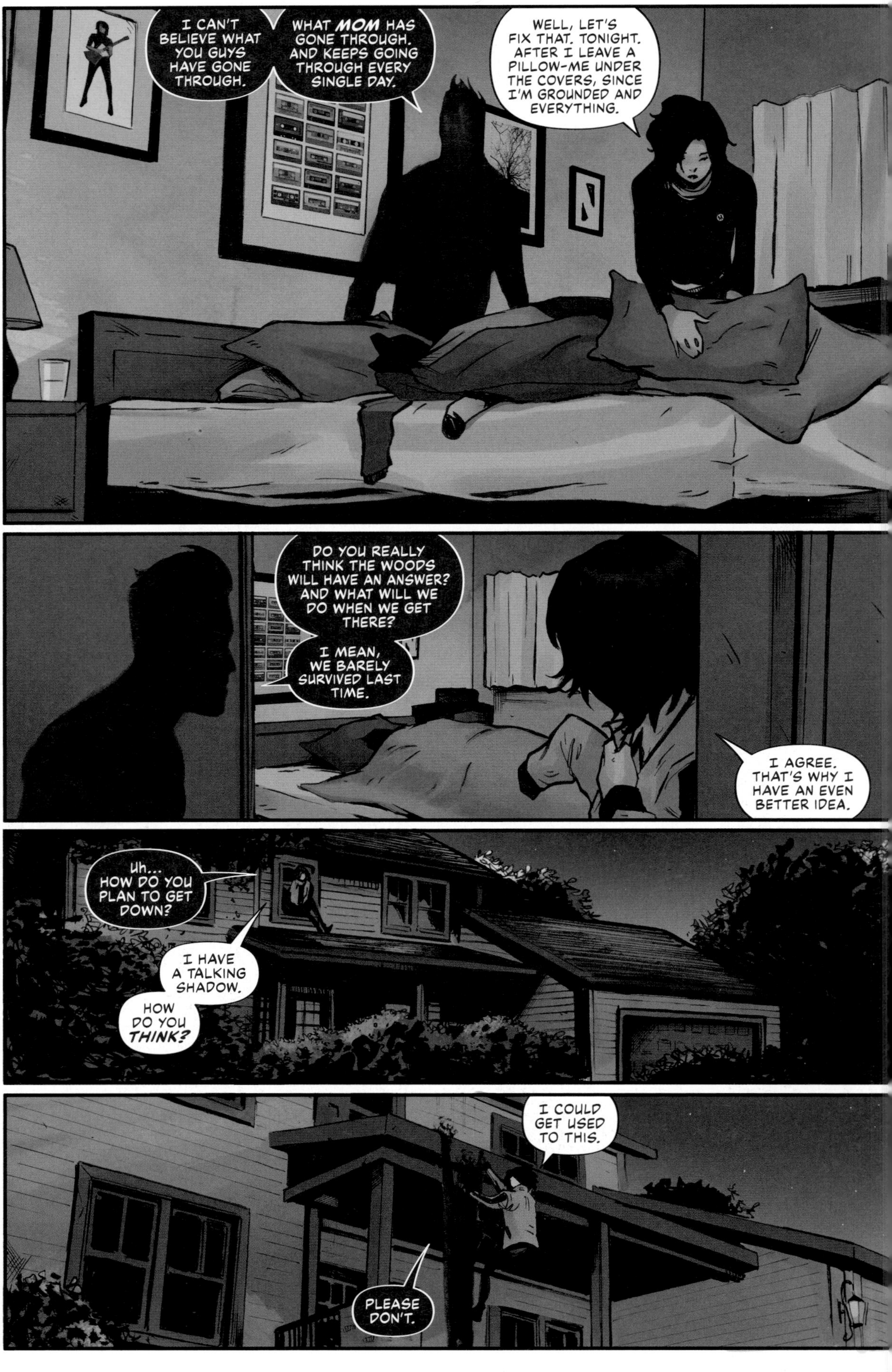
I CAN'T BELIEVE WHAT YOU GUYS HAVE GONE THROUGH.
WHAT MOM HAS GONE THROUGH. AND KEEPS GOING THROUGH EVERY SINGLE DAY.
WELL, LET'S FIX THAT. TONIGHT. AFTER I LEAVE A PILLOW-ME UNDER THE COVERS, SINCE I'M GROUNDED AND EVERYTHING.
DO YOU REALLY THINK THE WOODS WILL HAVE AN ANSWER? AND WHAT WILL WE DO WHEN WE GET THERE?
I MEAN, WE BARELY SURVIVED LAST TIME.
I AGREE. THAT'S WHY I HAVE AN EVEN BETTER IDEA.
UH... HOW DO YOU PLAN TO GET DOWN?
I HAVE A TALKING SHADOW.
HOW DO YOU THINK?
I COULD GET USED TO THIS.
PLEASE DON'T.

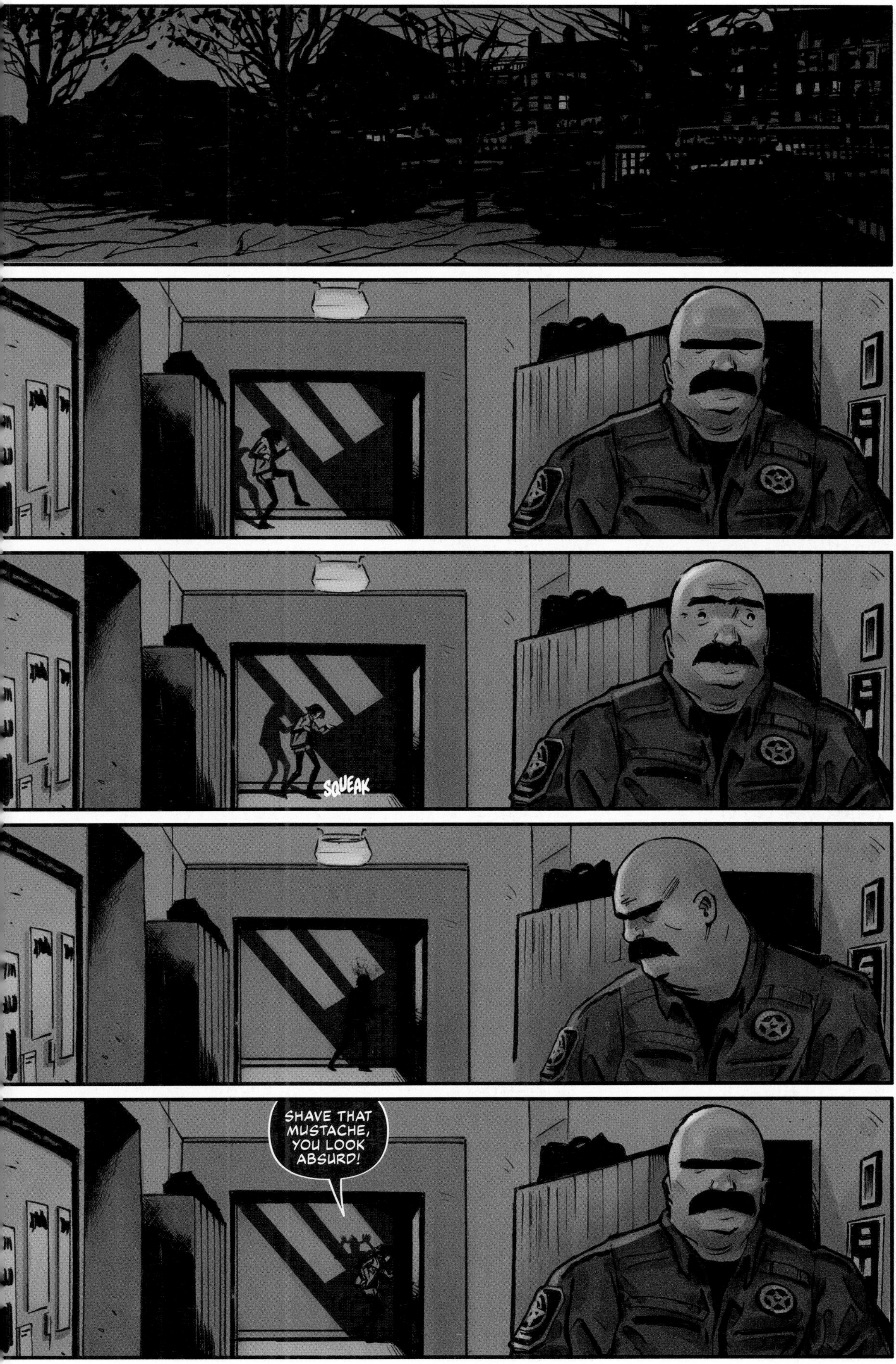
SQUEAK
SHAVE THAT MUSTACHE, YOU LOOK ABSURD!

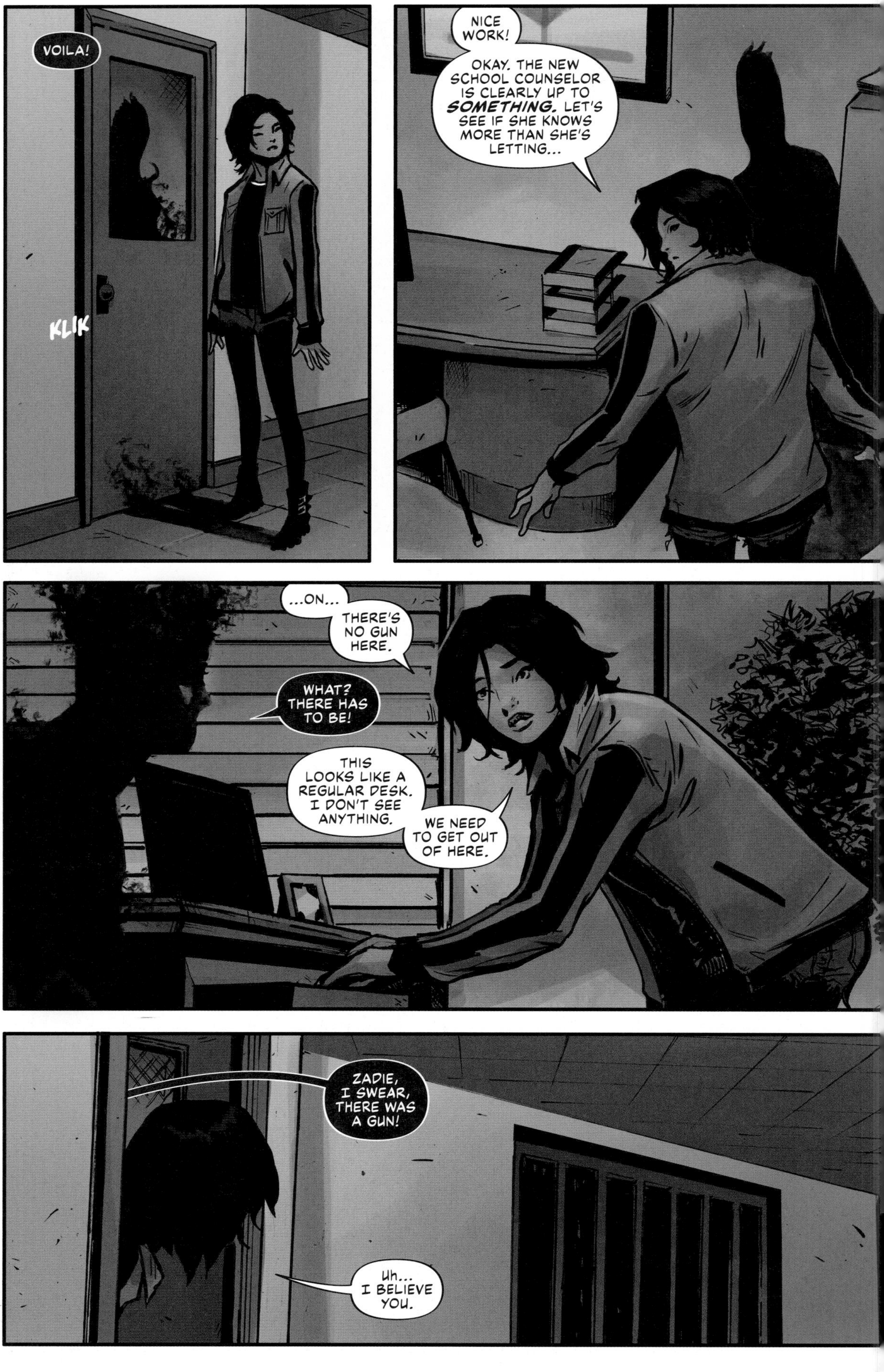
VOILA!
KLIK
NICE WORK!
OKAY. THE NEW SCHOOL COUNSELOR IS CLEARLY UP TO SOMETHING. LET'S SEE IF SHE KNOWS MORE THAN SHE'S LETTING...
...ON...
THERE'S NO GUN HERE.
WHAT? THERE HAS TO BE!
THIS LOOKS LIKE A REGULAR DESK. I DON'T SEE ANYTHING.
WE NEED TO GET OUT OF HERE.
ZADIE, I SWEAR, THERE WAS A GUN!
Uh... I BELIEVE YOU.

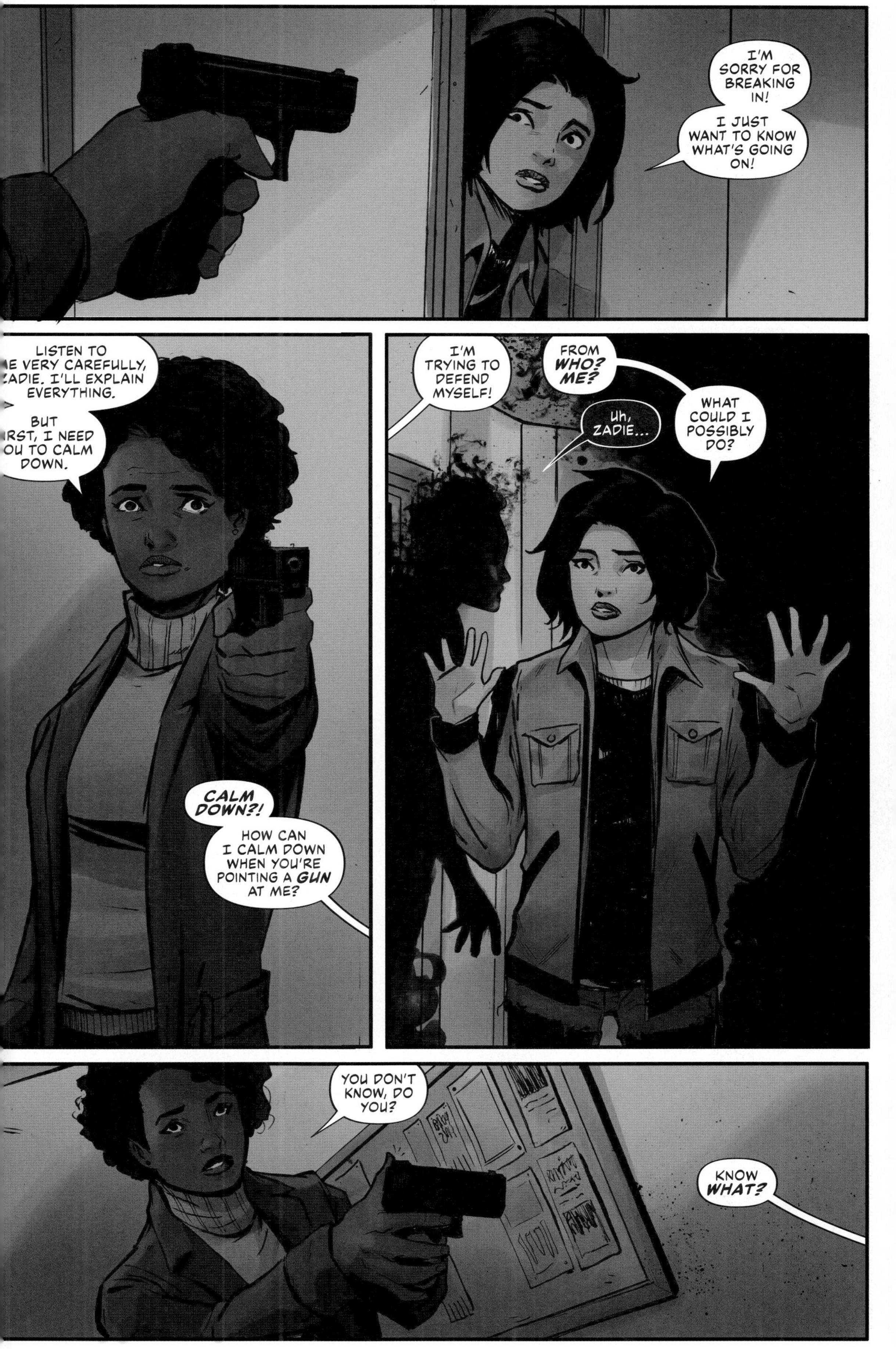
I'M SORRY FOR BREAKING IN!
I JUST WANT TO KNOW WHAT'S GOING ON!
LISTEN TO ЛE VERY CAREFULLY, ZADIE. I'LL EXPLAIN EVERYTHING.
BUT RST, I NEED OU TO CALM DOWN.
CALM DOWN?!
HOW CAN I CALM DOWN WHEN YOU'RE POINTING A GUN AT ME?
I'M TRYING TO DEFEND MYSELF!
FROM WHO? ME?
WHAT COULD I POSSIBLY DO?
Uh, ZADIE...
YOU DON'T KNOW, DO YOU?
KNOW WHAT?

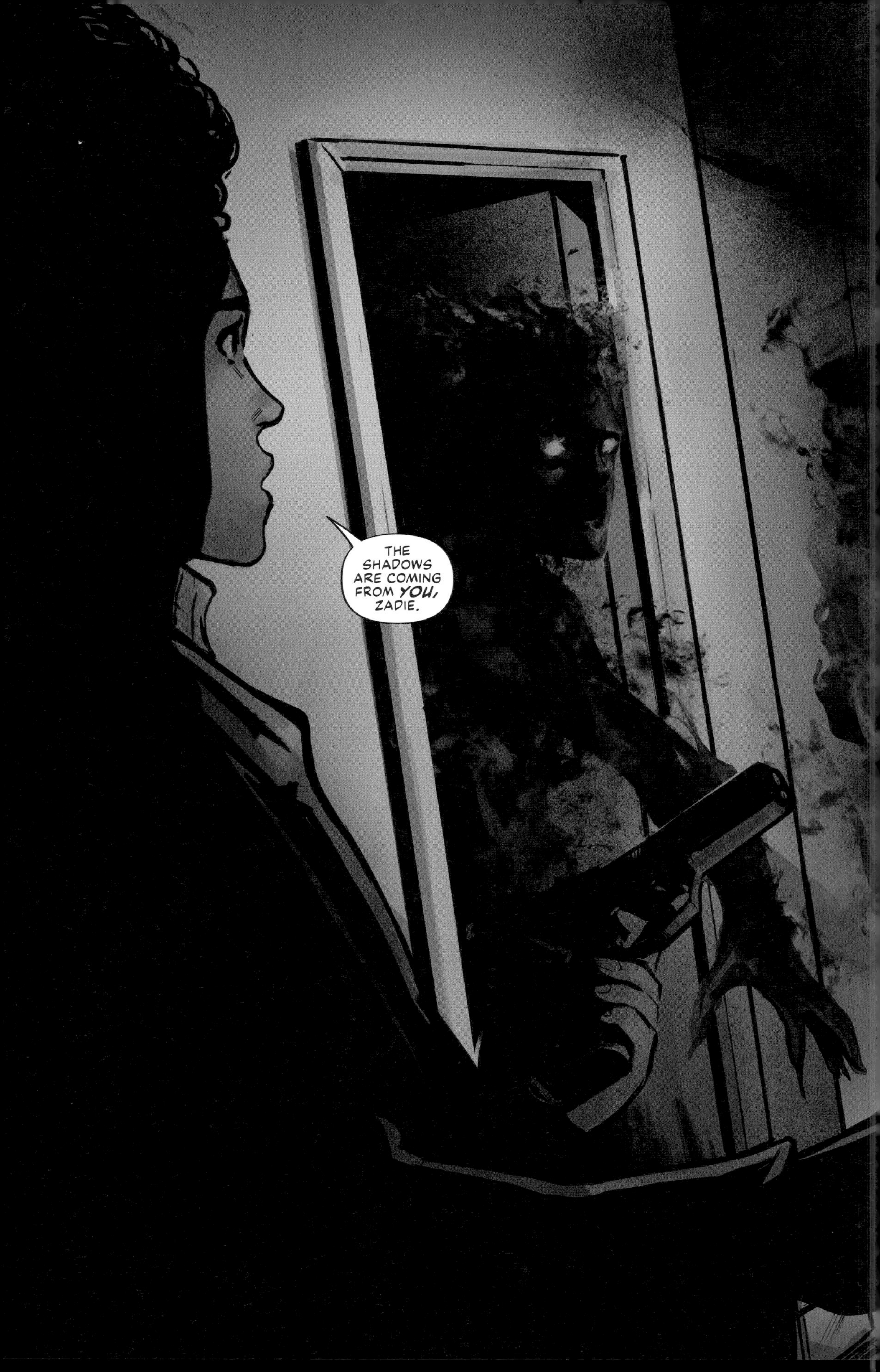
THE SHADOWS ARE COMING FROM *YOU,* ZADIE.

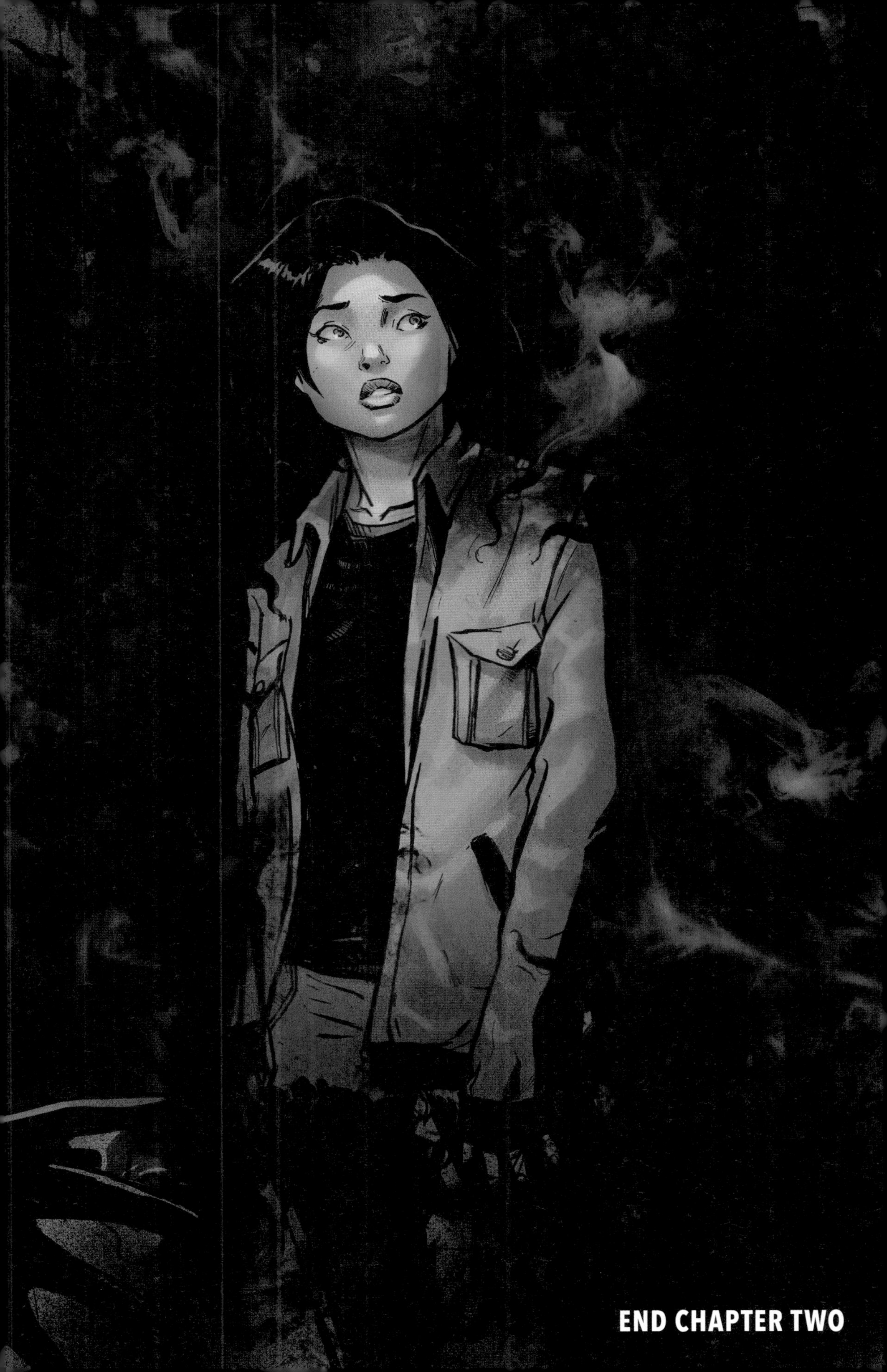
END CHAPTER TWO

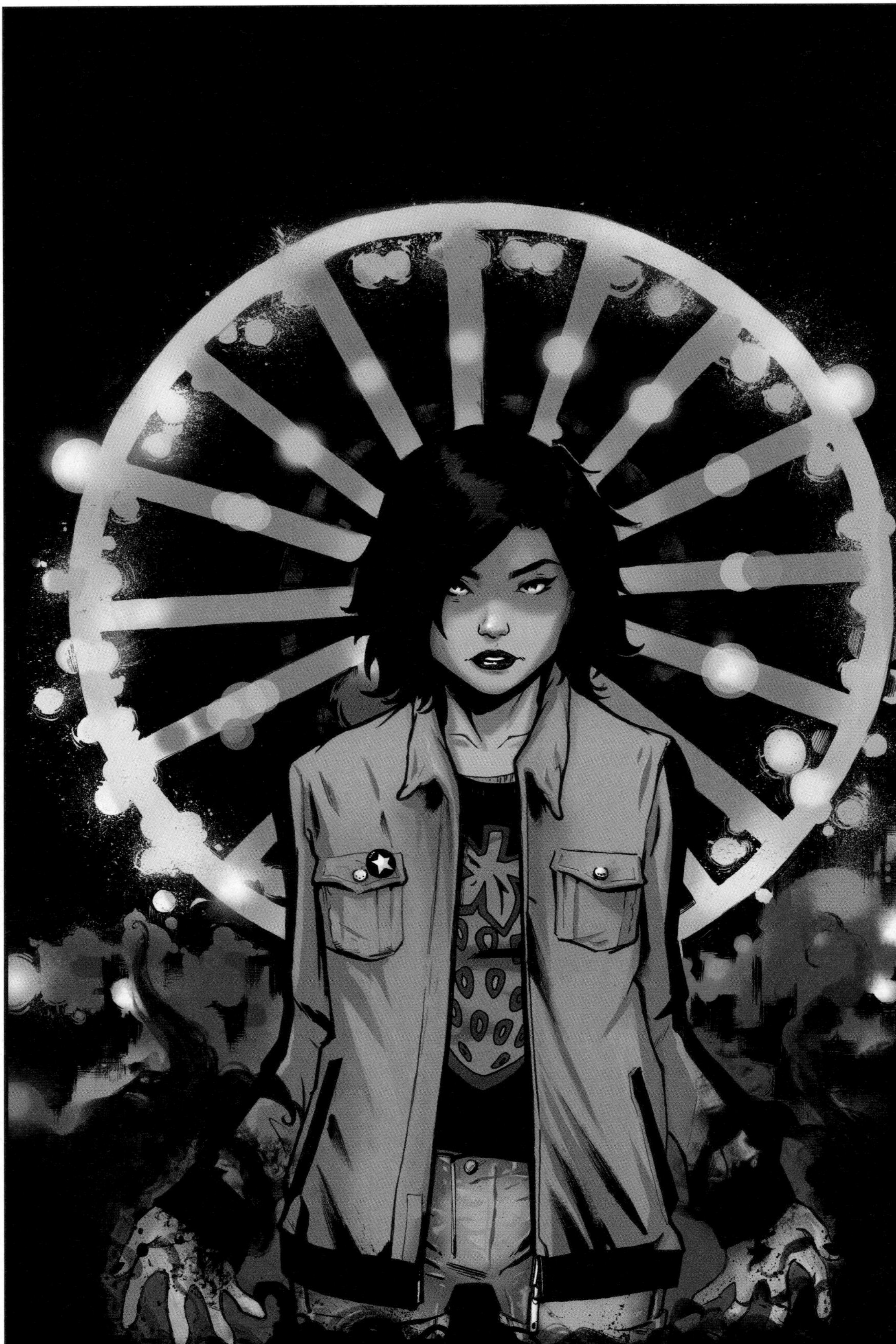

CHAPTER THREE

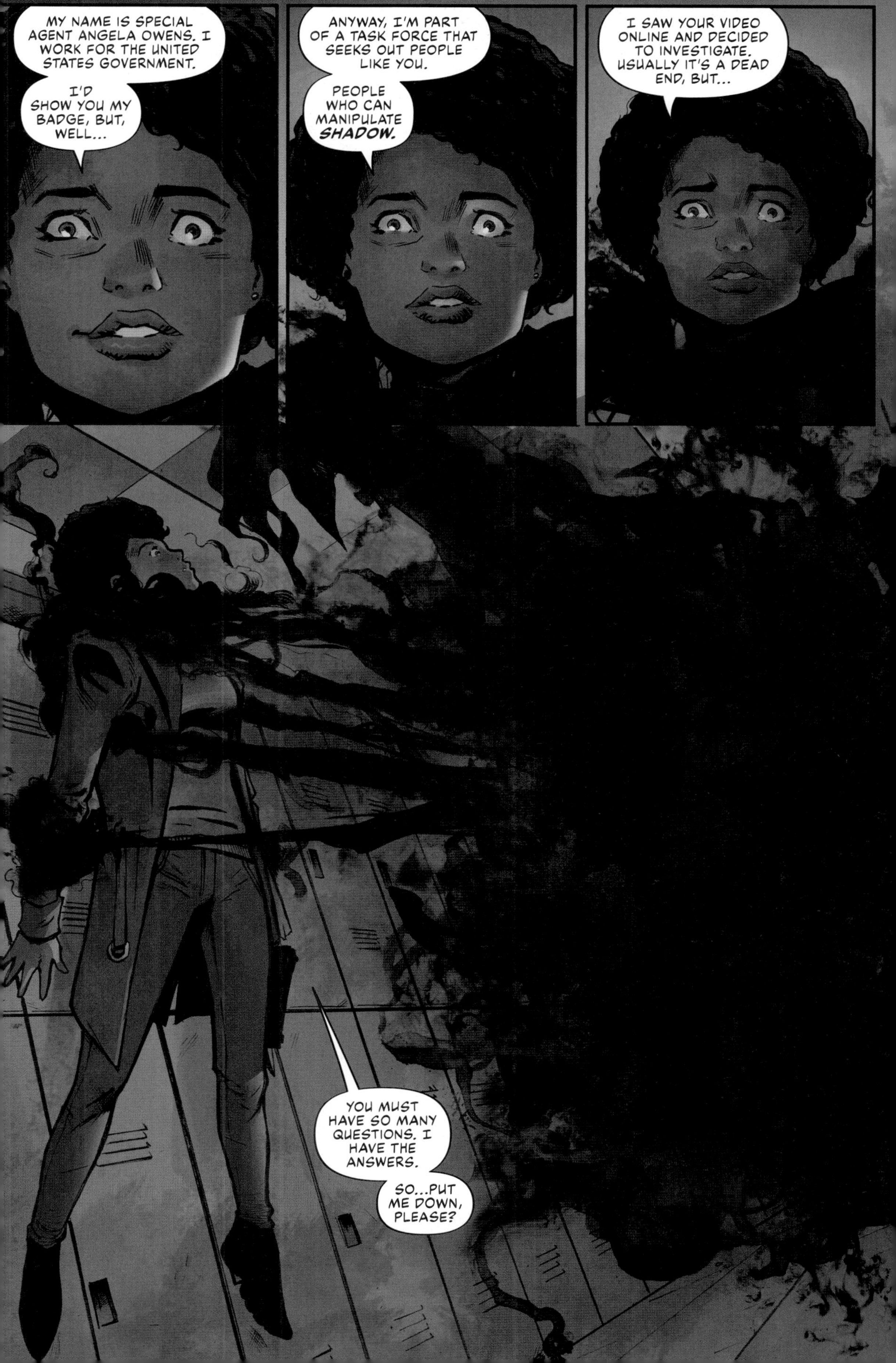
MY NAME IS SPECIAL AGENT ANGELA OWENS. I WORK FOR THE UNITED STATES GOVERNMENT.
I'D SHOW YOU MY BADGE, BUT, WELL...
ANYWAY, I'M PART OF A TASK FORCE THAT SEEKS OUT PEOPLE LIKE YOU.
PEOPLE WHO CAN MANIPULATE SHADOW.
I SAW YOUR VIDEO ONLINE AND DECIDED TO INVESTIGATE. USUALLY IT'S A DEAD END, BUT...
YOU MUST HAVE SO MANY QUESTIONS. I HAVE THE ANSWERS.
SO...PUT ME DOWN, PLEASE?

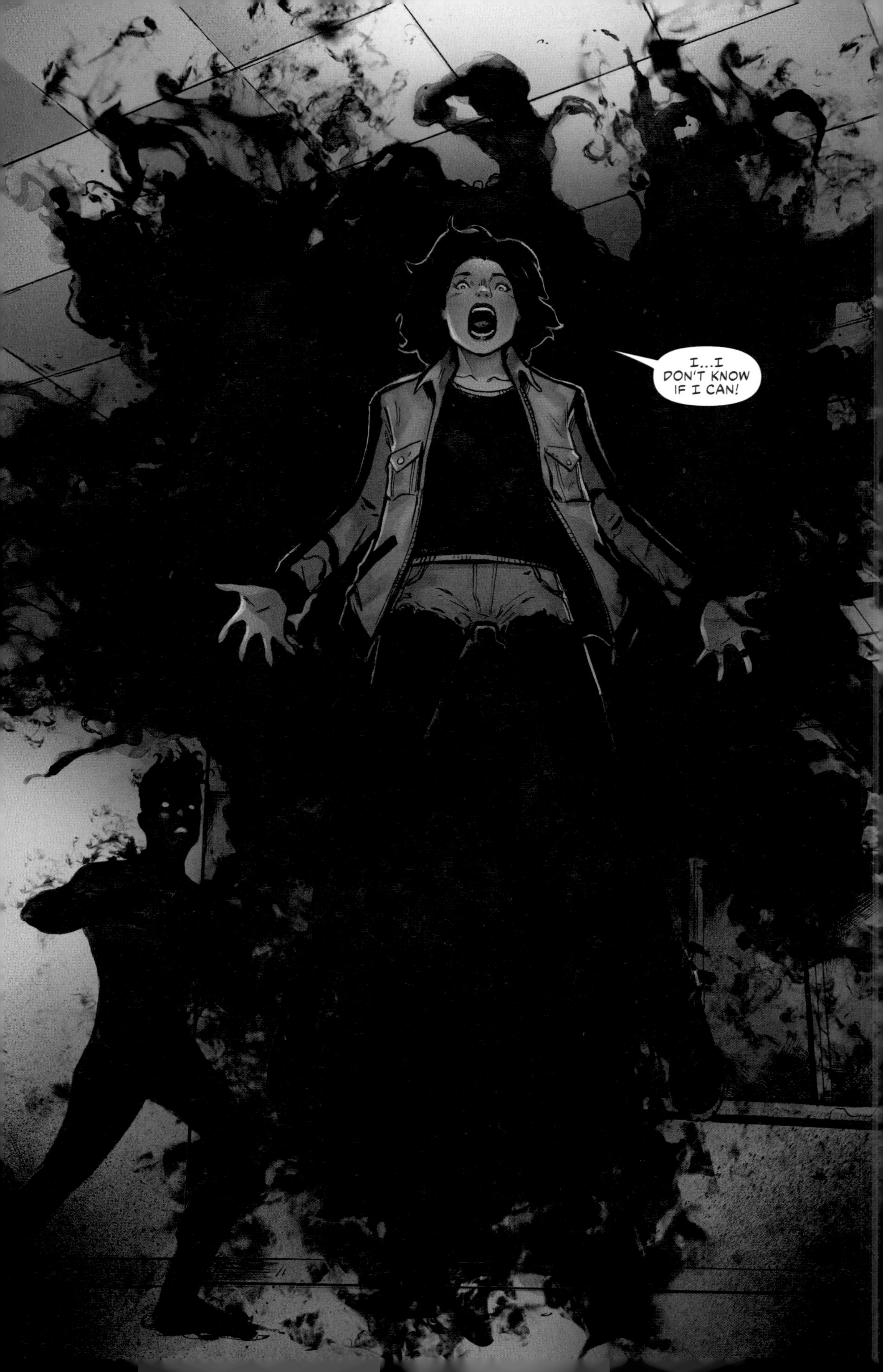
I...I DON'T KNOW IF I CAN!

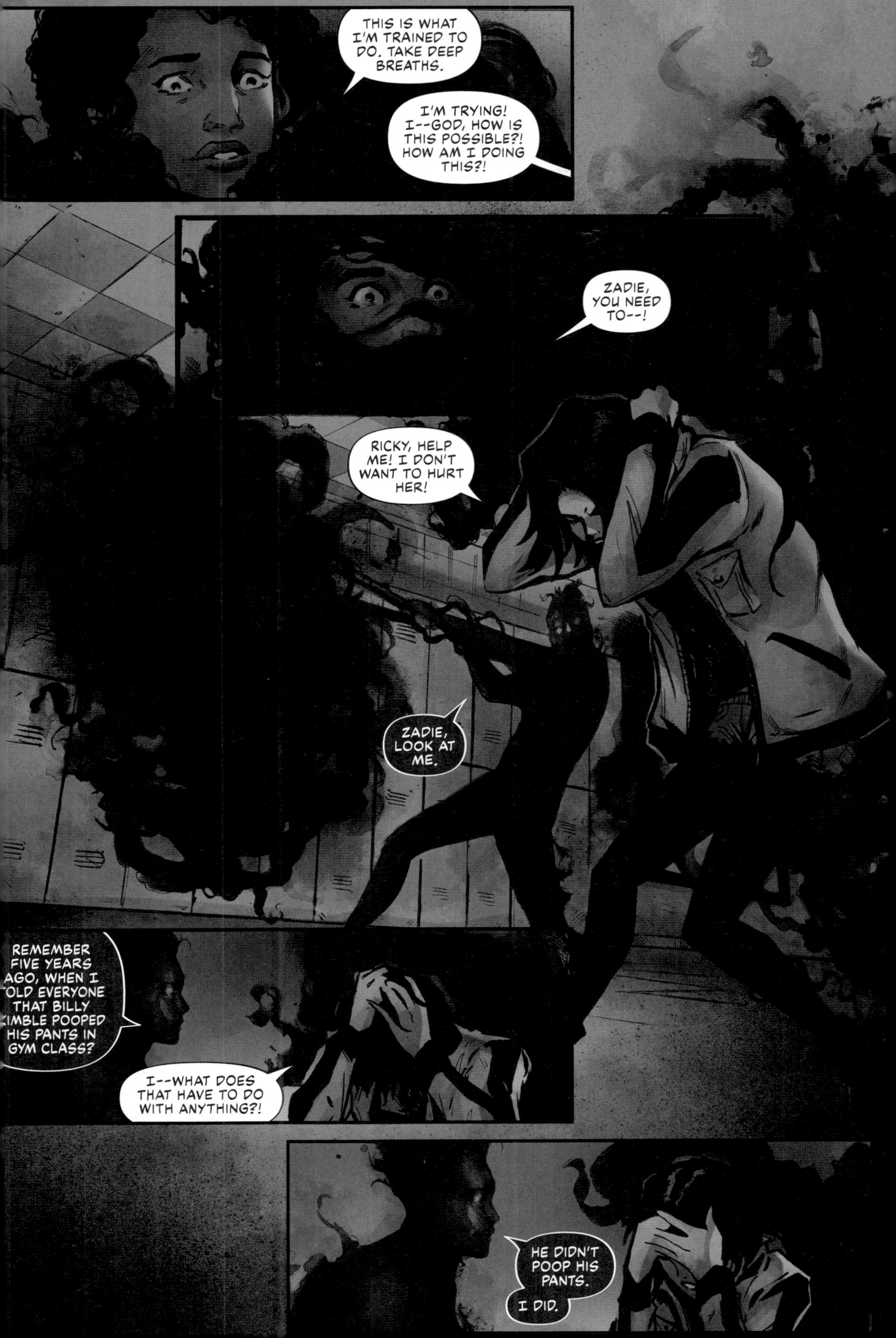
THIS IS WHAT I'M TRAINED TO DO. TAKE DEEP BREATHS.
I'M TRYING! I--GOD, HOW IS THIS POSSIBLE?! HOW AM I DOING THIS?!
ZADIE, YOU NEED TO--!
RICKY, HELP ME! I DON'T WANT TO HURT HER!
ZADIE, LOOK AT ME.
REMEMBER FIVE YEARS AGO, WHEN I TOLD EVERYONE THAT BILLY KIMBLE POOPED HIS PANTS IN GYM CLASS?
I--WHAT DOES THAT HAVE TO DO WITH ANYTHING?!
HE DIDN'T POOP HIS PANTS.
I DID.

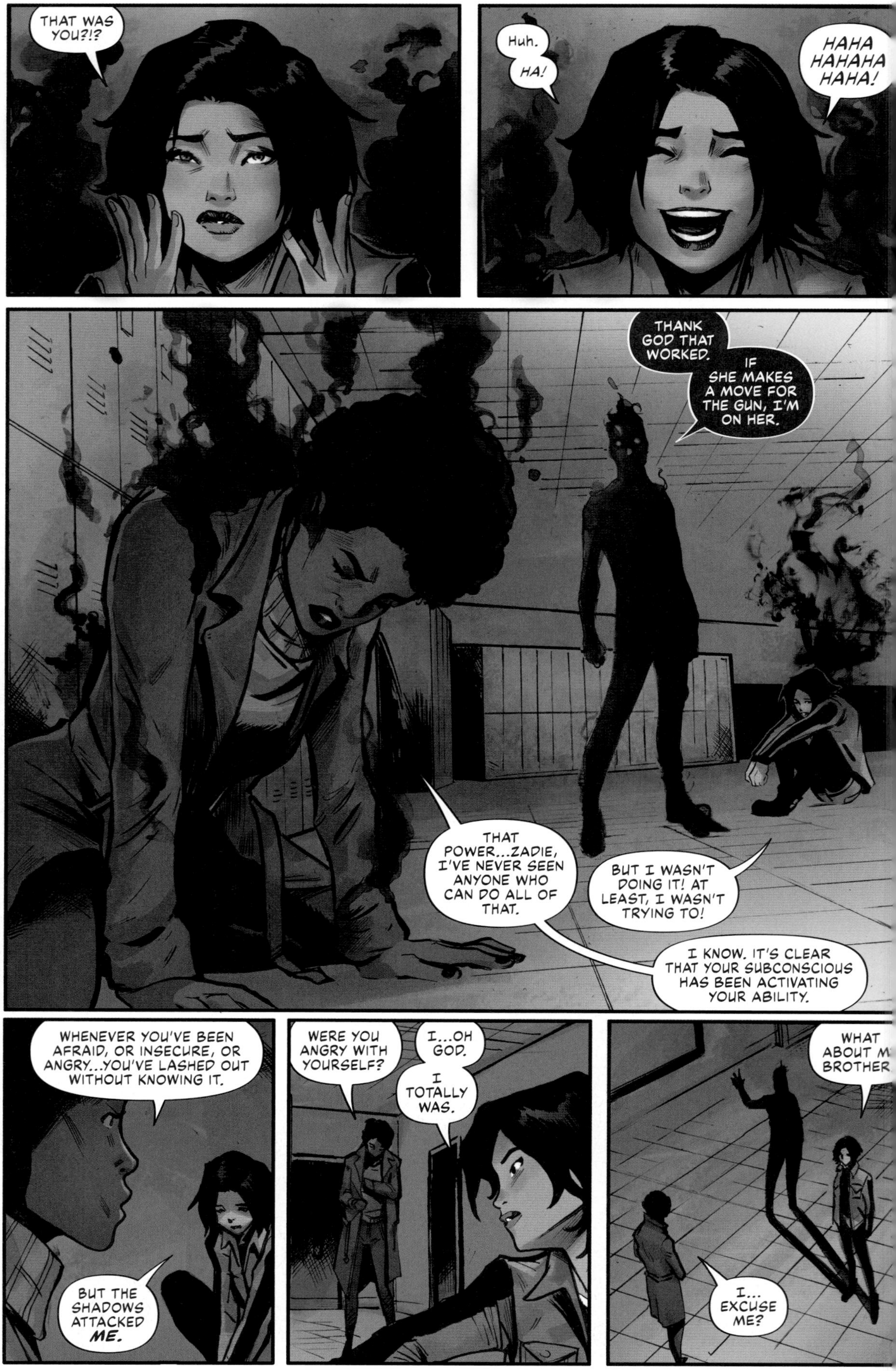
THAT WAS YOU?!?
Huh.
HA!
HAHA HAHAHA HAHA!
THANK GOD THAT WORKED.
IF SHE MAKES A MOVE FOR THE GUN, I'M ON HER.
THAT POWER...ZADIE, I'VE NEVER SEEN ANYONE WHO CAN DO ALL OF THAT.
BUT I WASN'T DOING IT! AT LEAST, I WASN'T TRYING TO!
I KNOW. IT'S CLEAR THAT YOUR SUBCONSCIOUS HAS BEEN ACTIVATING YOUR ABILITY.
WHENEVER YOU'VE BEEN AFRAID, OR INSECURE, OR ANGRY...YOU'VE LASHED OUT WITHOUT KNOWING IT.
BUT THE SHADOWS ATTACKED ME.
WERE YOU ANGRY WITH YOURSELF?
I...OH GOD.
I TOTALLY WAS.
I... EXCUSE ME?

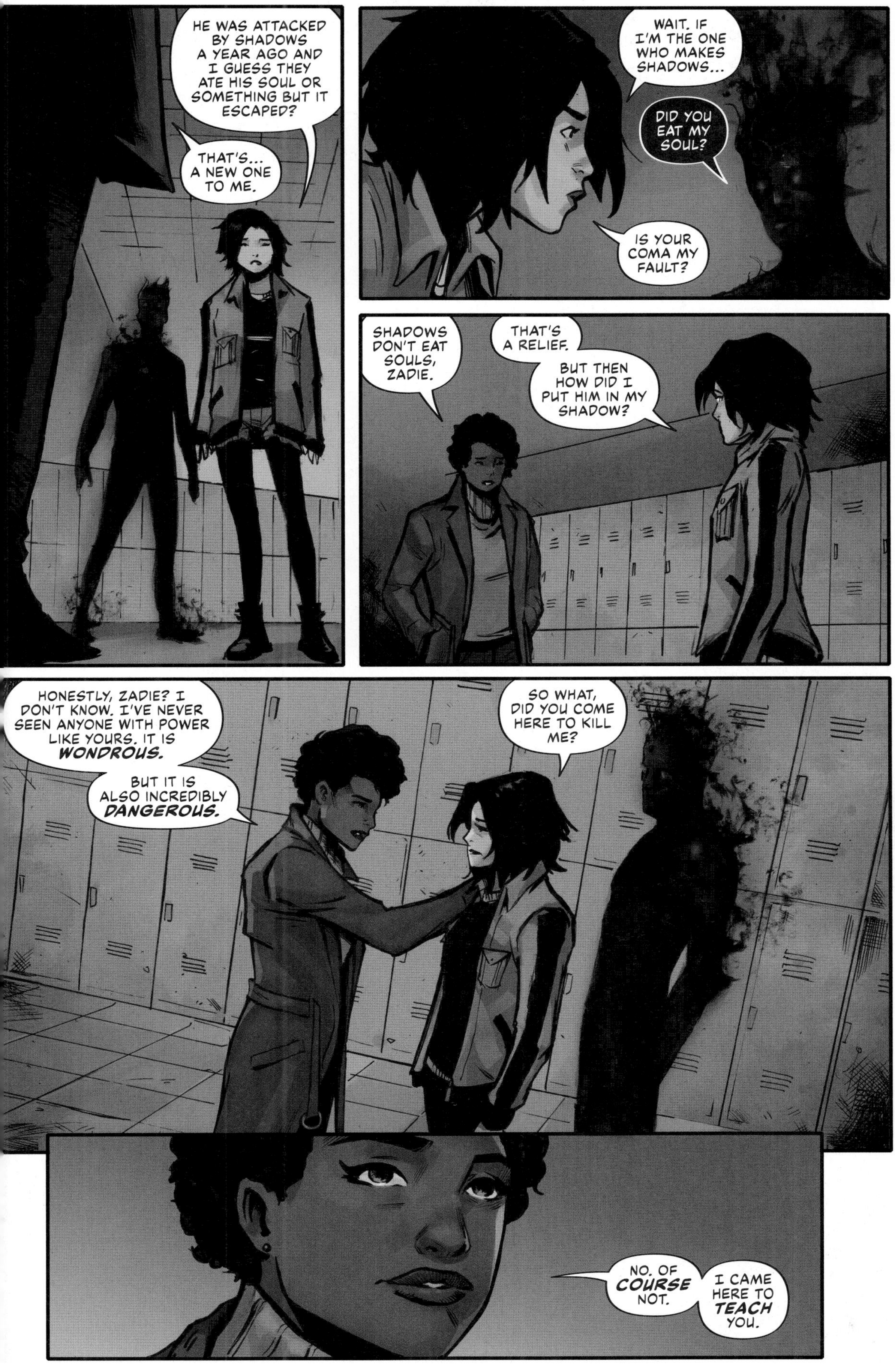
HE WAS ATTACKED BY SHADOWS A YEAR AGO AND I GUESS THEY ATE HIS SOUL OR SOMETHING BUT IT ESCAPED?
THAT'S... A NEW ONE TO ME.
WAIT. IF I'M THE ONE WHO MAKES SHADOWS...
DID YOU EAT MY SOUL?
IS YOUR COMA MY FAULT?
SHADOWS DON'T EAT SOULS, ZADIE.
THAT'S A RELIEF.
BUT THEN HOW DID I PUT HIM IN MY SHADOW?
HONESTLY, ZADIE? I DON'T KNOW. I'VE NEVER SEEN ANYONE WITH POWER LIKE YOURS. IT IS WONDROUS.
BUT IT IS ALSO INCREDIBLY DANGEROUS.
SO WHAT, DID YOU COME HERE TO KILL ME?
NO. OF COURSE NOT.
I CAME HERE TO TEACH YOU.

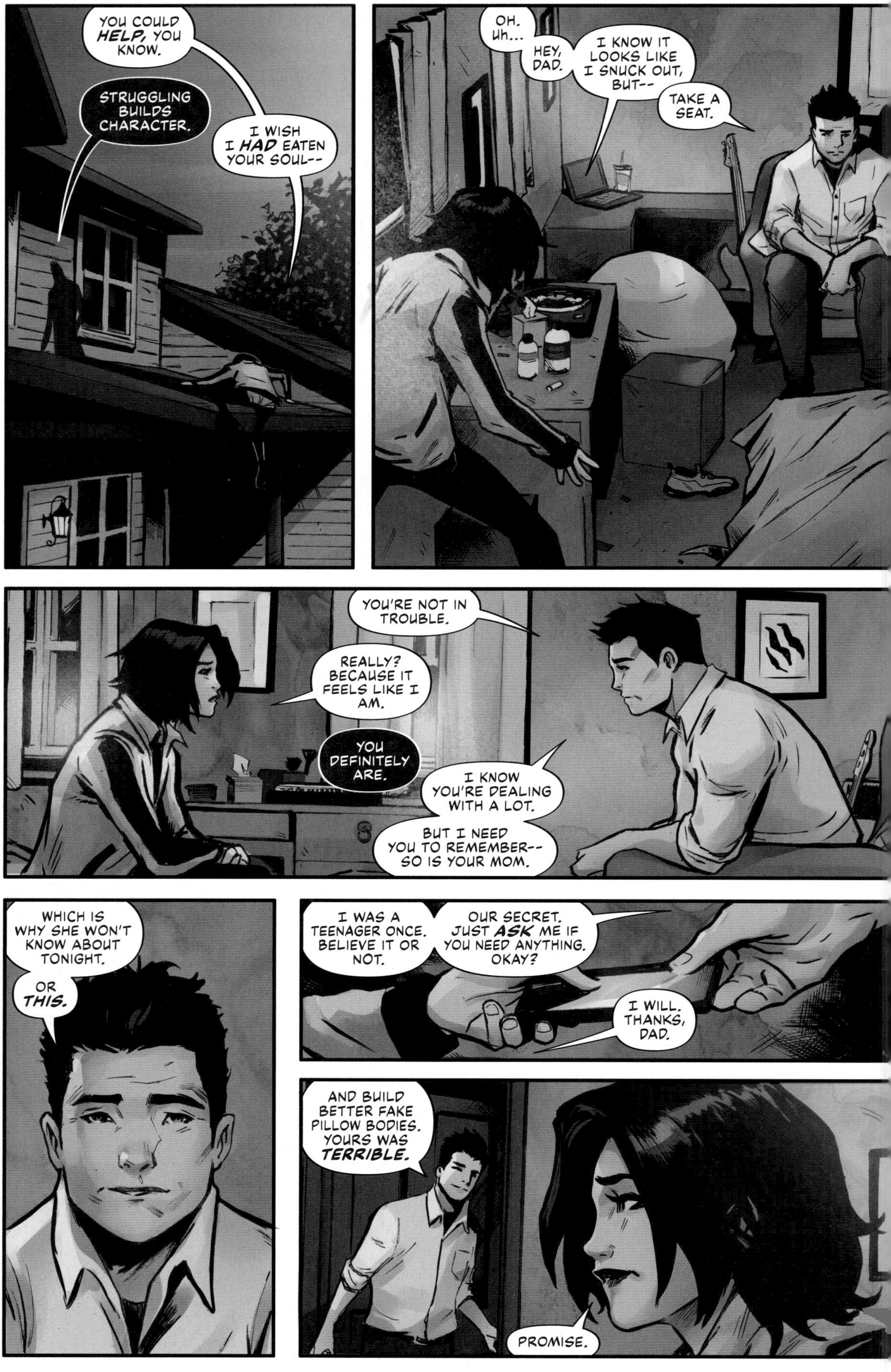
YOU COULD HELP, YOU KNOW.
STRUGGLING BUILDS CHARACTER.
I WISH I HAD EATEN YOUR SOUL--
OH. UH...
HEY, DAD.
I KNOW IT LOOKS LIKE I SNUCK OUT, BUT--
TAKE A SEAT.
YOU'RE NOT IN TROUBLE.
REALLY? BECAUSE IT FEELS LIKE I AM.
YOU DEFINITELY ARE.
I KNOW YOU'RE DEALING WITH A LOT.
BUT I NEED YOU TO REMEMBER-- SO IS YOUR MOM.
WHICH IS WHY SHE WON'T KNOW ABOUT TONIGHT.
OR THIS.
I WAS A TEENAGER ONCE. BELIEVE IT OR NOT.
OUR SECRET. JUST ASK ME IF YOU NEED ANYTHING. OKAY?
I WILL. THANKS, DAD.
AND BUILD BETTER FAKE PILLOW BODIES. YOURS WAS TERRIBLE.
PROMISE.

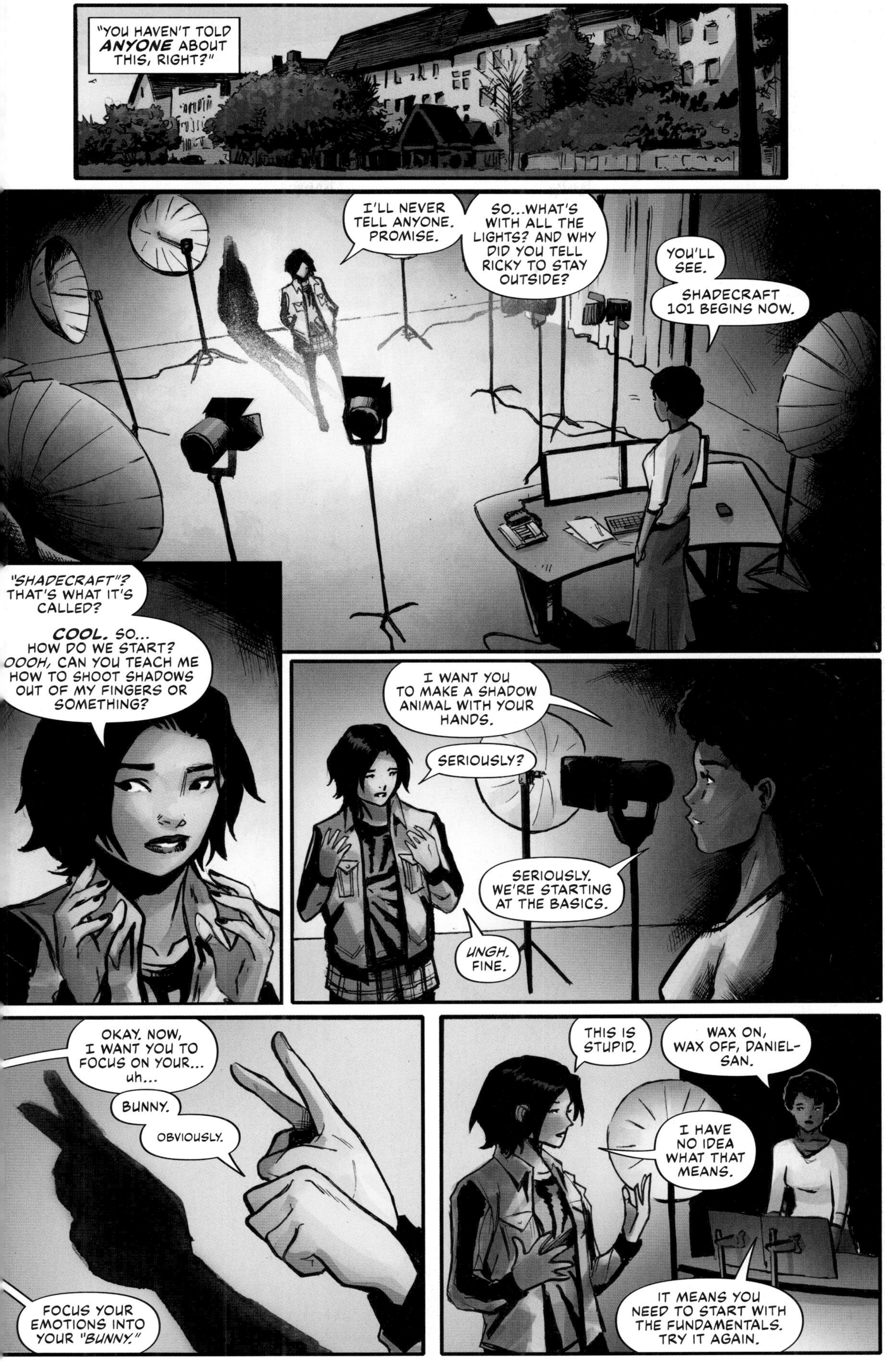
"YOU HAVEN'T TOLD *ANYONE* ABOUT THIS, RIGHT?"
I'LL NEVER TELL ANYONE. PROMISE.
SO...WHAT'S WITH ALL THE LIGHTS? AND WHY DID YOU TELL RICKY TO STAY OUTSIDE?
YOU'LL SEE.
SHADECRAFT 101 BEGINS NOW.
"SHADECRAFT"? THAT'S WHAT IT'S CALLED?
COOL. SO... HOW DO WE START? *OOOH*, CAN YOU TEACH ME HOW TO SHOOT SHADOWS OUT OF MY FINGERS OR SOMETHING?
I WANT YOU TO MAKE A SHADOW ANIMAL WITH YOUR HANDS.
SERIOUSLY?
SERIOUSLY. WE'RE STARTING AT THE BASICS.
UNGH. FINE.
OKAY. NOW, I WANT YOU TO FOCUS ON YOUR... uh...
BUNNY.
OBVIOUSLY.
FOCUS YOUR EMOTIONS INTO YOUR *"BUNNY."*
THIS IS STUPID.
WAX ON, WAX OFF, DANIEL-SAN.
I HAVE NO IDEA WHAT THAT MEANS.
IT MEANS YOU NEED TO START WITH THE FUNDAMENTALS. TRY IT AGAIN.

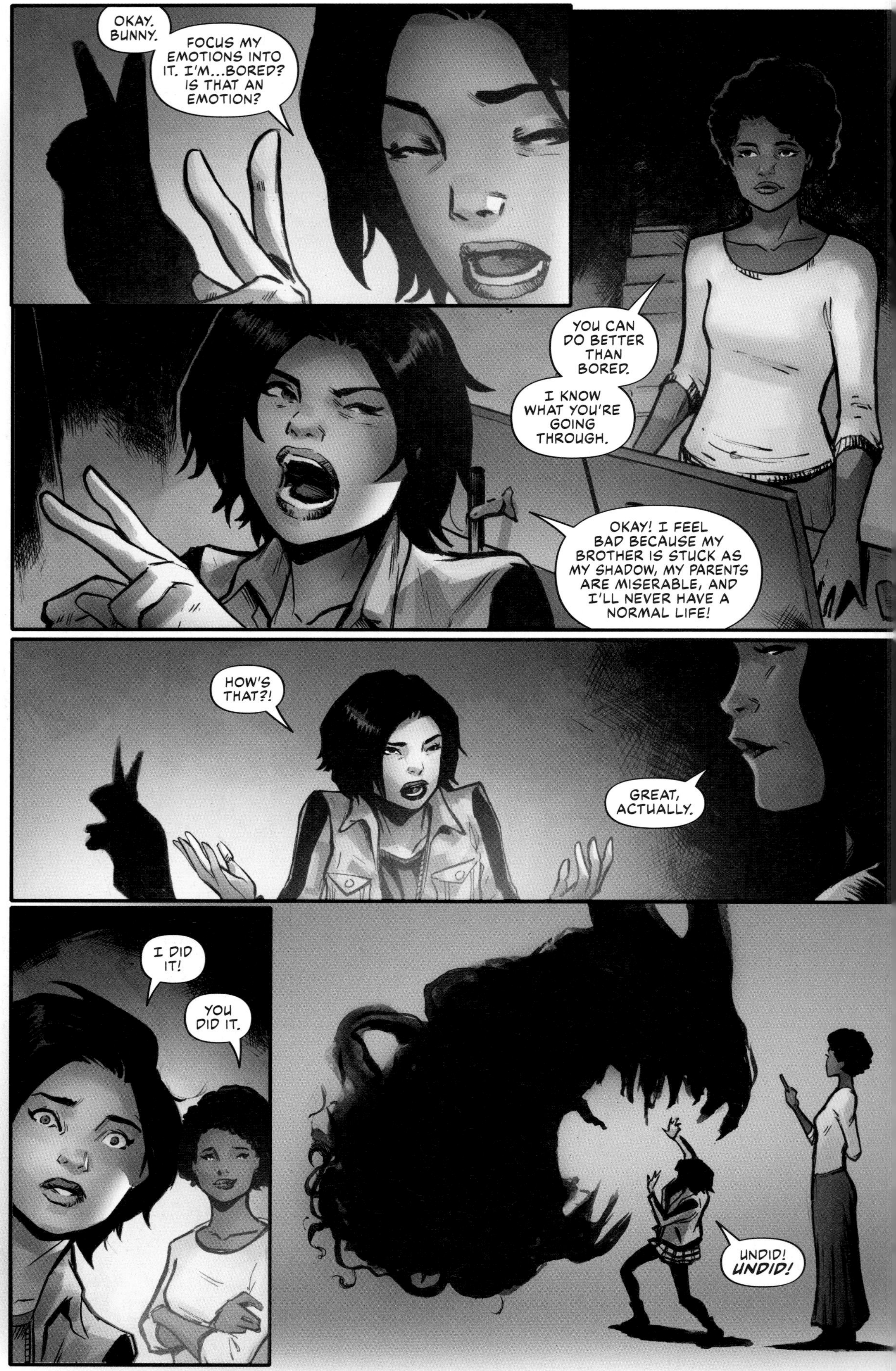
OKAY. BUNNY.
FOCUS MY EMOTIONS INTO IT. I'M...BORED? IS THAT AN EMOTION?
YOU CAN DO BETTER THAN BORED.
I KNOW WHAT YOU'RE GOING THROUGH.
OKAY! I FEEL BAD BECAUSE MY BROTHER IS STUCK AS MY SHADOW, MY PARENTS ARE MISERABLE, AND I'LL NEVER HAVE A NORMAL LIFE!
HOW'S THAT?!
GREAT, ACTUALLY.
I DID IT!
YOU DID IT.
UNDID! ***UNDID!***

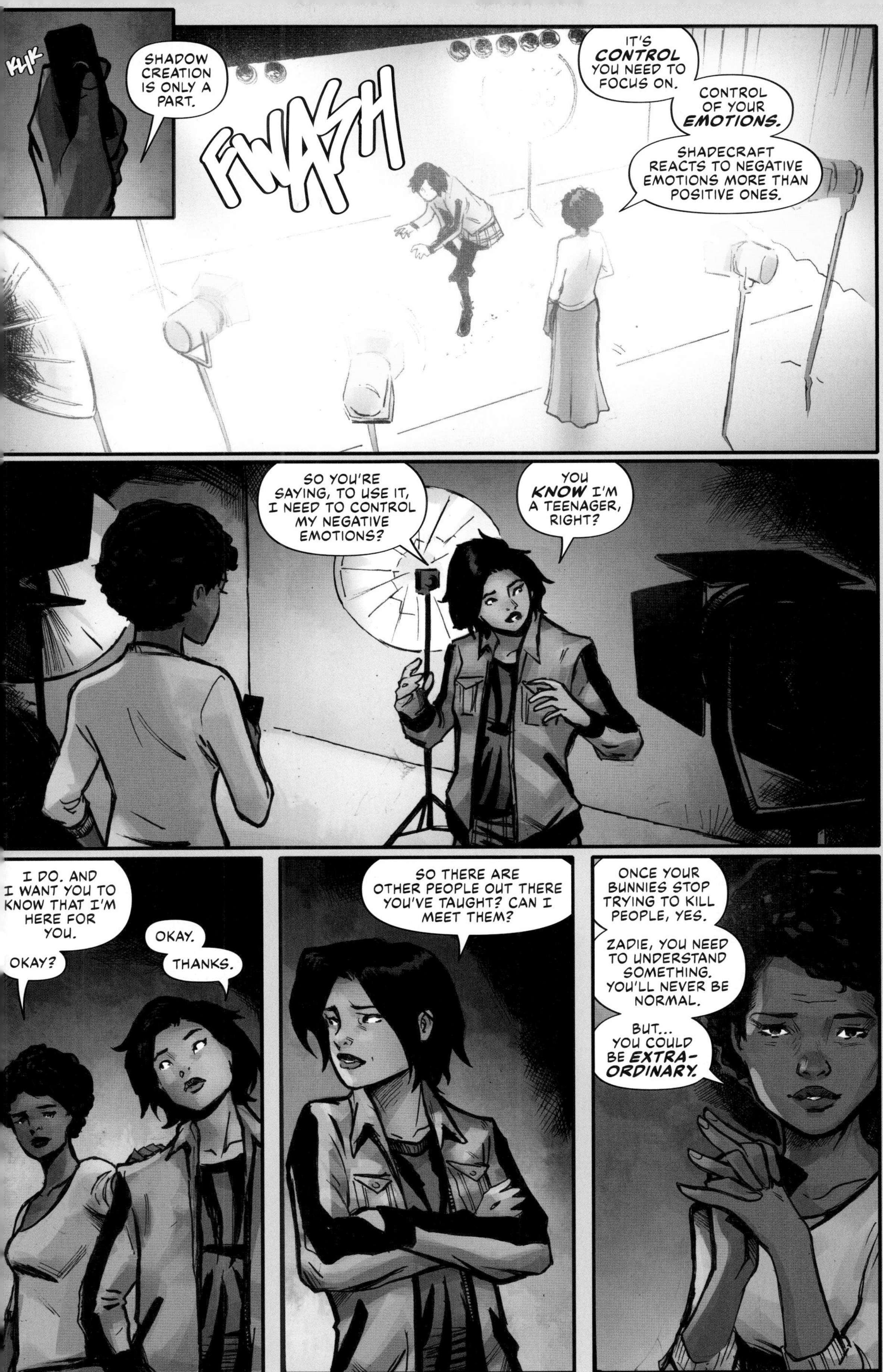
KLIK
SHADOW CREATION IS ONLY A PART.
FWASH
IT'S CONTROL YOU NEED TO FOCUS ON.
CONTROL OF YOUR EMOTIONS.
SHADECRAFT REACTS TO NEGATIVE EMOTIONS MORE THAN POSITIVE ONES.
SO YOU'RE SAYING, TO USE IT, I NEED TO CONTROL MY NEGATIVE EMOTIONS?
YOU KNOW I'M A TEENAGER, RIGHT?
I DO. AND I WANT YOU TO KNOW THAT I'M HERE FOR YOU.
OKAY?
OKAY.
THANKS.
SO THERE ARE OTHER PEOPLE OUT THERE YOU'VE TAUGHT? CAN I MEET THEM?
ONCE YOUR BUNNIES STOP TRYING TO KILL PEOPLE, YES.
ZADIE, YOU NEED TO UNDERSTAND SOMETHING. YOU'LL NEVER BE NORMAL.
BUT... YOU COULD BE EXTRA-ORDINARY.

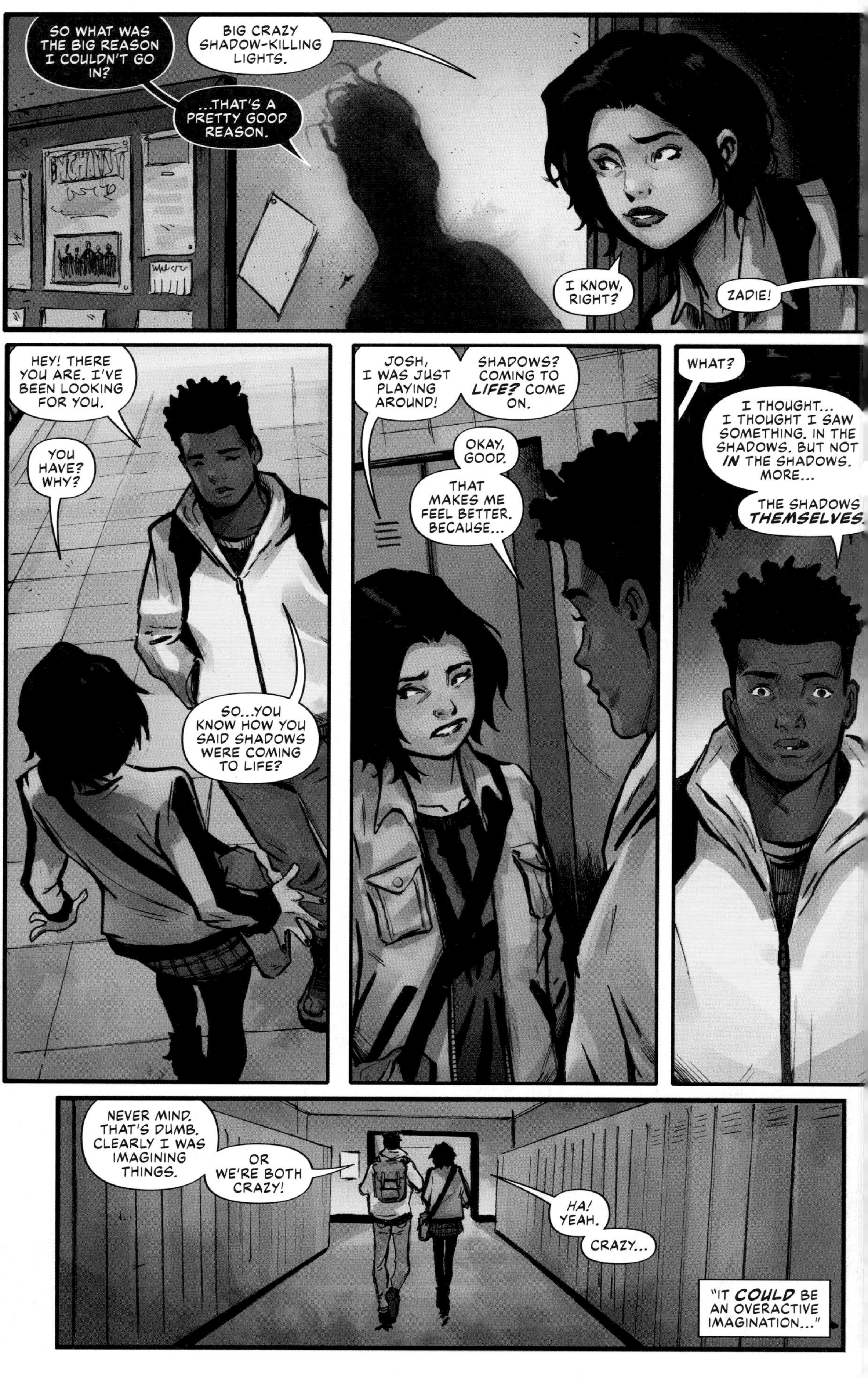
SO WHAT WAS THE BIG REASON I COULDN'T GO IN?
BIG CRAZY SHADOW-KILLING LIGHTS.
...THAT'S A PRETTY GOOD REASON.
I KNOW, RIGHT?
ZADIE!
HEY! THERE YOU ARE. I'VE BEEN LOOKING FOR YOU.
YOU HAVE? WHY?
SO...YOU KNOW HOW YOU SAID SHADOWS WERE COMING TO LIFE?
JOSH, I WAS JUST PLAYING AROUND!
SHADOWS? COMING TO *LIFE?* COME ON.
OKAY, GOOD.
THAT MAKES ME FEEL BETTER. BECAUSE...
WHAT?
I THOUGHT... I THOUGHT I SAW SOMETHING. IN THE SHADOWS. BUT NOT *IN* THE SHADOWS. MORE...
THE SHADOWS *THEMSELVES.*
NEVER MIND. THAT'S DUMB. CLEARLY I WAS IMAGINING THINGS.
OR WE'RE BOTH CRAZY!
HA! YEAH.
CRAZY...
"IT *COULD* BE AN OVERACTIVE IMAGINATION..."

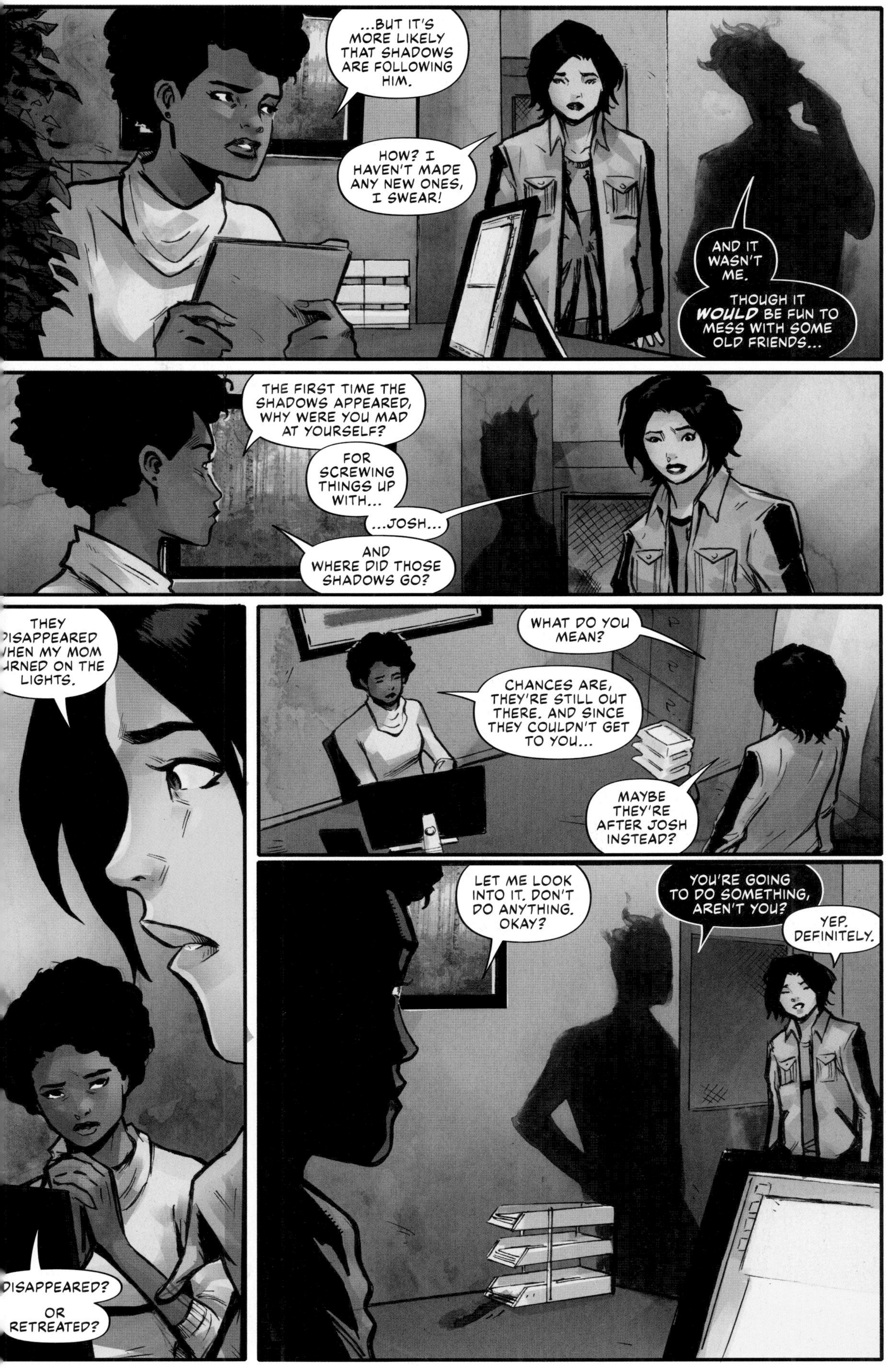
...BUT IT'S MORE LIKELY THAT SHADOWS ARE FOLLOWING HIM.
HOW? I HAVEN'T MADE ANY NEW ONES, I SWEAR!
AND IT WASN'T ME.
THOUGH IT WOULD BE FUN TO MESS WITH SOME OLD FRIENDS...
THE FIRST TIME THE SHADOWS APPEARED, WHY WERE YOU MAD AT YOURSELF?
FOR SCREWING THINGS UP WITH...
...JOSH...
AND WHERE DID THOSE SHADOWS GO?
THEY DISAPPEARED WHEN MY MOM TURNED ON THE LIGHTS.
DISAPPEARED? OR RETREATED?
WHAT DO YOU MEAN?
CHANCES ARE, THEY'RE STILL OUT THERE. AND SINCE THEY COULDN'T GET TO YOU...
MAYBE THEY'RE AFTER JOSH INSTEAD?
LET ME LOOK INTO IT. DON'T DO ANYTHING. OKAY?
YOU'RE GOING TO DO SOMETHING, AREN'T YOU?
YEP. DEFINITELY.

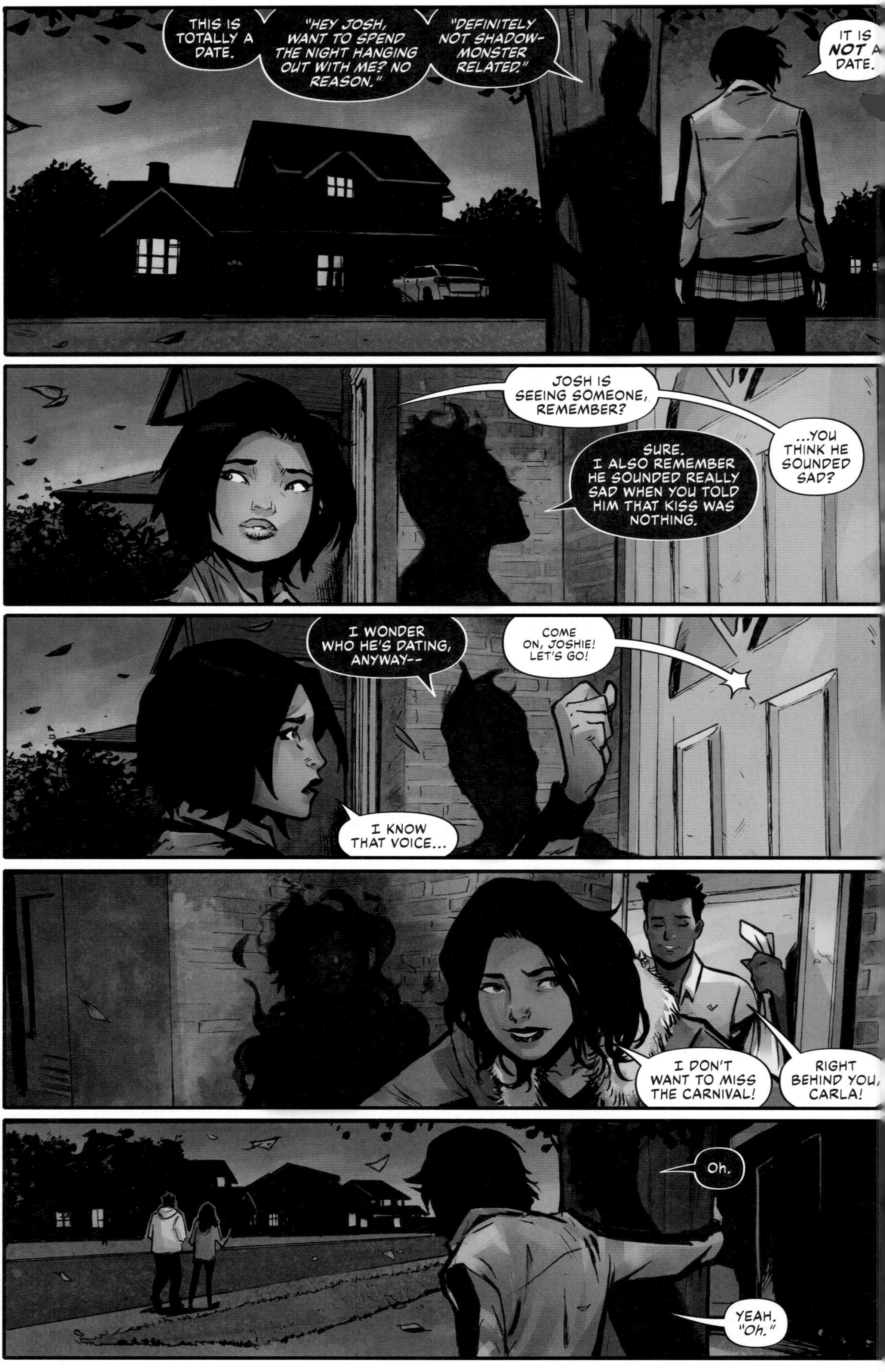
THIS IS TOTALLY A DATE.
"HEY JOSH, WANT TO SPEND THE NIGHT HANGING OUT WITH ME? NO REASON."
"DEFINITELY NOT SHADOW-MONSTER RELATED."
IT IS NOT A DATE.
JOSH IS SEEING SOMEONE, REMEMBER?
SURE. I ALSO REMEMBER HE SOUNDED REALLY SAD WHEN YOU TOLD HIM THAT KISS WAS NOTHING.
...YOU THINK HE SOUNDED SAD?
I WONDER WHO HE'S DATING, ANYWAY--
COME ON, JOSHIE! LET'S GO!
I KNOW THAT VOICE...
I DON'T WANT TO MISS THE CARNIVAL!
RIGHT BEHIND YOU, CARLA!
Oh.
YEAH. "Oh."

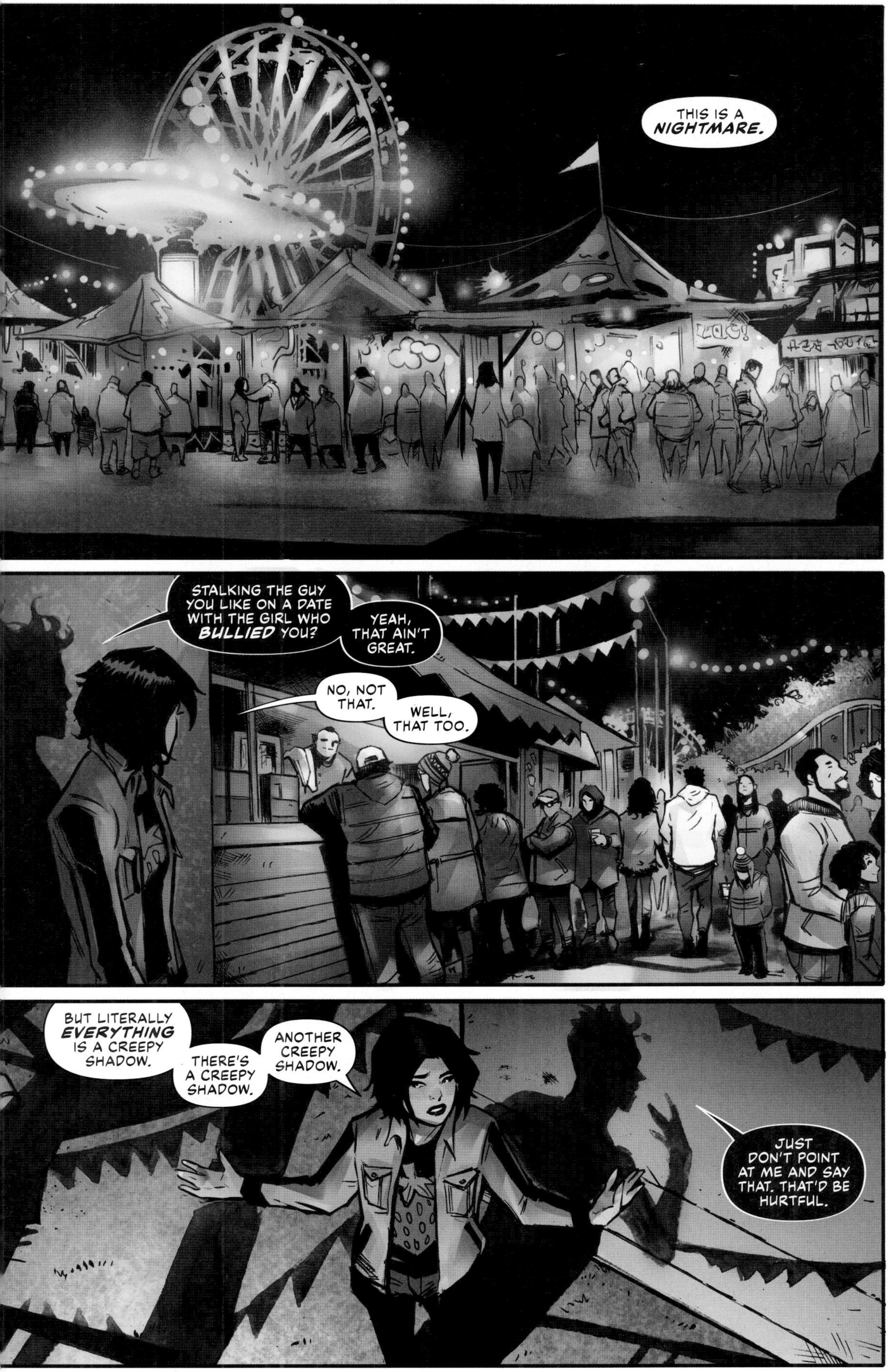
THIS IS A NIGHTMARE.
STALKING THE GUY YOU LIKE ON A DATE WITH THE GIRL WHO BULLIED YOU?
YEAH, THAT AIN'T GREAT.
NO, NOT THAT.
WELL, THAT TOO.
BUT LITERALLY EVERYTHING IS A CREEPY SHADOW.
THERE'S A CREEPY SHADOW.
ANOTHER CREEPY SHADOW.
JUST DON'T POINT AT ME AND SAY THAT. THAT'D BE HURTFUL.

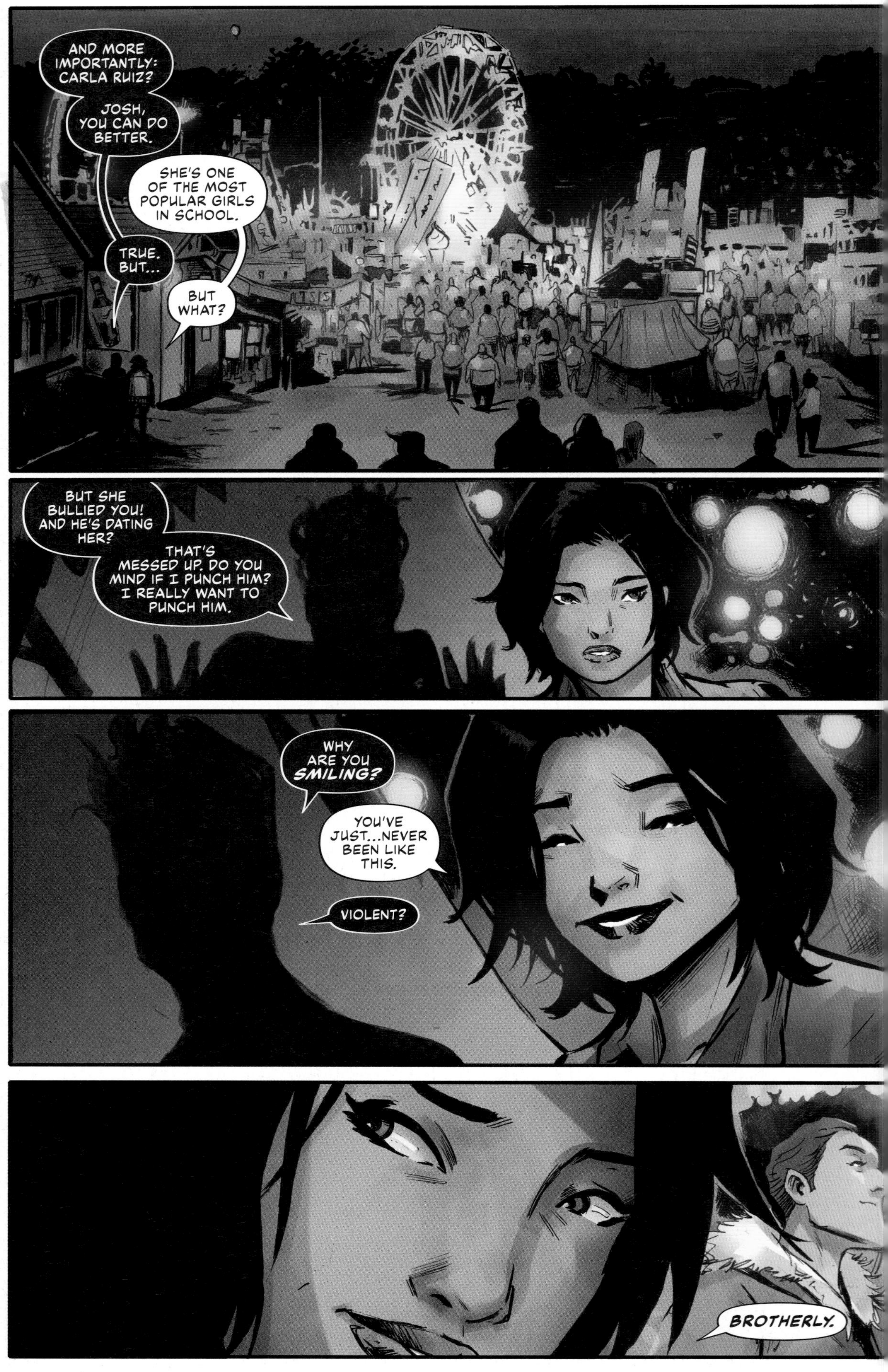
AND MORE IMPORTANTLY: CARLA RUIZ?
JOSH, YOU CAN DO BETTER.
SHE'S ONE OF THE MOST POPULAR GIRLS IN SCHOOL.
TRUE. BUT...
BUT WHAT?
BUT SHE BULLIED YOU! AND HE'S DATING HER?
THAT'S MESSED UP. DO YOU MIND IF I PUNCH HIM? I REALLY WANT TO PUNCH HIM.
WHY ARE YOU *SMILING?*
YOU'VE JUST...NEVER BEEN LIKE THIS.
VIOLENT?
BROTHERLY.

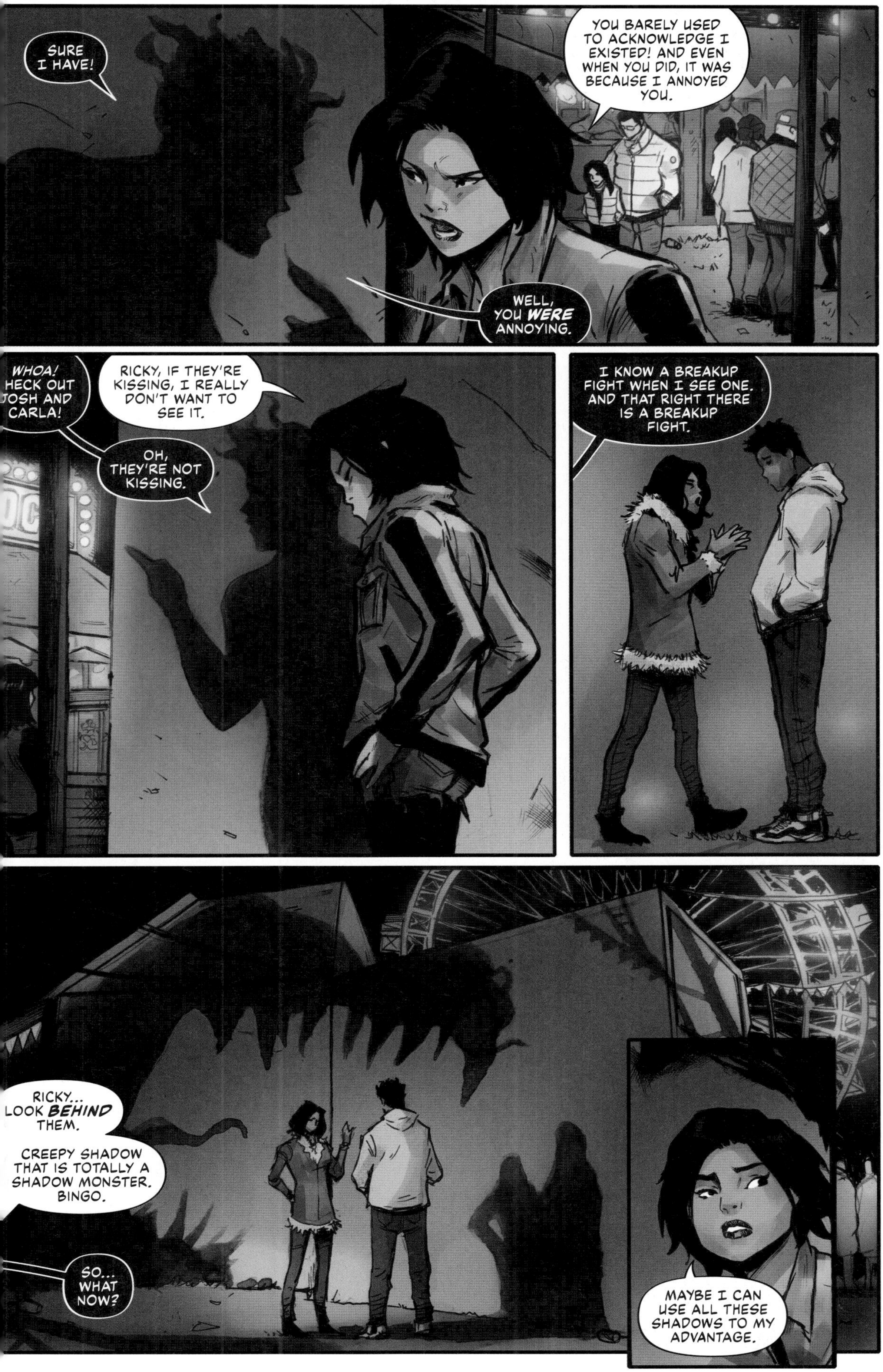
SURE I HAVE!
YOU BARELY USED TO ACKNOWLEDGE I EXISTED! AND EVEN WHEN YOU DID, IT WAS BECAUSE I ANNOYED YOU.
WELL, YOU *WERE* ANNOYING.
WHOA! HECK OUT JOSH AND CARLA!
RICKY, IF THEY'RE KISSING, I REALLY DON'T WANT TO SEE IT.
OH, THEY'RE NOT KISSING.
I KNOW A BREAKUP FIGHT WHEN I SEE ONE. AND THAT RIGHT THERE IS A BREAKUP FIGHT.
RICKY... LOOK *BEHIND* THEM.
CREEPY SHADOW THAT IS TOTALLY A SHADOW MONSTER. BINGO.
SO... WHAT NOW?
MAYBE I CAN USE ALL THESE SHADOWS TO MY ADVANTAGE.

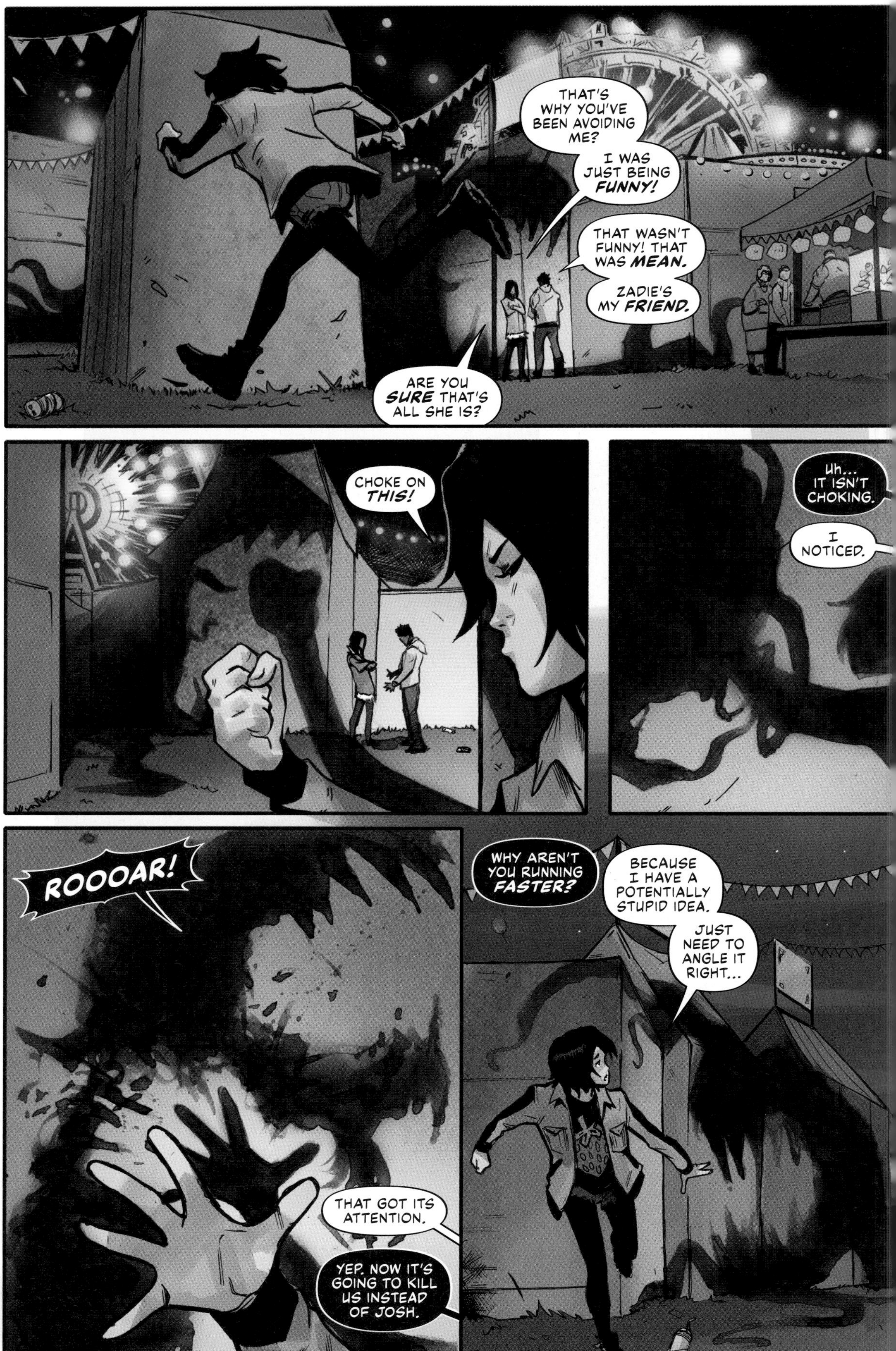
THAT'S WHY YOU'VE BEEN AVOIDING ME?
I WAS JUST BEING FUNNY!
THAT WASN'T FUNNY! THAT WAS MEAN.
ZADIE'S MY FRIEND.
ARE YOU SURE THAT'S ALL SHE IS?
CHOKE ON THIS!
Uh... IT ISN'T CHOKING.
I NOTICED.
ROOOAR!
THAT GOT ITS ATTENTION.
YEP. NOW IT'S GOING TO KILL US INSTEAD OF JOSH.
WHY AREN'T YOU RUNNING FASTER?
BECAUSE I HAVE A POTENTIALLY STUPID IDEA.
JUST NEED TO ANGLE IT RIGHT...

OKAY! NOW IT'S *ANGRY*.

YEAH? WELL, SAME.

THIS IS ALL ABOUT DEALING WITH YOUR EMOTIONS, RIGHT?

WHAT WERE YOU FEELING WHEN YOU CREATED IT?

I WAS SUPER EMBARRASSED THAT I KISSED JOSH AND HE DIDN'T KISS ME BACK!

WELL, I'M PRETTY SURE JOSH JUST BROKE UP WITH CARLA BECAUSE OF YOU!

WAIT, DO YOU THINK SO--?

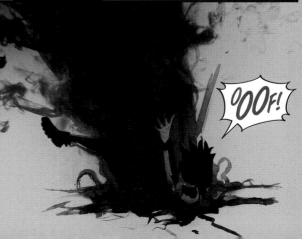

OOF!

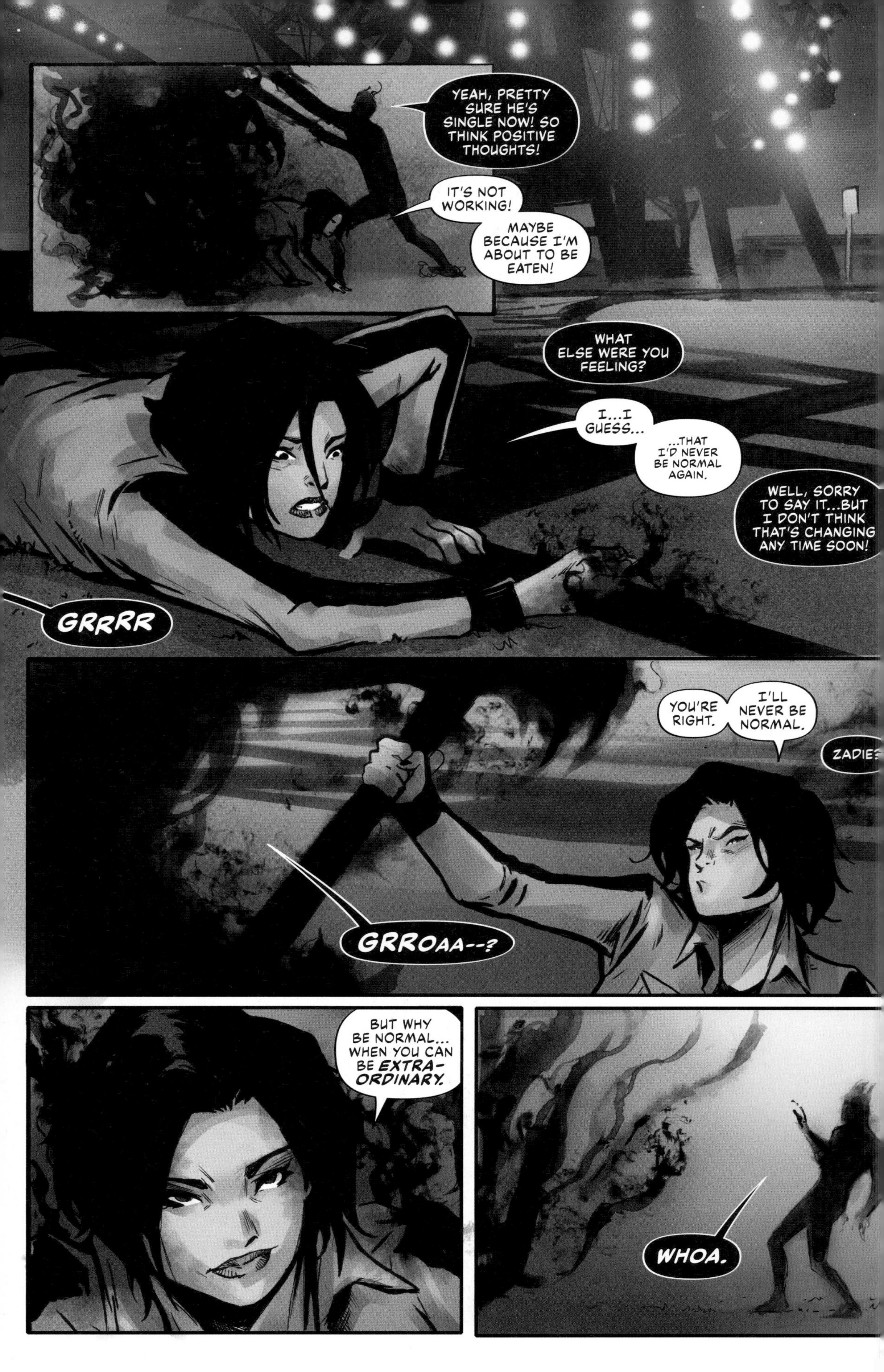
YEAH, PRETTY SURE HE'S SINGLE NOW! SO THINK POSITIVE THOUGHTS!
IT'S NOT WORKING!
MAYBE BECAUSE I'M ABOUT TO BE EATEN!
WHAT ELSE WERE YOU FEELING?
I...I GUESS...
...THAT I'D NEVER BE NORMAL AGAIN.
WELL, SORRY TO SAY IT...BUT I DON'T THINK THAT'S CHANGING ANY TIME SOON!
GRRRR
YOU'RE RIGHT.
I'LL NEVER BE NORMAL.
GRROAA--?
BUT WHY BE NORMAL... WHEN YOU CAN BE EXTRA-ORDINARY.
WHOA.

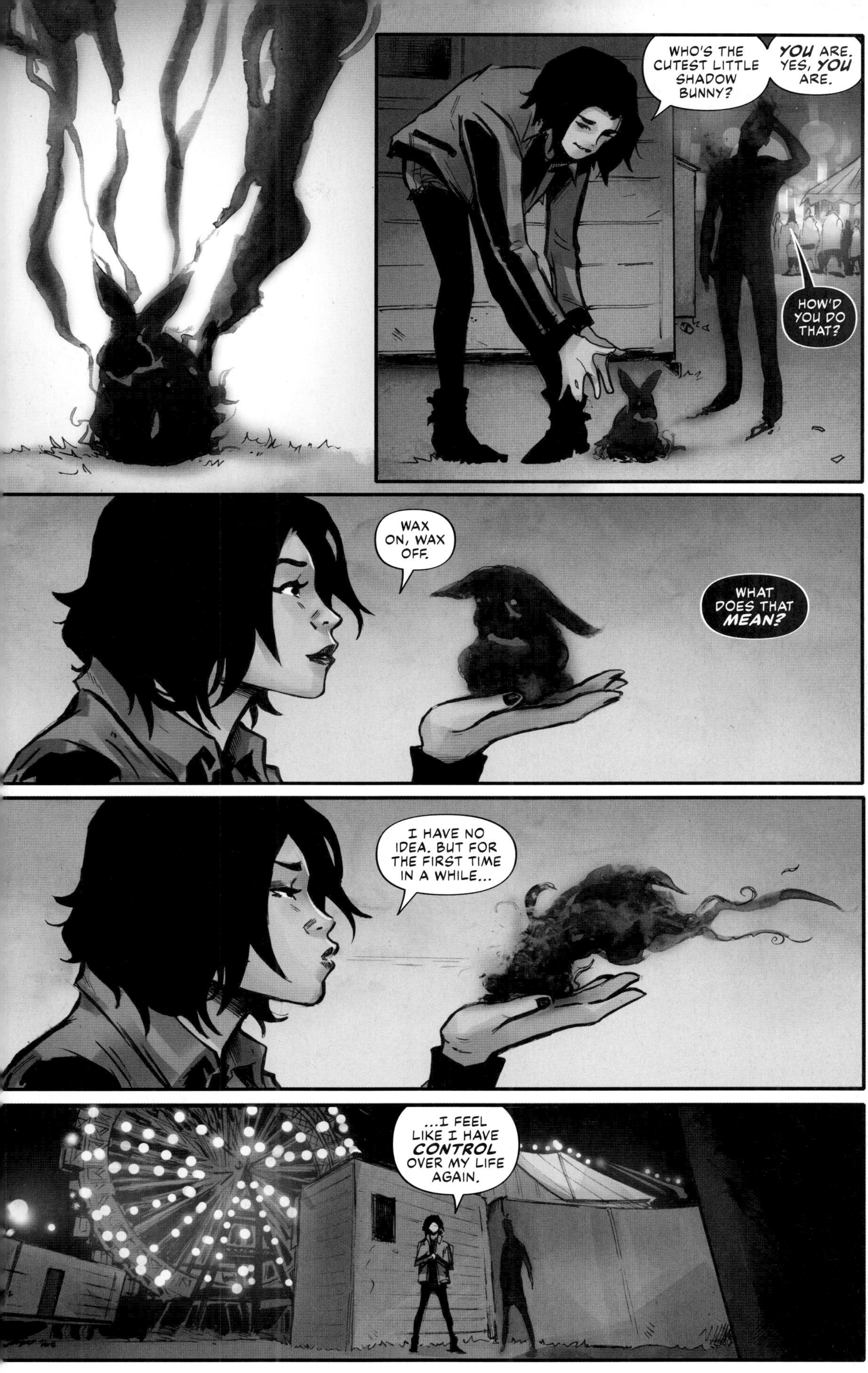
WHO'S THE CUTEST LITTLE SHADOW BUNNY?
YOU ARE. YES, YOU ARE.
HOW'D YOU DO THAT?
WAX ON, WAX OFF.
WHAT DOES THAT MEAN?
I HAVE NO IDEA. BUT FOR THE FIRST TIME IN A WHILE...
...I FEEL LIKE I HAVE CONTROL OVER MY LIFE AGAIN.

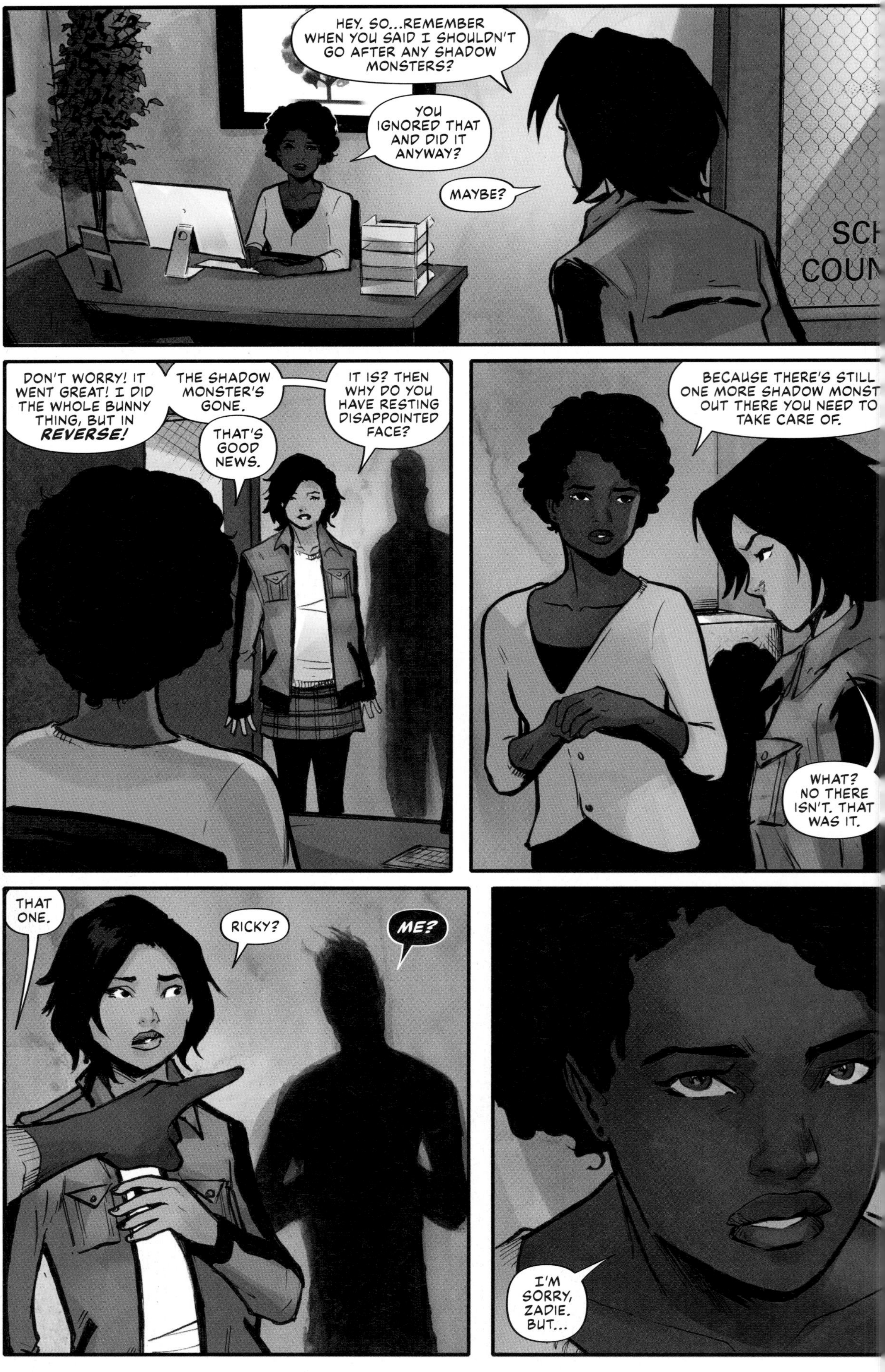
HEY. SO...REMEMBER WHEN YOU SAID I SHOULDN'T GO AFTER ANY SHADOW MONSTERS?
YOU IGNORED THAT AND DID IT ANYWAY?
MAYBE?
SCH
COUN
DON'T WORRY! IT WENT GREAT! I DID THE WHOLE BUNNY THING, BUT IN *REVERSE!*
THE SHADOW MONSTER'S GONE.
THAT'S GOOD NEWS.
IT IS? THEN WHY DO YOU HAVE RESTING DISAPPOINTED FACE?
BECAUSE THERE'S STILL ONE MORE SHADOW MONST OUT THERE YOU NEED TO TAKE CARE OF.
WHAT? NO THERE ISN'T. THAT WAS IT.
THAT ONE.
RICKY?
ME?
I'M SORRY, ZADIE. BUT...

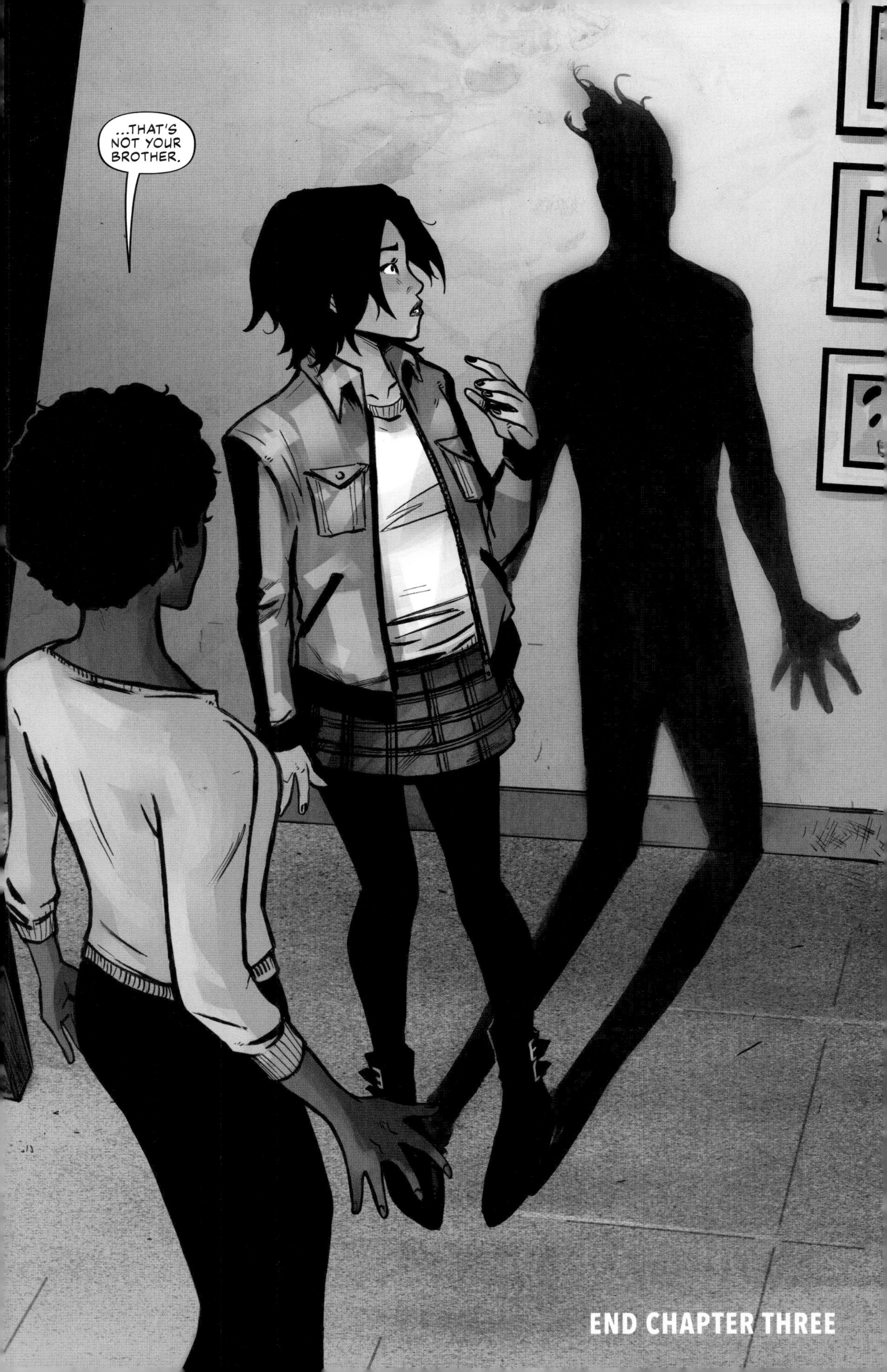
...THAT'S NOT YOUR BROTHER.
END CHAPTER THREE

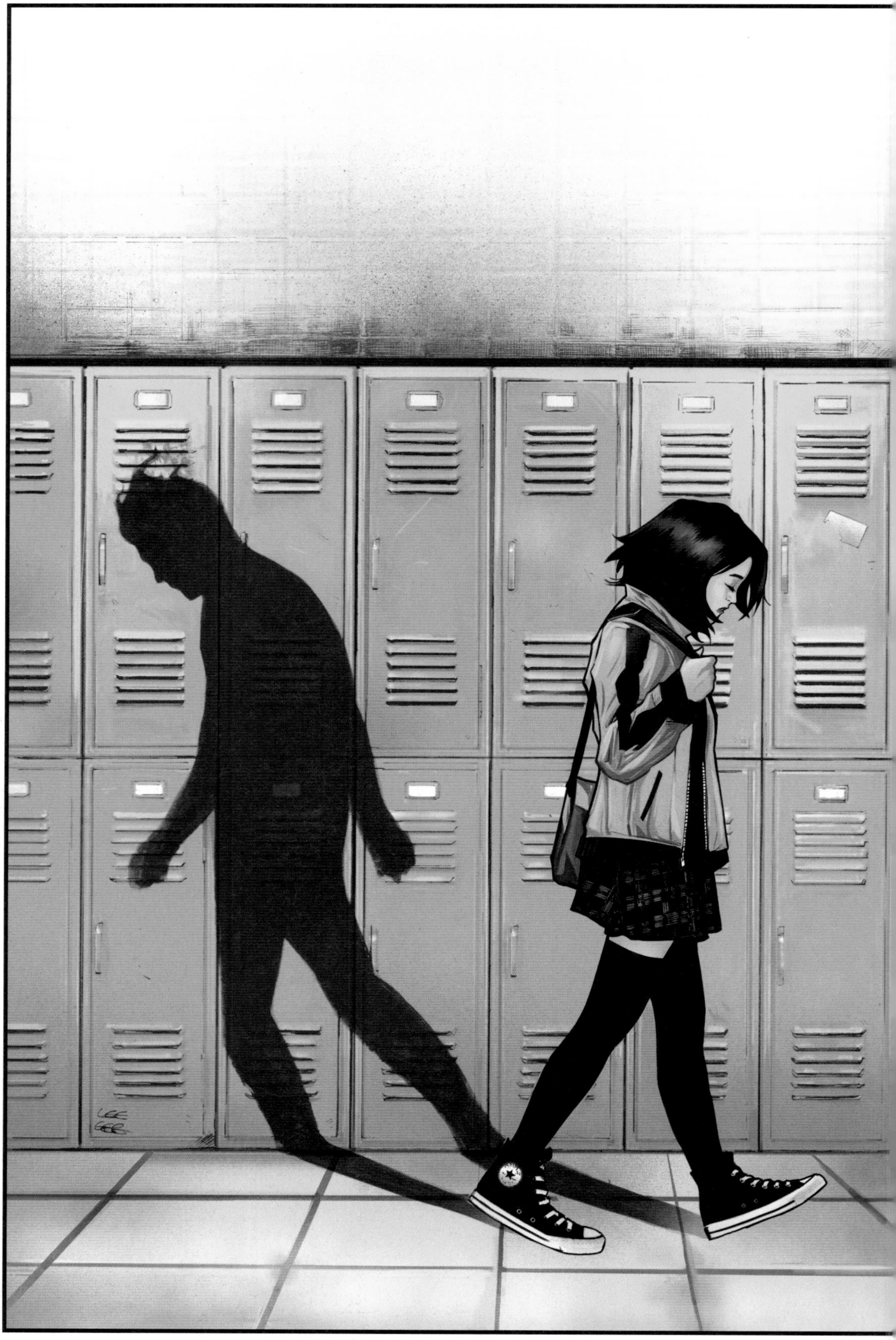

CHAPTER FOUR

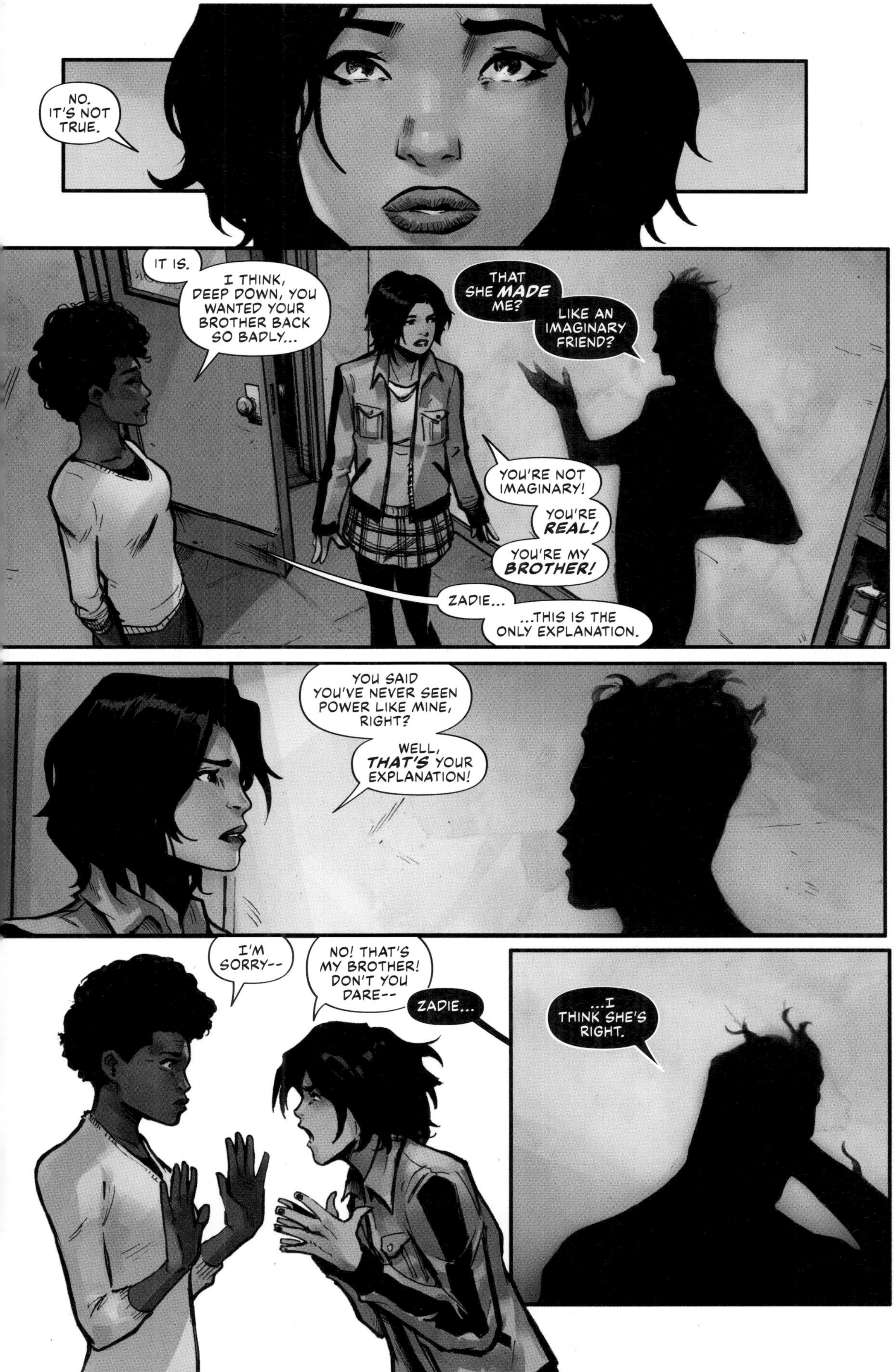
NO. IT'S NOT TRUE.
IT IS.
I THINK, DEEP DOWN, YOU WANTED YOUR BROTHER BACK SO BADLY...
THAT SHE MADE ME?
LIKE AN IMAGINARY FRIEND?
YOU'RE NOT IMAGINARY!
YOU'RE REAL!
YOU'RE MY BROTHER!
ZADIE...
...THIS IS THE ONLY EXPLANATION.
YOU SAID YOU'VE NEVER SEEN POWER LIKE MINE, RIGHT?
WELL, THAT'S YOUR EXPLANATION!
I'M SORRY--
NO! THAT'S MY BROTHER! DON'T YOU DARE--
ZADIE...
...I THINK SHE'S RIGHT.

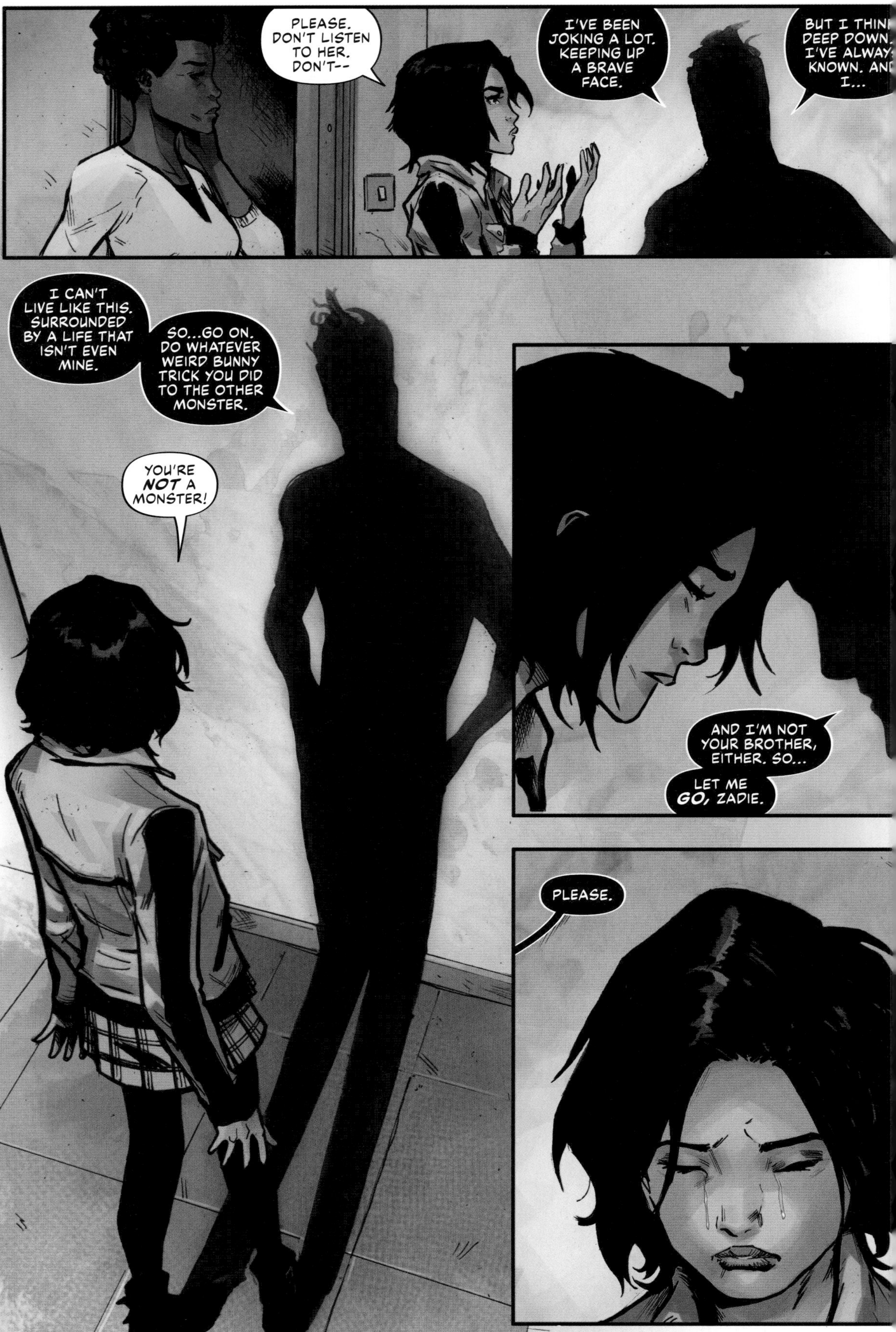
PLEASE. DON'T LISTEN TO HER. DON'T--
I'VE BEEN JOKING A LOT. KEEPING UP A BRAVE FACE.
BUT I THIN DEEP DOWN. I'VE ALWAY KNOWN. AN I...
I CAN'T LIVE LIKE THIS. SURROUNDED BY A LIFE THAT ISN'T EVEN MINE.
SO...GO ON. DO WHATEVER WEIRD BUNNY TRICK YOU DID TO THE OTHER MONSTER.
YOU'RE NOT A MONSTER!
AND I'M NOT YOUR BROTHER, EITHER. SO...
LET ME GO, ZADIE.
PLEASE.

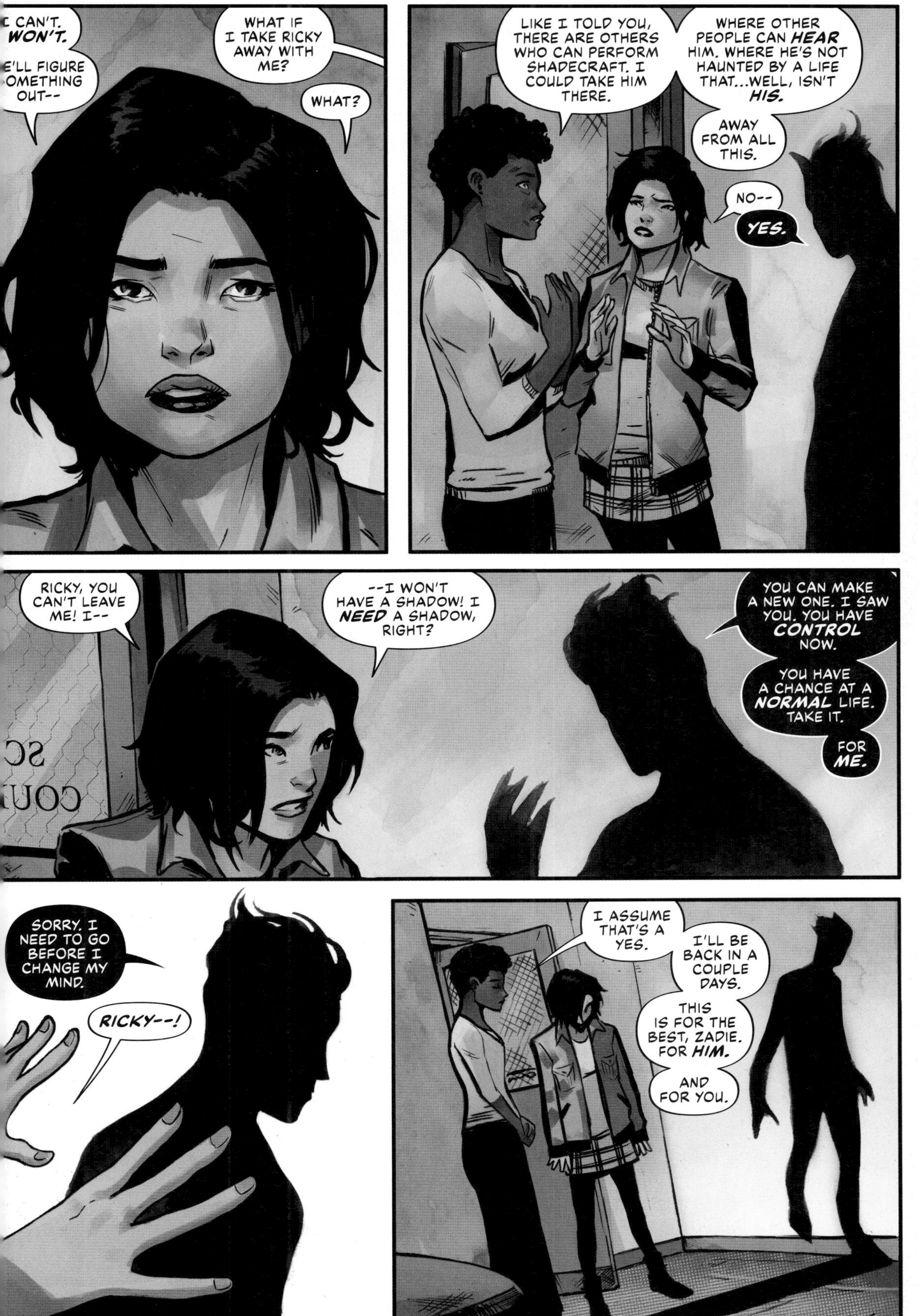
CAN'T. WON'T.
E'LL FIGURE OMETHING OUT--
WHAT IF I TAKE RICKY AWAY WITH ME?
WHAT?
LIKE I TOLD YOU, THERE ARE OTHERS WHO CAN PERFORM SHADECRAFT. I COULD TAKE HIM THERE.
WHERE OTHER PEOPLE CAN HEAR HIM. WHERE HE'S NOT HAUNTED BY A LIFE THAT...WELL, ISN'T HIS.
AWAY FROM ALL THIS.
NO--
YES.
RICKY, YOU CAN'T LEAVE ME! I--
--I WON'T HAVE A SHADOW! I NEED A SHADOW, RIGHT?
YOU CAN MAKE A NEW ONE. I SAW YOU. YOU HAVE CONTROL NOW.
YOU HAVE A CHANCE AT A NORMAL LIFE. TAKE IT.
FOR ME.
SORRY. I NEED TO GO BEFORE I CHANGE MY MIND.
RICKY--!
I ASSUME THAT'S A YES.
I'LL BE BACK IN A COUPLE DAYS.
THIS IS FOR THE BEST, ZADIE. FOR HIM.
AND FOR YOU.

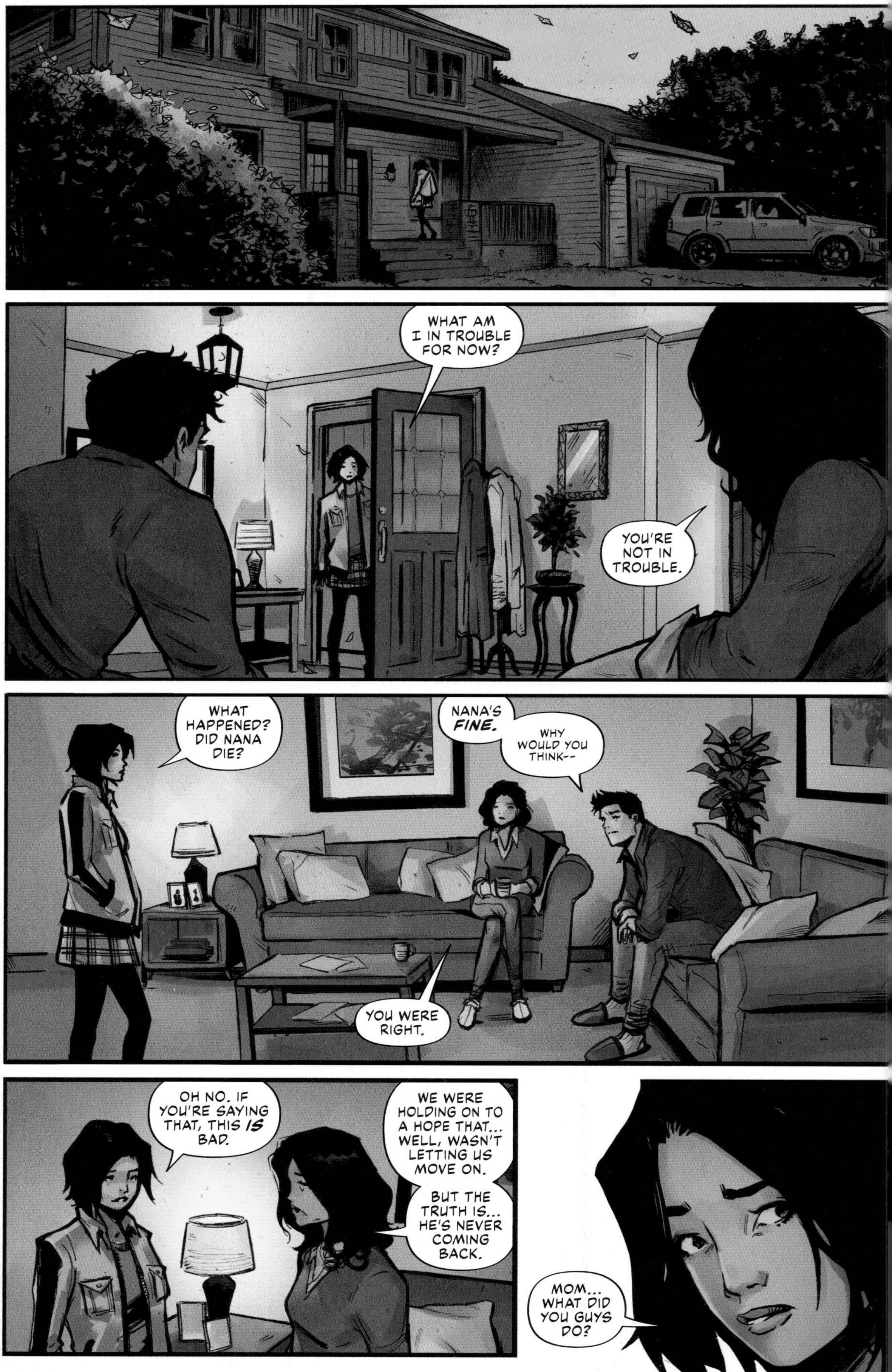

WHAT AM I IN TROUBLE FOR NOW?
YOU'RE NOT IN TROUBLE.
WHAT HAPPENED? DID NANA DIE?
NANA'S **FINE.**
WHY WOULD YOU THINK--
YOU WERE RIGHT.
OH NO. IF YOU'RE SAYING THAT, THIS ***IS*** BAD.
WE WERE HOLDING ON TO A HOPE THAT... WELL, WASN'T LETTING US MOVE ON.
BUT THE TRUTH IS... HE'S NEVER COMING BACK.
MOM... WHAT DID YOU GUYS DO?

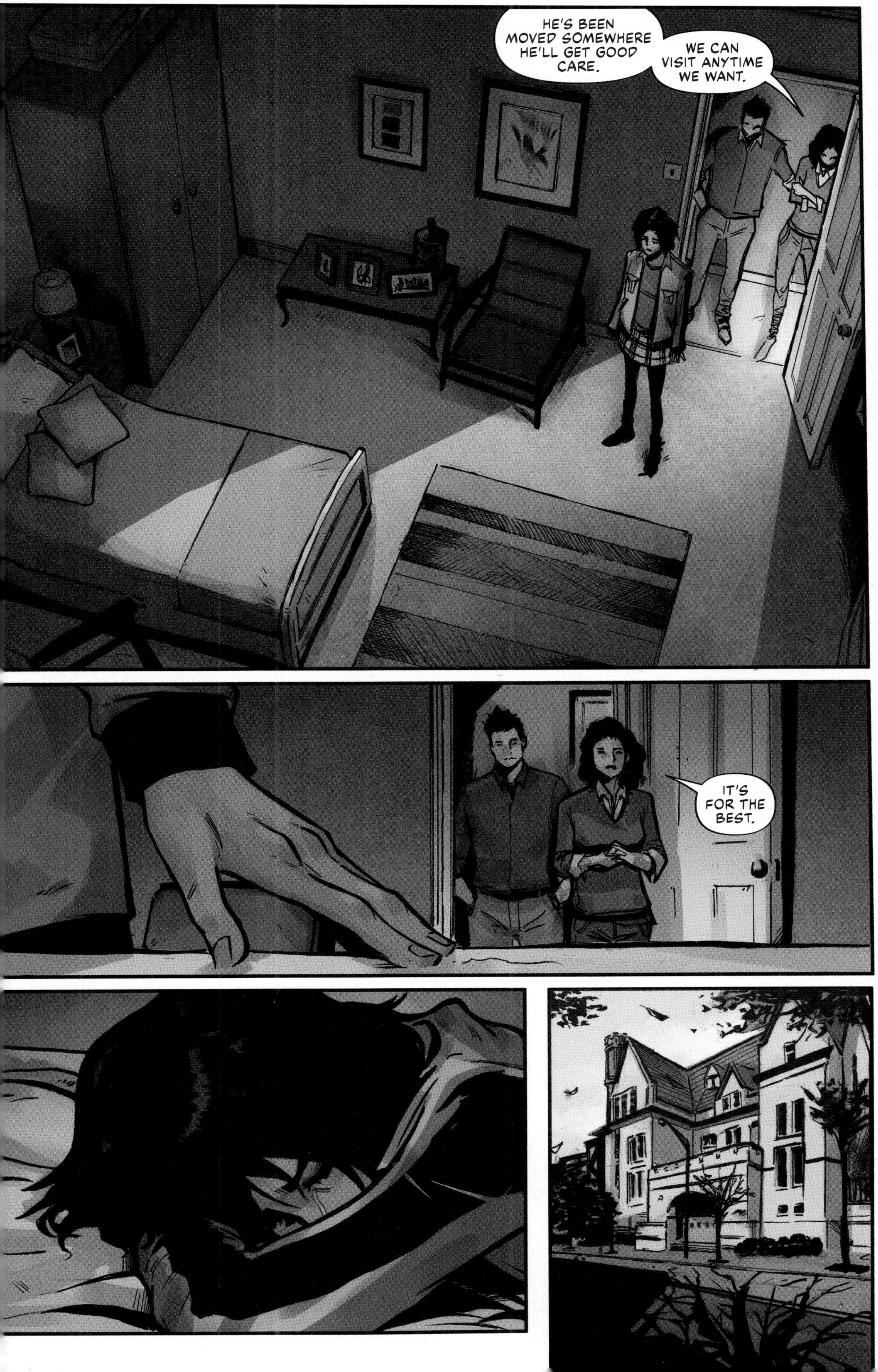
HE'S BEEN MOVED SOMEWHERE HE'LL GET GOOD CARE.
WE CAN VISIT ANYTIME WE WANT.
IT'S FOR THE BEST.

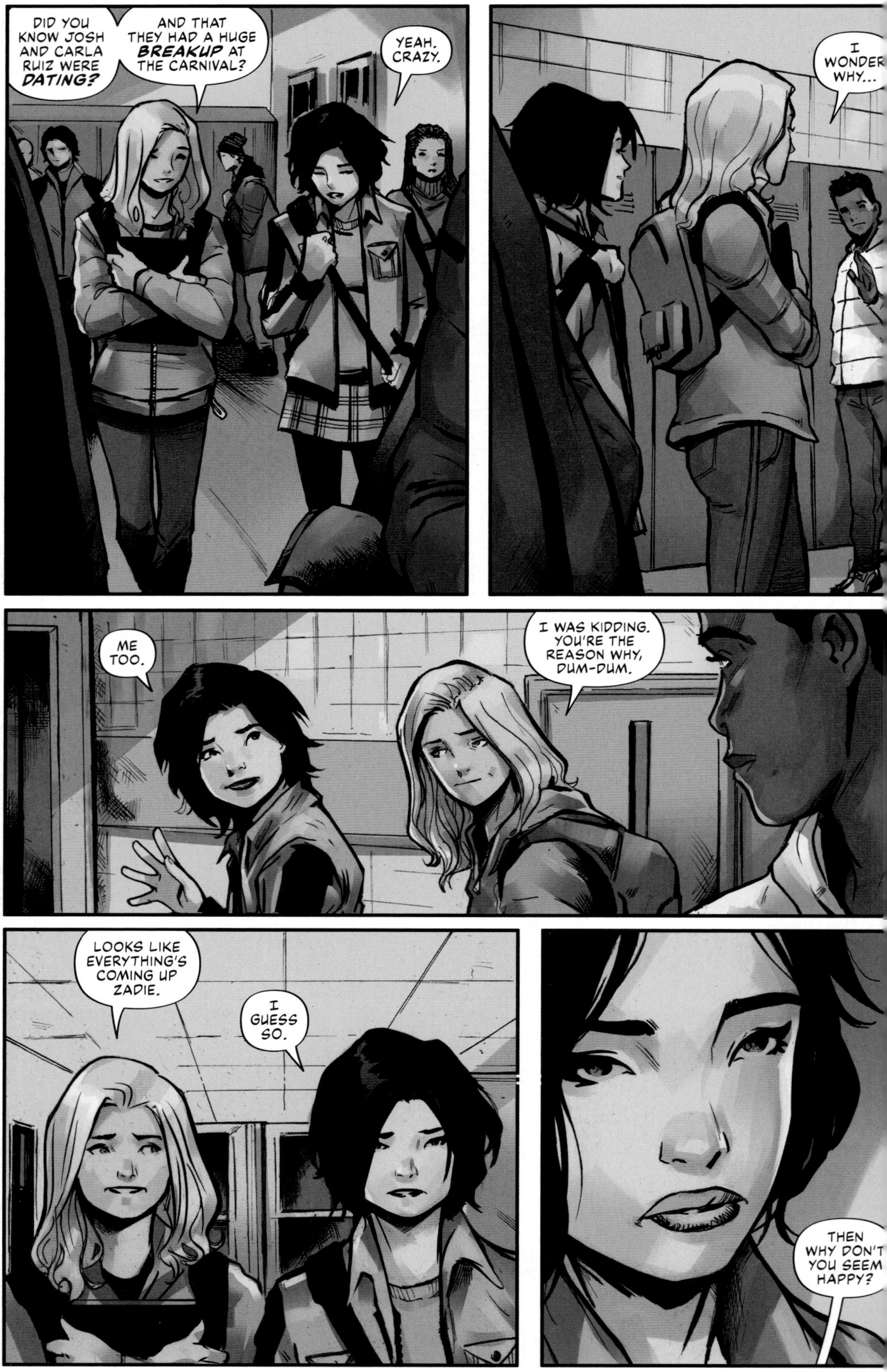

DID YOU KNOW JOSH AND CARLA RUIZ WERE *DATING?*
AND THAT THEY HAD A HUGE *BREAKUP* AT THE CARNIVAL?
YEAH. CRAZY.
I WONDER WHY...
ME TOO.
I WAS KIDDING. YOU'RE THE REASON WHY, DUM-DUM.
LOOKS LIKE EVERYTHING'S COMING UP ZADIE.
I GUESS SO.
THEN WHY DON'T YOU SEEM HAPPY?

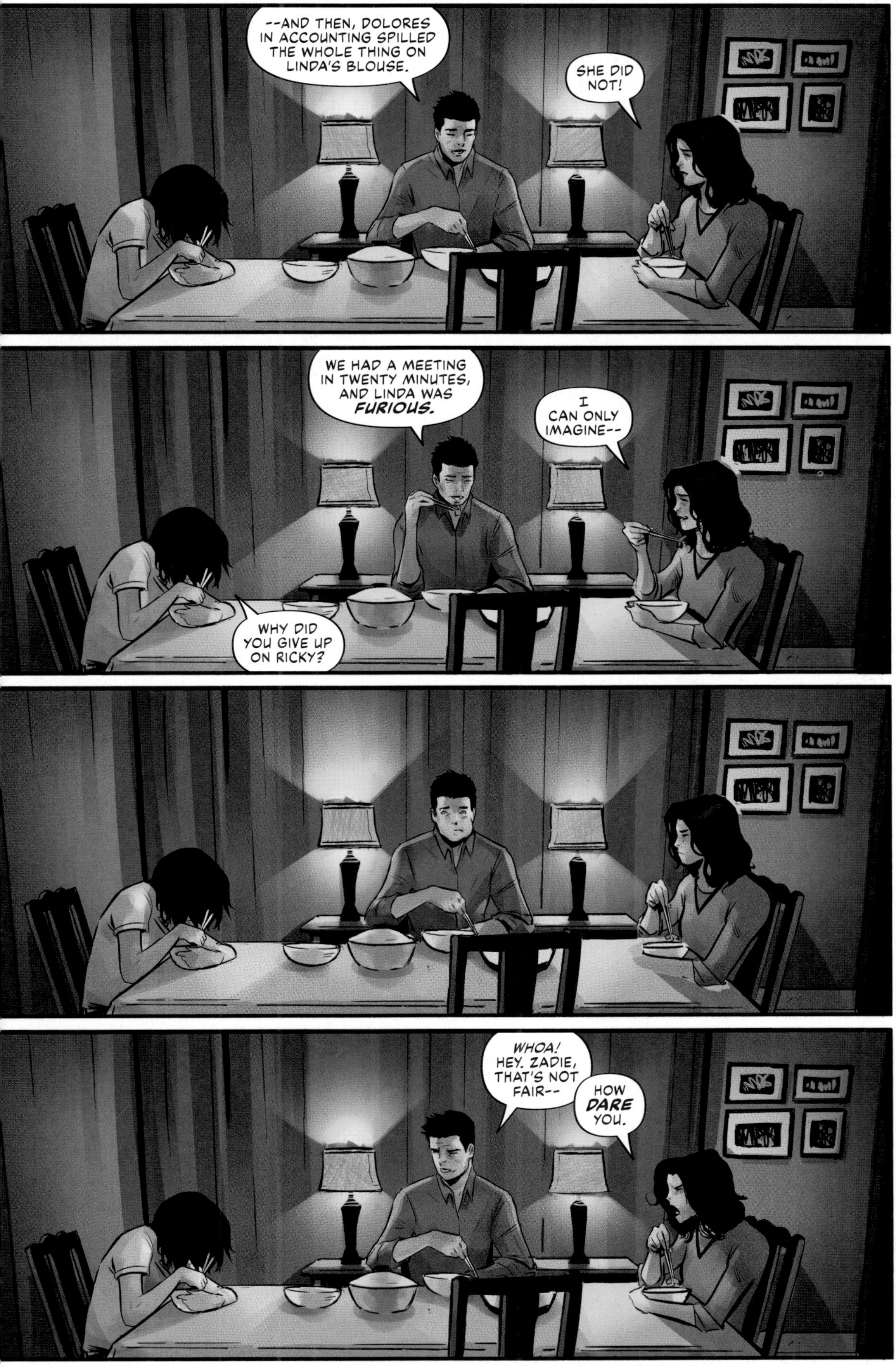
--AND THEN, DOLORES IN ACCOUNTING SPILLED THE WHOLE THING ON LINDA'S BLOUSE.
SHE DID NOT!
WE HAD A MEETING IN TWENTY MINUTES, AND LINDA WAS FURIOUS.
I CAN ONLY IMAGINE--
WHY DID YOU GIVE UP ON RICKY?
WHOA! HEY. ZADIE, THAT'S NOT FAIR--
HOW DARE YOU.

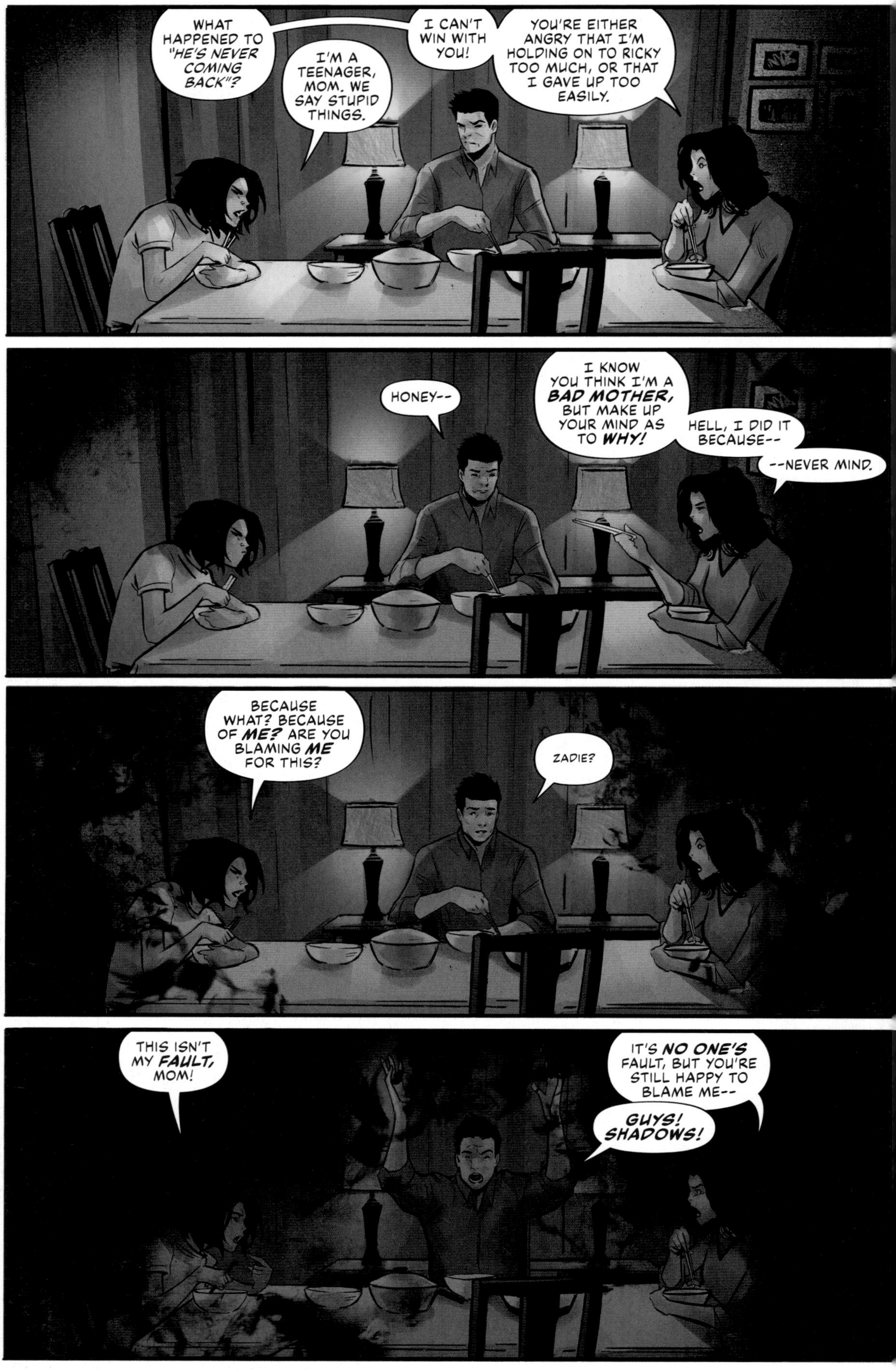
WHAT HAPPENED TO "HE'S NEVER COMING BACK"?
I'M A TEENAGER, MOM. WE SAY STUPID THINGS.
I CAN'T WIN WITH YOU!
YOU'RE EITHER ANGRY THAT I'M HOLDING ON TO RICKY TOO MUCH, OR THAT I GAVE UP TOO EASILY.
HONEY--
I KNOW YOU THINK I'M A BAD MOTHER, BUT MAKE UP YOUR MIND AS TO WHY!
HELL, I DID IT BECAUSE--
--NEVER MIND.
BECAUSE WHAT? BECAUSE OF ME? ARE YOU BLAMING ME FOR THIS?
ZADIE?
THIS ISN'T MY FAULT, MOM!
IT'S NO ONE'S FAULT, BUT YOU'RE STILL HAPPY TO BLAME ME--
GUYS! SHADOWS!

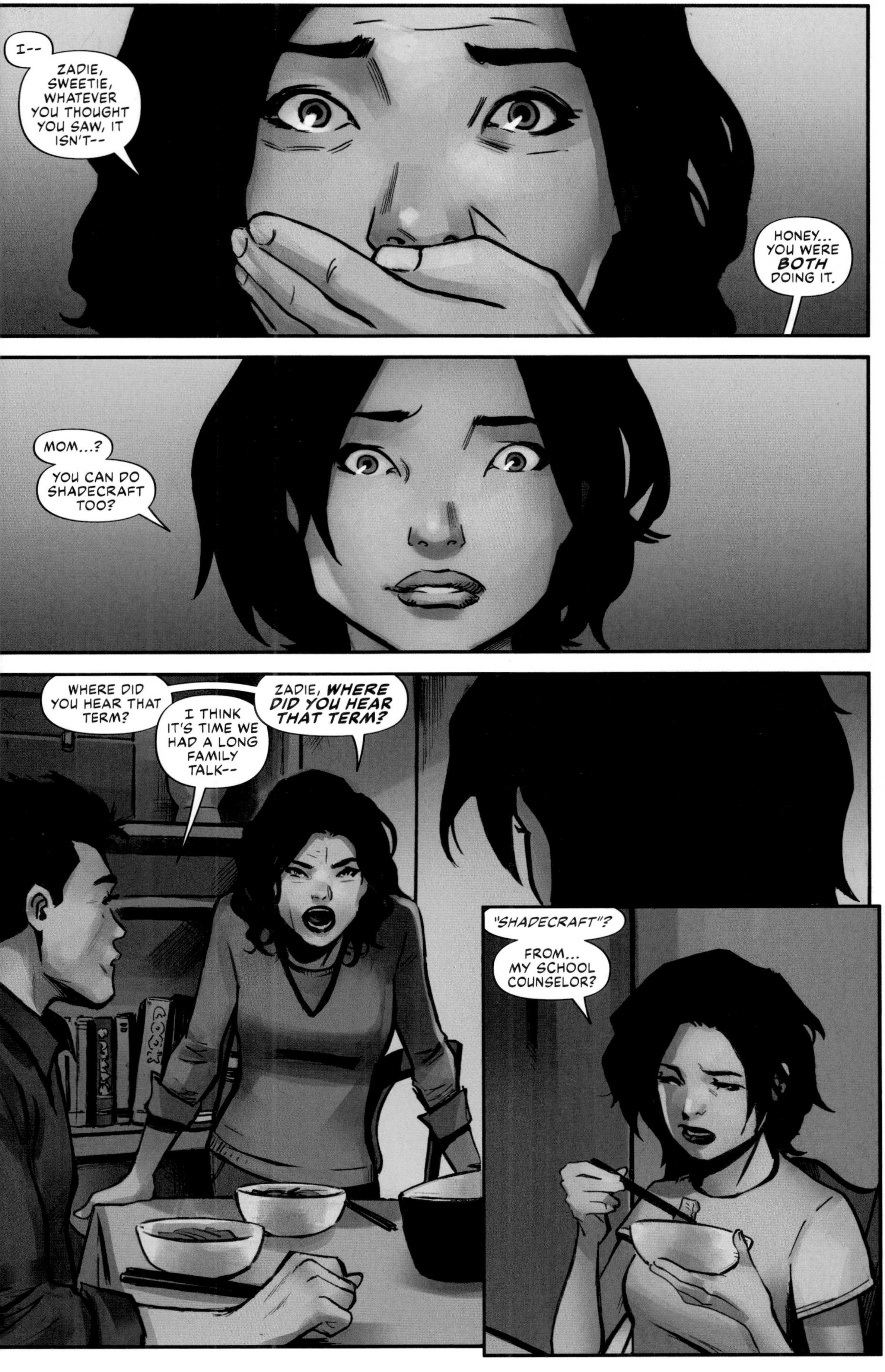
I--
ZADIE, SWEETIE, WHATEVER YOU THOUGHT YOU SAW, IT ISN'T--
HONEY... YOU WERE BOTH DOING IT.
MOM...?
YOU CAN DO SHADECRAFT TOO?
WHERE DID YOU HEAR THAT TERM?
I THINK IT'S TIME WE HAD A LONG FAMILY TALK--
ZADIE, WHERE DID YOU HEAR THAT TERM?
"SHADECRAFT"?
FROM... MY SCHOOL COUNSELOR?

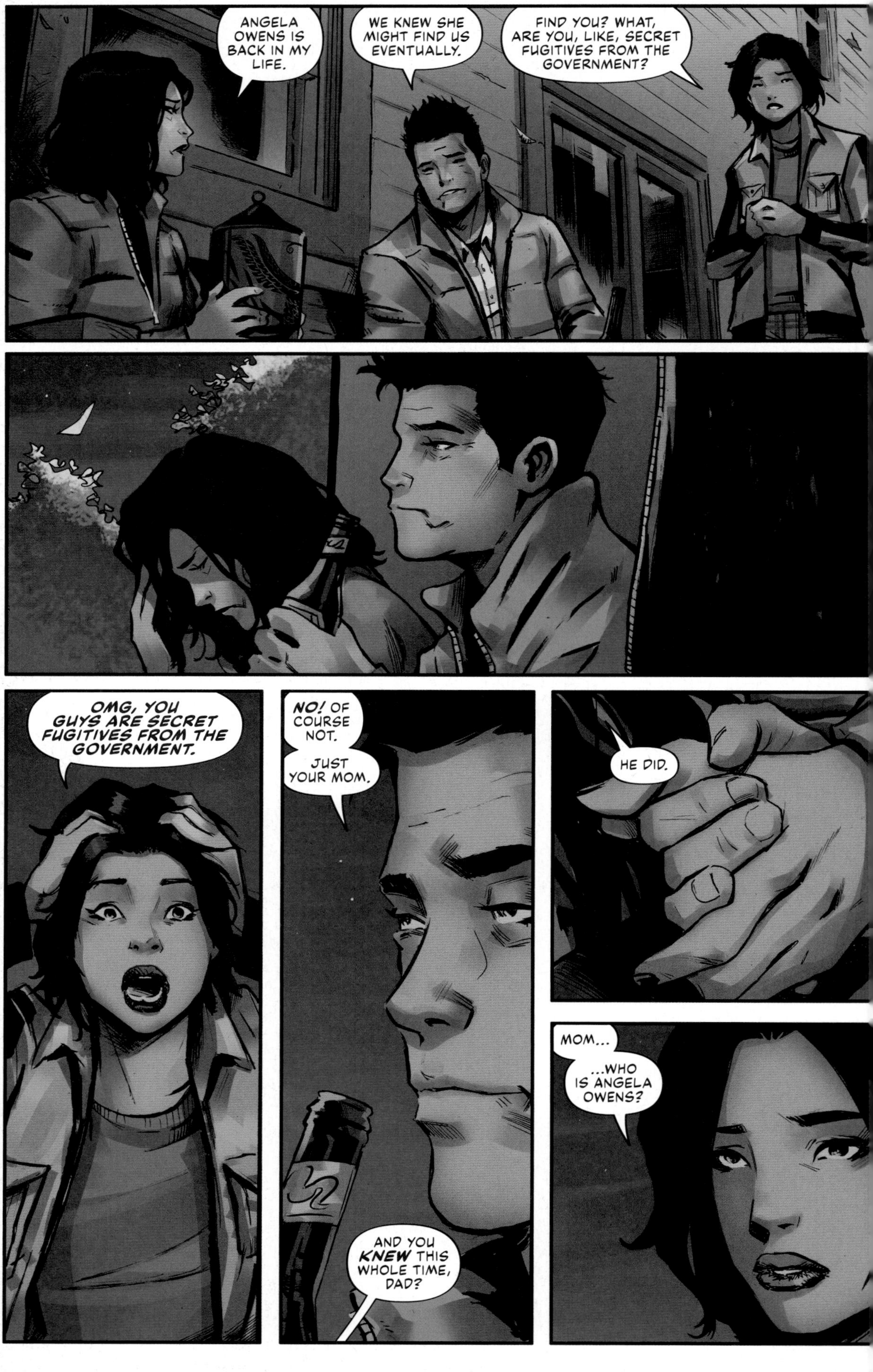
ANGELA OWENS IS BACK IN MY LIFE.
WE KNEW SHE MIGHT FIND US EVENTUALLY.
FIND YOU? WHAT, ARE YOU, LIKE, SECRET FUGITIVES FROM THE GOVERNMENT?
OMG, YOU GUYS ARE SECRET FUGITIVES FROM THE GOVERNMENT.
NO! OF COURSE NOT.
JUST YOUR MOM.
AND YOU KNEW THIS WHOLE TIME, DAD?
HE DID.
MOM...
...WHO IS ANGELA OWENS?

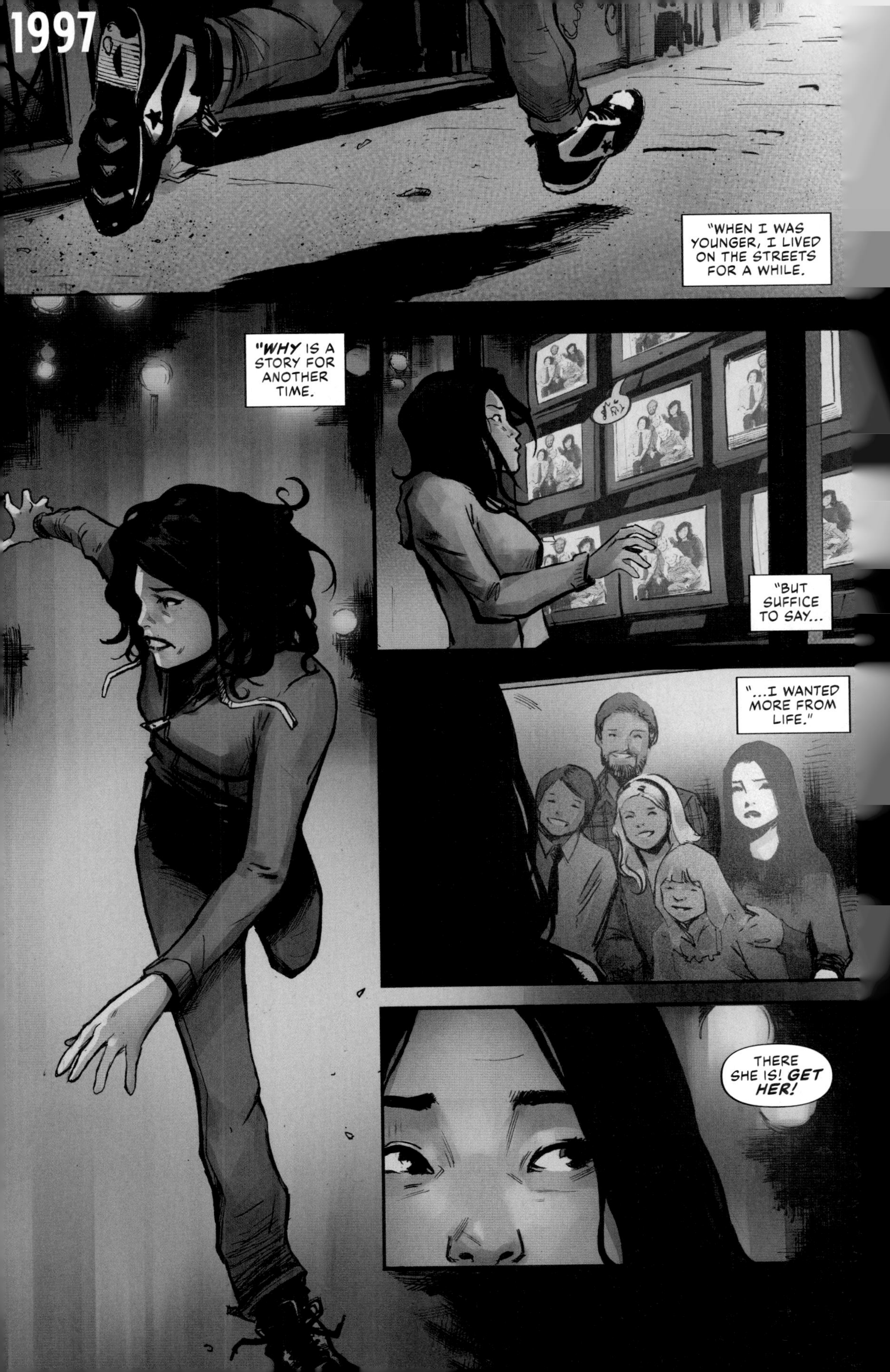
1997
"WHEN I WAS YOUNGER, I LIVED ON THE STREETS FOR A WHILE.
"WHY IS A STORY FOR ANOTHER TIME.
"BUT SUFFICE TO SAY...
"...I WANTED MORE FROM LIFE."
THERE SHE IS! GET HER!

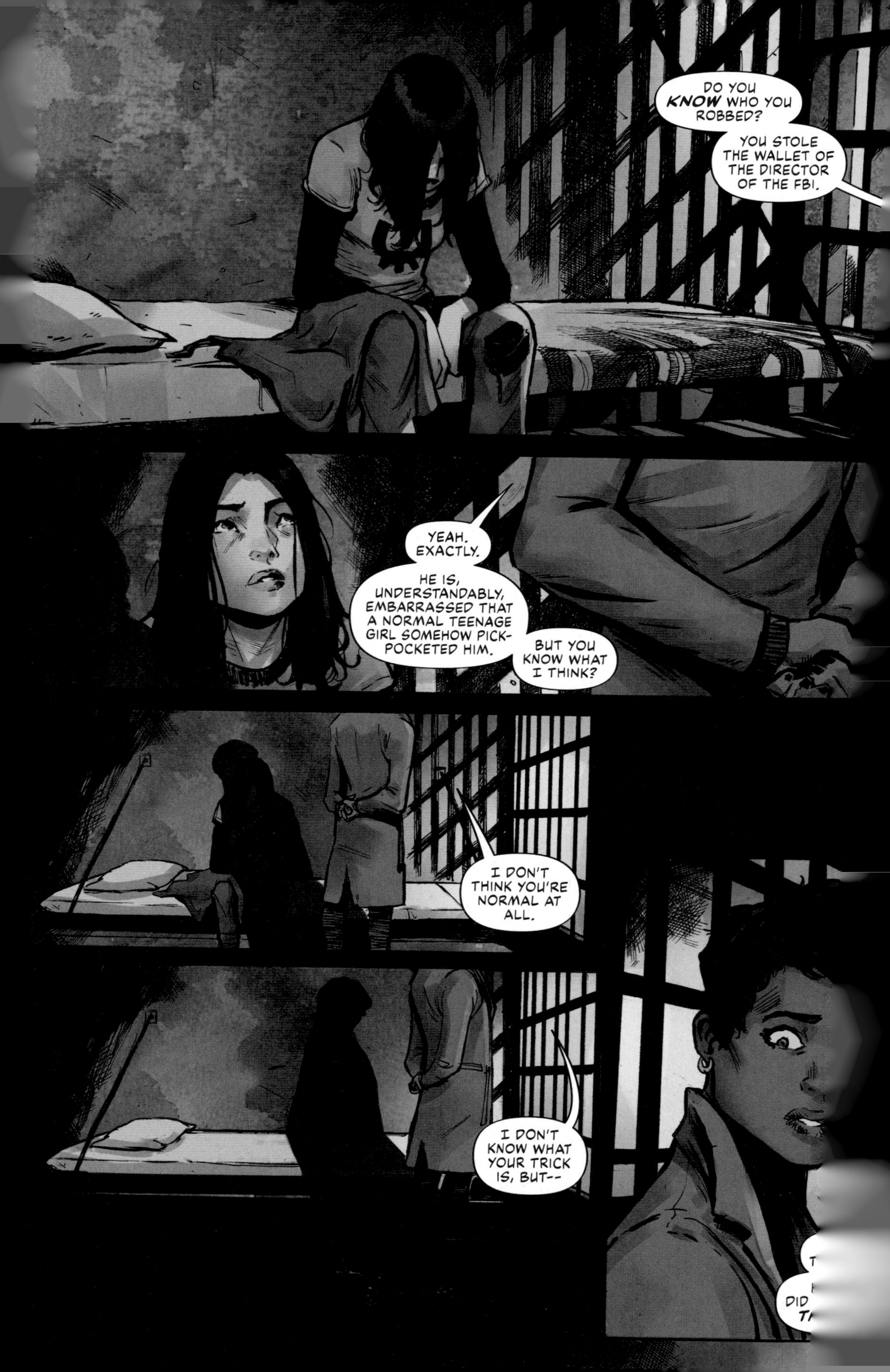
DO YOU KNOW WHO YOU ROBBED?
YOU STOLE THE WALLET OF THE DIRECTOR OF THE FBI.
YEAH. EXACTLY.
HE IS, UNDERSTANDABLY, EMBARRASSED THAT A NORMAL TEENAGE GIRL SOMEHOW PICK-POCKETED HIM.
BUT YOU KNOW WHAT I THINK?
I DON'T THINK YOU'RE NORMAL AT ALL.
I DON'T KNOW WHAT YOUR TRICK IS, BUT--

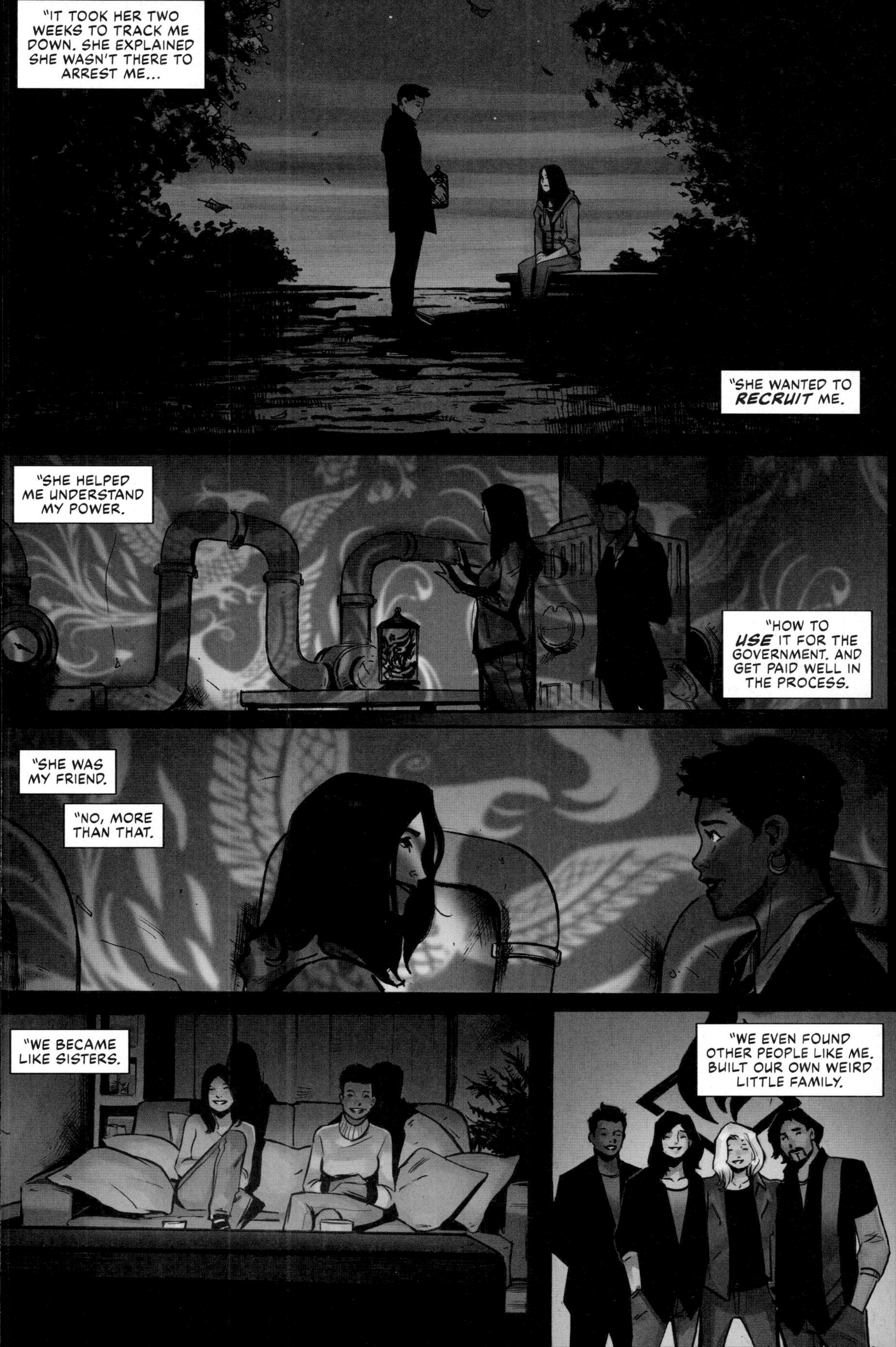
"IT TOOK HER TWO WEEKS TO TRACK ME DOWN. SHE EXPLAINED SHE WASN'T THERE TO ARREST ME...
"SHE WANTED TO RECRUIT ME.
"SHE HELPED ME UNDERSTAND MY POWER.
"HOW TO USE IT FOR THE GOVERNMENT. AND GET PAID WELL IN THE PROCESS.
"SHE WAS MY FRIEND.
"NO, MORE THAN THAT.
"WE BECAME LIKE SISTERS.
"WE EVEN FOUND OTHER PEOPLE LIKE ME. BUILT OUR OWN WEIRD LITTLE FAMILY.

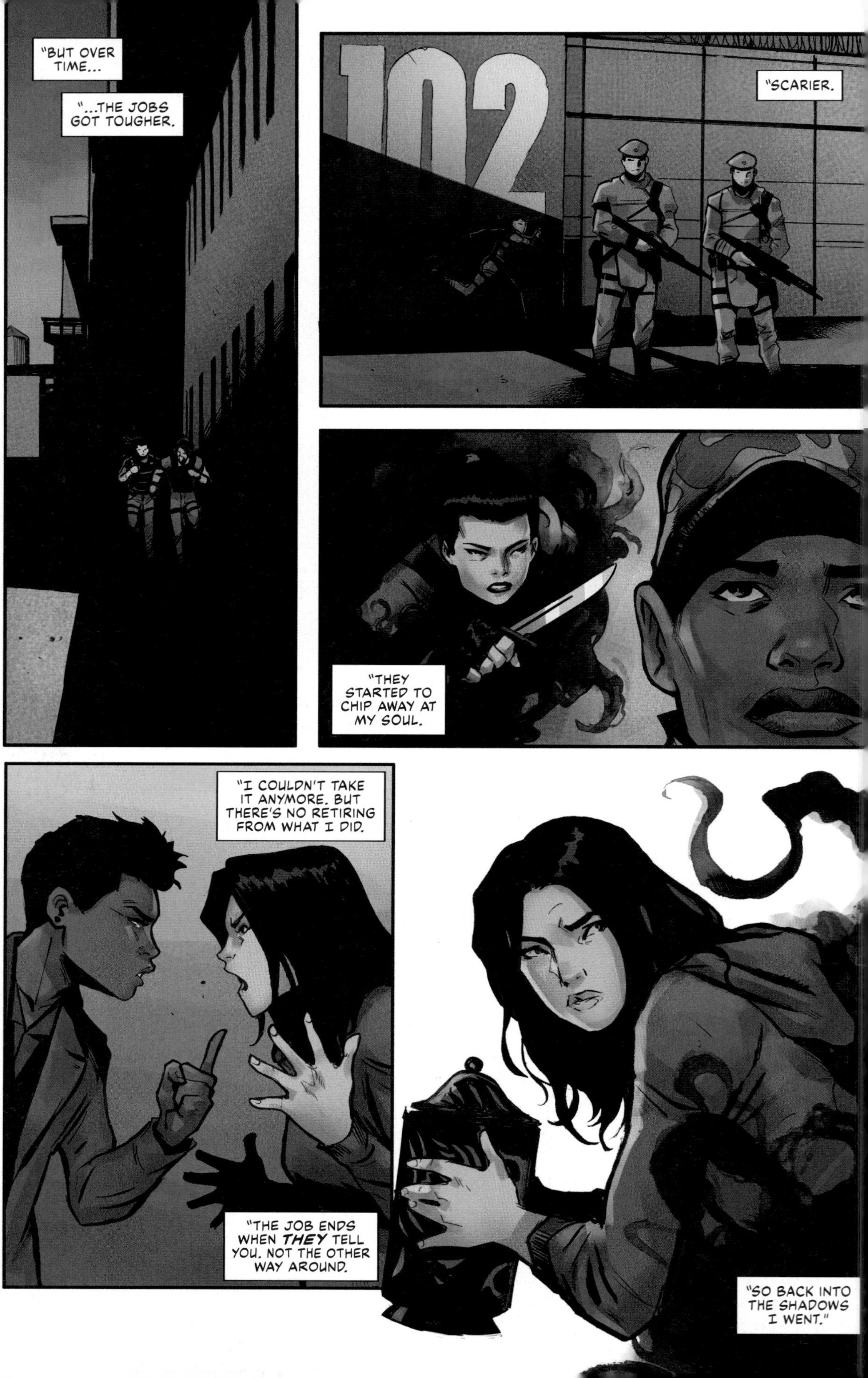
"BUT OVER TIME...
"...THE JOBS GOT TOUGHER.
102
"SCARIER.
"THEY STARTED TO CHIP AWAY AT MY SOUL.
"I COULDN'T TAKE IT ANYMORE. BUT THERE'S NO RETIRING FROM WHAT I DID.
"THE JOB ENDS WHEN ***THEY*** TELL YOU. NOT THE OTHER WAY AROUND.
"SO BACK INTO THE SHADOWS I WENT."

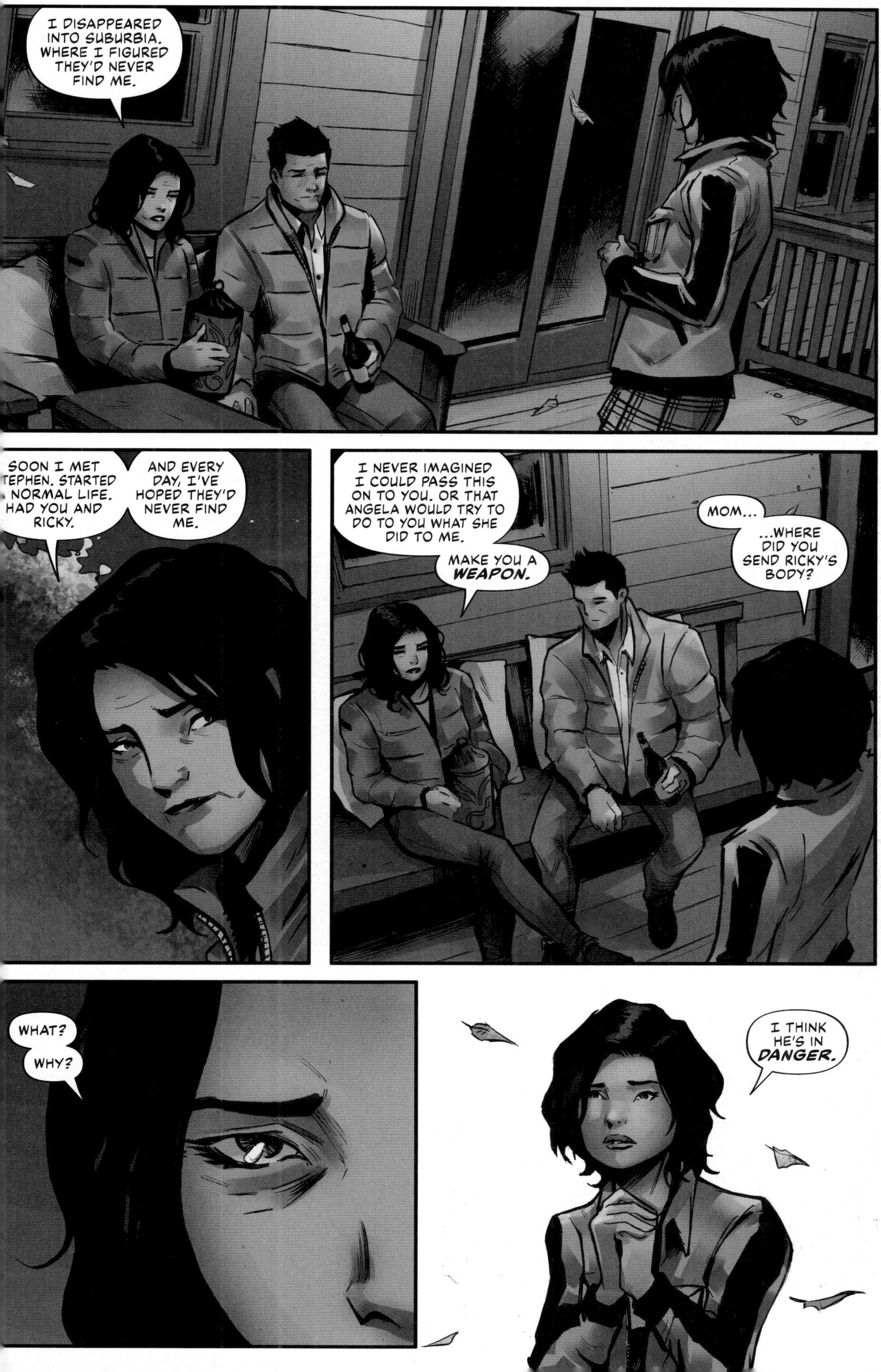
I DISAPPEARED INTO SUBURBIA. WHERE I FIGURED THEY'D NEVER FIND ME.
SOON I MET STEPHEN. STARTED A NORMAL LIFE. HAD YOU AND RICKY.
AND EVERY DAY, I'VE HOPED THEY'D NEVER FIND ME.
I NEVER IMAGINED I COULD PASS THIS ON TO YOU. OR THAT ANGELA WOULD TRY TO DO TO YOU WHAT SHE DID TO ME.
MAKE YOU A WEAPON.
MOM...
...WHERE DID YOU SEND RICKY'S BODY?
WHAT?
WHY?
I THINK HE'S IN DANGER.

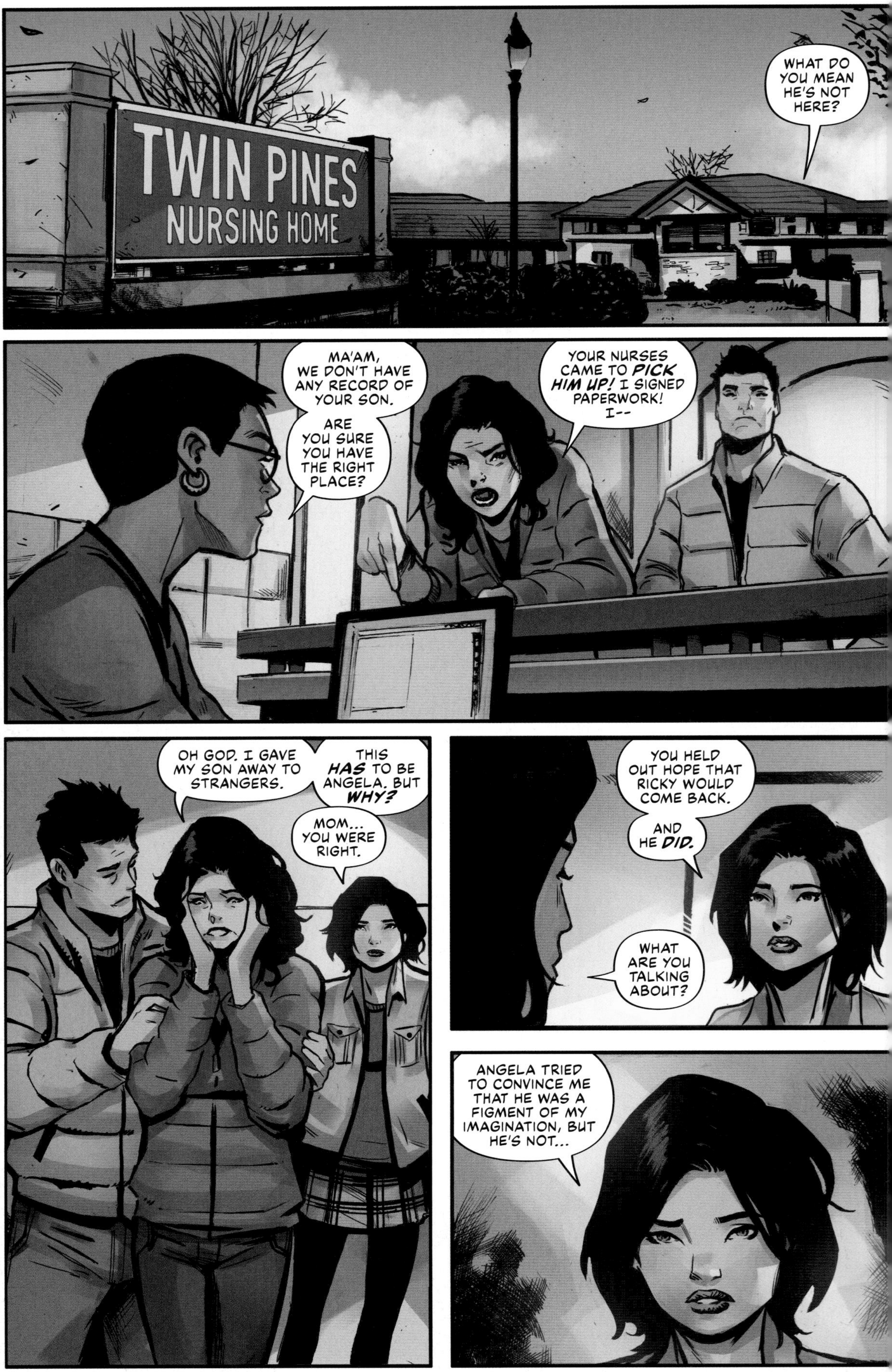
TWIN PINES
NURSING HOME
WHAT DO YOU MEAN HE'S NOT HERE?
MA'AM, WE DON'T HAVE ANY RECORD OF YOUR SON.
ARE YOU SURE YOU HAVE THE RIGHT PLACE?
YOUR NURSES CAME TO *PICK HIM UP!* I SIGNED PAPERWORK! I--
OH GOD. I GAVE MY SON AWAY TO STRANGERS.
THIS *HAS* TO BE ANGELA. BUT *WHY?*
MOM... YOU WERE RIGHT.
YOU HELD OUT HOPE THAT RICKY WOULD COME BACK.
AND HE *DID.*
WHAT ARE YOU TALKING ABOUT?
ANGELA TRIED TO CONVINCE ME THAT HE WAS A FIGMENT OF MY IMAGINATION, BUT HE'S NOT...

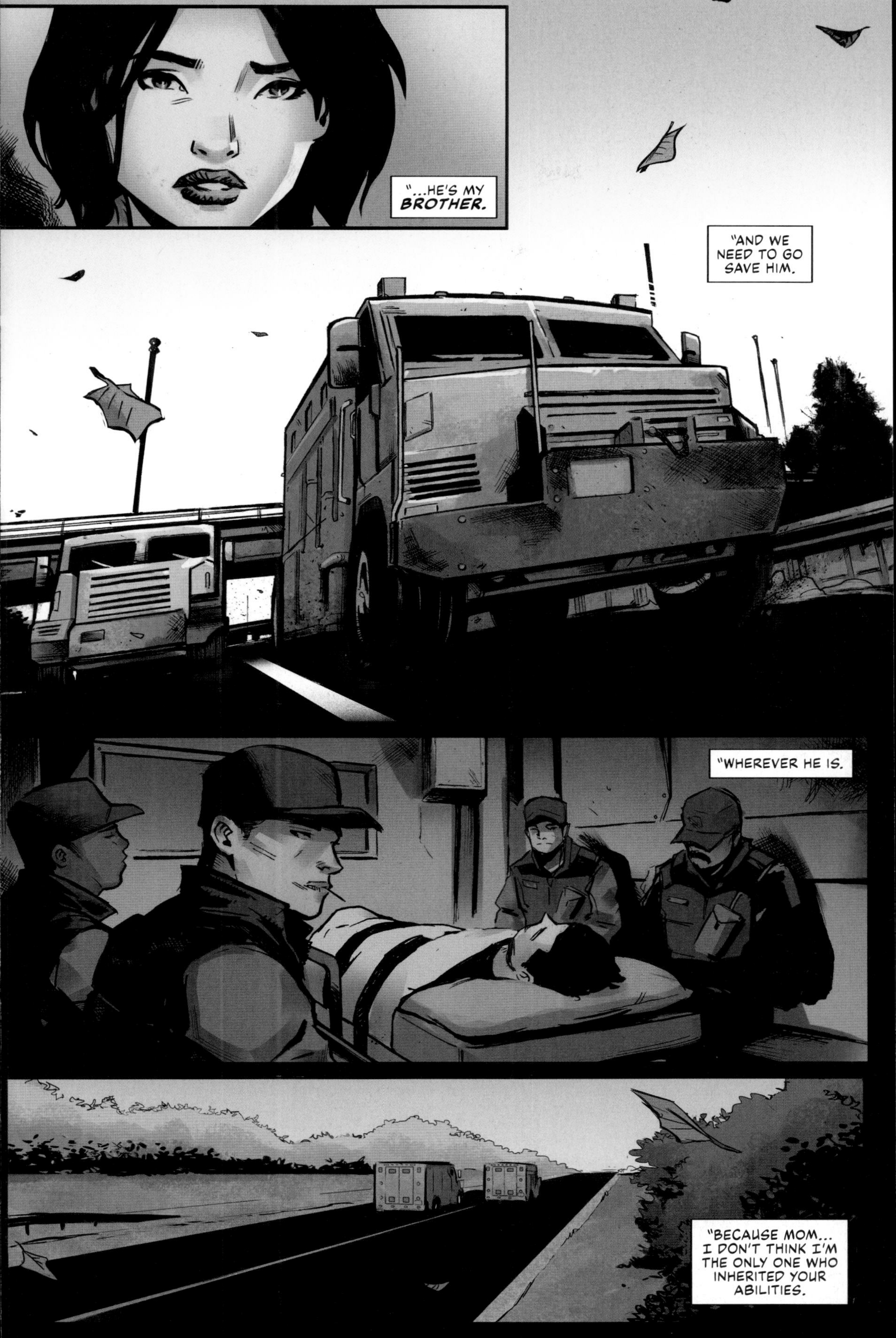
"...HE'S MY **BROTHER.**
"AND WE NEED TO GO SAVE HIM.
"WHEREVER HE IS.
"BECAUSE MOM... I DON'T THINK I'M THE ONLY ONE WHO INHERITED YOUR ABILITIES.

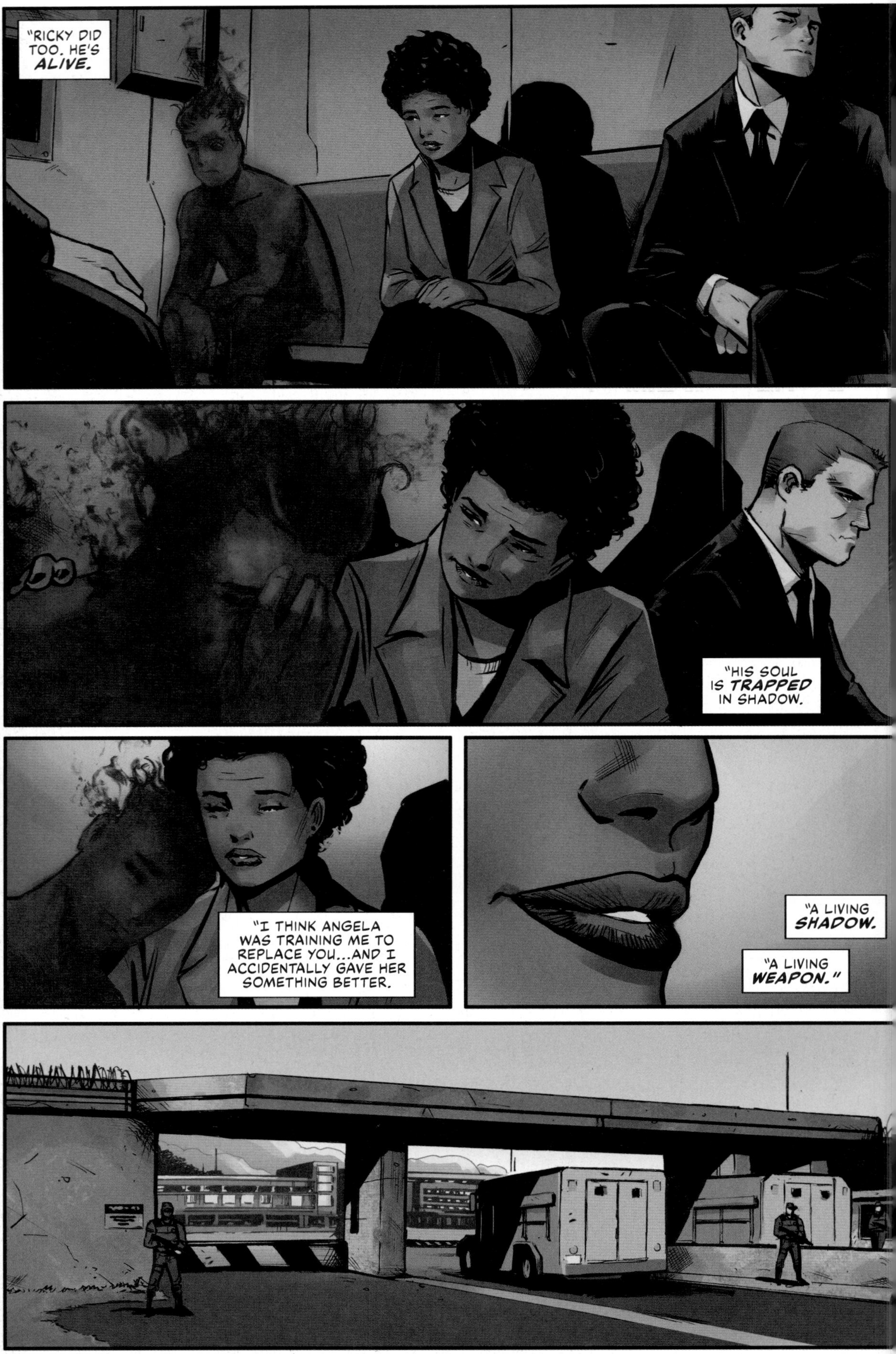
"RICKY DID TOO. HE'S *ALIVE.*
"HIS SOUL IS *TRAPPED* IN SHADOW.
"I THINK ANGELA WAS TRAINING ME TO REPLACE YOU...AND I ACCIDENTALLY GAVE HER SOMETHING BETTER.
"A LIVING *SHADOW.*
"A LIVING *WEAPON.*"

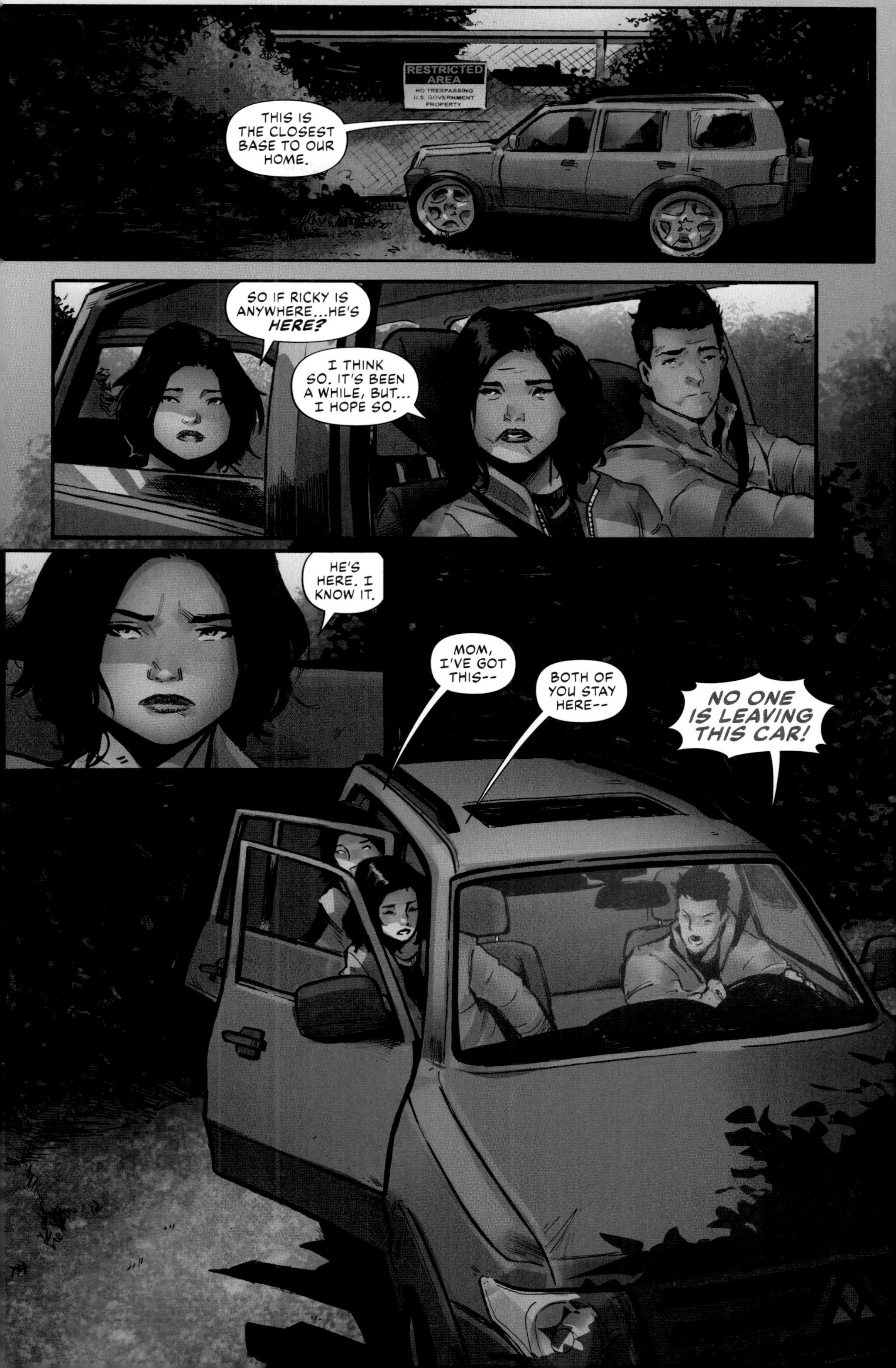
RESTRICTED AREA
NO TRESPASSING U.S. GOVERNMENT PROPERTY
THIS IS THE CLOSEST BASE TO OUR HOME.
SO IF RICKY IS ANYWHERE...HE'S *HERE?*
I THINK SO. IT'S BEEN A WHILE, BUT... I HOPE SO.
HE'S HERE. I KNOW IT.
MOM, I'VE GOT THIS--
BOTH OF YOU STAY HERE--
NO ONE IS LEAVING THIS CAR!

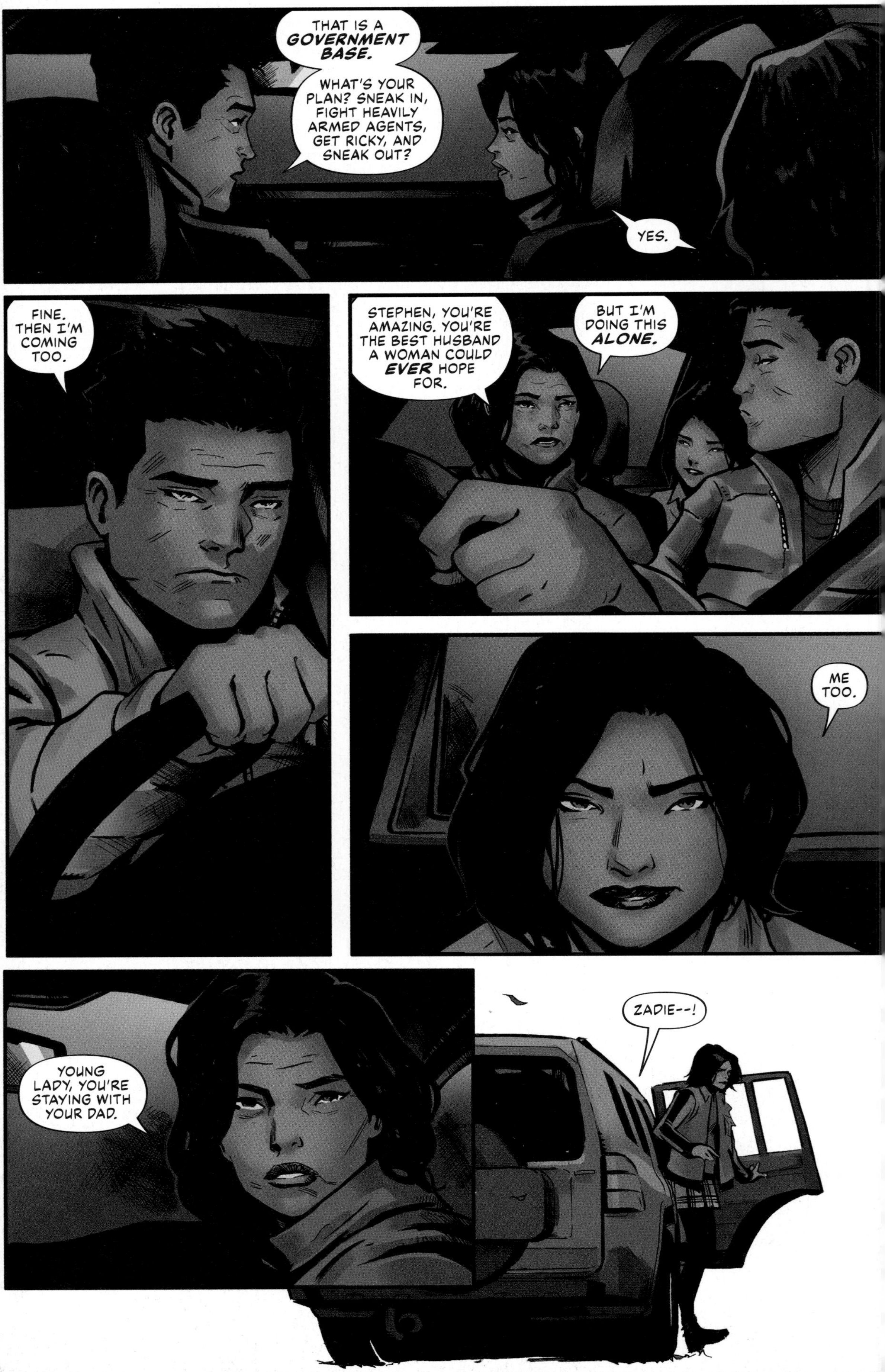
THAT IS A *GOVERNMENT BASE.*
WHAT'S YOUR PLAN? SNEAK IN, FIGHT HEAVILY ARMED AGENTS, GET RICKY, AND SNEAK OUT?
YES.
FINE. THEN I'M COMING TOO.
STEPHEN, YOU'RE AMAZING. YOU'RE THE BEST HUSBAND A WOMAN COULD *EVER* HOPE FOR.
BUT I'M DOING THIS *ALONE.*
ME TOO.
YOUNG LADY, YOU'RE STAYING WITH YOUR DAD.
ZADIE--!

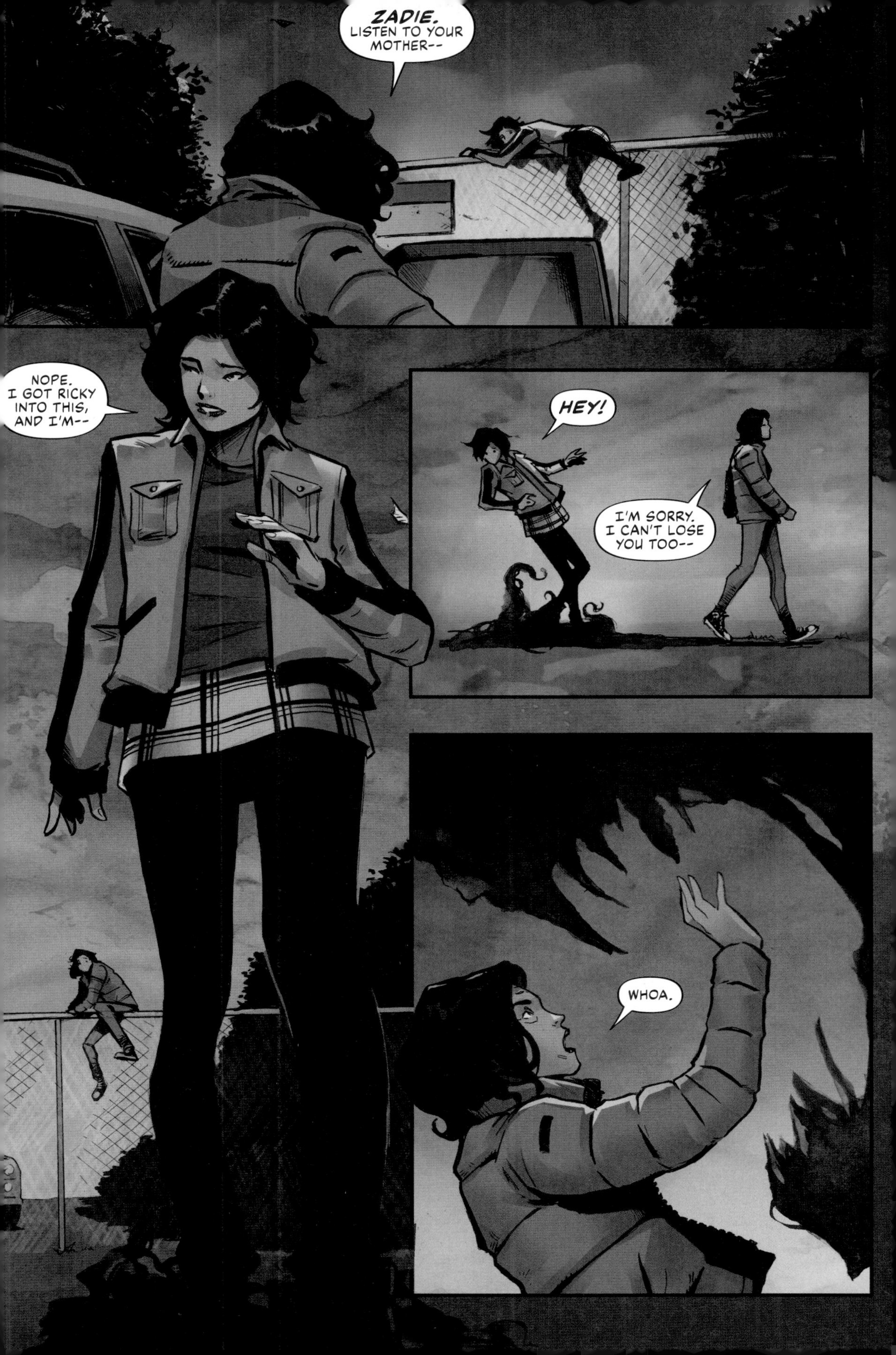
ZADIE. LISTEN TO YOUR MOTHER--
NOPE. I GOT RICKY INTO THIS, AND I'M--
HEY!
I'M SORRY. I CAN'T LOSE YOU TOO--
WHOA.

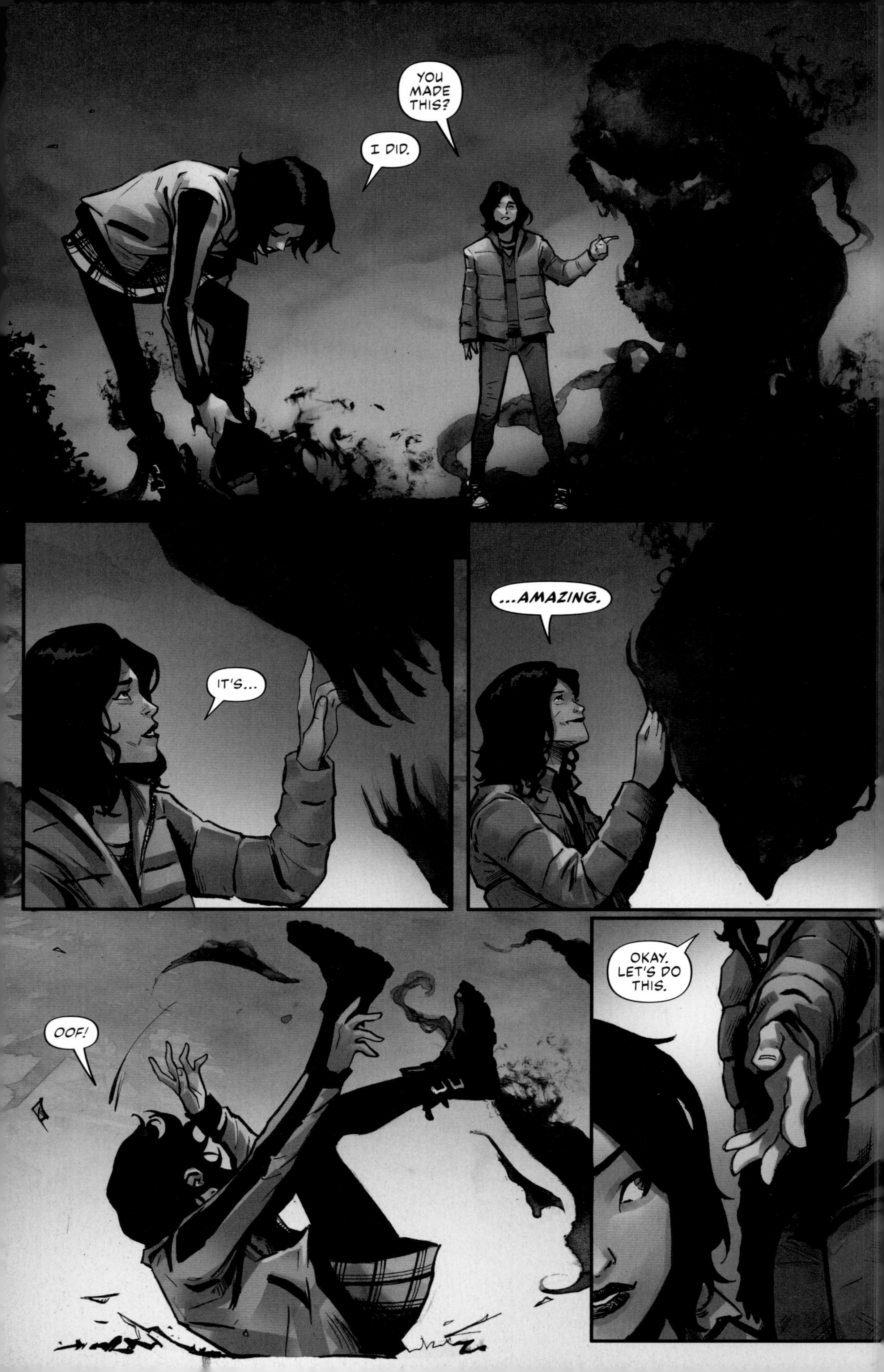
YOU MADE THIS?
I DID.
IT'S...
...AMAZING.
OOF!
OKAY. LET'S DO THIS.

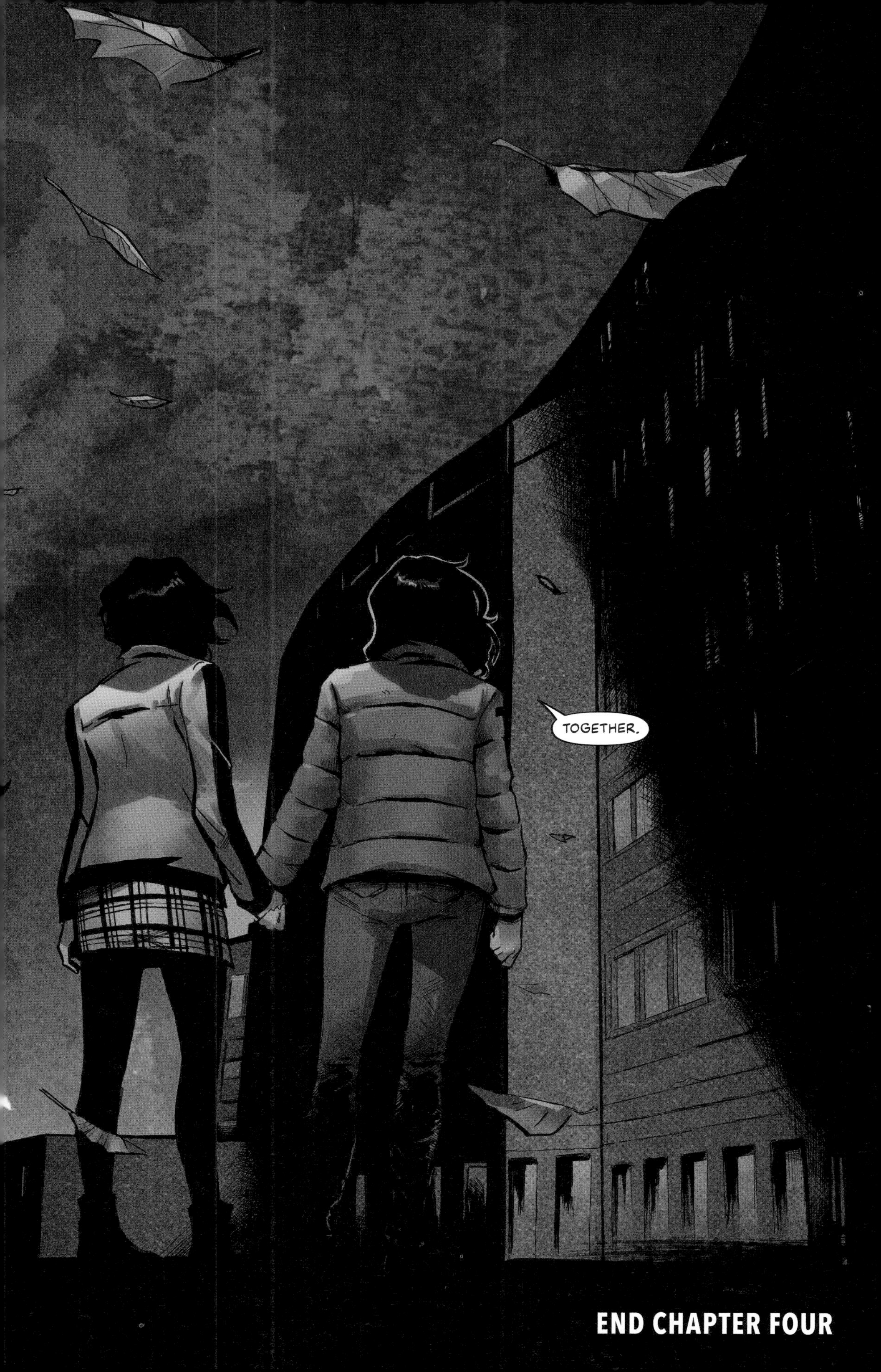
TOGETHER.

END CHAPTER FOUR

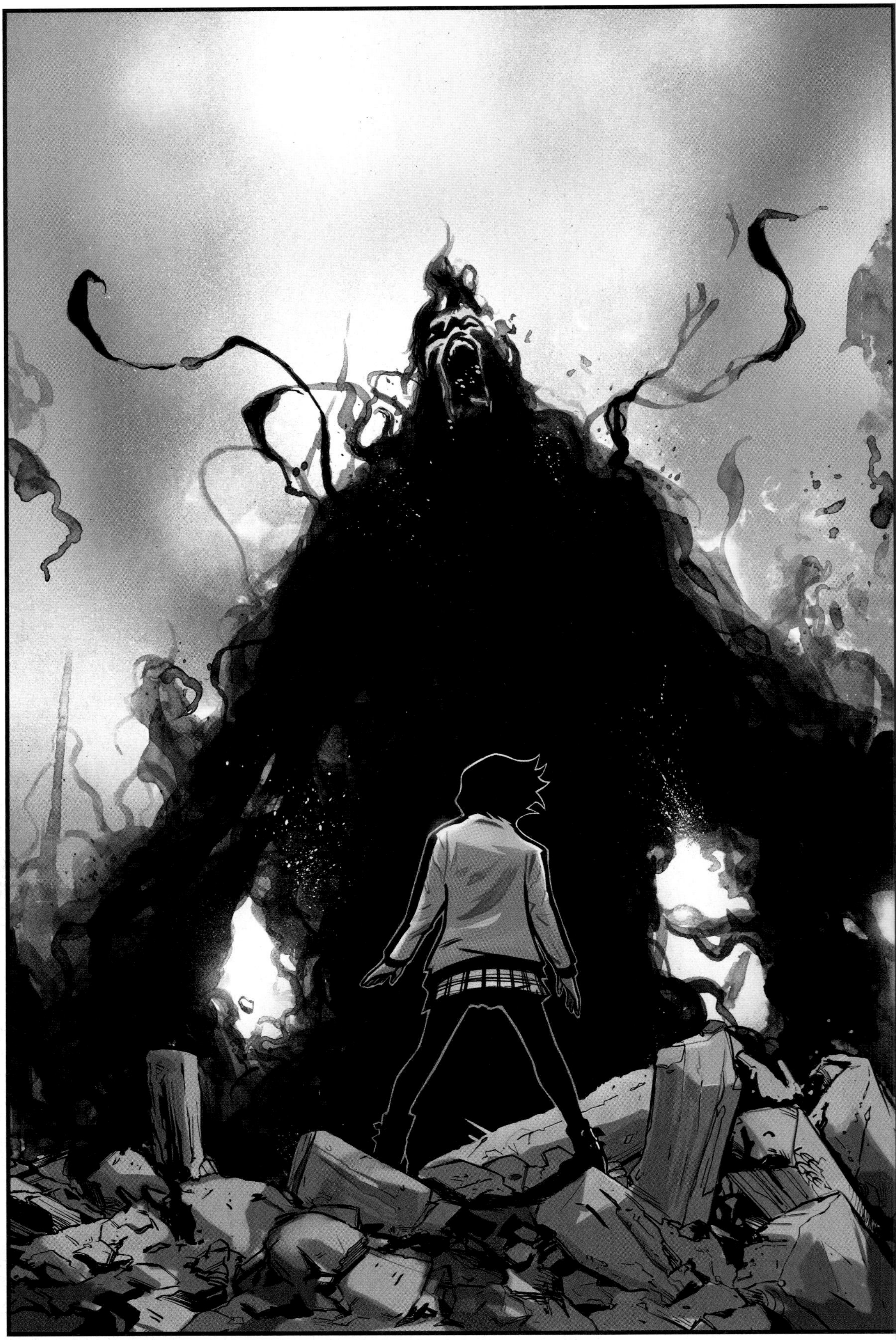

CHAPTER FIVE

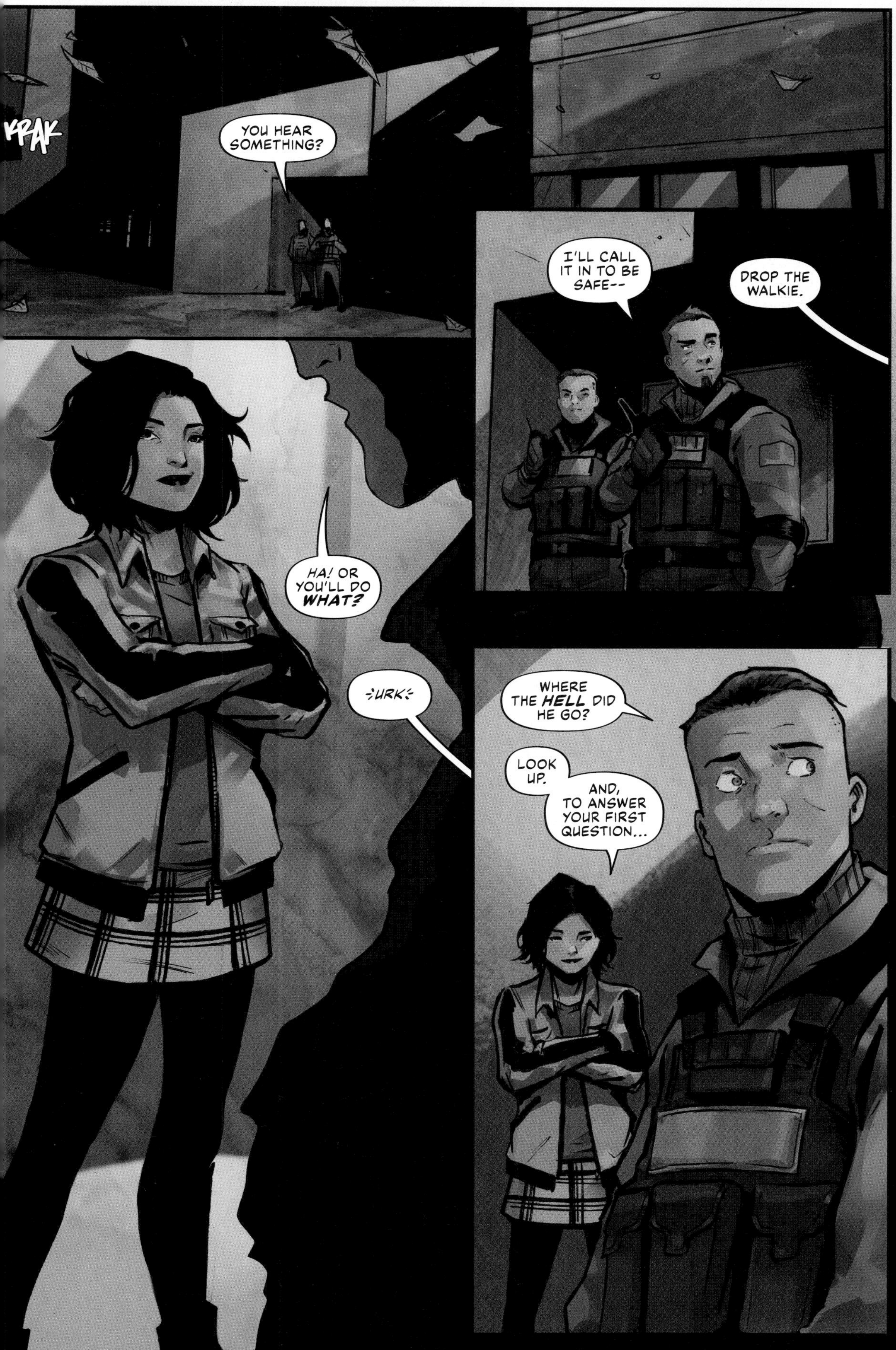
KRAK
YOU HEAR SOMETHING?
I'LL CALL IT IN TO BE SAFE--
DROP THE WALKIE.
HA! OR YOU'LL DO WHAT?
URK
WHERE THE HELL DID HE GO?
LOOK UP.
AND, TO ANSWER YOUR FIRST QUESTION...

...OR WE'LL DO THAT.

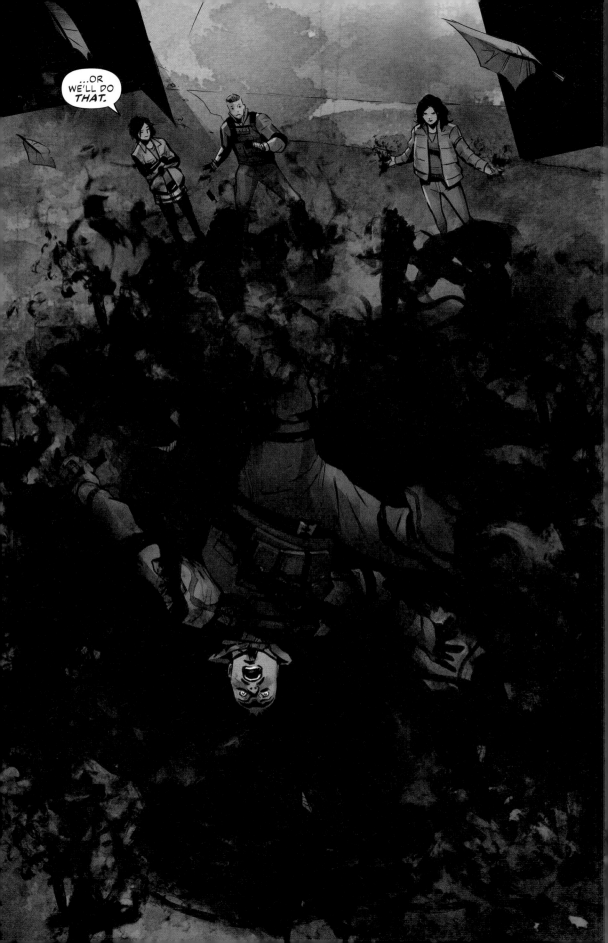

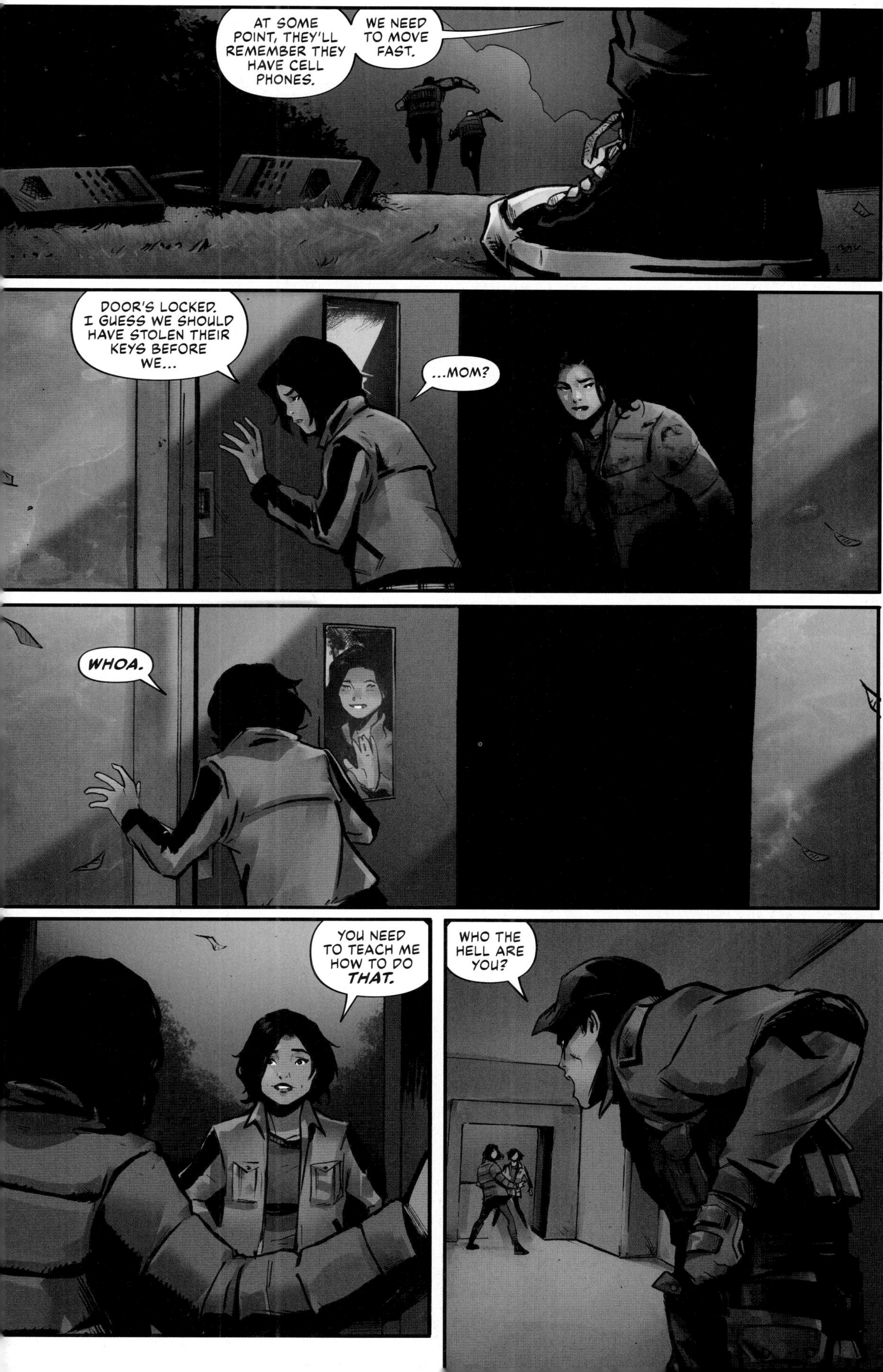
AT SOME POINT, THEY'LL REMEMBER THEY HAVE CELL PHONES.
WE NEED TO MOVE FAST.
DOOR'S LOCKED. I GUESS WE SHOULD HAVE STOLEN THEIR KEYS BEFORE WE...
...MOM?
WHOA.
YOU NEED TO TEACH ME HOW TO DO *THAT.*
WHO THE HELL ARE YOU?

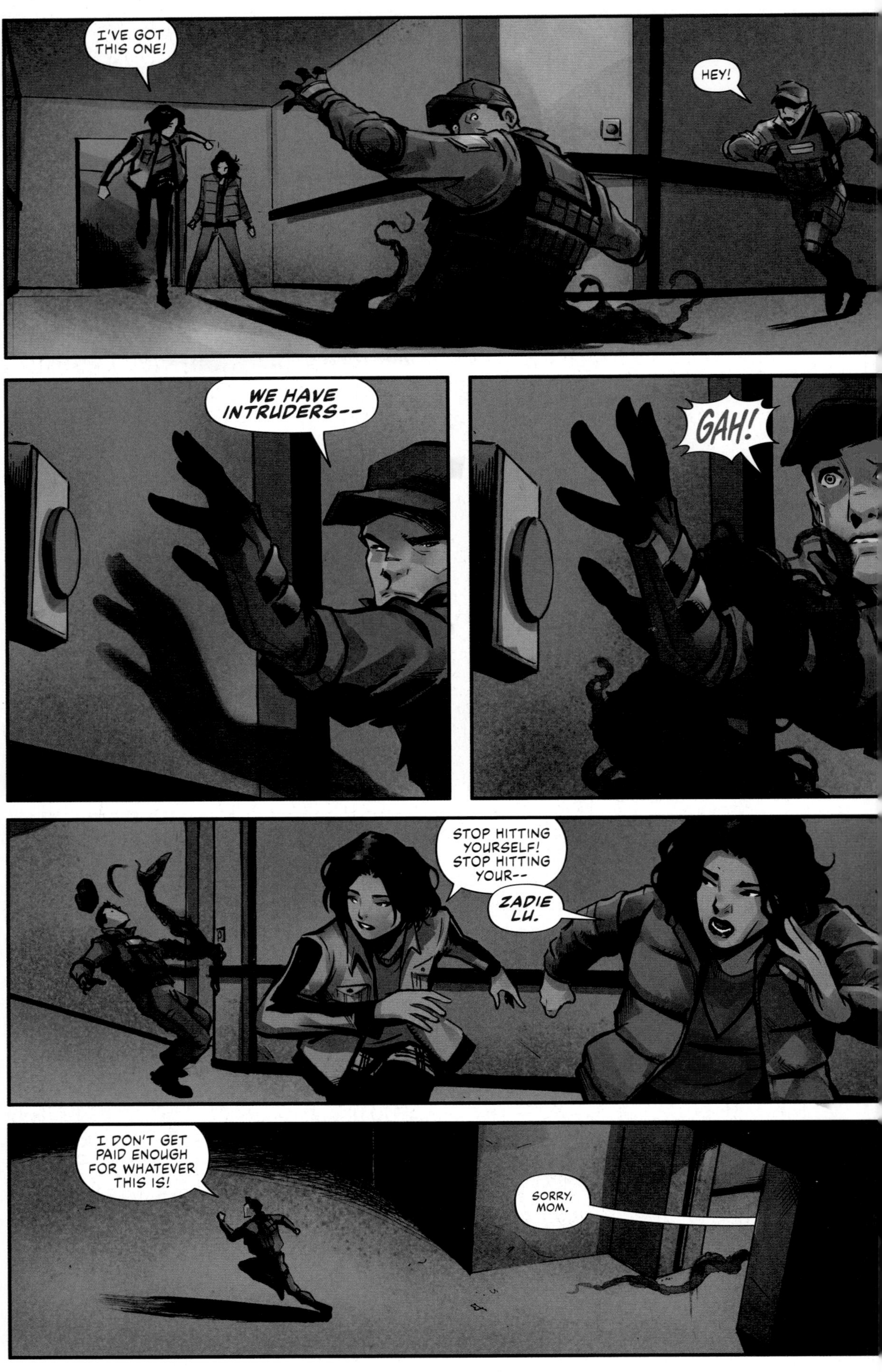
I'VE GOT THIS ONE!
HEY!
WE HAVE INTRUDERS--
GAH!
STOP HITTING YOURSELF! STOP HITTING YOUR--
ZADIE LU.
I DON'T GET PAID ENOUGH FOR WHATEVER THIS IS!
SORRY, MOM.

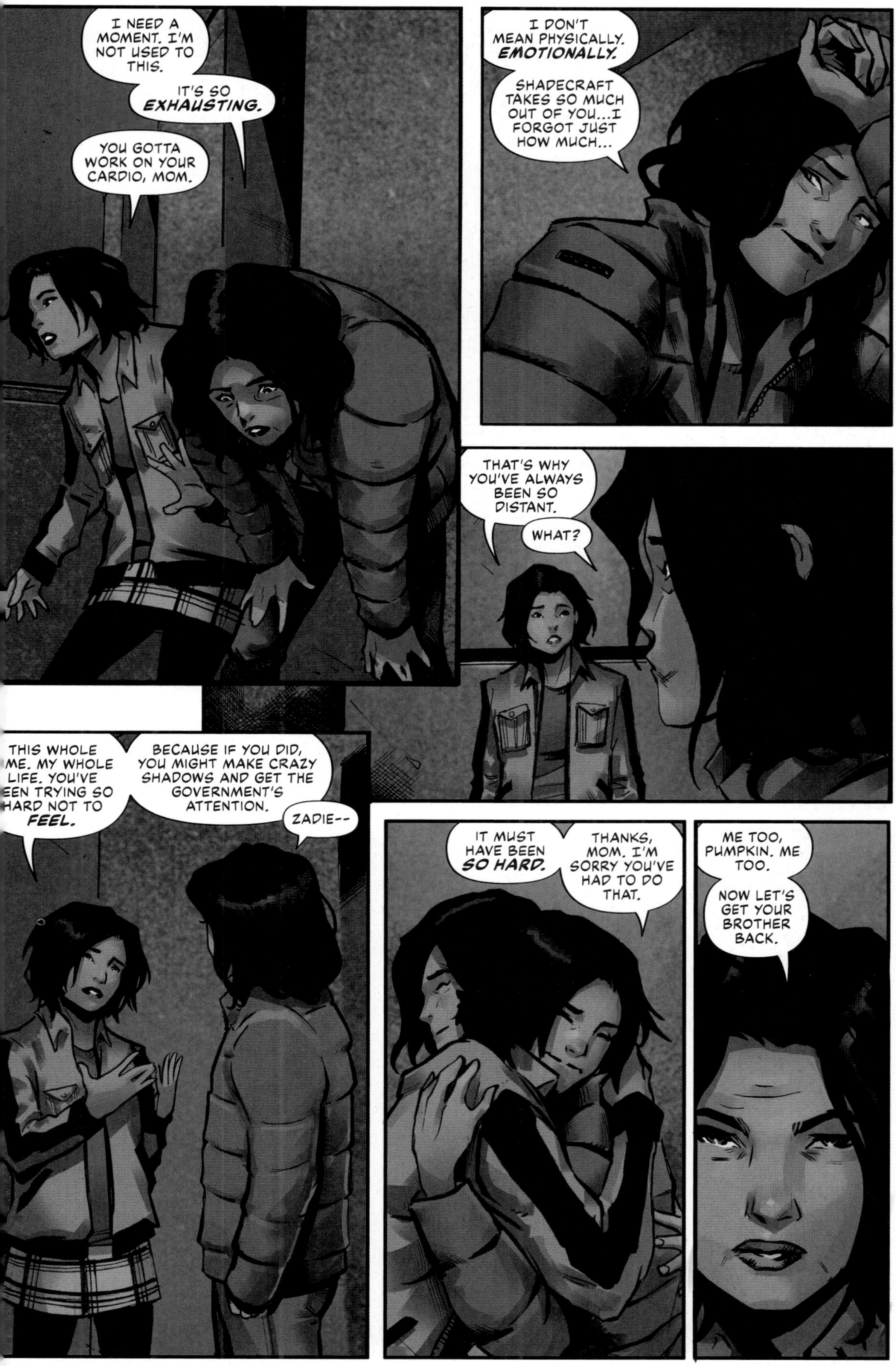
I NEED A MOMENT. I'M NOT USED TO THIS.
IT'S SO EXHAUSTING.
YOU GOTTA WORK ON YOUR CARDIO, MOM.
I DON'T MEAN PHYSICALLY. EMOTIONALLY.
SHADECRAFT TAKES SO MUCH OUT OF YOU...I FORGOT JUST HOW MUCH...
THAT'S WHY YOU'VE ALWAYS BEEN SO DISTANT.
WHAT?
THIS WHOLE TIME. MY WHOLE LIFE. YOU'VE BEEN TRYING SO HARD NOT TO FEEL.
BECAUSE IF YOU DID, YOU MIGHT MAKE CRAZY SHADOWS AND GET THE GOVERNMENT'S ATTENTION.
ZADIE--
IT MUST HAVE BEEN SO HARD.
THANKS, MOM. I'M SORRY YOU'VE HAD TO DO THAT.
ME TOO, PUMPKIN. ME TOO.
NOW LET'S GET YOUR BROTHER BACK.

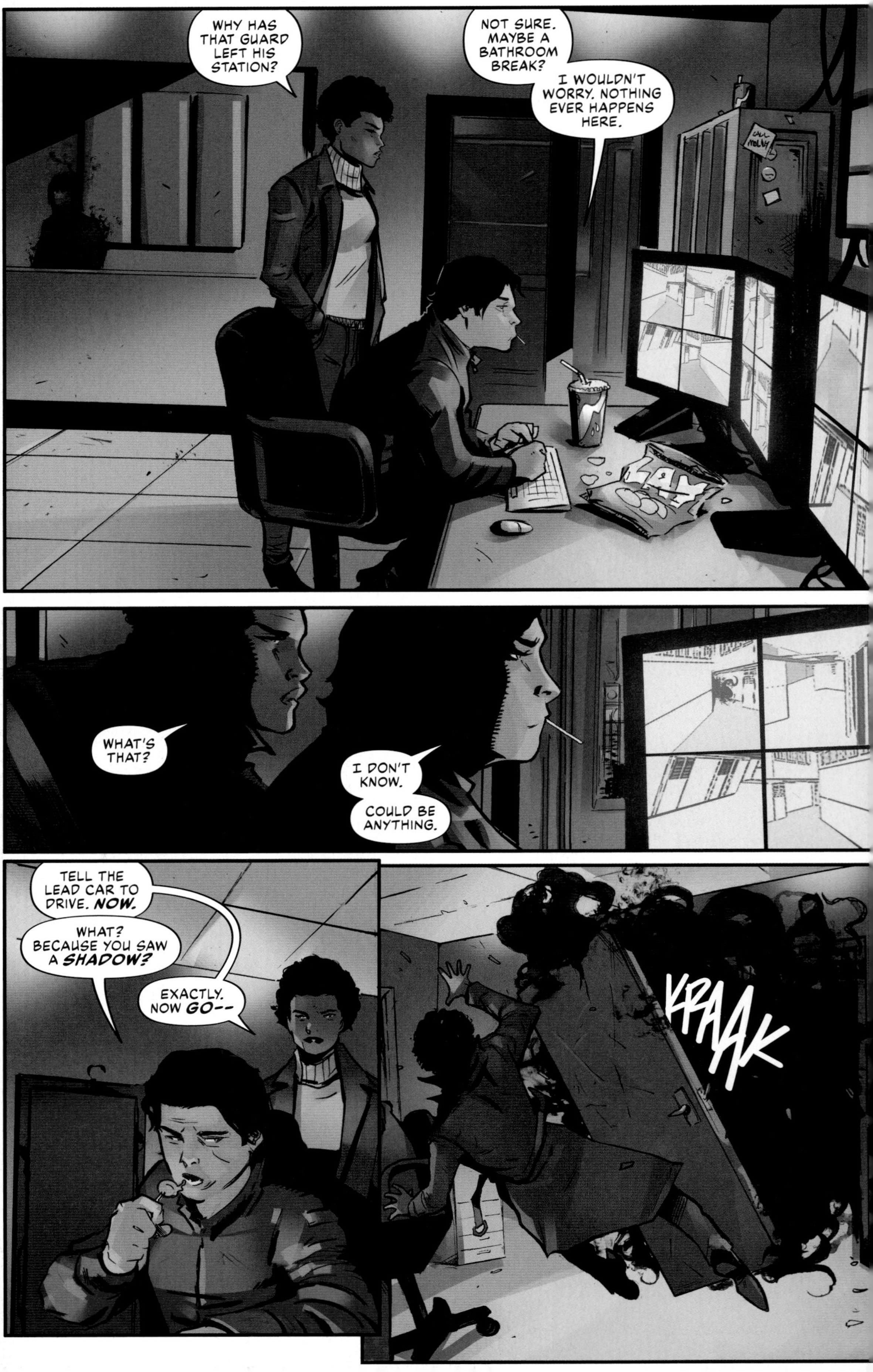
WHY HAS THAT GUARD LEFT HIS STATION?
NOT SURE. MAYBE A BATHROOM BREAK?
I WOULDN'T WORRY. NOTHING EVER HAPPENS HERE.
WHAT'S THAT?
I DON'T KNOW.
COULD BE ANYTHING.
TELL THE LEAD CAR TO DRIVE. NOW.
WHAT? BECAUSE YOU SAW A SHADOW?
EXACTLY. NOW GO--
KRAAAK

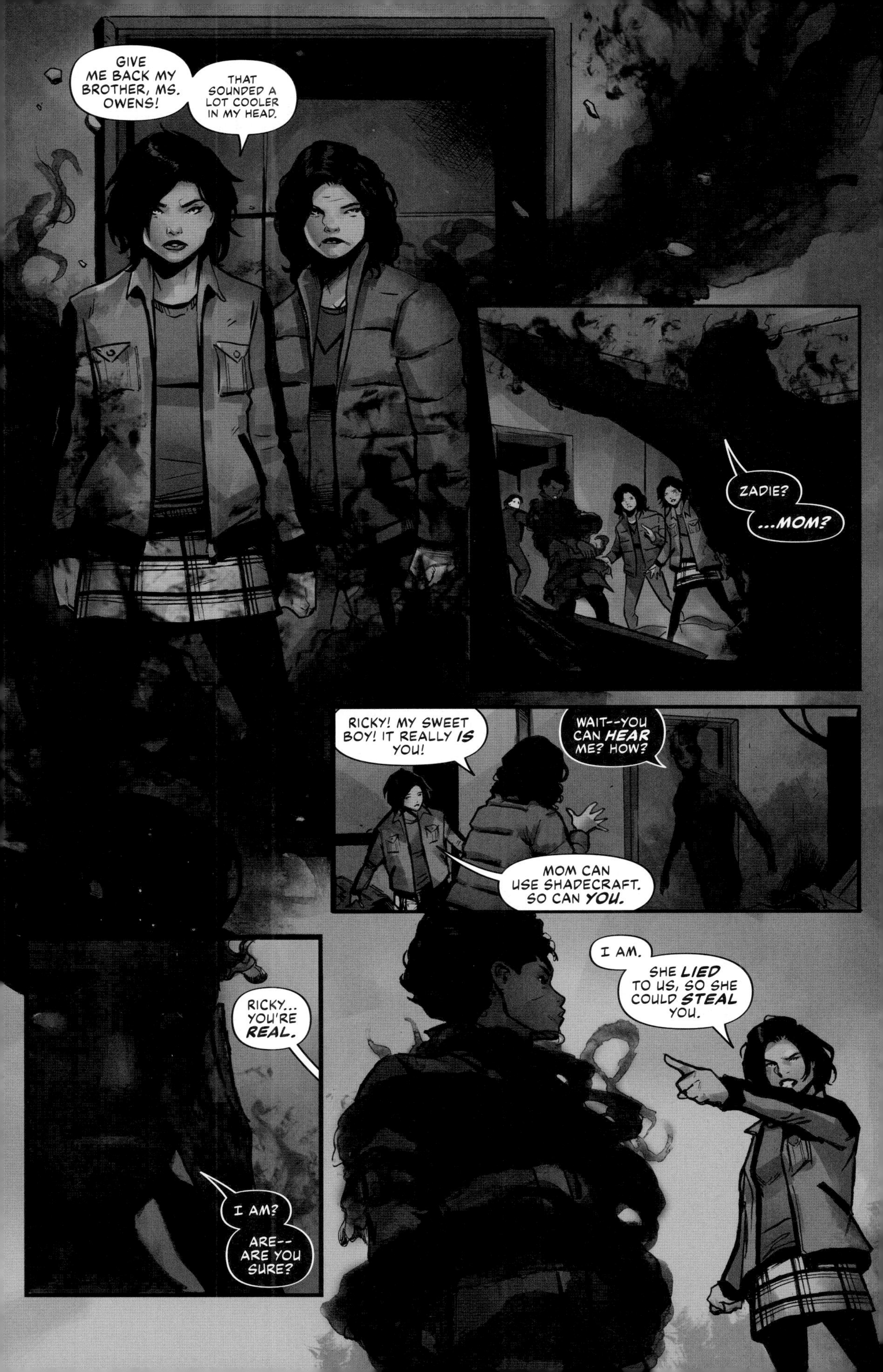
GIVE ME BACK MY BROTHER, MS. OWENS!
THAT SOUNDED A LOT COOLER IN MY HEAD.
ZADIE?
...MOM?
RICKY! MY SWEET BOY! IT REALLY IS YOU!
WAIT--YOU CAN HEAR ME? HOW?
MOM CAN USE SHADECRAFT. SO CAN YOU.
RICKY... YOU'RE REAL.
I AM?
ARE-- ARE YOU SURE?
I AM.
SHE LIED TO US, SO SHE COULD STEAL YOU.

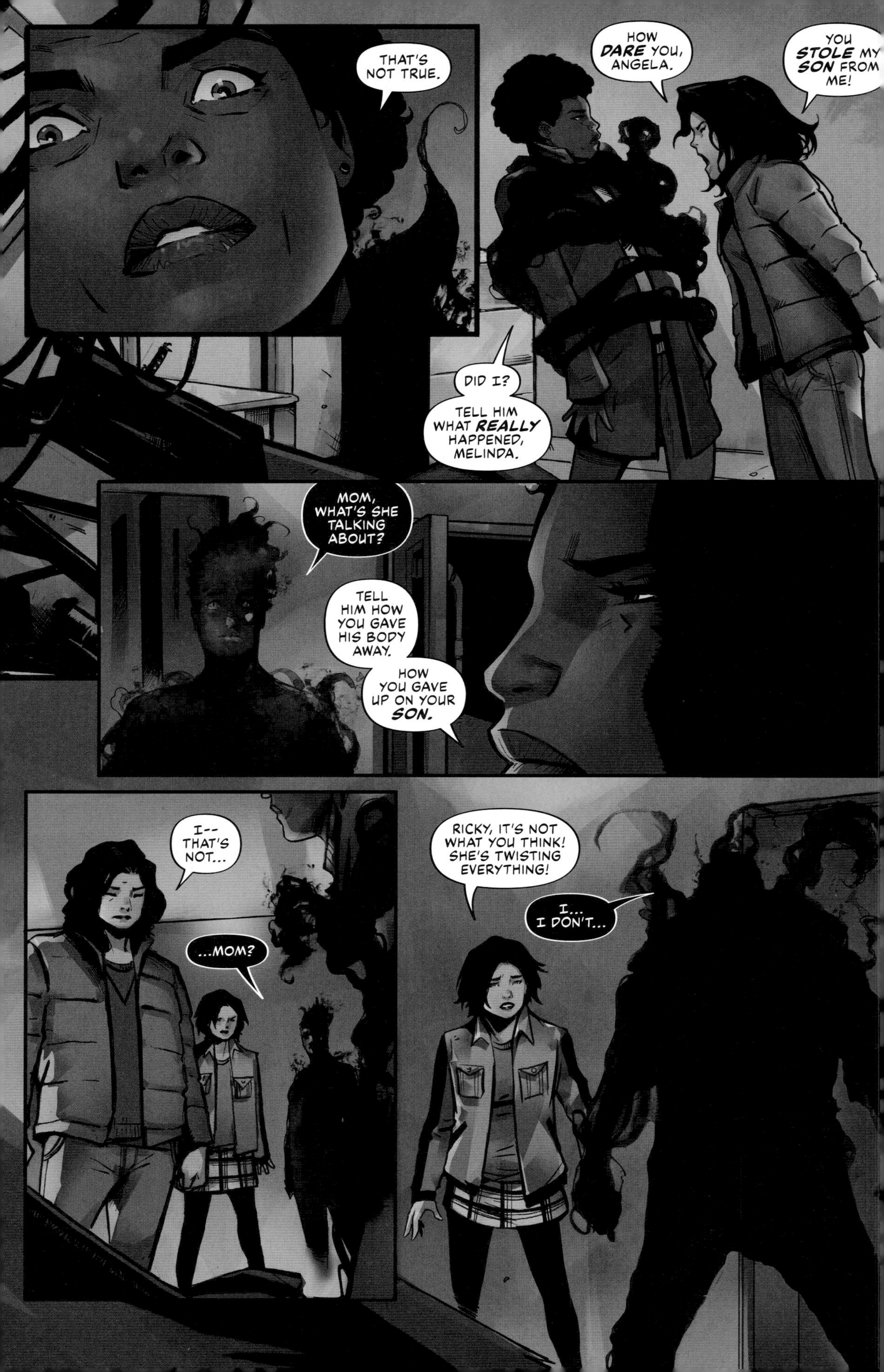
THAT'S NOT TRUE.
HOW DARE YOU, ANGELA.
YOU STOLE MY SON FROM ME!
DID I?
TELL HIM WHAT REALLY HAPPENED, MELINDA.
MOM, WHAT'S SHE TALKING ABOUT?
TELL HIM HOW YOU GAVE HIS BODY AWAY.
HOW YOU GAVE UP ON YOUR SON.
I-- THAT'S NOT...
...MOM?
RICKY, IT'S NOT WHAT YOU THINK! SHE'S TWISTING EVERYTHING!
I... I DON'T...

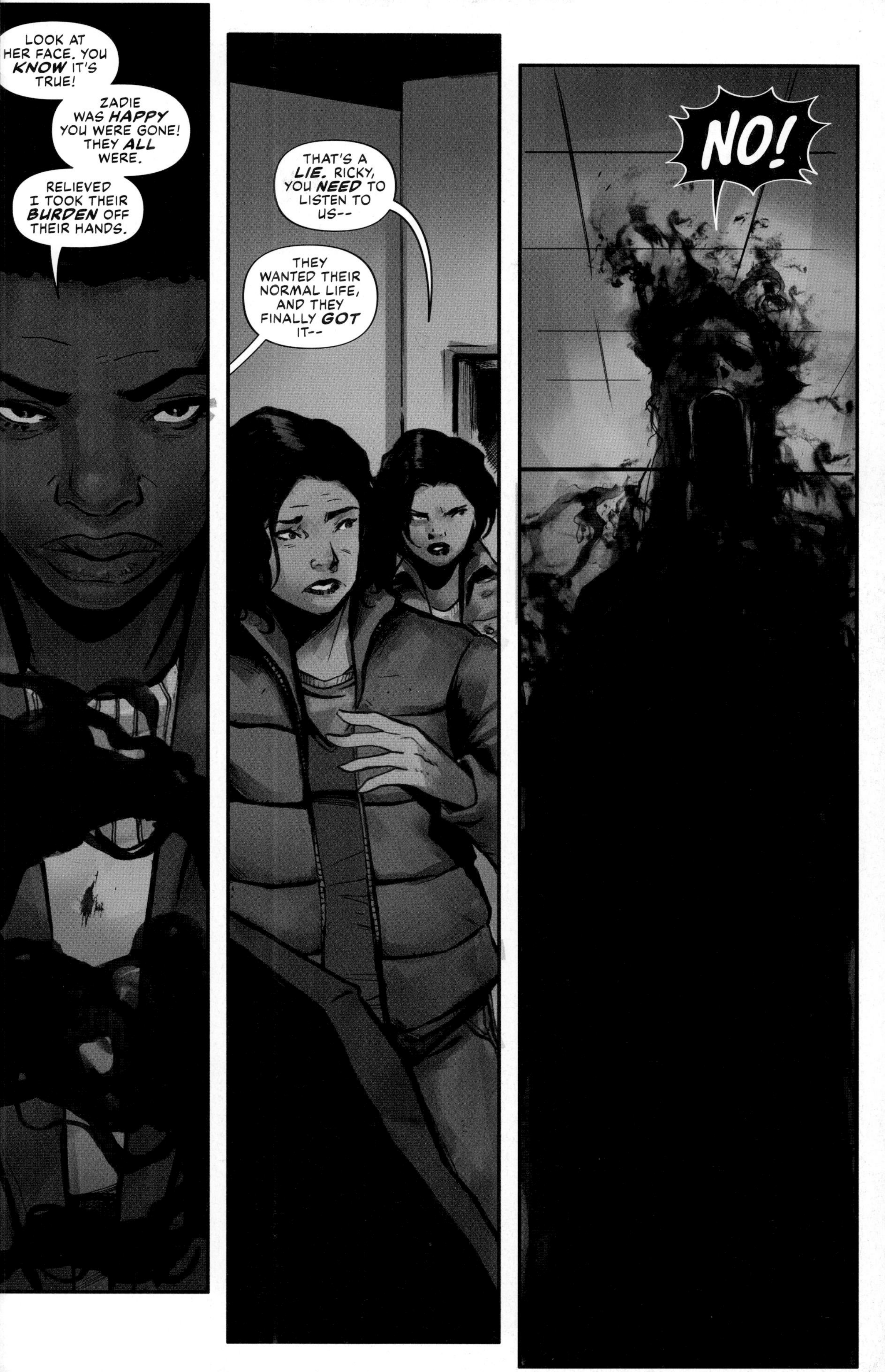

LOOK AT HER FACE. YOU KNOW IT'S TRUE!
ZADIE WAS HAPPY YOU WERE GONE! THEY ALL WERE.
RELIEVED I TOOK THEIR BURDEN OFF THEIR HANDS.
THAT'S A LIE. RICKY, YOU NEED TO LISTEN TO US--
THEY WANTED THEIR NORMAL LIFE, AND THEY FINALLY GOT IT--
NO!

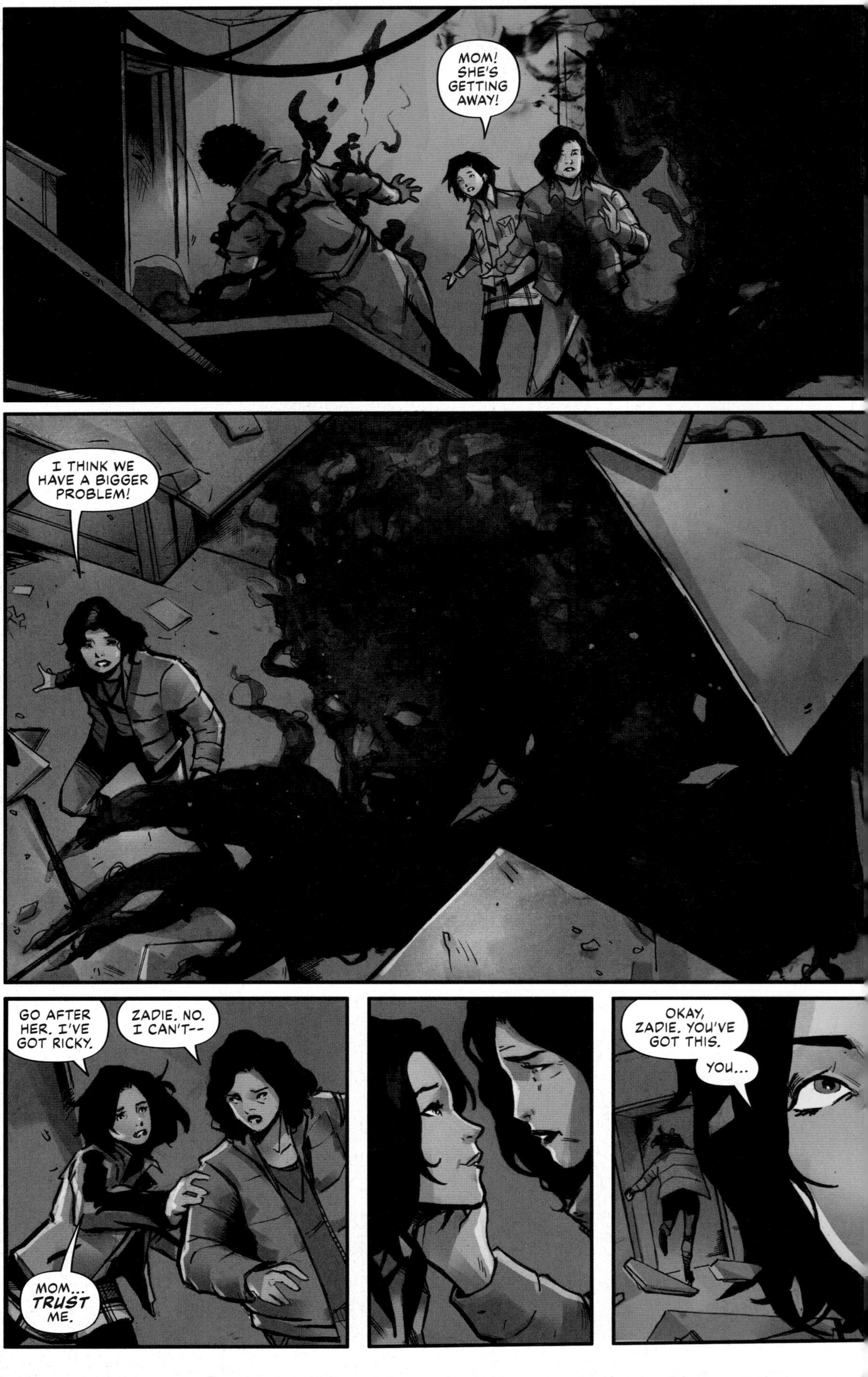
MOM! SHE'S GETTING AWAY!
I THINK WE HAVE A BIGGER PROBLEM!
GO AFTER HER. I'VE GOT RICKY.
ZADIE. NO. I CAN'T--
MOM... *TRUST* ME.
OKAY, ZADIE. YOU'VE GOT THIS.
YOU...

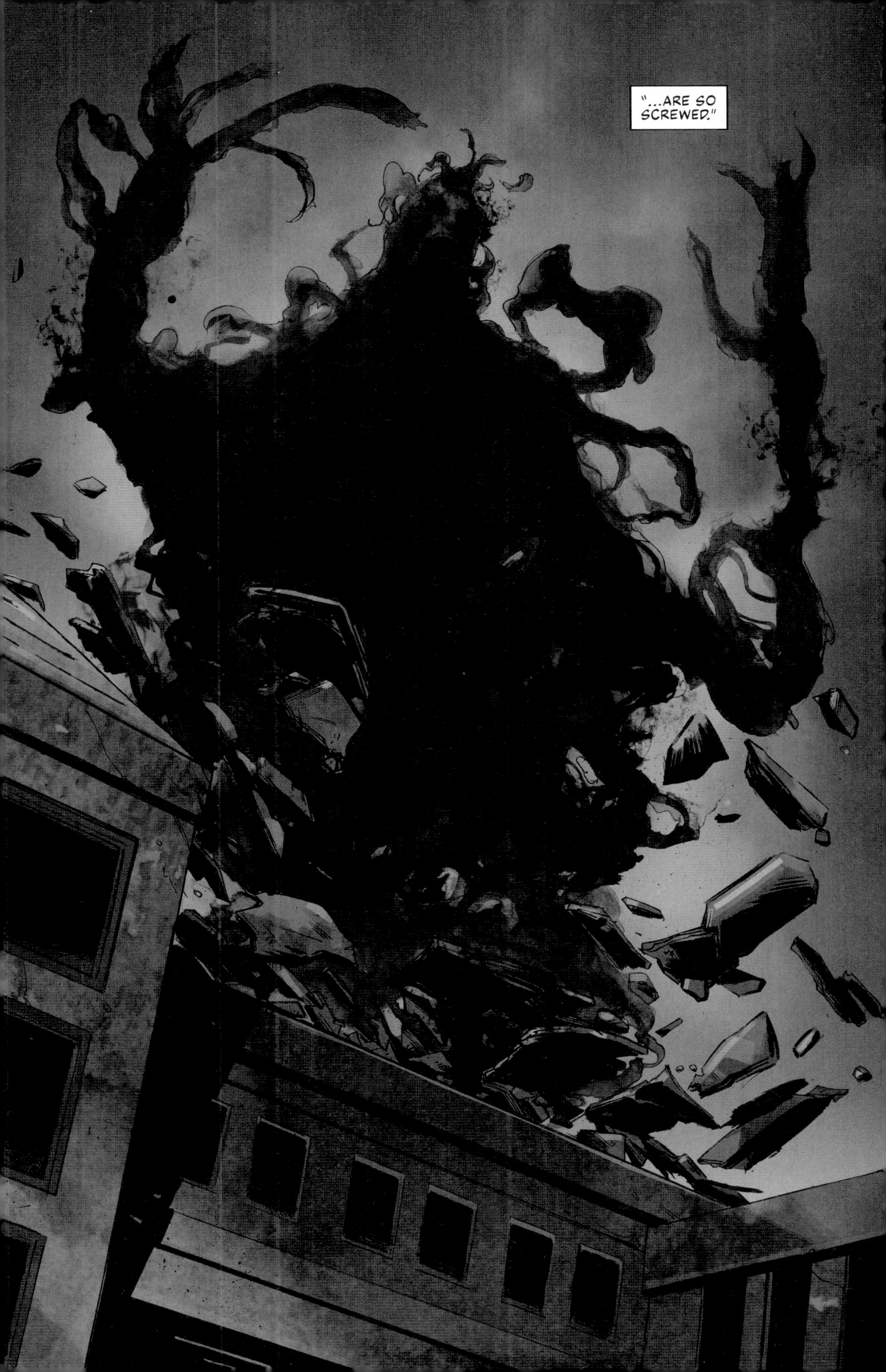
"...ARE SO SCREWED."

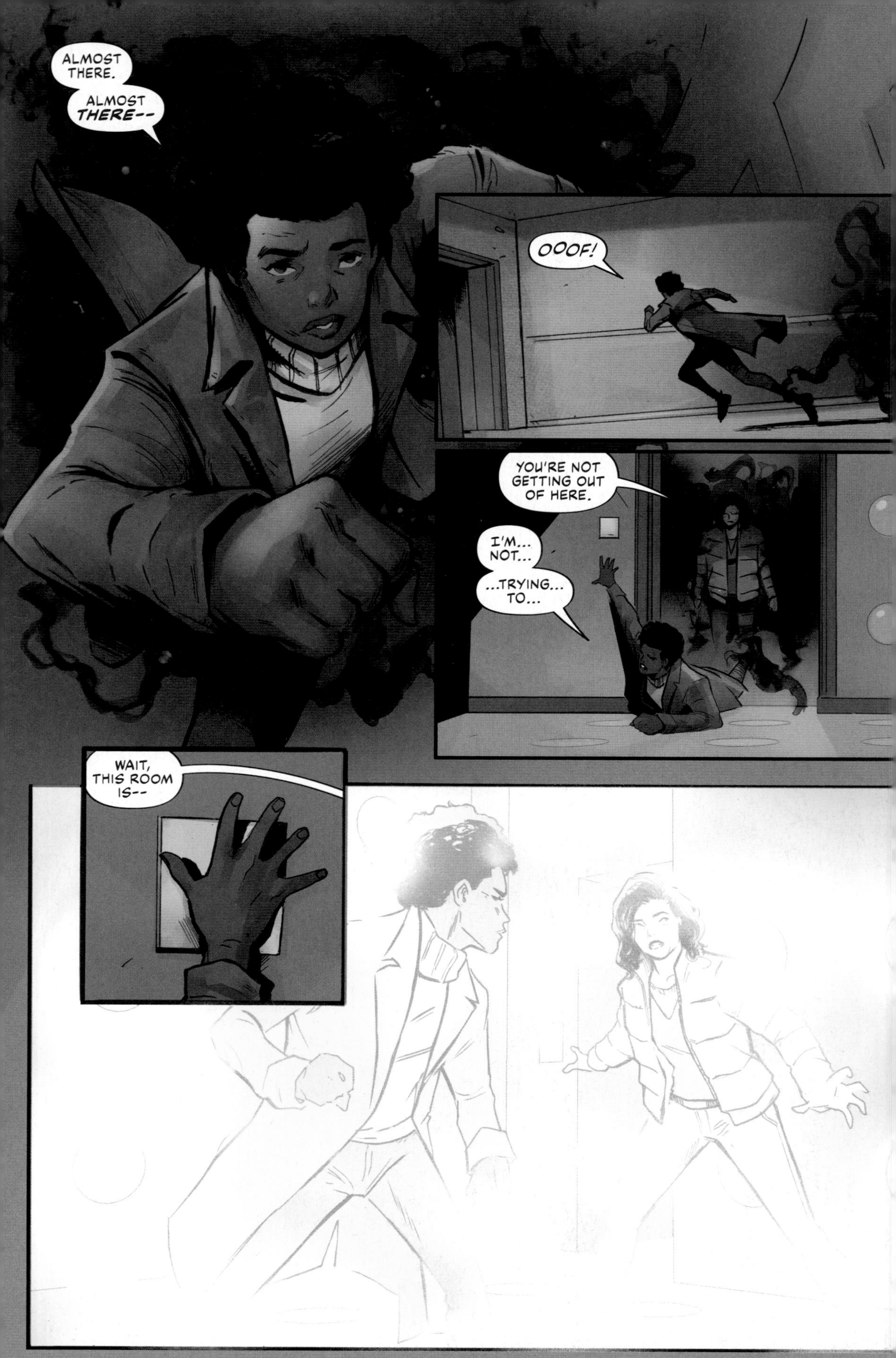
ALMOST THERE.
ALMOST *THERE--*
OOOF!
YOU'RE NOT GETTING OUT OF HERE.
I'M... NOT...
...TRYING... TO...
WAIT, THIS ROOM IS--

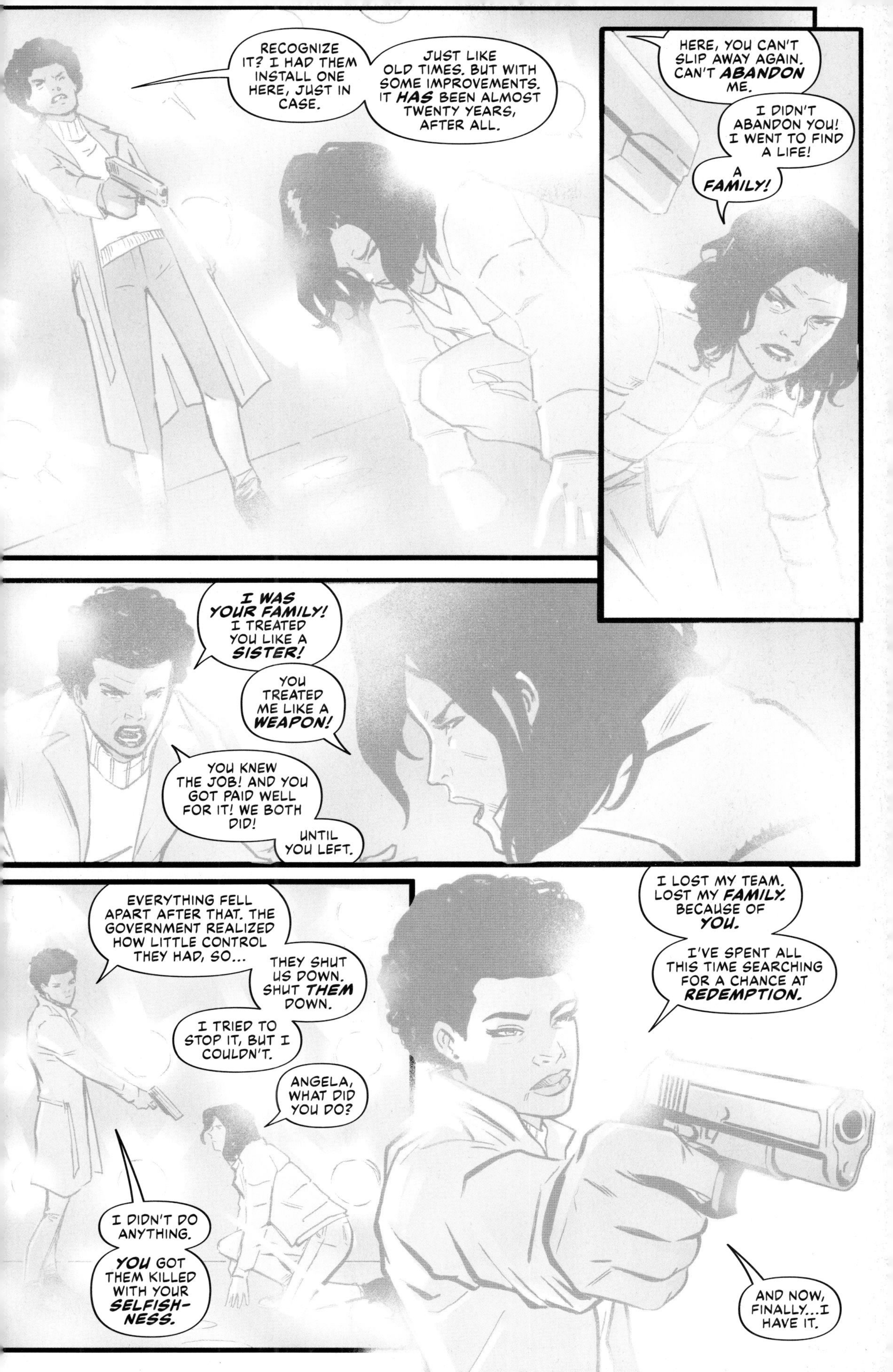
RECOGNIZE IT? I HAD THEM INSTALL ONE HERE, JUST IN CASE.
JUST LIKE OLD TIMES. BUT WITH SOME IMPROVEMENTS. IT HAS BEEN ALMOST TWENTY YEARS, AFTER ALL.
HERE, YOU CAN'T SLIP AWAY AGAIN. CAN'T ABANDON ME.
I DIDN'T ABANDON YOU! I WENT TO FIND A LIFE!
A FAMILY!
I WAS YOUR FAMILY! I TREATED YOU LIKE A SISTER!
YOU TREATED ME LIKE A WEAPON!
YOU KNEW THE JOB! AND YOU GOT PAID WELL FOR IT! WE BOTH DID!
UNTIL YOU LEFT.
EVERYTHING FELL APART AFTER THAT. THE GOVERNMENT REALIZED HOW LITTLE CONTROL THEY HAD, SO...
THEY SHUT US DOWN. SHUT THEM DOWN.
I TRIED TO STOP IT, BUT I COULDN'T.
ANGELA, WHAT DID YOU DO?
I DIDN'T DO ANYTHING.
YOU GOT THEM KILLED WITH YOUR SELFISH-NESS.
I LOST MY TEAM. LOST MY FAMILY. BECAUSE OF YOU.
I'VE SPENT ALL THIS TIME SEARCHING FOR A CHANCE AT REDEMPTION.
AND NOW, FINALLY...I HAVE IT.

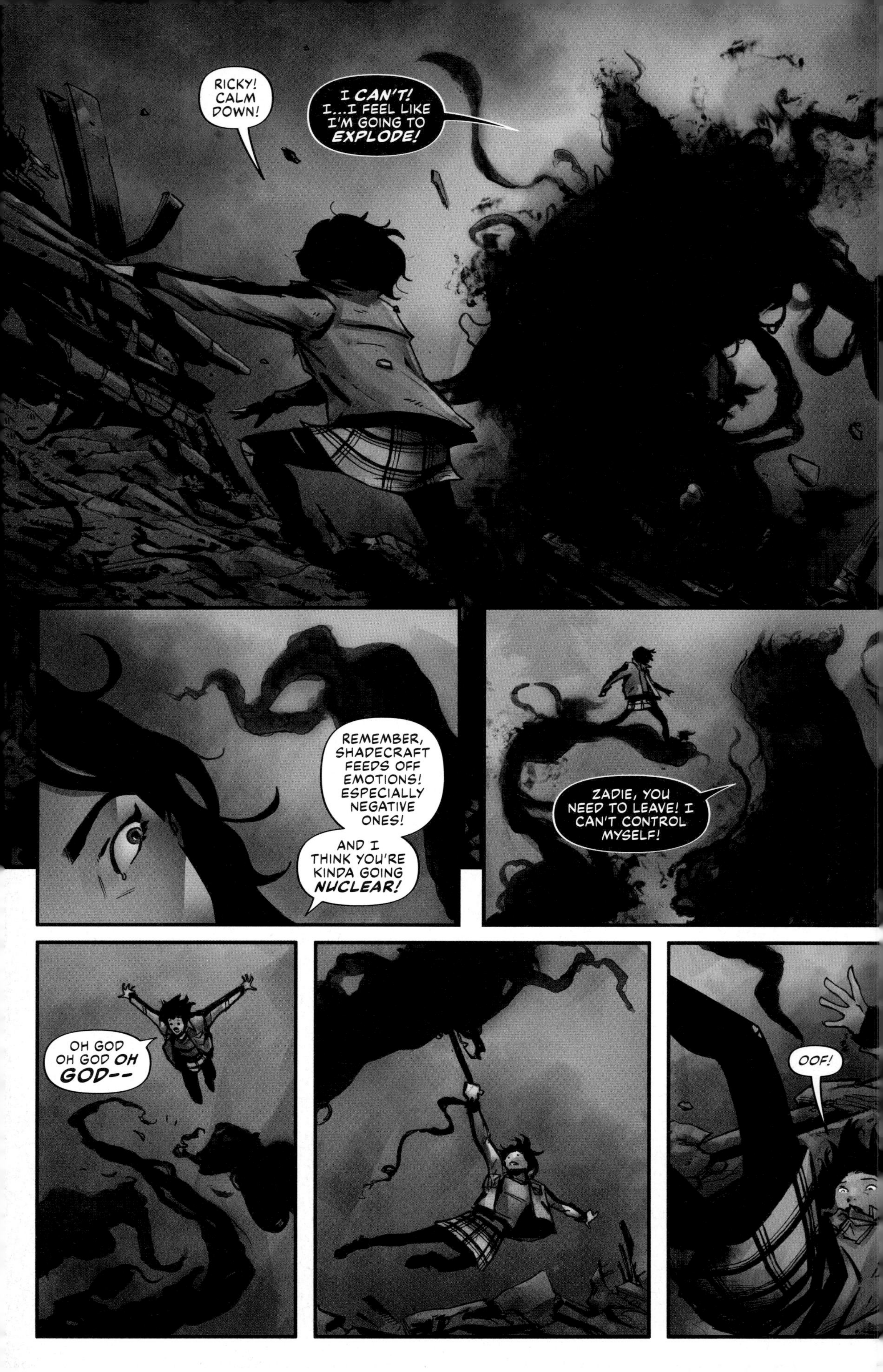
RICKY! CALM DOWN!
I CAN'T! I...I FEEL LIKE I'M GOING TO EXPLODE!
REMEMBER, SHADECRAFT FEEDS OFF EMOTIONS! ESPECIALLY NEGATIVE ONES!
AND I THINK YOU'RE KINDA GOING NUCLEAR!
ZADIE, YOU NEED TO LEAVE! I CAN'T CONTROL MYSELF!
OH GOD OH GOD OH GOD--
OOF!

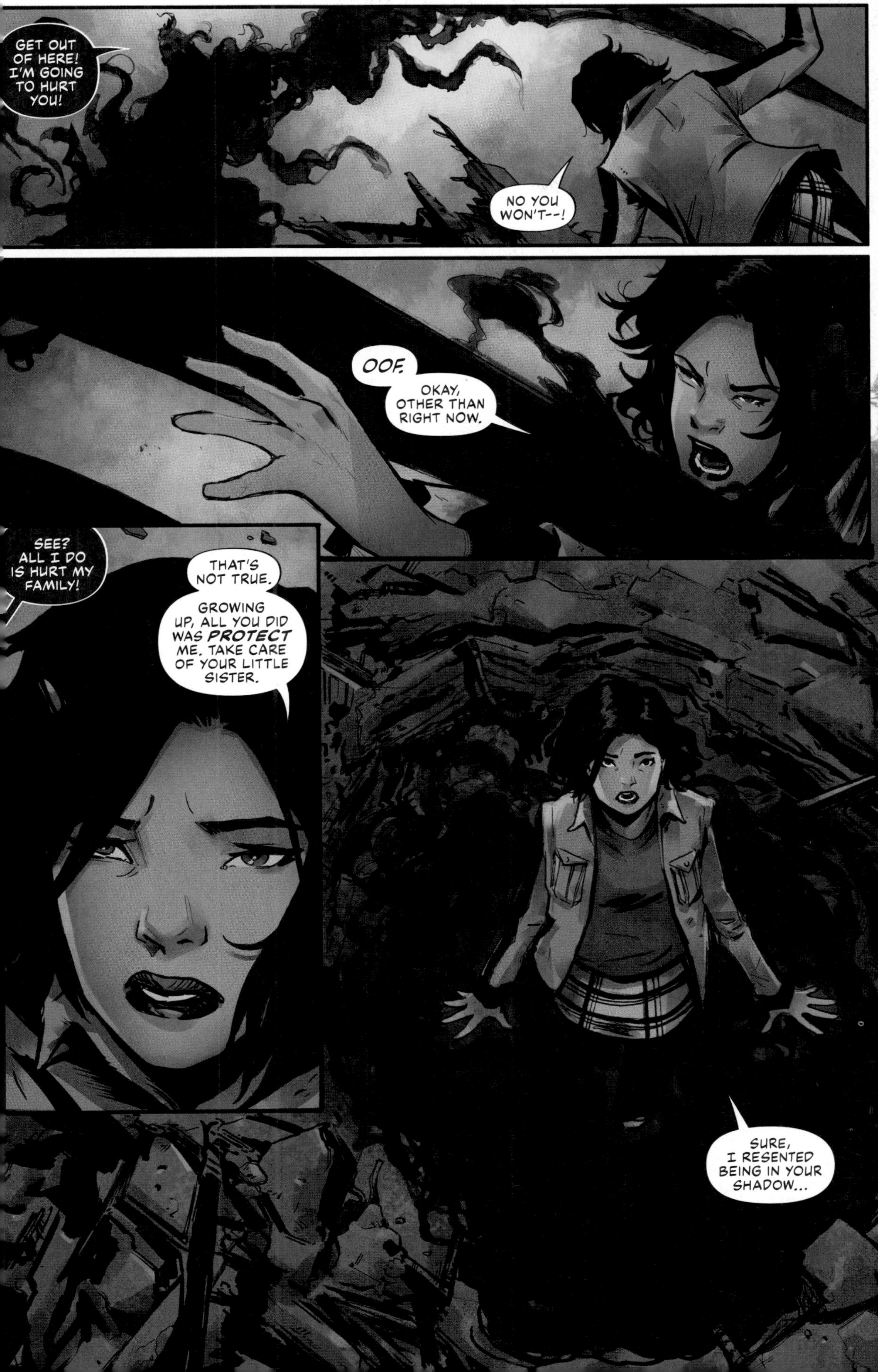
GET OUT OF HERE! I'M GOING TO HURT YOU!
NO YOU WON'T--!
OOF.
OKAY, OTHER THAN RIGHT NOW.
SEE? ALL I DO IS HURT MY FAMILY!
THAT'S NOT TRUE.
GROWING UP, ALL YOU DID WAS PROTECT ME. TAKE CARE OF YOUR LITTLE SISTER.
SURE, I RESENTED BEING IN YOUR SHADOW...

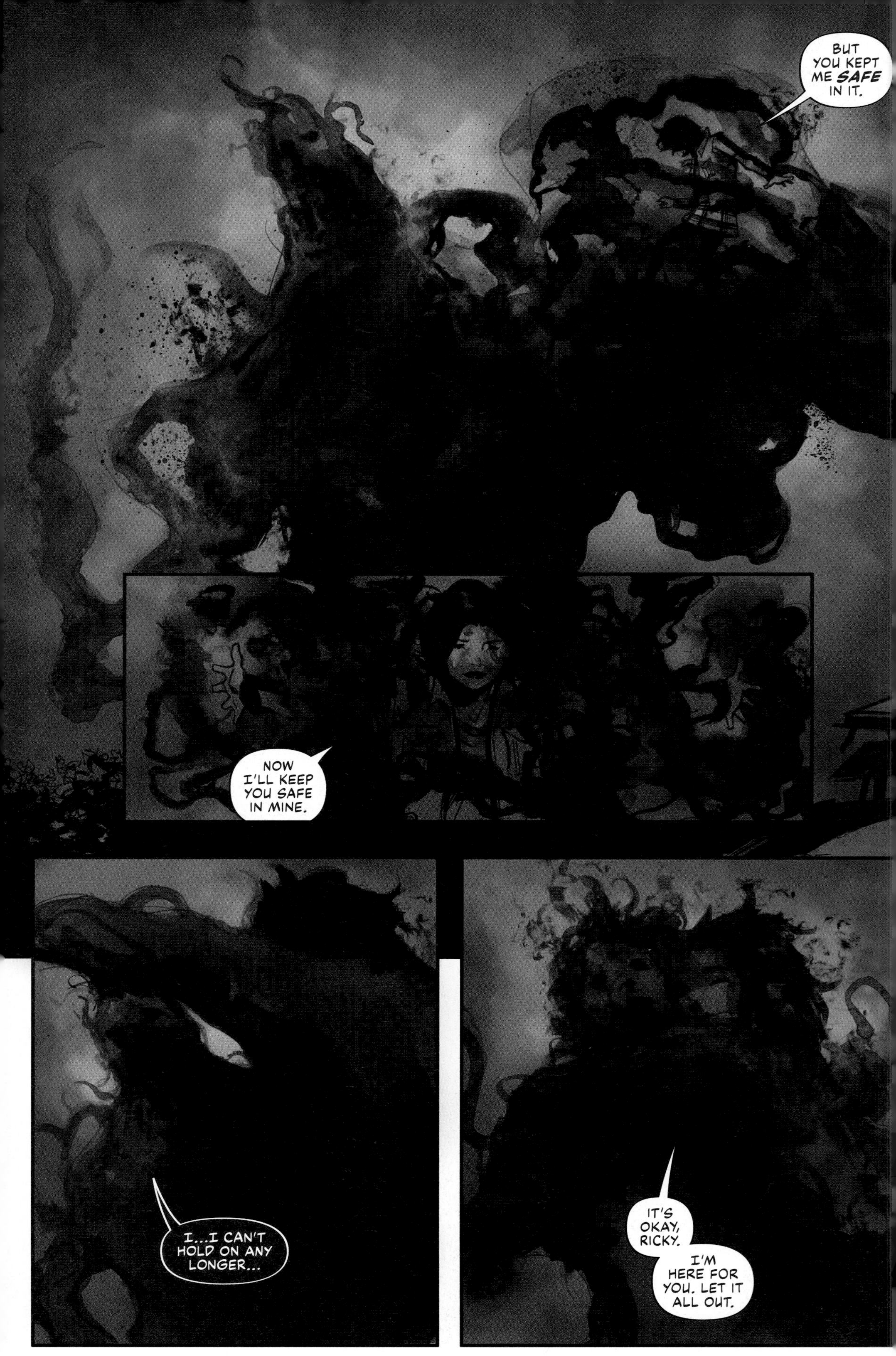
BUT YOU KEPT ME SAFE IN IT.
NOW I'LL KEEP YOU SAFE IN MINE.
I...I CAN'T HOLD ON ANY LONGER...
IT'S OKAY, RICKY.
I'M HERE FOR YOU. LET IT ALL OUT.

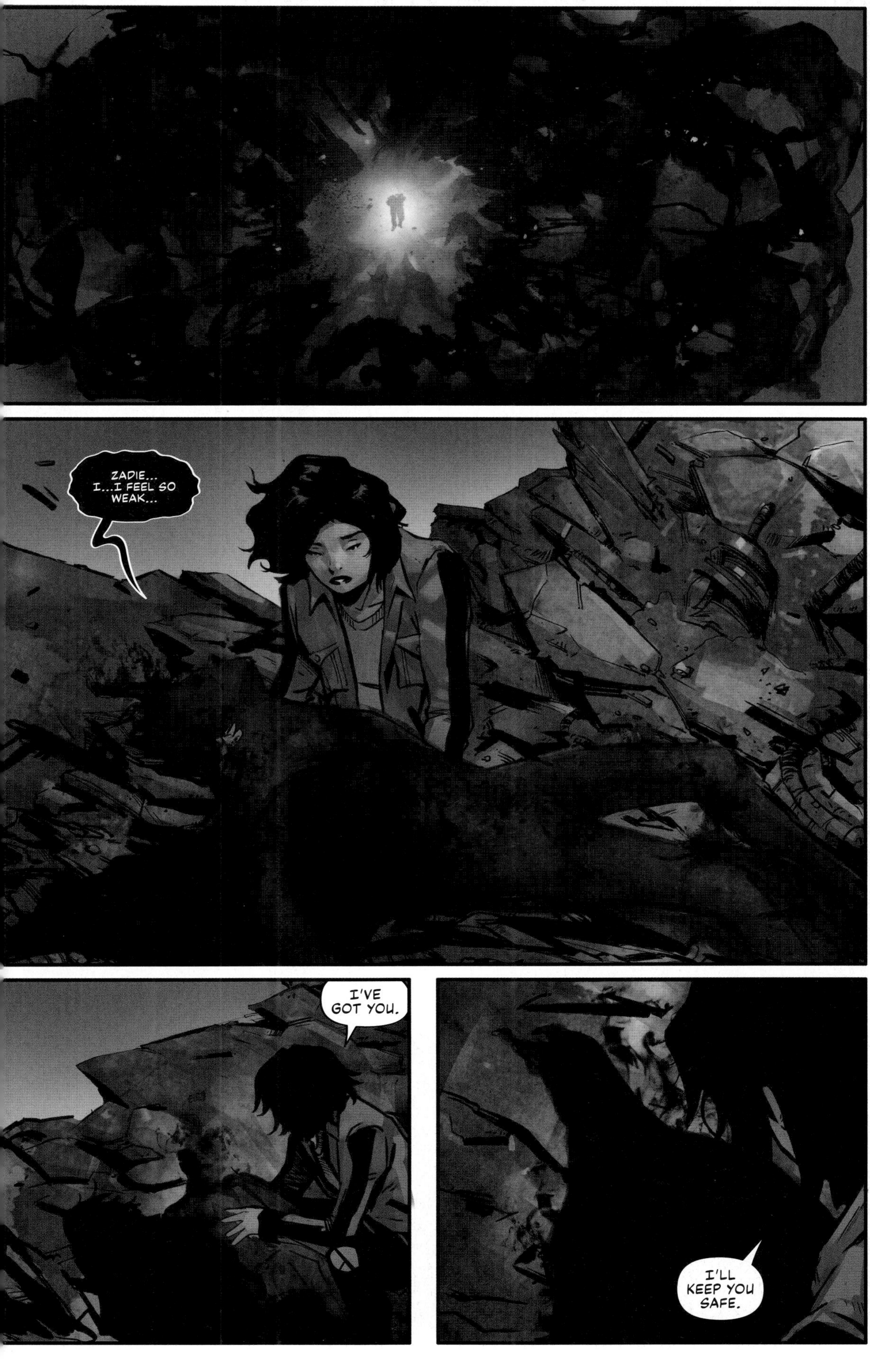
ZADIE... I...I FEEL SO WEAK...
I'VE GOT YOU.
I'LL KEEP YOU SAFE.

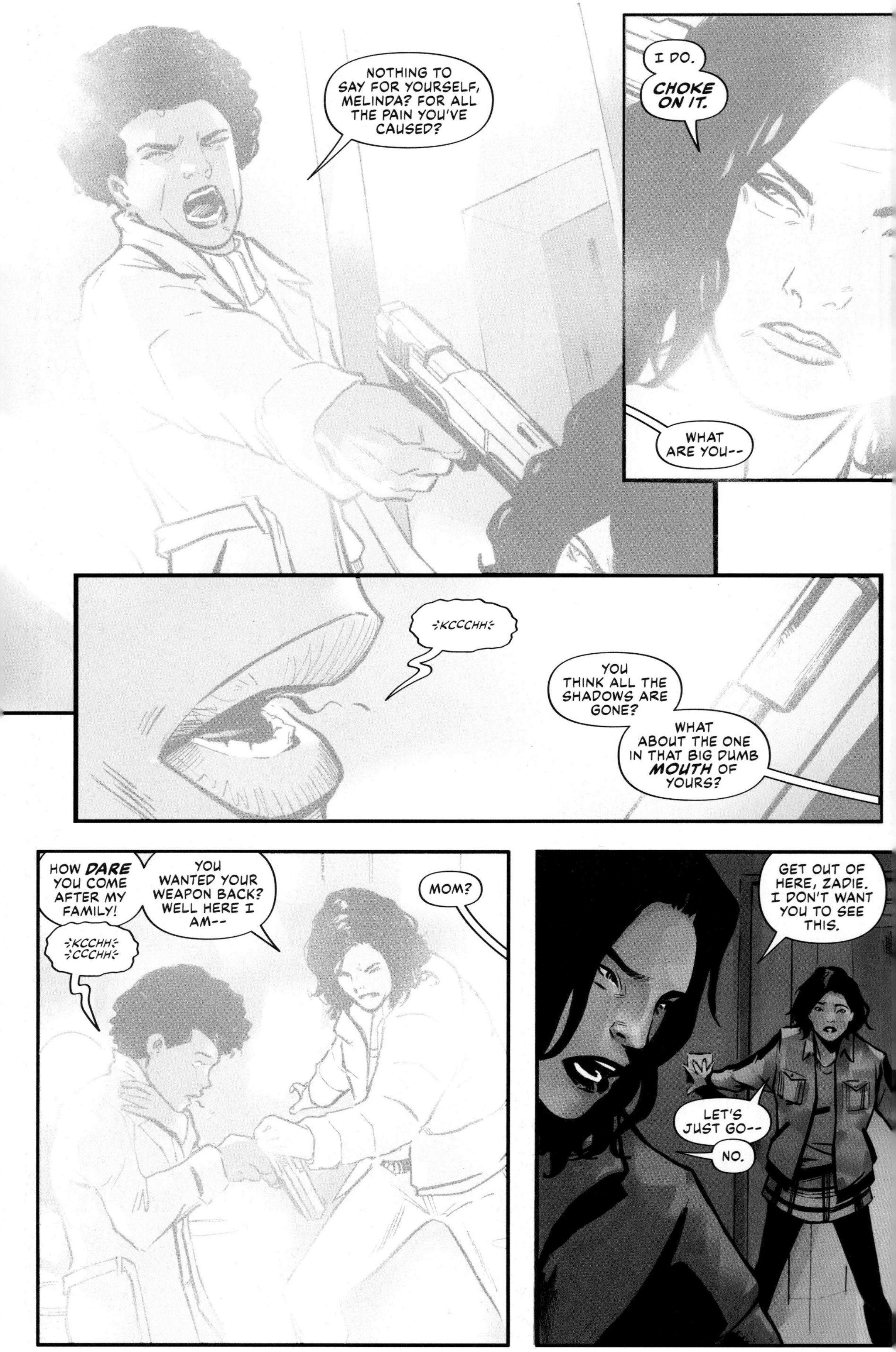
NOTHING TO SAY FOR YOURSELF, MELINDA? FOR ALL THE PAIN YOU'VE CAUSED?
I DO.
CHOKE ON IT.
WHAT ARE YOU--
KCCCHH
YOU THINK ALL THE SHADOWS ARE GONE?
WHAT ABOUT THE ONE IN THAT BIG DUMB MOUTH OF YOURS?
HOW DARE YOU COME AFTER MY FAMILY!
KCCHH CCCHH
YOU WANTED YOUR WEAPON BACK? WELL HERE I AM--
MOM?
GET OUT OF HERE, ZADIE. I DON'T WANT YOU TO SEE THIS.
LET'S JUST GO--
NO.

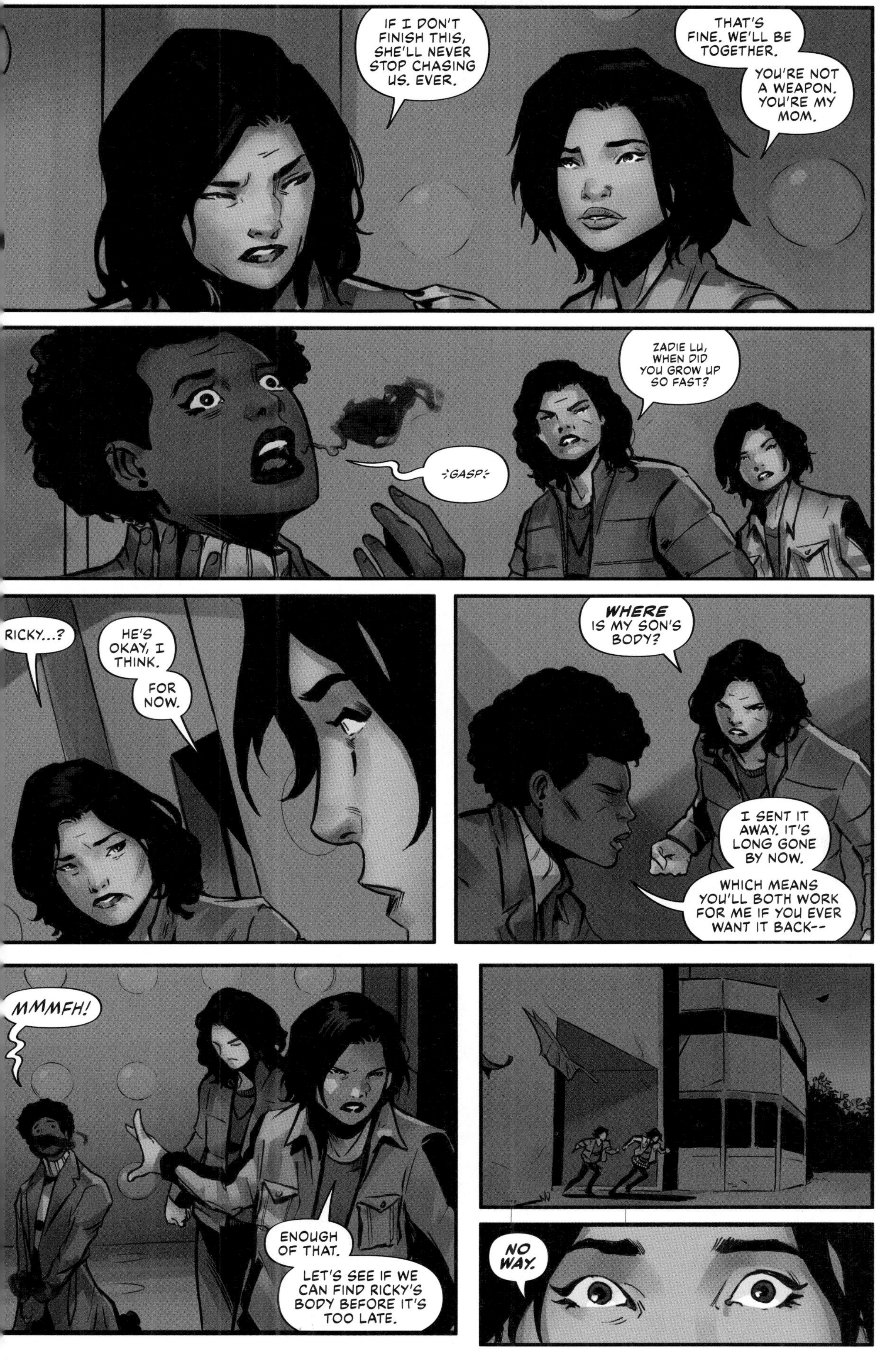
IF I DON'T FINISH THIS, SHE'LL NEVER STOP CHASING US. EVER.
THAT'S FINE. WE'LL BE TOGETHER.
YOU'RE NOT A WEAPON. YOU'RE MY MOM.
ZADIE LU, WHEN DID YOU GROW UP SO FAST?
GASP
RICKY...?
HE'S OKAY, I THINK.
FOR NOW.
WHERE IS MY SON'S BODY?
I SENT IT AWAY. IT'S LONG GONE BY NOW.
WHICH MEANS YOU'LL BOTH WORK FOR ME IF YOU EVER WANT IT BACK--
MMMFH!
ENOUGH OF THAT.
LET'S SEE IF WE CAN FIND RICKY'S BODY BEFORE IT'S TOO LATE.
NO WAY.

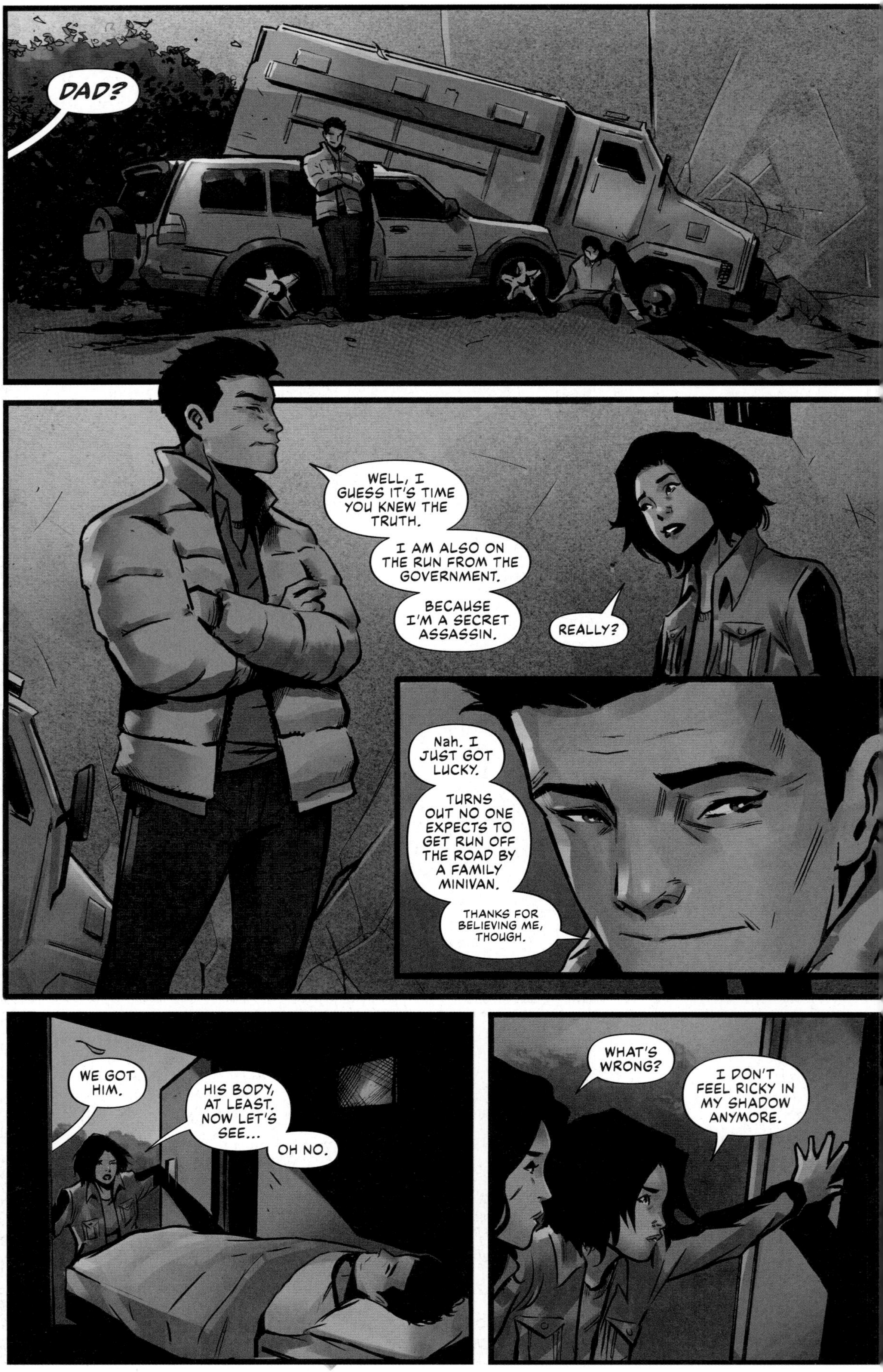
DAD?
WELL, I GUESS IT'S TIME YOU KNEW THE TRUTH.
I AM ALSO ON THE RUN FROM THE GOVERNMENT.
BECAUSE I'M A SECRET ASSASSIN.
REALLY?
Nah. I JUST GOT LUCKY.
TURNS OUT NO ONE EXPECTS TO GET RUN OFF THE ROAD BY A FAMILY MINIVAN.
THANKS FOR BELIEVING ME, THOUGH.
WE GOT HIM.
HIS BODY, AT LEAST. NOW LET'S SEE...
OH NO.
WHAT'S WRONG?
I DON'T FEEL RICKY IN MY SHADOW ANYMORE.

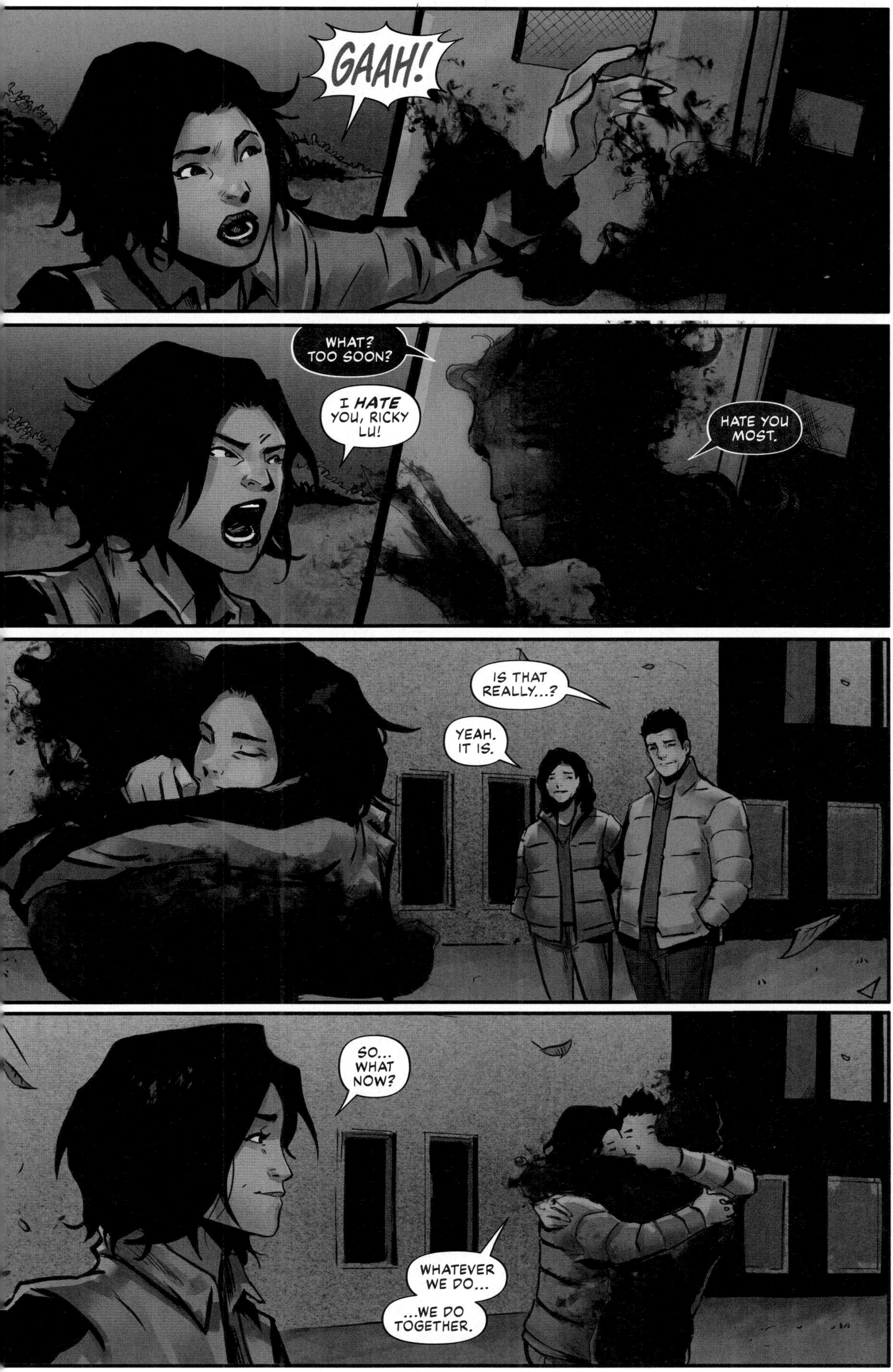
GAAH!
WHAT? TOO SOON?
I HATE YOU, RICKY LU!
HATE YOU MOST.
IS THAT REALLY...?
YEAH. IT IS.
SO... WHAT NOW?
WHATEVER WE DO...
...WE DO TOGETHER.

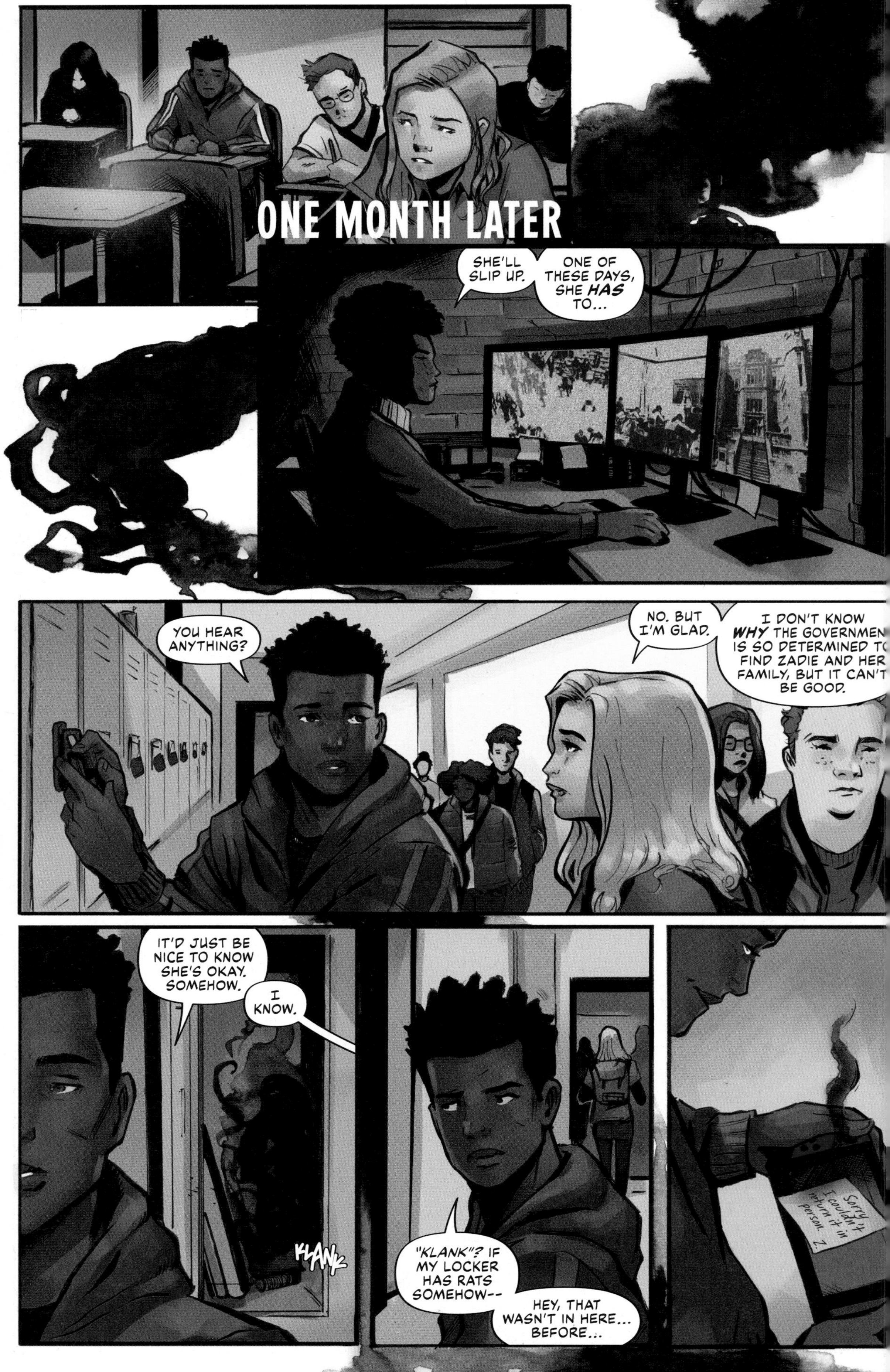
ONE MONTH LATER
SHE'LL SLIP UP.
ONE OF THESE DAYS, SHE HAS TO...
YOU HEAR ANYTHING?
NO. BUT I'M GLAD.
I DON'T KNOW WHY THE GOVERNMEN IS SO DETERMINED T FIND ZADIE AND HER FAMILY, BUT IT CAN'T BE GOOD.
IT'D JUST BE NICE TO KNOW SHE'S OKAY. SOMEHOW.
I KNOW.
KLANK
"KLANK"? IF MY LOCKER HAS RATS SOMEHOW--
HEY, THAT WASN'T IN HERE... BEFORE...
Sorry I couldn't return it in person. Z.

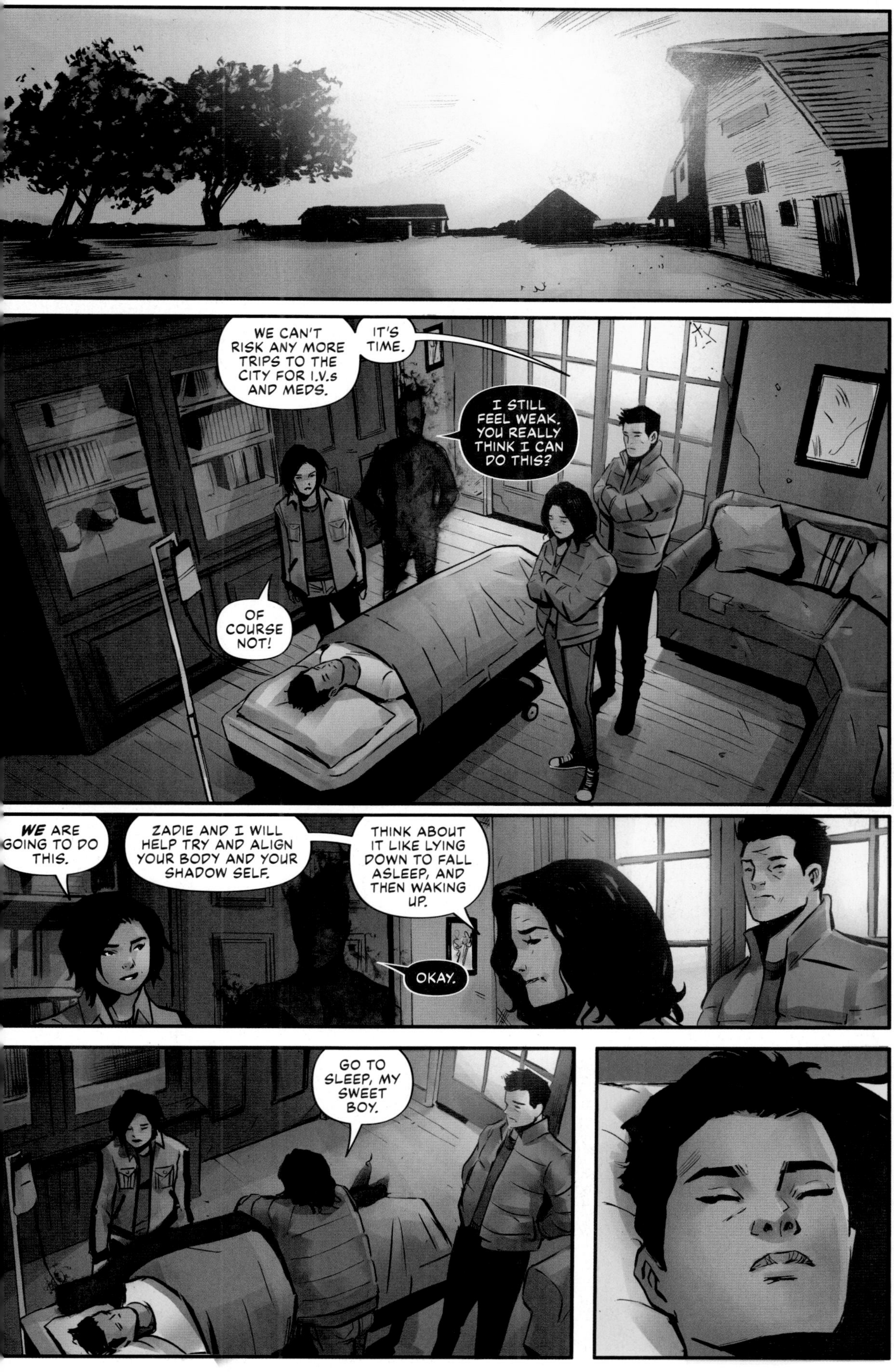
WE CAN'T RISK ANY MORE TRIPS TO THE CITY FOR I.V.s AND MEDS.
IT'S TIME.
I STILL FEEL WEAK. YOU REALLY THINK I CAN DO THIS?
OF COURSE NOT!
WE ARE GOING TO DO THIS.
ZADIE AND I WILL HELP TRY AND ALIGN YOUR BODY AND YOUR SHADOW SELF.
THINK ABOUT IT LIKE LYING DOWN TO FALL ASLEEP, AND THEN WAKING UP.
OKAY.
GO TO SLEEP, MY SWEET BOY.

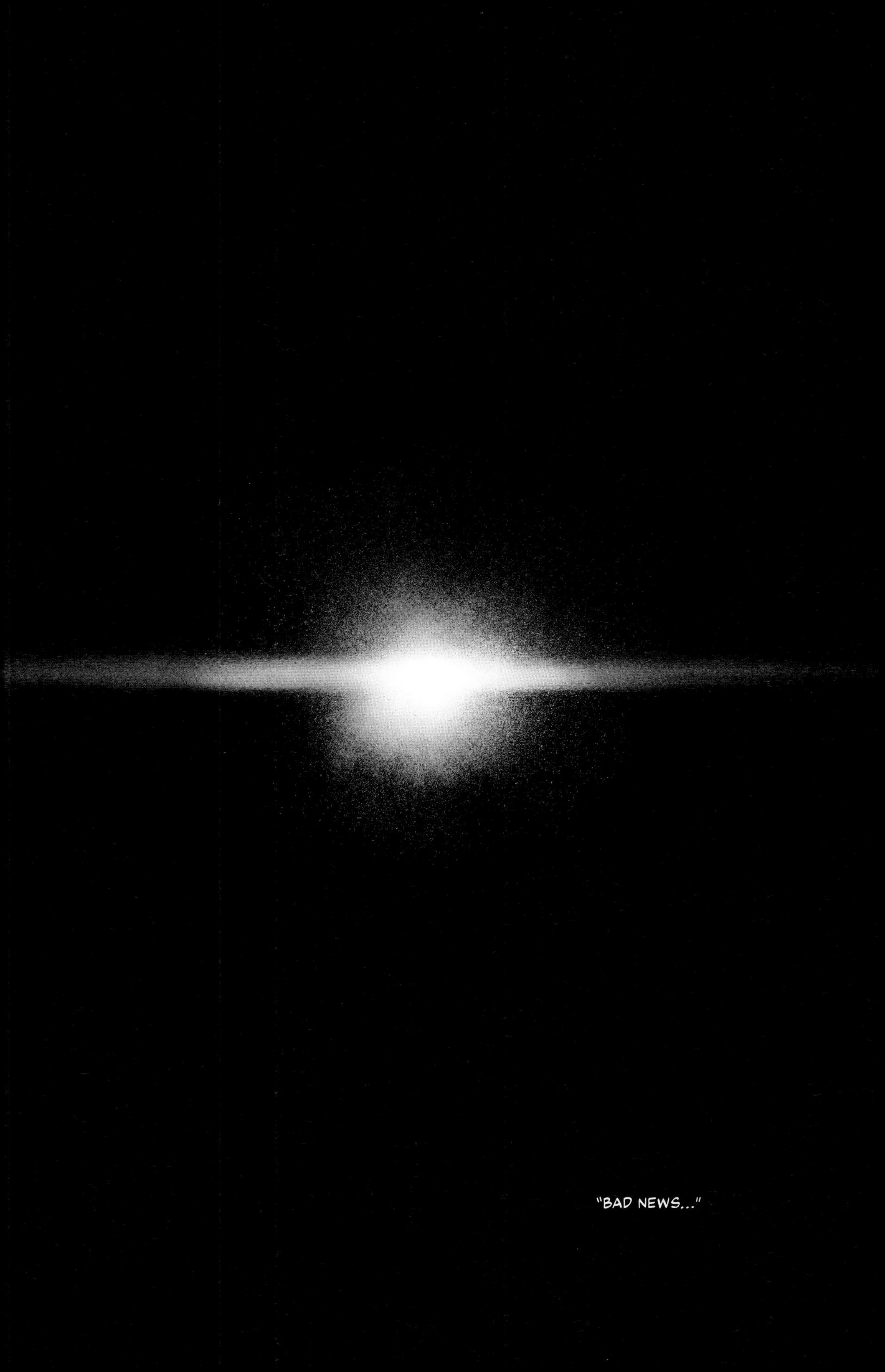
"BAD NEWS..."

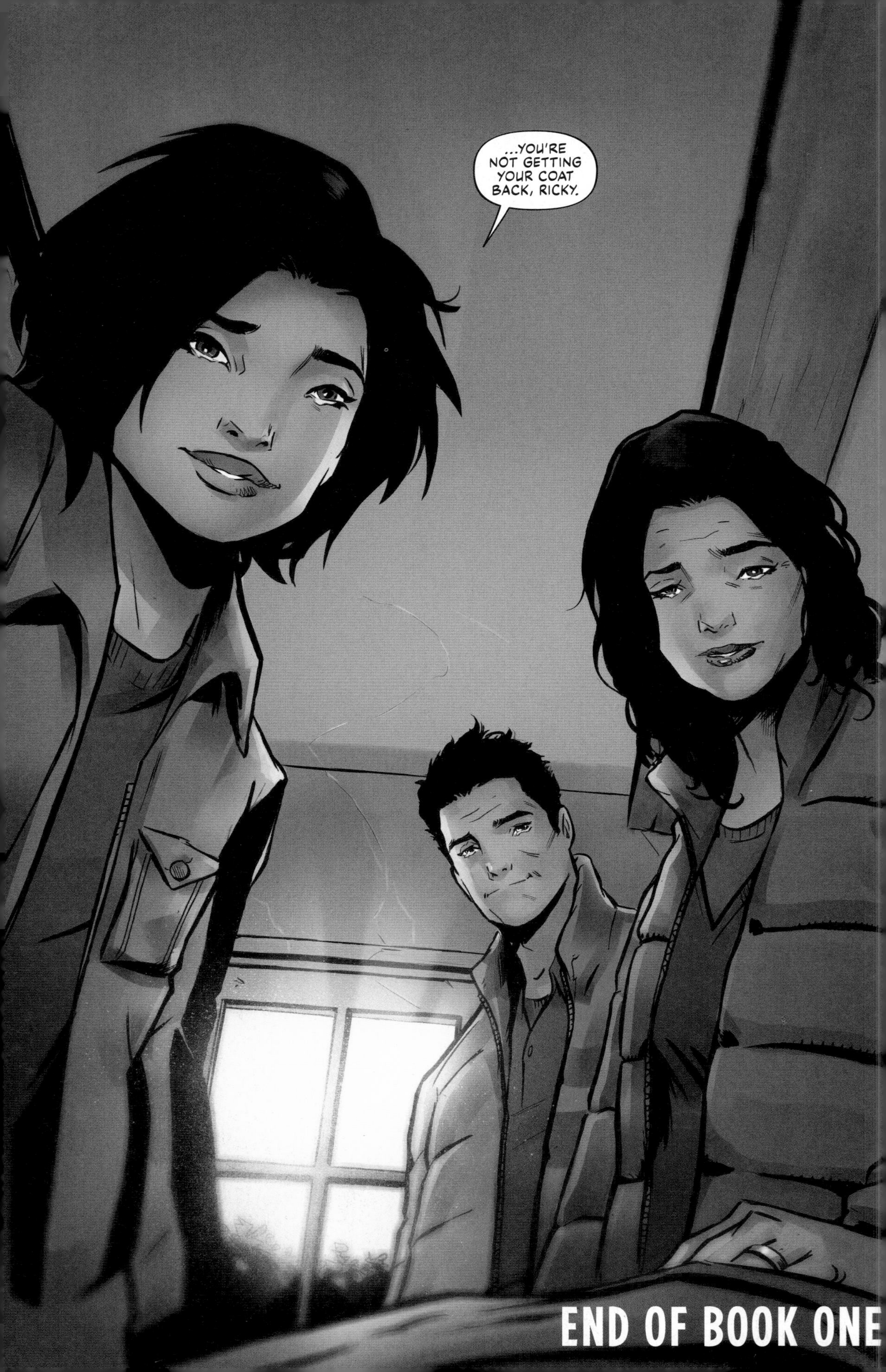
...YOU'RE NOT GETTING YOUR COAT BACK, RICKY.
END OF BOOK ONE

COVER
GALLERY

ISSUE ONE
COVER B
BY JOCK

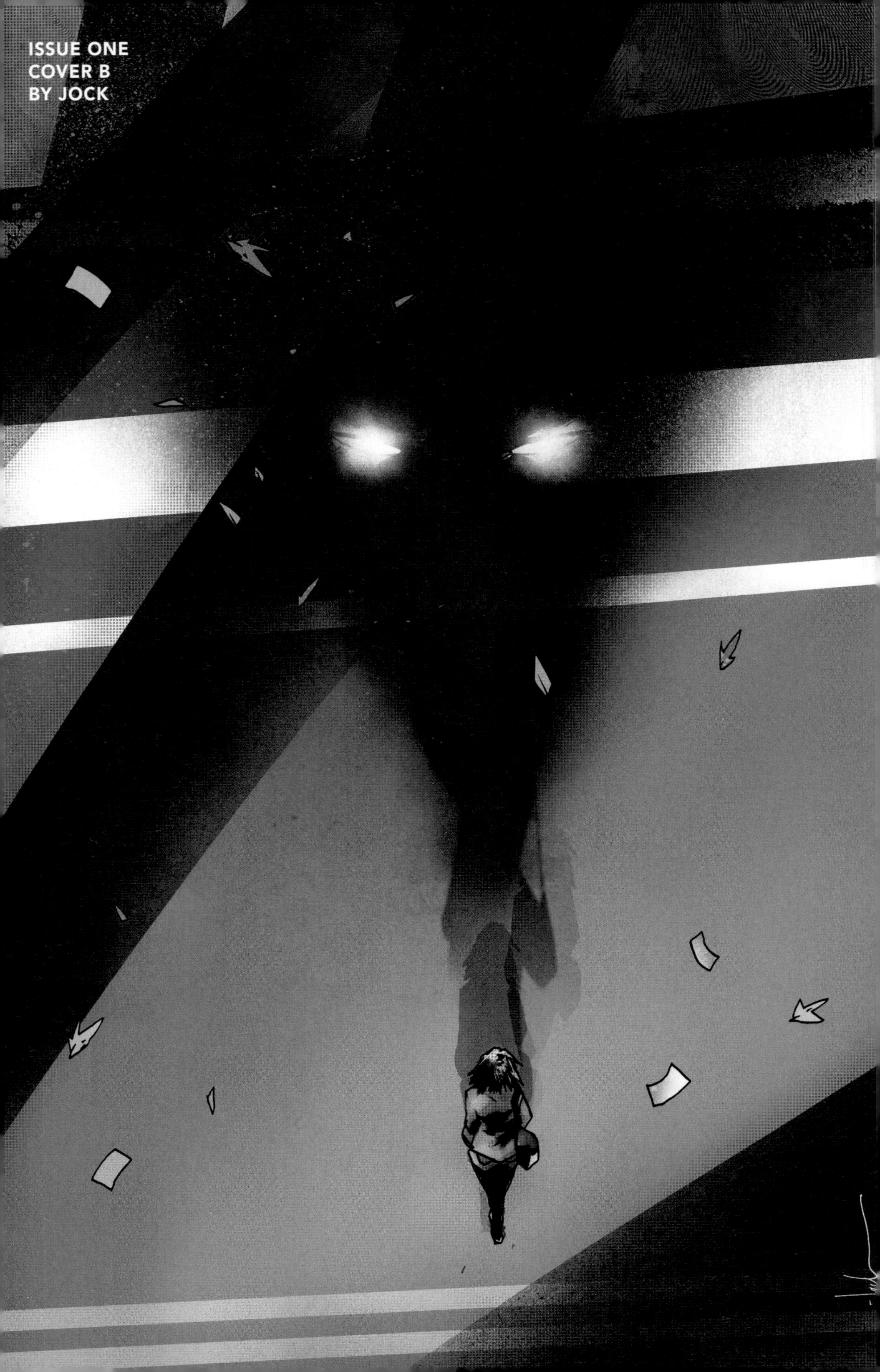

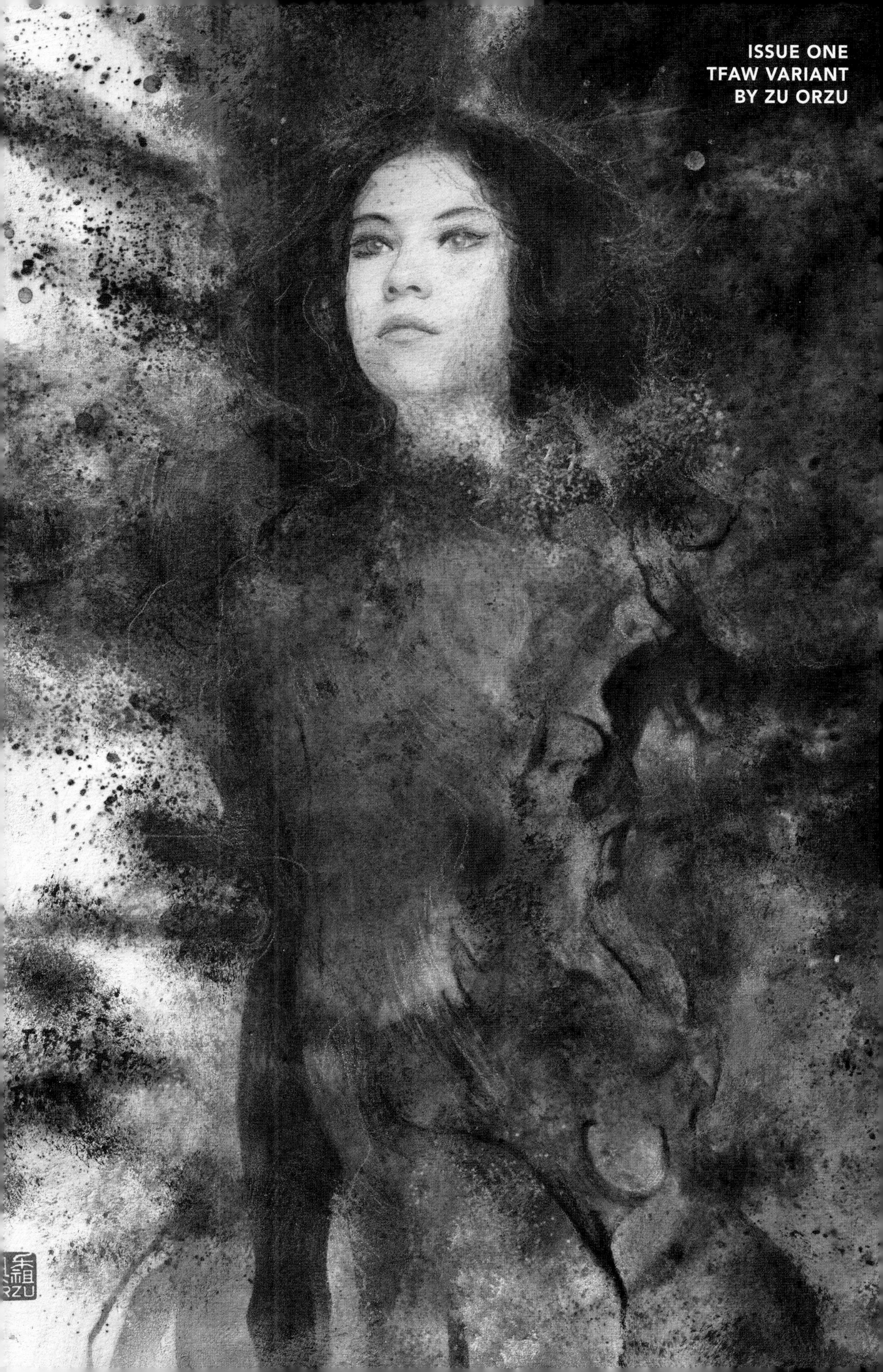
ISSUE ONE
TFAW VARIANT
BY ZU ORZU

ISSUE ONE
SANCTUM SANCTORUM VARIANT
BY FRANY

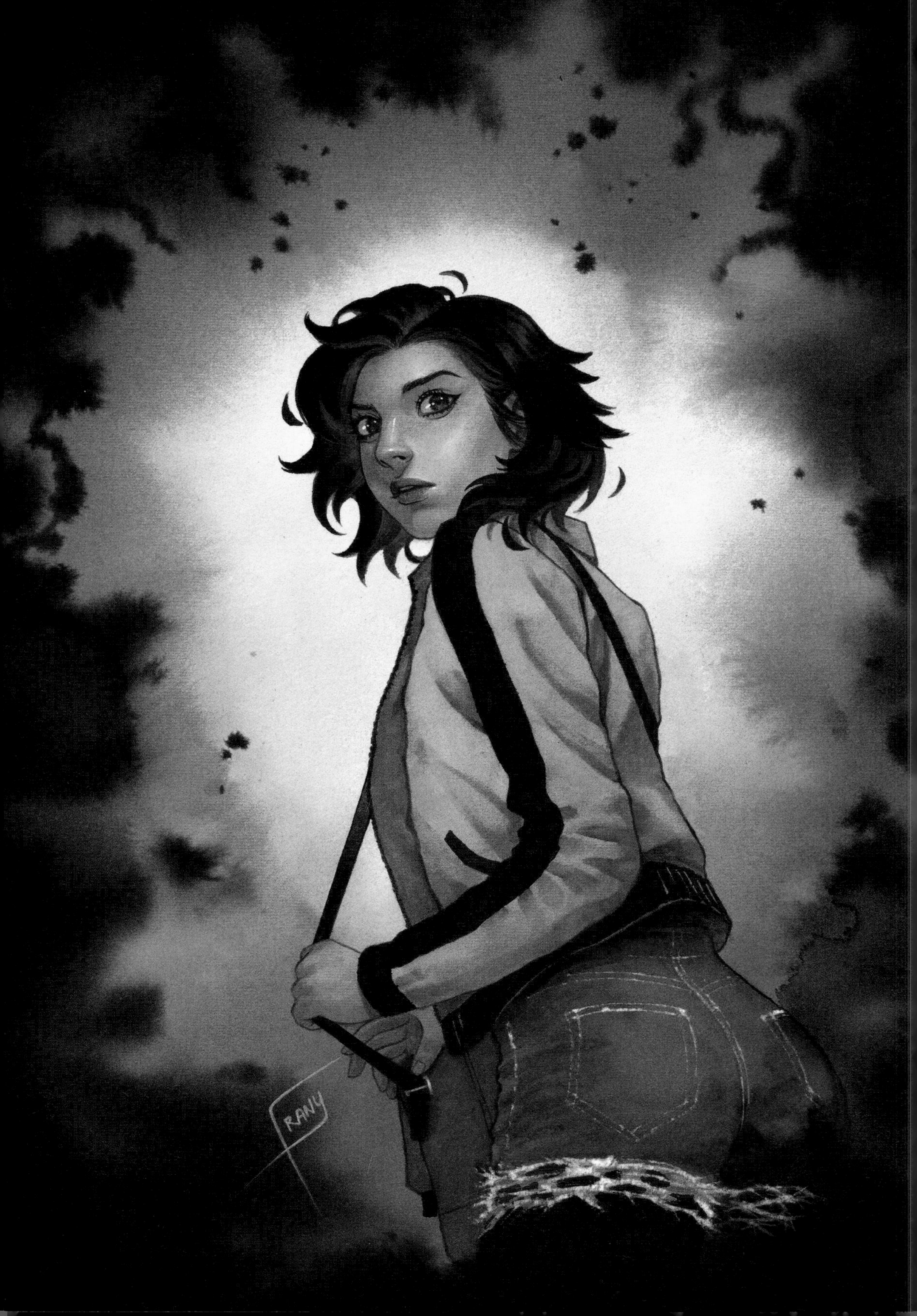

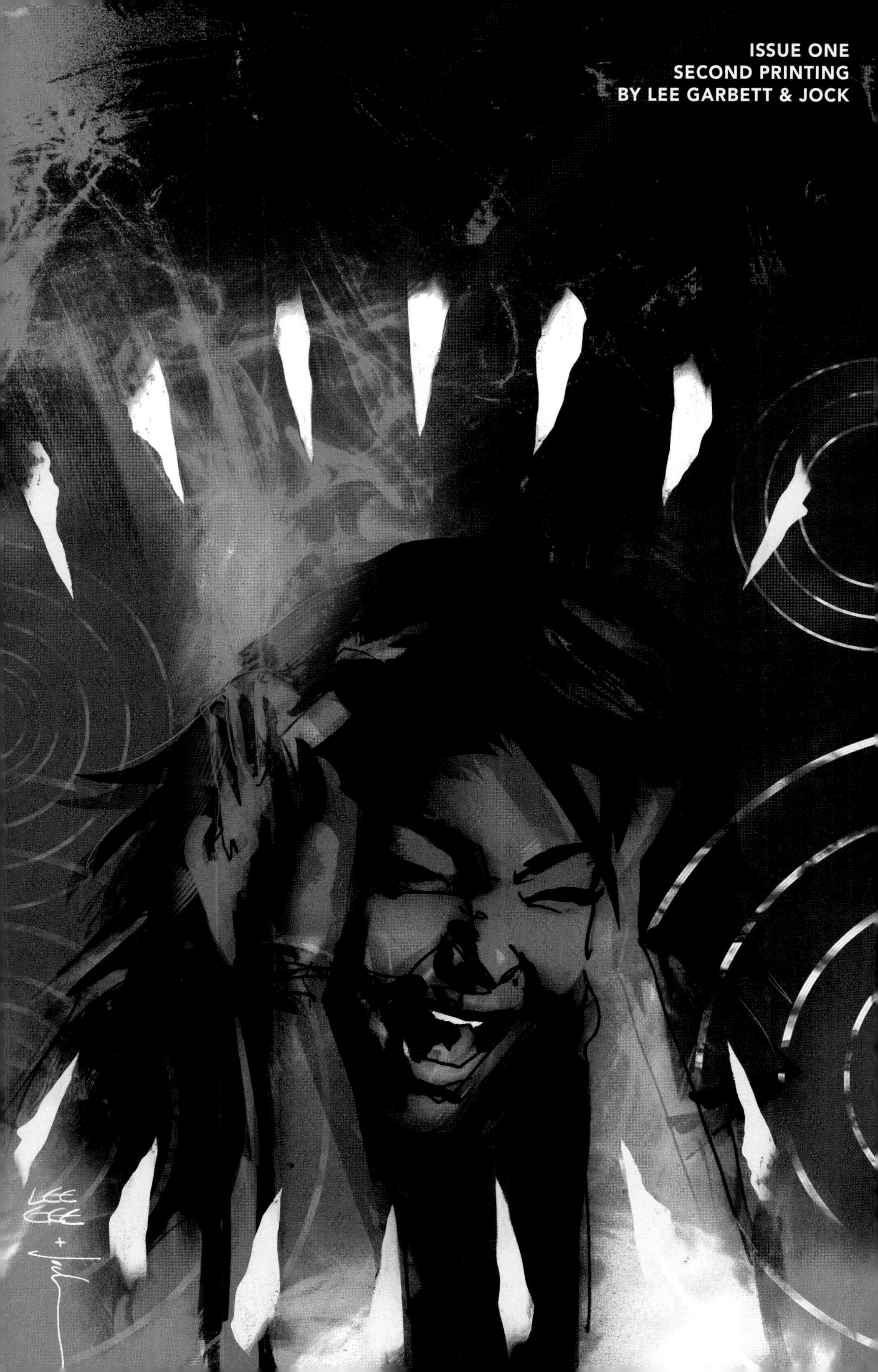
ISSUE ONE
SECOND PRINTING
BY LEE GARBETT & JOCK

ISSUE TWO
COVER B
BY TULA LOTAY

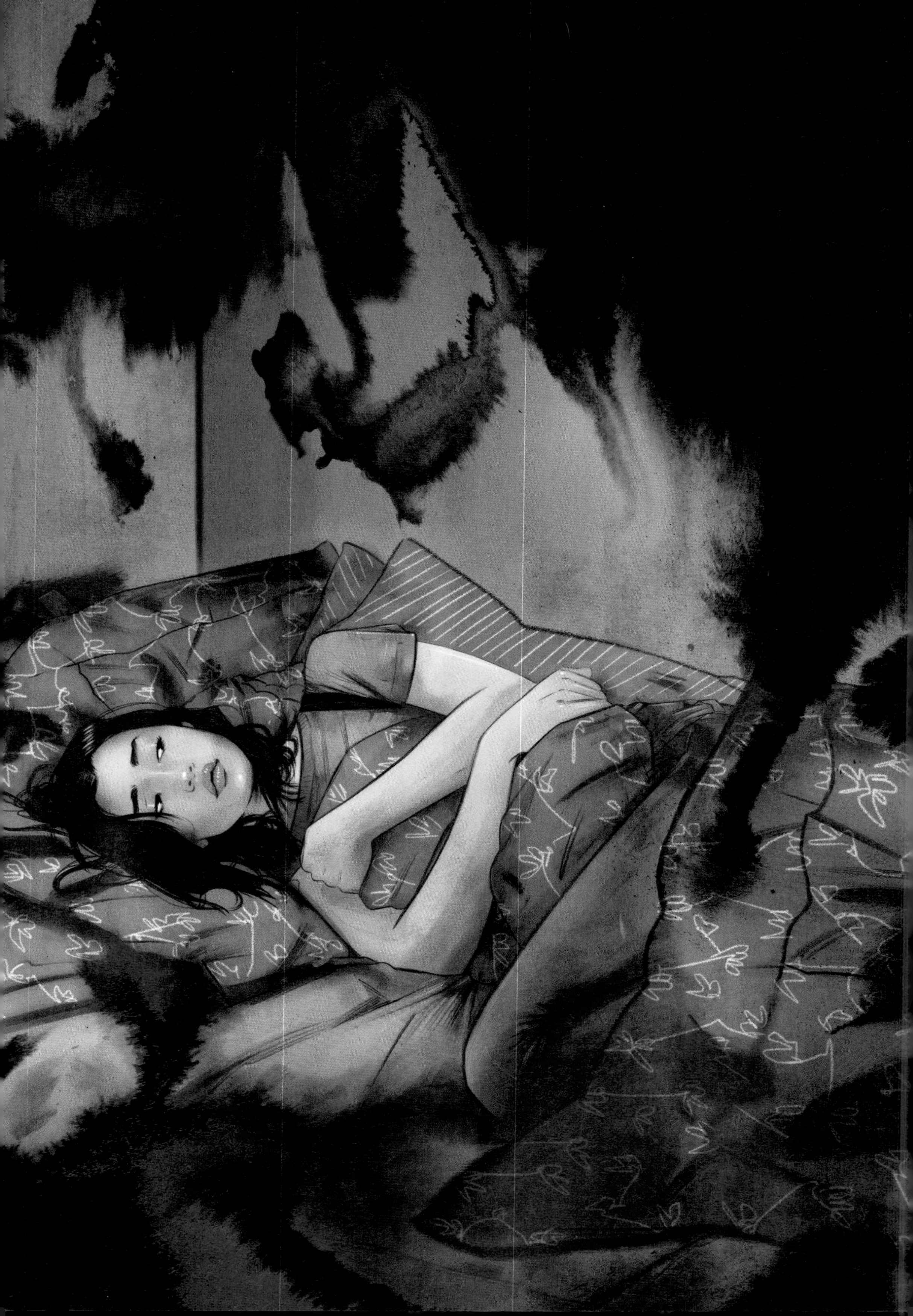

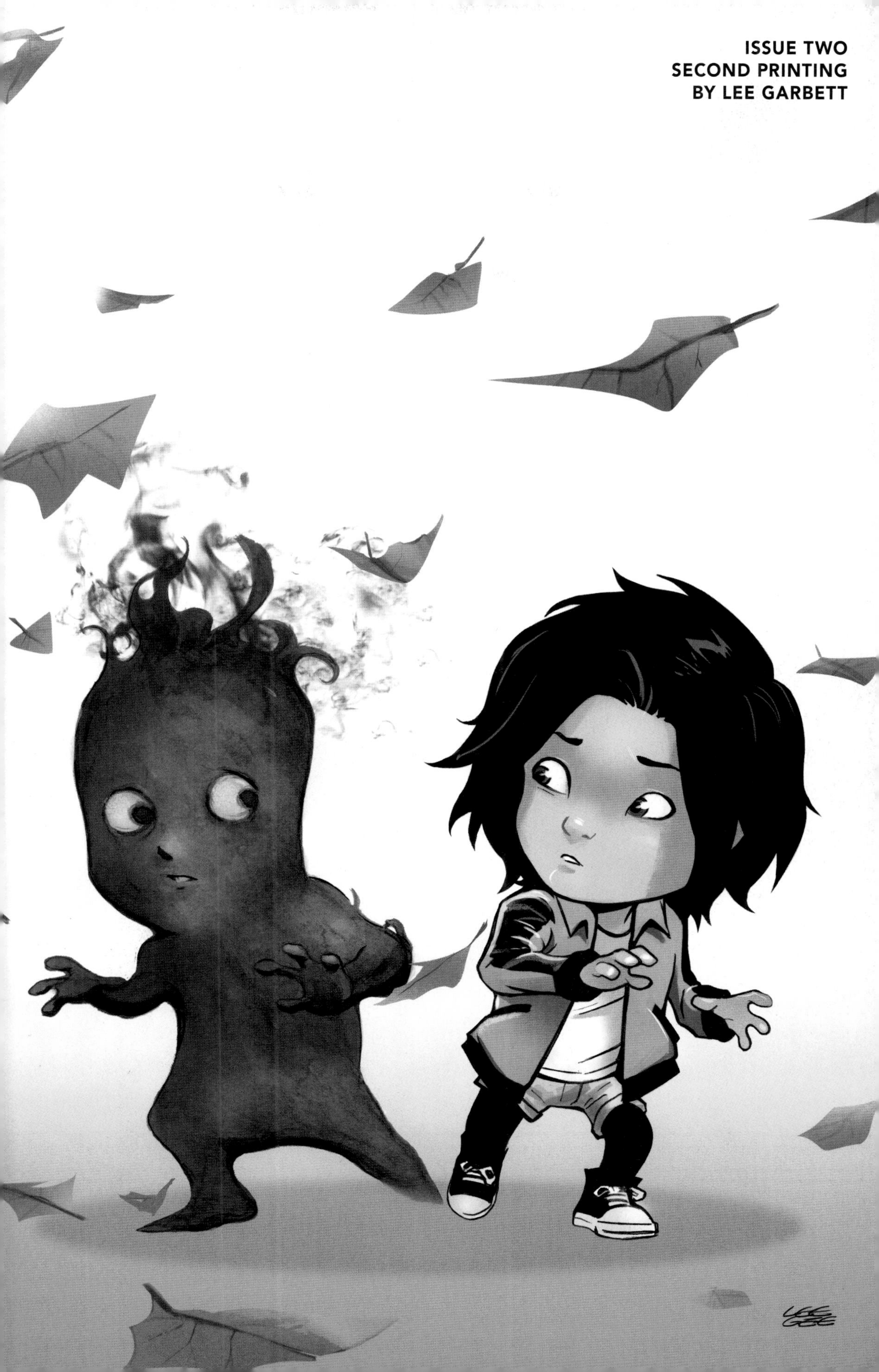
ISSUE TWO
SECOND PRINTING
BY LEE GARBETT

ISSUE THREE
COVER B
BY JIM CHEUNG & LEE GARBETT

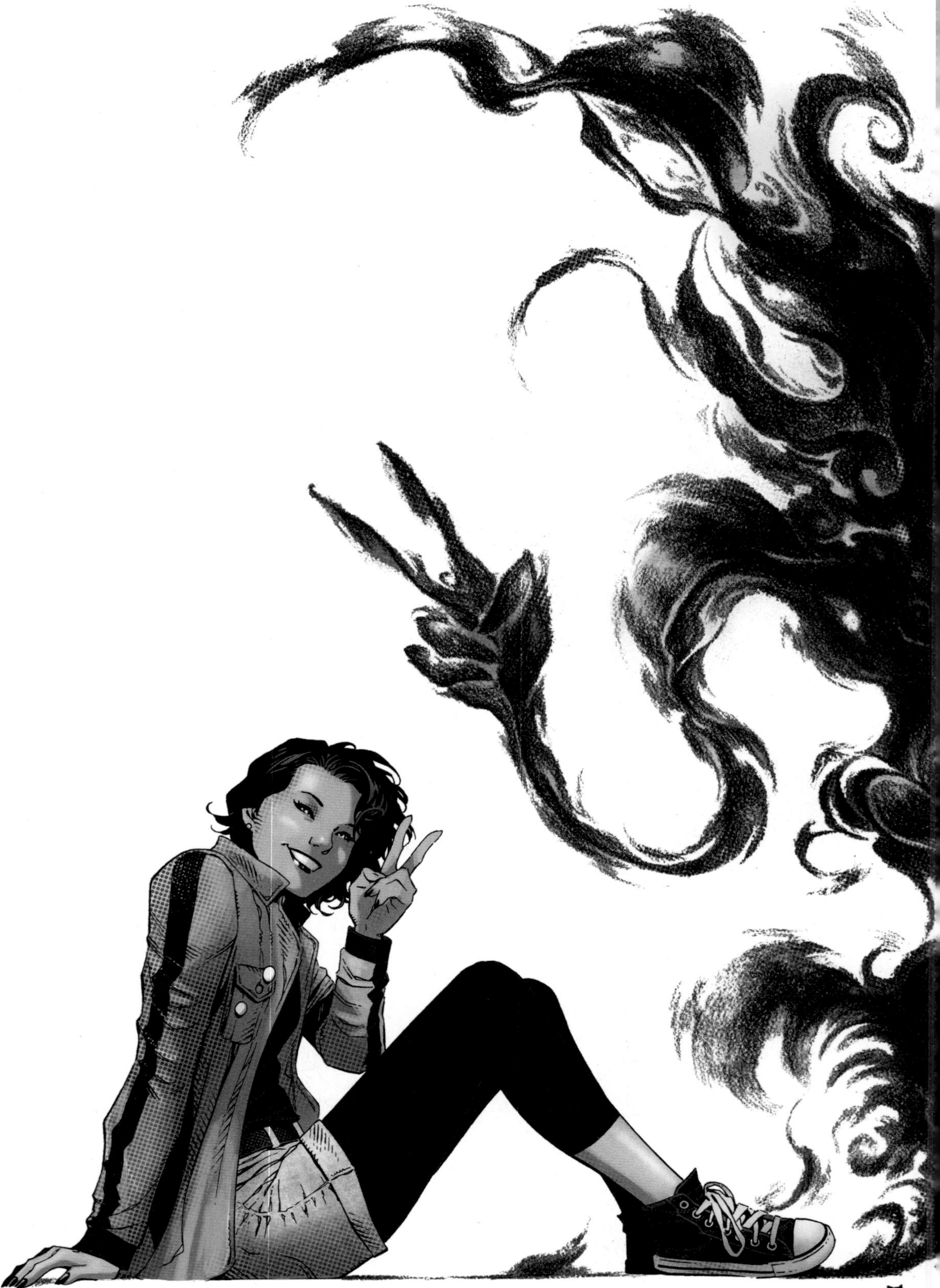

ISSUE THREE
OASAS COMICS VARIANT
BY JAE LEE

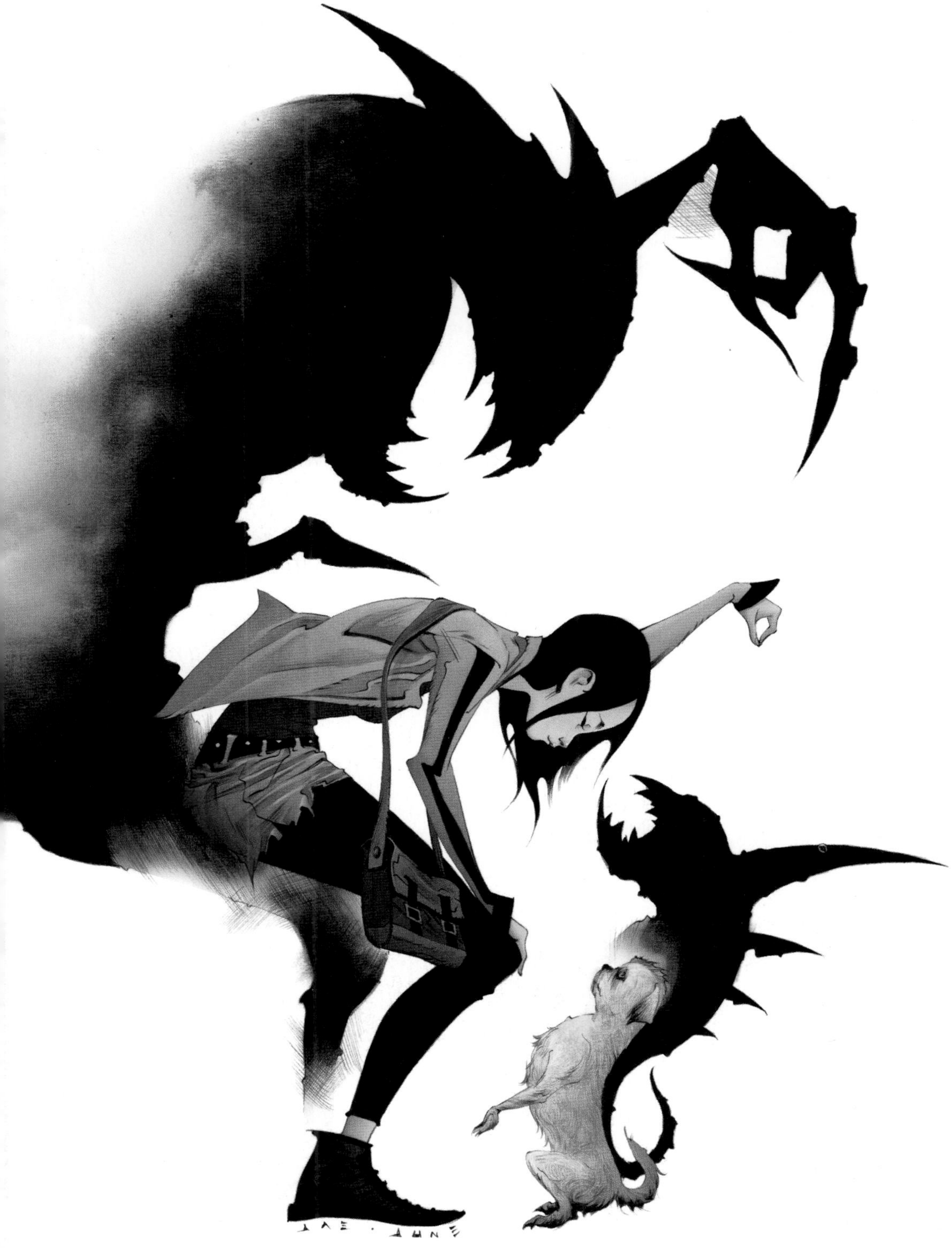

ISSUE THREE
SECOND PRINTING
BY LEE GARBETT

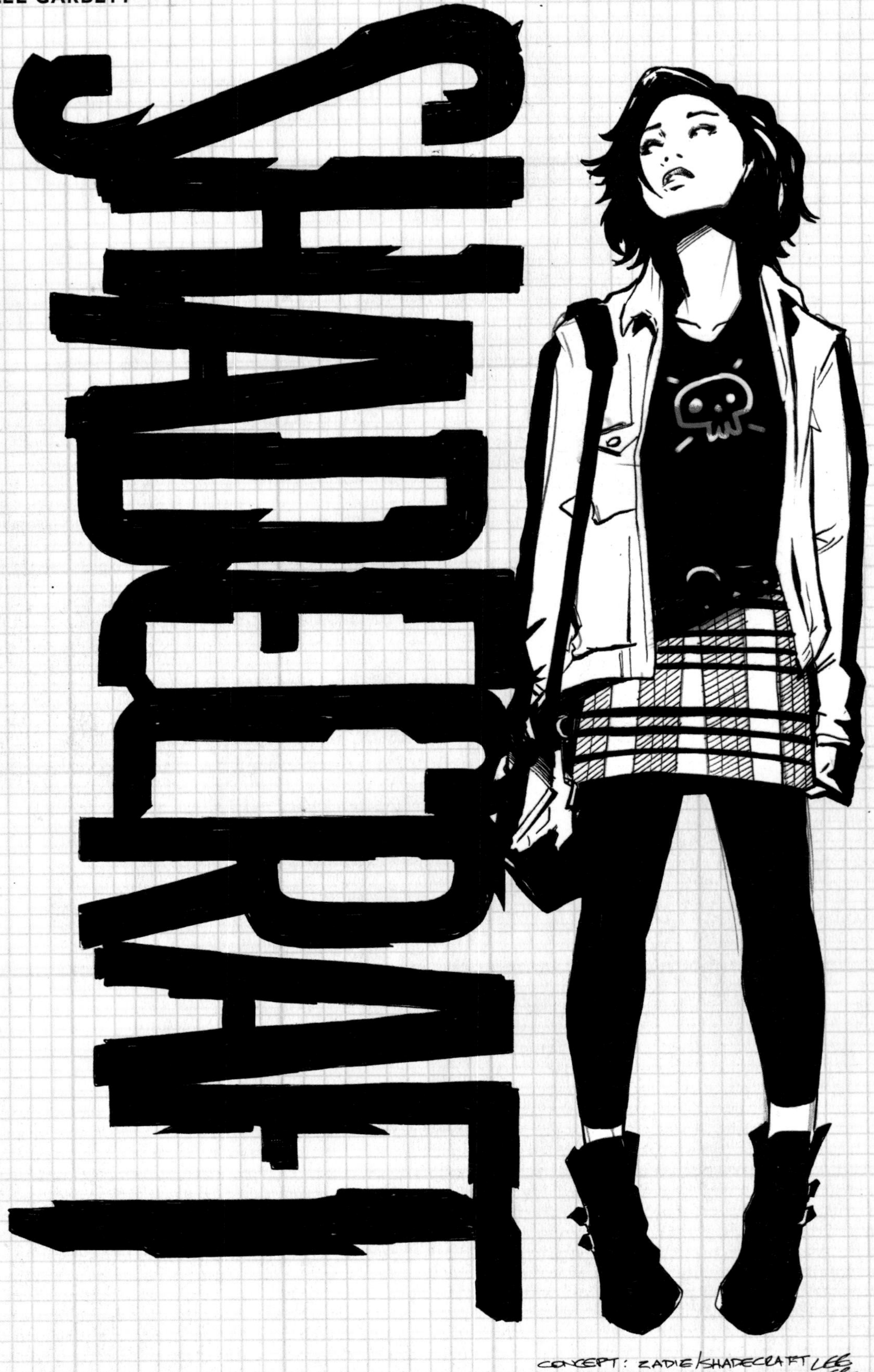
SHADECRAFT
CONCEPT: ZADIE/SHADECRAFT

ISSUE FOUR
COVER B
BY JAMIE McKELVIE

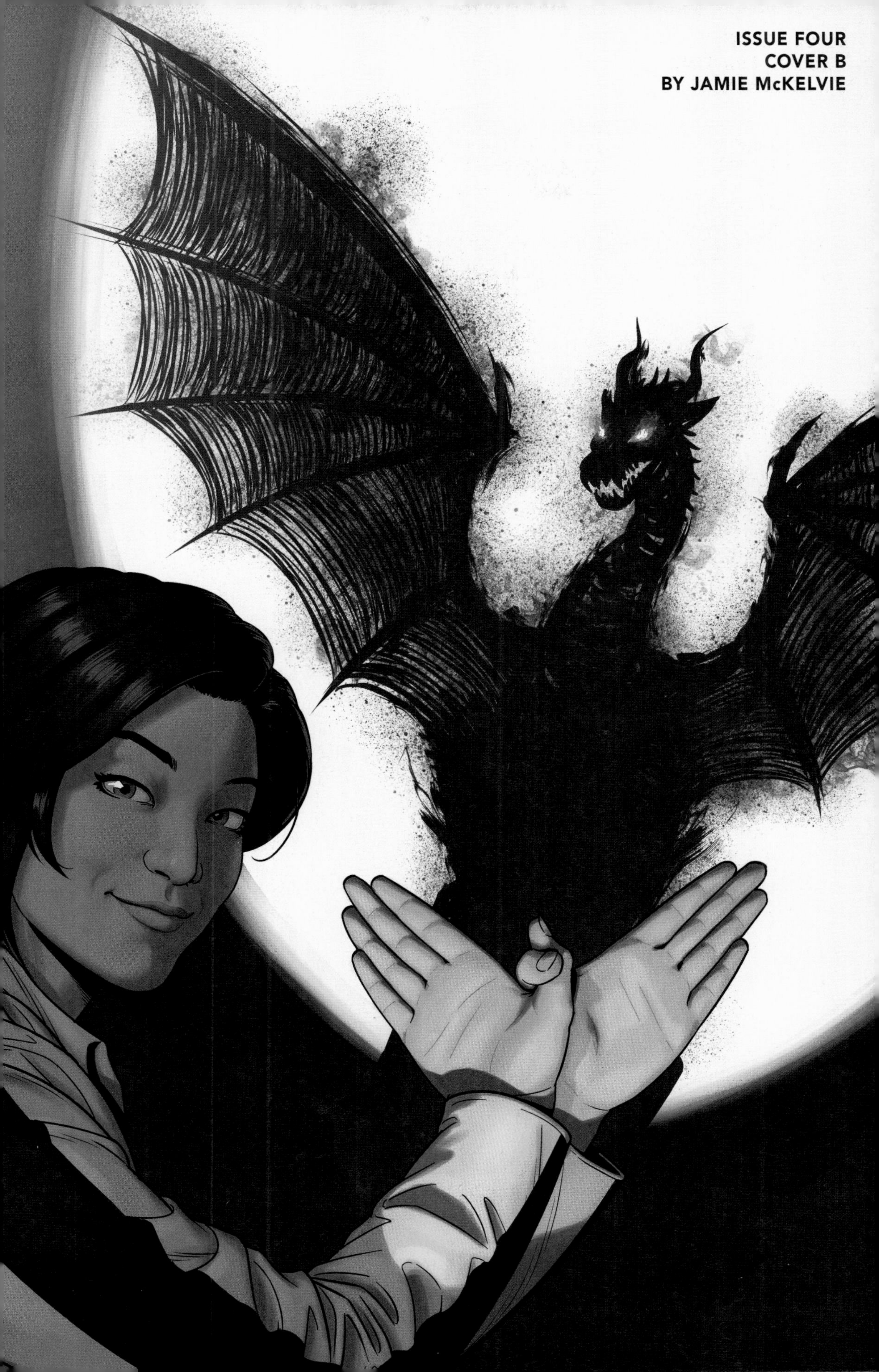

UR
ABER VARIANT
EN MOONEY

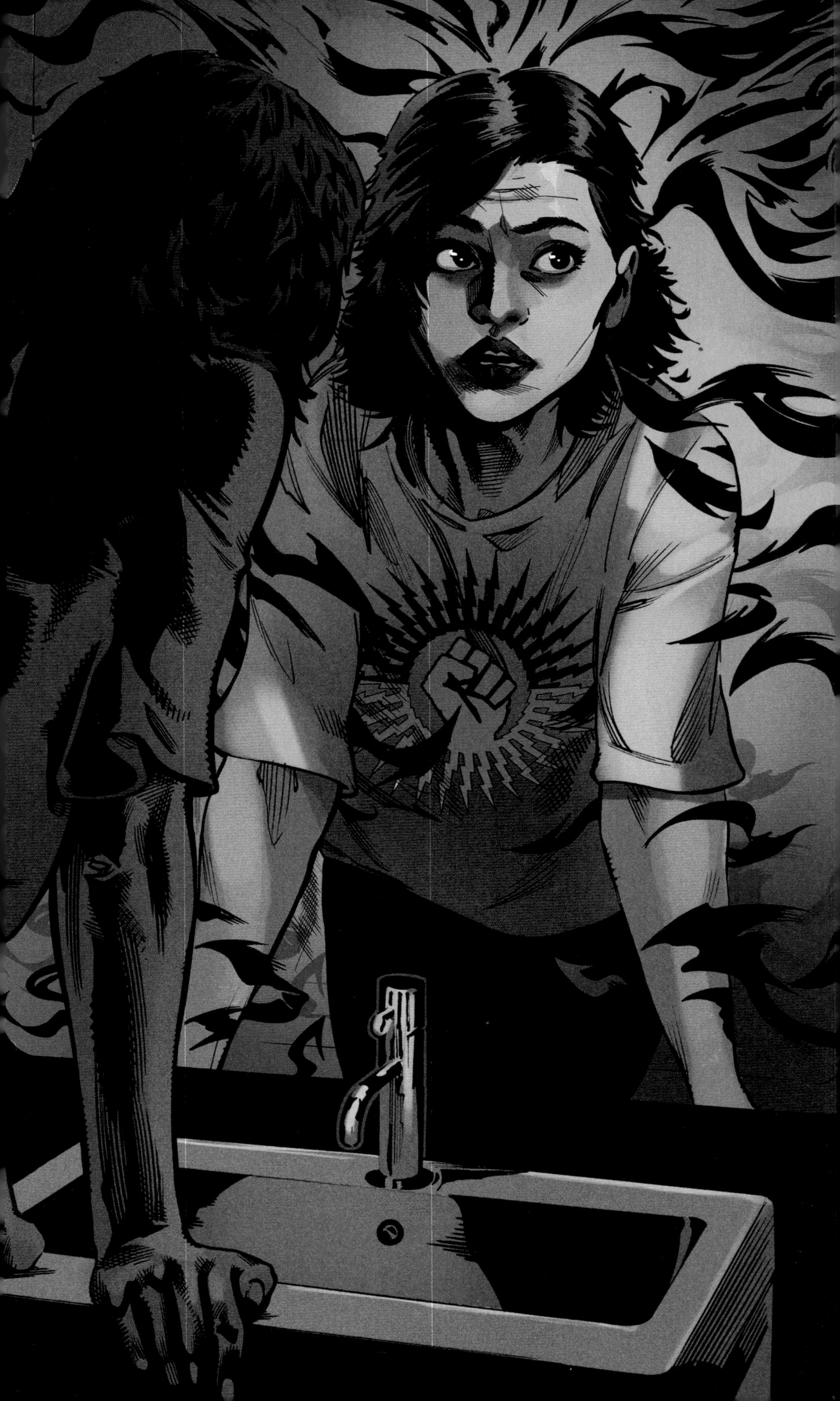

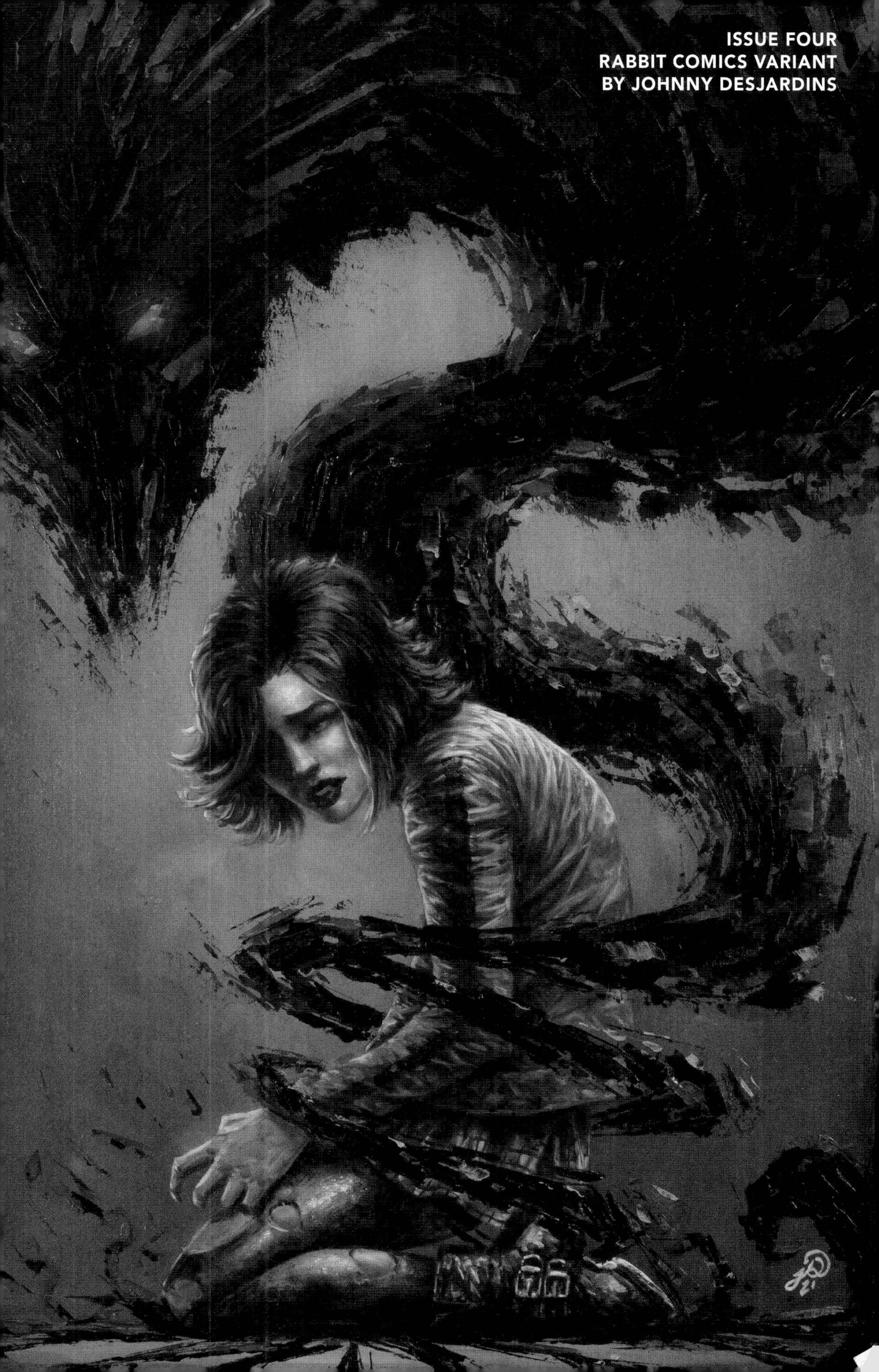

ISSUE FOUR
RABBIT COMICS VARIANT
BY JOHNNY DESJARDINS

ISSUE FOUR
OASAS COMICS VARIANT
BY JAE LEE

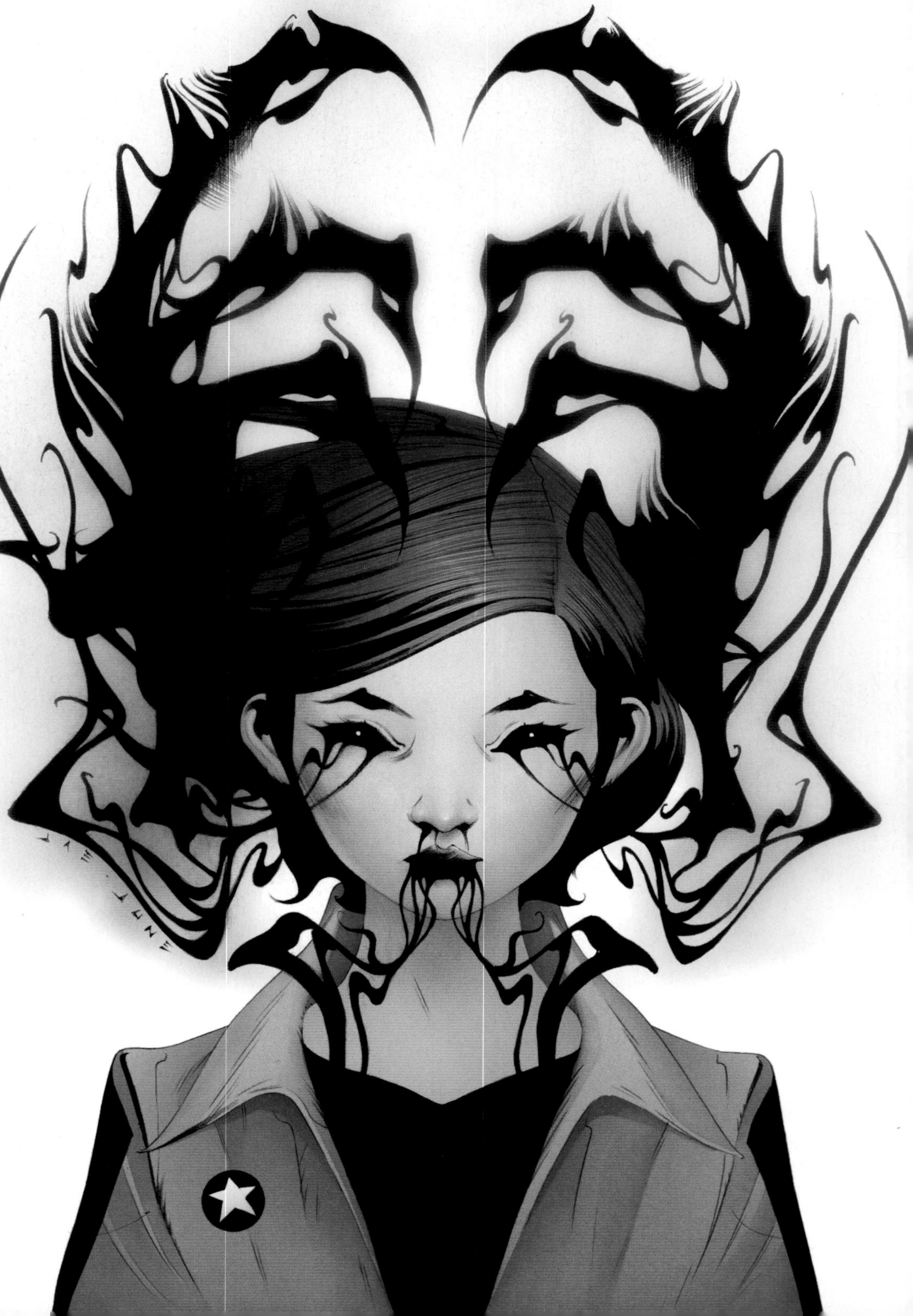

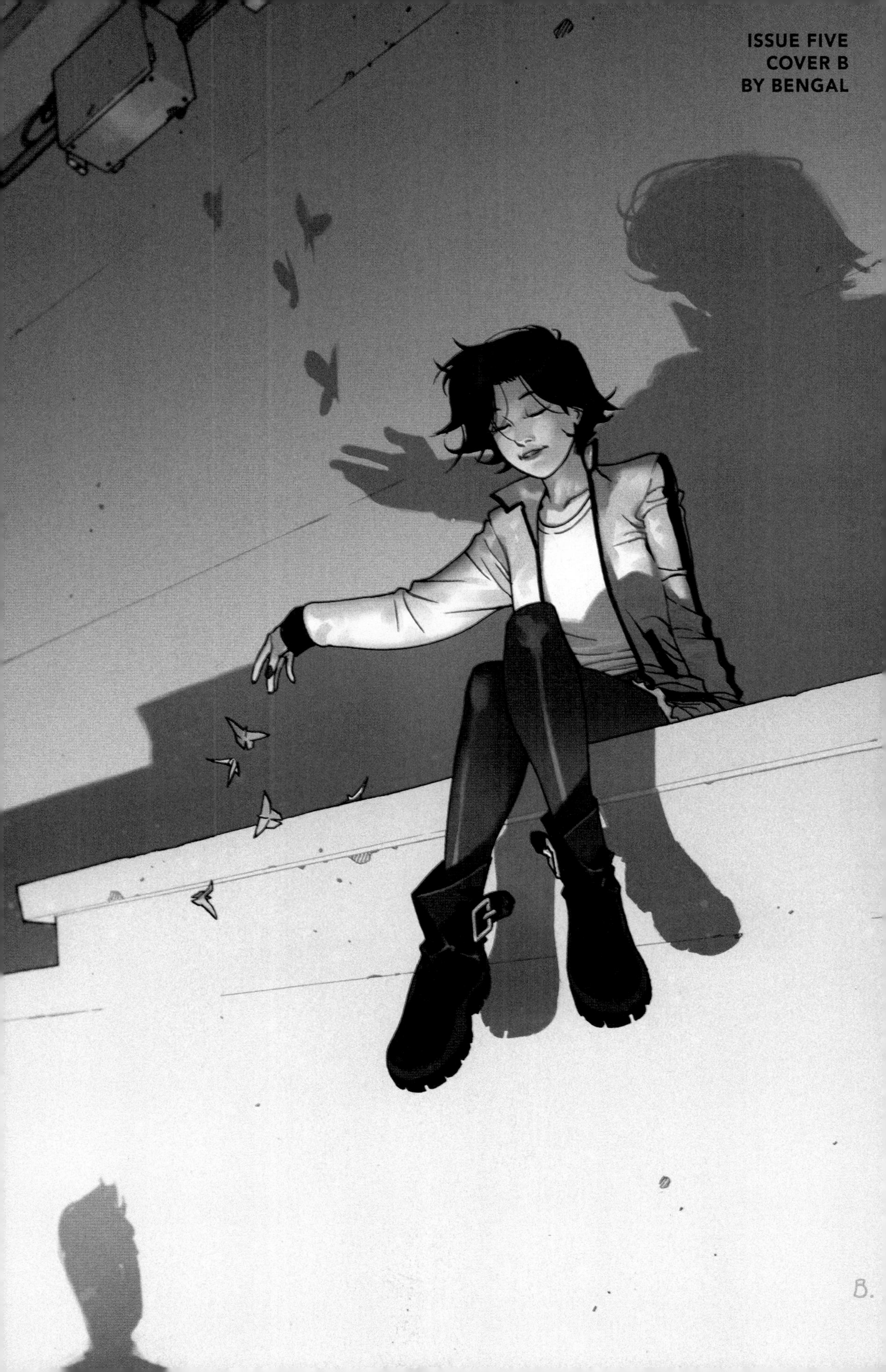
B.

ISSUE FIVE
COVER B
BY BENGAL

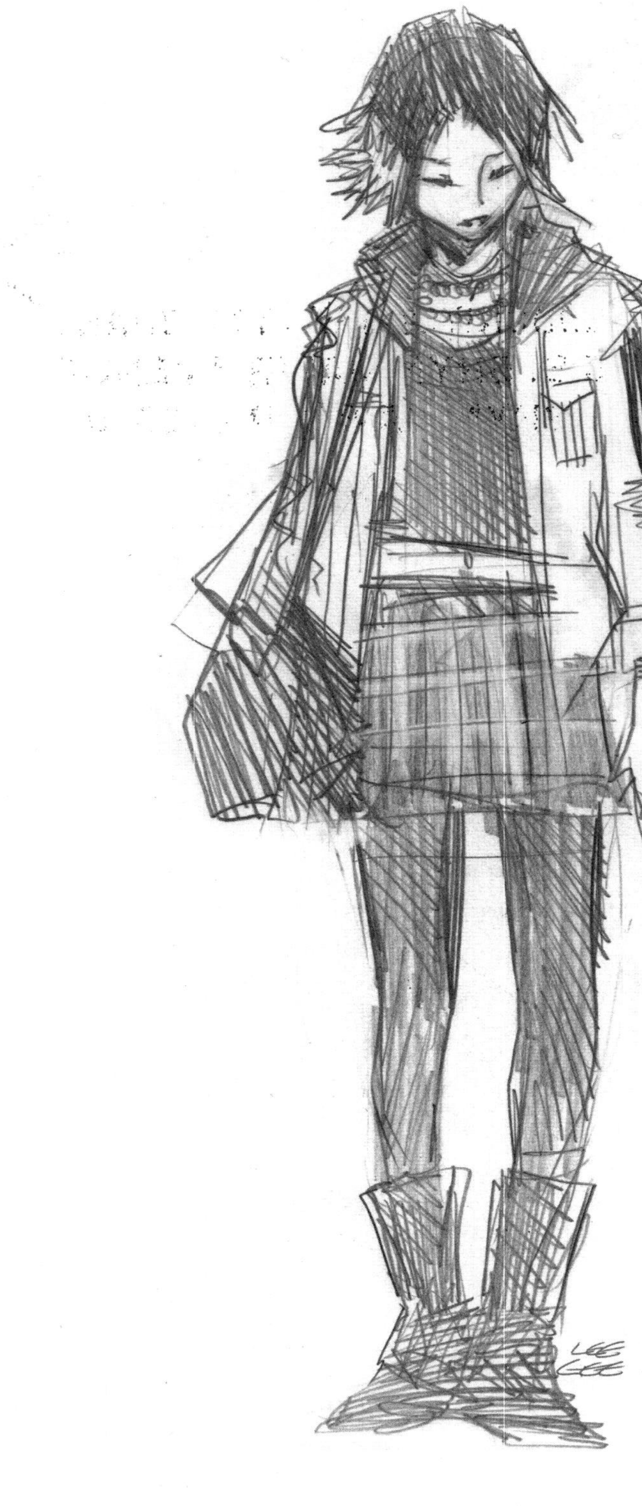
ZADIE